In No Time At All

In No
Time
At All

N A Millington

Matador
9 Priory Business Park,
Wistow Road, Kibworth Beauchamp,
Leicestershire. LE8 0RX
Tel: 0116 279 2299
Email: books@troubador.co.uk
Web: www.troubador.co.uk/matador
Twitter: @matadorbooks

ISBN 978 1785893 346

British Library Cataloguing in Publication Data.
A catalogue record for this book is available from the British Library.

Printed and bound in the UK by TJ International, Padstow, Cornwall
Typeset in 11pt Minion Pro by Troubador Publishing Ltd, Leicester, UK

Matador is an imprint of Troubador Publishing Ltd

Dedicated to my mother Esme, you are loved and missed.

"Pain and suffering are always inevitable
for large intelligence and a deep heart.
The really great men must, I think
have great sadness on earth."

FYODOR DOSTOYEVSKY

Prologue

Harry and Magda Ginsberg were once in possession of a beautiful little egg timer. Harry had 'stumbled' upon the little golden egg timer while in Johannesburg on the very day he had first met Magda; very soon after that, they were married. Harry in those days was a specialist in the buying and selling of special time pieces, especially men's antique pocket watches. "I love the feel of it in the palm of my hand," he would say to his wife when taking possession of an especially fine piece. "The way it sounds when I close it – you just don't get that quality of 'click' sound anymore!" Magda would smile and shake her head. She loved her odd and eccentric husband; as the years passed, their love for each other grew beyond measure. At first, out of caution they did not use the timer very often, for their egg timer was useless for the timing of boiled eggs: its powder would frequently and inexplicably become damp, therefore unable to pass from phial to phial. The egg timer that had chosen Harry and Magda to possess it, was one of two in the world capable of transporting them through time. At first they were scared, though sometimes amused, at the things it showed them. Then slowly, as the number of their trips increased, they began to trust their timer as if it had become their friend.

Unfortunately for Harry and Magda, they had not been blessed with the gift of children, so as the years passed they had plenty of time and energy to explore the places of history that they were interested in. Sometimes though, and much to their alarm, they soon found that if they didn't use the timer themselves it would take them on a 'trip' anyway, whether they liked it or not, and at the most inconvenient of times.

It was shortly after one of these 'involuntary trips' that their relationship with the timer seemed to change. This had been a trip to London on a viciously cold winter's day somewhere at the end of the nineteenth century. (They were never sure exactly which year it was!) As usual when the timer sent them on a trip of this kind, they explored their immediate surroundings – the impoverished back streets of the city, rather like a scene from a Dickens story. It was here that they found the little girl. She was a beautiful child and could have been no more than four or five years of age; she had obviously been abandoned. Her strawberry blonde hair was dirty, matted and tangled, her face covered with what looked like soot. Her clothing was soiled, ragged and torn.

"Who on earth does the little thing belong to?" cried Magda, filled with pity. They asked her where she lived but couldn't get two words out of her. They even asked a scruffy-looking boy of ten or eleven if he knew who she belonged to and where she lived.

"She don't live nowhere, miss," he had answered. "She's an urchin, like me!" He had then laughed at the top of his voice and disappeared down one of the many dark little alley ways before they could ask him anything else.

It was then that the little girl began to cry. Great tears rolled down her cheeks from her large round, shining blue eyes. Not able to see any other reason for the trip, they reasoned that the timer had sent them to take the little girl home with them.

"I cannot leave the little darling here to die of cold or starve to death," Magda said as she snuggled the pale, dirty little girl beneath her thick warm coat. Harry was uneasy, but he agreed that they could not leave her. They held hands tightly as the familiar colourful display of red, silver and gold sparks spewed from the timer. Magda felt that she and Harry could be complete at last and that the sense of 'something missing' would leave her now. As the dull gray, cobbled streets of London began to disappear, Magda held her husband's and the little girl's hands tightly. But as the sound of the sea came crashing and the wind roared, she felt her grip on the little girl's hand begin to loosen, as if being prised apart by an unseen force. When they finally stood in the dining room of their apartment, they were alone – the little girl had been left behind. Their first thought was to immediately return to find her and try to bring her back again. Maybe the sound of the sea and the wind had frightened her and she had let go herself.

Harry held the timer in his hand; with his other he gripped Magda's as they tried to think of the dull grey, cobbled streets of London so that they could return. But mysteriously, their thoughts were filled with only shadows and darkness and they had trouble remembering any real detail of where they had just been. The timer itself was also lifeless; the powder in the phials had become clammy and damp and there was not a hint of a glow or a spark. It would or could not allow them to return to the same place immediately. Sick with worry for their little girl, who they felt sure was meant to be theirs to love and to look after, they tried the very next day, but with the same results. Indeed, every day afterwards they tried to return to that same dull grey, cobbled street somewhere in time, somewhere in London. They could think of nothing else and had no desire to travel anywhere else in history. The timer also, it seemed, had no desire to send them anywhere for its own devices either. Every day they tried to visualise the street on which they had met the little girl, but each time their minds were filled with the same shadows and darkness. Exactly one year after they had first made their trip, the memory suddenly became clear in their minds, as if a bright light had been turned on in a room of darkness and shadows. Bright sparks emanated from the egg timer. Their hearts rose with anticipation as the sound of the wind and sea filled their ears. But when they arrived, the street looked different. It was not cold and grey at all. The sun was shining in a sky of summer blue; they could feel its warmth on their faces immediately. The street they had been expecting to see seemed to have become an avenue of smart-looking, double-fronted, Victorian style, red brick villas. Their doors and window frames were all painted white. The gardens were filled with the colours of red and white roses, while the tiny lawns were bordered by high-gloss, black iron railings.

"Have we come to the correct street?" asked Magda, her confusion quite evident on her face, "or even the correct time?"

Harry pointed up to the sign that was fixed to the wall of the end house.

SYCAMORE STREET

"The street is the correct one," he answered, "and we were never sure of the exact year. We trusted the timer to bring us back to the right place and time." He looked at the timer where it sat in the palm of his hand. As they both continued to wonder where they were and what had happened, they were suddenly approached by an elegant young woman dressed in the typical attire of a well-to-do lady of the late nineteenth century. She was wheeling a Victorian-style pram. The baby inside was covered with knitted, pink woollen blankets and was fast asleep. Just as she was passing, she stopped and turned to face them.

"Good day, madam," she said addressing Magda. "May I help you? Are you perhaps looking for somebody?" Harry and Magda both gasped with surprise. Even though the person in front of them was grown and matured there was no mistaking those clear blue, shining eyes looking at them from beneath the brim of her wide, white hat.

"No thank you, madam," answered Harry, staring at her in wonder. "We had been worried about somebody that once lived here, but we have just found out that they are quite alright. No madam, but thank you."

The young woman smiled softly at them. "I am so glad to hear that," she said and then continued to walk past them down the avenue. As they both watched her disappear around the corner at the end of the road, the timer sprang into life.

They stood in their dining room, bemused and sad. Even though they were tremendously relieved to learn that the little girl had somehow been well cared for, they were baffled by what the timer had put them through! But as time went by and the expectation of their next trip filled their minds, the feelings of sadness and emptiness grew a little less. Harry, though, could not help but harbour resentment towards the timer, even though he knew that it did not make mistakes. Shortly after this, the egg timer seemed to stop working.

Over the years, Magda had become a lecturer in medieval history, and she particularly wanted to visit the battle of Hastings to see whether King Harold had, in fact, been shot by an arrow in the eye as most modern historians record. They stood in their dining room as usual and thought of the coast of Hastings in 1066. Nothing appeared to happen. They had used the timer so many times now, this 'loose' coordinate was usually enough. So they tried to be more specific. Sunday, 14 October 1066, Hastings, Sussex, England. Again, nothing happened. It began to dawn on them that perhaps the timer was unhappy with them; that they had done something wrong! It was Harry that pointed out that they shouldn't, after all, have tried to bring the little girl back to their own time.

"Obviously, it would unbalance things!" he said. "And

anyway, her life certainly seemed to turn out all right without us!" But still the timer refused to transport them.

Though they missed their trips to the past, their love for each other was complete and though the timer seemed to be inactive, they were always fully aware of its presence and they always kept it near them. In fact, when one or the other of them was troubled they would hold the little thing in their hand, and be comforted.

The years passed, and while they were at home the beautiful little egg timer became an ornament on their mantelpiece. They would often look at it and sigh, for they felt they missed its true friendship dreadfully. When they travelled, which was quite often, they would always take it with them. Over these years, Magda decided to return to college and using the knowledge she had learned from her trips, she soon qualified as a professor in medieval history. Her colleagues at the university where she eventually worked were astounded at the knowledge she possessed of all history. But they were disconcerted and even became very angry when she claimed to know things that had never been recorded in the history books. It bothered Magda that she was not able to share the 'truth' about history with others; that they would not believe her and that they thought her quite mad. She tried to explain that history was relative, and that it relied on the biased or unbiased opinion of the person that recorded it. This caused many arguments. She had then written a book, which included the omitted parts that she and Harry had witnessed in history, and sent them to potential publishers but they were returned as rubbish.

"So what had it all been about?" Harry had said. Shortly after Harry had first 'found' the timer, an old shabby-looking, brown leather-bound book had mysteriously appeared in his flat. On opening it, he found that all the handwritten entries began to disappear before his eyes as he read them, until all the pages became blank. He realised that this book was connected to the timer and that they should record all the events of their trips. Magda named it 'the Book of Truth,' and she faithfully recorded all the details of their trips in it. At the time of them trying to bring the little girl back, it was over half full.

"We have all this information, yet no one else can read what we have written and no one believes us when we try to tell them!"

So the years passed; both were now in their mid-sixties. Their love for each other was as strong if not stronger than ever. Harry would tell his wife that she had never been more beautiful, and Magda would squeeze his hand and tell him that he was a crazy old fool and should put on his glasses.

The reason for their visit to Johannesburg was twofold. Harry had seen advertised in the 'Timers Weekly' a very special men's pocket watch. It had apparently been made by Victor Kuhlberg of London in 1910, and was described as having a white enamel dial, with subsidiary dials for power reserve at 12.00 and constant seconds at 6.00. It was also wound by either the stem or by a key. But there were two things that attracted him the most about the watch: one of its movement plates had the mark of Joseph Preston of Prescott who was the eminent ébauche maker (an incomplete watch movement still to be fitted with jewels, escapement, mainspring, hands and dial) which confirmed the superb craftsmanship of its movement; and secondly, it was said to have once belonged to the last tsar of Russia. The other reason for their visit was due to Magda finally deciding to tell all publicly – the truth about history. They had hired the conference room of the Rosebank Hotel in the leafy northern suburbs of Johannesburg, and placed an advertisement in the national newspaper. "The timer has been growing on my mind, my darling," she said to Harry as she picked up the phone to book the venue, "I feel we have let it down. I feel we need to do something."

As he walked along the tree-lined streets of Rosebank, Harry remembered that this was where he had first met his precious Magda. Indeed, as the delicious aroma of newly baked bread, croissants and rich coffee filled his nostrils, he realised that he was walking past the very café in which she had been sitting all those years ago. He could hear the distinctive rhythm of the year's pop music, with which he was not impressed, for he was a Sinatra fan. He stopped and looked over at the front of the café. There was a large poster of the Beatles in the window next to one of a young outlandish-looking young man. His hair was wild and curly, his painfully thin body packaged in a 'Chinese style' suit. A thin, pasty-looking face stared out at the passersby through thick-rimmed sunglasses. Times are always changing, thought Harry, thinking of all the different styles and fashions he had witnessed through history, but that guy looks like a spider in a raincoat.

Harry took his seat in the front row of the conference room. He had arrived early and was the first there. There had been no tickets issued and entrance was to be paid at the door. Would anyone even attend, he thought. He looked at a cutting of the advertisement that had been placed in the newspaper:

HISTORY AS YOU <u>DON'T</u> KNOW IT
PRESENTED BY PROFESSOR MAGDA GINSBERG

ALL THOSE ATTENDING PLEASE BE ATTENTIVE:

AGENDA:

QUESTIONS AND ANSWERES
PLEASE ASK QUESTIONS ON HISTORY'S <u>VAGUE</u> MOMENTS
- TOPICS OF SPECIAL INTEREST
- WAS THE MAID OF ORLEANS A FRAUD?
- WHAT WAS THE NAME OF THE DRAGON THAT

SAINT GEORGE SLEW?
- "LET THEM EAT CAKE" – DID THAT FAMOUS REMARK REFER TO CARROT CAKE OF FISH CAKE?
- WHO WAS ROBIN HOOD? WAS HE REALLY THE GOOD GUY OR WAS HE JUST ROBBIN'?
- WHAT IS THE PARCHMENT OF LIFE?
- THE WORLD – PRE FLOOD

NB: BRING AN OPEN MIND BUT CRAMMED WITH QUESTIONS

ENTRANCE FEE:
HISTORIANS: R100/each
STUDENTS: R 50/each
ALL OTHERS: VERY WELCOME AND FREE OF CHARGE

He smiled to himself, folded the piece of paper and slipped it into his jacket pocket. Magda would be nervous, he knew, but he agreed with her; it was time to tell the world. He took out his new pocket watch, sighing with satisfaction at the feel of it in his palm. He flipped it open with his thumb nail and read the time on the pearl-inlaid face. 6.55 p.m. He sighed again. She's going to be dreadfully disappointed, he thought to himself as he looked around at all the empty seats. He was roused from his thoughts by a rush of movement and noise behind him as the doors to the conference room were flung open. To his amazement, a crowd of people, young, middle-aged and old, made their way to their seats. Some of them obviously knew each other and were chatting together earnestly. But as 7 p.m. approached, all had taken their seats and were waiting for Magda patiently.

At precisely 7 p.m., Magda entered the room and walked up to the podium. Her long, wavy, grey hair sprang to life as she walked. She had grown rather plump as she had grown older, but Harry was very happy with that; there was even more of her now to love. He stared and smiled at his beloved wife proudly.

"Good evening people, and welcome!" she said, her voice resonating clearly through the microphone in her hand. "Some of you may know me and some of you may not. I certainly recognise one or two faces out there, but either way, all of you will deem me unqualified to make some of the statements that I will make tonight. That is not what we should be concerned with. I ask you to open your minds and place yourselves mentally in the time periods we will visit tonight. Qualifications on paper in this case mean nothing, I am afraid. In these matters, I am qualified by other means."

There was a low murmur among the participants and a few puzzled expressions, especially among the historians and students.

"I am going to open this discussion a little differently," she continued. "I would like to start with questions from the audience on any topic of well-known or even not so well-known history. I will try to answer all your questions, of course, but I have a special interest from the year AD 1000 to our present year of 1965. Ask me something that maybe seems to be a little vague in the history books of today and I will try to clarify it for you if I can. However, please note that there will be the usual time spot allocated for more questions at the end of this seminar." There was silence. Then a low murmur rose from the audience as a young woman raised her hand. Magda nodded in her direction.

"Good evening, Professor Ginsberg!"

"Good evening," nodded Magda, taking her first sip of water.

"My name is Joy Taylor, and I am a student of medieval history at Oxford University. I am visiting friends in your beautiful country and was lucky enough to see the advertisement, so here I am and I hope you can help me with a question."

"Welcome to South Africa, and I certainly hope I can!" answered Magda.

Harry looked over his shoulder at the frumpy-looking, bespectacled student that stood a few rows behind him.

"'And none of you will bid the winter come, to thrust his icy fingers in my maw; ... I beg cold comfort; and you are so strait, and so ungrateful, you deny me that,'" she began, with suitable dramatics. "It refers to the death of King John, ma'am. In your opinion, why was there not a change from the Plantagenet rule at the time of John's death, he being such an unpopular king and in many eyes rather useless? His son Henry was only nine years old at the time – it would have been easy for the barons to dispose of him and then aid Louis to the throne of both France and England." The young woman sat down, grinning broadly. She removed her steamed up glasses and cleaned them quickly. Then, very pleased with herself, she looked up expectantly at Magda.

"First of all, let me say it sounds like you know the history of our old 'friend' King John and his times well, and may I say your Shakespeare too, by the sound of things, young lady. But I must emphasise that the following is not merely my opinion. Were you aware, Joy, that John didn't die of the dysentery, aggravated by fatigue and too much food and drink, as recorded in most history books?" The young woman immediately looked puzzled. She opened her mouth to say something, then snapped it shut. The room was still and silent. "A poison, Henbane to be precise, was mixed with a dish of peaches and given to him by William the Marshal. This, as well as the copious amounts of ale he consumed, disrupted the delicate equilibria of his body and he died in agonising convulsions," Magda continued. "But what is interesting I think, is not so much the fact that he *was* poisoned, but the reason for it. William knew that sooner or later the fiend of a king would have been assassinated by a supporter of the French and therefore pave a way for Louis, the king of France, to take up the crown. Being a staunch supporter of John's father Henry and brother Richard, William was going to do all he could to make sure the Plantagenet dynasty would not end with his death. He rallied an army and the people of England behind the young boy Henry well before he committed the ghastly deed. But in my opinion, he did the right thing, and I told him so." There was a titter of laughter from most of the audience. Obviously, she was joking. They were beginning to warm to this humorous lecturer's style. But Harry held his pocket watch in his hand for comfort. Magda took a sip of water from the glass on the podium. The student smiled at Magda, pleased with the answer.

"Next question?" cried Magda.

A tall man stood up, one of the older people of the audience. "I am from the publication 'History as It Happened,' madam. I see on the advertisement for this seminar that there is a reference to the mythical 'George and the dragon' saga. I would therefore like to ask you to name the so-called dragon that the so-called George is supposed to have slain."

"Thank you, sir. Your question is understood and most welcome," acknowledged Magda. She looked in Harry's direction suddenly. There, on the wooden armrest dividing his seat from the one next to him, for some reason he had placed the little egg timer. She stared at it a moment, it seemed larger, shinier and more golden than usual. (Harry had felt uncomfortable; the timer had seemed to grow large and heavy in his pocket.)

With confidence and a loud and clear voice, Magda continued:

"Firstly sir, let me tell you there are well over forty patronages of Saint George still in existence around the world today. Quite unusual for a mythical character, wouldn't you say?"

The man who had asked the question rolled his eyes dramatically and took his seat, chuckling loudly.

"If you were to study the seventeenth century works of Daniel Papebroch, Jean Bolland and Godfrey Henschen, you would learn that the mythical character of the medieval legends is dismissed as such. The real Saint George was born to a Greek Christian noble family of Lydda, Palestine on 4 November, 280 AD."

The man stood up again, clearly agitated. "Yes madam, there is no need to tell us what we already know, though you seem to have *exact* details of his date of birth. Surely you are guessing! We know it was somewhere between 275 and 285 AD. Where did you get this information?"

Harry looked over his shoulder and gave the 'historian' a stern look. He hated it when someone attempted to give Magda a hard time. Then he sat back and stared up at the ceiling at some long ago memory.

"So you and maybe others here will know that he became a soldier under the Roman emperor Diocletian," Magda continued unfazed, " and that his skills were so great that he was soon promoted to the rank of tribune and was then stationed in the imperial guard of Diocletian at Nicomedia. On the 27 February 303 AD, the emperor issued an edict that every Christian soldier should be arrested, but George objected and presented himself to his emperor. He renounced the edict and declared himself a faithful follower of Jesus Christ in front of all his fellow soldiers and tribunes. But as Diocletian had known George's father, who had also been one of his finest soldiers, he attempted to persuade George to convert by offering him land, money and servants. But his efforts were in vain. Did you know sir, Diocletian wept with frustration?"

"Really!" answered the man. "I suppose you dried his tears with your handkerchief!" he continued with contempt, clearly now thinking that Magda was some sort of 'joke.'

"Left with no choice, the emperor now issued an execution order," Magda continued, ignoring him, "but due to the embarrassment he caused the emperor and his fellow tribunes, George was grotesquely tortured." Magda's voice broke a little. Steadying herself by holding on to the podium with one hand, she stared at Harry. He stared back, his eyes flooded with tears. She slowly took another sip of water and then, composing herself, she continued: "The torture of George was a terrible spectacle," she said, her voice wavering again, "including laceration on a wheel of swords, from which he was resuscitated three times!" She took another sip of water. The historian stood up again. "I suppose it was you that resuscitated him as well!" he declared sarcastically. Again, he chuckled loudly as he took his seat. The audience, though, were mesmerised and silent.

"On the 23 April at 9 a.m. in the morning, before the city walls of Nicomedia, saint George was beheaded, but ..."

"There you go again," the historian shouted out rudely, not even bothering to stand up this time, "how do you claim to know the actual time of the execution? Did a little bird tell you?"

Harry was now about to jump out of his seat and 'sort' the historian out, but just as he started to rise, he became aware of a faint familiar glow from the timer on the armrest. It had been so long since he had seen those eerie interwoven colours of green, silver and gold. He really did not know why he had brought it along, except that he felt compelled to keep it with him, to keep it safe. He resumed his seat, looking at it from the corner of his eyes.

"However, his sufferings did not go unnoticed," Magda again continued, also noticing the faint glow from the timer. "For Diocletian's wife Alexandra and a pagan priest were so moved by the way he bravely endured his agonies that they were converted to Christianity, and then of course they themselves were martyred for their faith by her husband."

"Madam!" declared the man, this time standing up, "you have certainly not told me or I suspect anyone else in this room anything we did not already know. Though I did notice that you seemed to leave out the dragon, not to mention naming it."

Harry stood up. He could restrain himself no longer. "Obviously, you weren't listening you oaf! The dragon is clearly present all through the story of Saint George and particularly during his final ordeal."

"Oh, really!" cried the man, a wide grin on his face, "Invisible, was he? And if so, what was the *invisible* dragon's name?"

"His name is *Satan*, sir," interrupted Magda.

The man threw his hands up in the air. He looked around briefly at the other people in the auditorium and then sat down again. The audience now buzzed alive; everybody seemed to start talking at once. Most of them clearly found the debate amusing, but some had become pensive and uneasy. Magda waited patiently for the noise to die down. Just as the audience began to quieten, a loud and clear voice with a clipped English accent rang out from the front left side of the room. "Would you by any chance know where the missing Fabergé eggs are, or the Parchment of Life?"

CHAPTER 1
VASSILI

The truck crawled along the narrow dirt road, forcing its way through torrential rain. Its wheels struggled to find traction in the thick yellow mire. Visibility was poor. Plant gritted his teeth and hunched up his shoulders in agitation. The pelting rain on the roof resonated like a thousand golf balls bouncing on it simultaneously. He screwed up his face, struggling to make sense of the latest twist in events. Where had that fellow disappeared to, and with Tatiana Nicolaevna? He knew that she had not been abducted by him – she had obviously gone with him willingly. Her second and latest mysterious disappearance had upset her sisters terribly; Olga it seemed in particular. Indeed, he was worried about Olga. Of the three, she had by far lost the most weight, her once pretty face now hollow, gaunt and somewhat ravaged. It was more the face of one approaching middle age than that of a twenty-three-year-old young woman. She was struggling with the news of the death of her father in silent trauma. Those eyes could break the heart of the coldest of assassins. He strove to put it at the back of his mind; there was nothing he could do about it now. He had to take charge of the situation, but he was edgy with concern. This damned rain had held them up far too long. They would miss the deadline if it continued. He'd had word yesterday of news that he would keep to himself for the time being. The boy had died. He had gone to sleep soon after he and his mother had boarded the Red Cross train for Odessa, and never woke up again. The image of the young tsarevich with his saucer-like eyes and white, paper-thin skin flashed into his mind. He swallowed hard. What was it about this family that touched him so? Now the tsarina was on her way alone to Odessa with the body of her beloved child. She would need her daughters around her. He also knew there was only so long the British warship could wait, so time was of the essence. He was so deep in thought that he had been unaware of the officer sitting next to him in the passenger seat, staring at him.

"It seems I should have splattered his brains after all," said the officer.

Plant turned briefly to look at him and then peered through the windscreen again to resume his gruelling task. "That man did us a great service, Owen. We wouldn't have got any of them out of there if it hadn't been for him. His manner and ways were a little unorthodox I admit, but effective."

"Unorthodox or not, it seems he's just kidnapped the 'prized grand duchess' and I don't know what … "

"'*Prized* grand duchess' Captain Tudor!" interrupted Plant, turning to his colleague, a perturbed look on his face, "a prize maybe; but surely no more a prize than the ones we have in the back here. Unless of course she is a personal prize?" Plant looked a little longer and harder at Tudor than he should have, and had to steer the truck abruptly back into the middle of the road.

"You know the deal, Reg. They will all need to melt into an obscure life back in old Blighty or wherever they end up. For we know the Bolshies are already planning something particularly nasty for them – not to mention you." Plant smiled to himself at the memory of the sound of the two gun shots that had undoubtedly finished off Yurovsky and Ermakov. Two *prized* revolutionaries executed by their own men!

"I have been promised by Louis and even higher," Tudor continued, "that she is mine if she'll have me, but I haven't even had the chance to talk to her, as some hothead from your lot decided to run off with her. Does he realise he's now got a price on his head from *both* sides?"

Plant looked over his shoulder to make sure the tarpaulin covering the girls in the back was still secure. It was. Disconcerted, he glanced again at Owen Tudor, the officer who he himself had prevented from blowing away a very serious problem.

"Look," he said, "I am not even sure he *is* with us! All I know is that he turned up in the nick of time; he certainly saved my bacon." He felt what was left of his scabbed and swollen left ear now missing its lobe. He also felt Tudor's burning stare into the side of his cheek as he peered through the screen again.

"You mean to tell me he's not even part of the mission? Then why the hell did you ... "

"I was *alone*, you buffoon, and he helped *me*!" Plant bellowed, his face turning purple. He gripped the steering wheel with all his pent-up anger, almost distorting its shape. "Have you ever been in that situation, Owen? You Sandhurst monkey!"

"Take it easy, take it easy my friend," said Tudor, somewhat taken aback and realising that he knew very little about the man he called Reg.

"And I can tell you something else," Plant continued, his anger still boiling. "You will have a fight on your hands for her affections," he said, remembering the note that had fallen out of Arty's pocket at their first meeting.

"There's more to this than you know, my friend," answered Tudor, "as a brother officer, whether you were schooled at Sandhurst with us chimps or not," he continued coolly, "or whether you were favoured by an influential friend in high

3

places to get where you are. I do know I can trust you, and under these circumstances I think you need to know."

"Know what?" replied Plant, collecting himself, quite aware that Tudor was going to confide in him something he shouldn't.

"They have all been designated husbands," said Tudor, staring ahead at his reflection in the windscreen. "Each one has her own story to hide behind; Olga is to be married to some politician in the states. She is apparently the daughter of a deposed Russian aristocrat who fled to America shortly after the October revolution. Not too far from the truth, wouldn't you say?"

"Very nice, very nice," answered Plant wryly, "and does she have any say in the matter?"

"Olga? No," answered Tudor. "She has been 'predestined' as they say."

"They?" shouted Plant above the din of the rain that was pelting the roof of the truck again.

Tudor looked down at his hands, struggling with some inner decision. "By the Club!" He gasped.

Plant had heard of the 'Club,' but wasn't sure of its function or who its members were. In the circles he had been frequenting since his sudden transfer from Scotland Yard six years previously to MI1, he had heard frequent references to the 'Club.' Indeed, he had slowly become aware the organisation was known by many different names. It had an air of mystery and undoubted affluence, and its functions and purpose were somehow kept secret. All his associates seemed to know of the organisation, but nobody seemed to know anything about it. It was in Plant's nature to dislike anything he could not access.

"So you are part of the 'Old Farts' club, are you?" he said sarcastically, not at all believing such a thing. "Go on! What other secrets are you going to tell me?"

"Don't make fun of something you don't know about, Reg," said Tudor. "Power is mightier than both the sword and the pen."

"If the sword and the pen were in unison, we probably wouldn't have a need for your power," cried Plant, "But as that day will never come on this blasted earth, just give me a colt forty-five like the one I saw in the Ipatiev House the other night and I would have all the power I need. No need for 'Clubs, swords or pens!" He laughed loudly, trying to cover his true feelings. He also needed Tudor to tell him more. "Go on my friend," he said, "You can trust me!"

Tudor looked straight ahead again through the windscreen of the truck, not really noticing that the rain was beginning to ease.

"Marie is to go Canada," he said. "A very wealthy landowner is patiently waiting for his new bride who apparently is not Russian at all, but French."

"Quite ironic," interrupted Plant, "as she looks the most Russian of all her sisters!"

"*They* know best my friend," answered Tudor airily. "She is now the daughter of a French diplomat who got caught in a Zeppelin raid whilst in Hull. Those idiot Krauts had been trying to hit London! Can you believe it? So penniless and homeless Marie will go to her new husband."

"Another irony," said Plant ruefully, "considering she should actually be one of the richest young women in the world today."

"Their lives were expensive," replied Tudor simply.

"Do *they* know we live in the twentieth century?" accused Plant, beginning to understand the situation. "And where is good old Uncle George in all this 'slave trading?'"

"Let me correct myself," said Tudor, "Power is mightier that the sword, the pen and the *king*."

Plant was silent, but there was a strange look in his eye as he tried to see ahead with the aid of the dim yellow lights of the headlamps that seemed to be dissolved by the atrocious conditions outside. For king and country, my arse!

"Anastasia will stay with her mother in Harrogate," continued

Tudor, "at least for a while. Her aunt, Grand Duchess George, is running a hospital on the outskirts of the town. We thought it a good idea for them to get involved."

"Incognito, of course," said Plant with undisguised sarcasm.

"Of course," said Tudor. "They will be given an allowance and they will be near to their relatives."

"How very thoughtful of you all," answered Plant, raising his voice as the rain began to pour heavily again. "So what new identity have you got for the incredible disappearing duchess?"

Tudor smiled to himself. He put his hand into the inside pocket of his jacket and produced a rather creased and crumpled black and white photo of Tatiana. She was standing in a white stone courtyard by a fountain.

"My friend Louis gave this to me," he said solemnly studying the photo, "They call him Dicky, you know … "

"I can't imagine why," said Plant sarcastically.

"He told me she is much more beautiful than most of her photos reflect. In fact, as you can see, all her sisters are," continued Tudor, ignoring the comment.

Plant had to agree. He had seen photographs of the imperial daughters, many of them as gawky teenagers. They had now grown into quite beautiful young women. Again he thought of Olga. Ravaged, yet still beautiful.

"Louis tells me we are a perfect match. He says she is pretty down to earth for a grand duchess, probably due to their austere upbringing. Though she is apparently rather deep and reserved, she is practical and a natural leader. Reg, what man wouldn't want a woman with such talents to be his wife?" Tudor looked at Plant questioningly.

Plant threw his head back and laughed. "So you had never met her, talked to her or conversed with her in anyway apart from just now, when you almost shot her trusty companion in front of her," Plant exploded incredulously. "You have to tell me Owen, what guise will she be in when you run away into the sunset together?" He looked briefly at the young woman in the photo. She could only have been about eighteen when it had been taken, her face so young and innocent as she posed primly in her virginal white dress. Tudor looked at the man he called Reg, and quite seriously replied.

"A belly dancer from Constantinople."

*

Smith's shoulder healed much quicker than expected. Of course, Peabody had used the excuse of 'a shooting accident' when accompanying him to the hospital. "Anyway, there is a war on; lots of people are getting shot and blown up these days!" he had argued with the matron.

"Yes sir," she had replied, "but not generally in the middle of the Lancashire countryside!"

The bullet had propelled clean through Smith's flesh; luckily for him it had missed vital organs. "It's a pity it didn't hit you on that skull of yours," Peabody had said. "It would have rebounded and hit that swine, Plant."

They were sitting together now in the dean's study in the college. Peabody was gazing at the front page of an old newspaper that he had found in the college library.

JAPAN ATTACKS RUSSIAN FLEET AT PORT ARTHUR WITHOUT WARNING

"I like their style!" Peabody muttered to himself.

Smith was taking the liberty of warming himself in front of the fire's gently collapsing embers. The amber glow cast flickering shadows on the wall. The room was dimly illuminated by the twilight that exuded from the large arched window overlooking the seemingly endless, straight driveway that lead up to the entrance of Stoneyhurst. Peabody gazed at Smith disapprovingly.

"Don't think you can make yourself too comfortable in this office, my man," he said, "just because you got a little scratch on the shoulder, which was entirely your own fault, may I add. That doesn't mean you can now roast that great big rump of yours to your heart's content!" He stood up from behind his desk and walked over to the window, muttering to himself.

"I hate this time of year!" he declared. "Blasted snow! February is not far enough away from the rubbish of Christmas (he hated Christmas and never celebrated it) and not near enough to the promise of May." He much preferred the warmer weather. He craned his neck as he looked up at the large swirling snowflakes that were beginning to fall again onto the existing white blanket. "I think it's time we made a trip, Mr Smith. Are you up to it?"

Peabody really didn't care about Smith's wellbeing, but he was concerned that his bodyguard was in a good enough shape to protect him in case things got a little rough.

"Just say the word, boss," said the gallant Smith. "I want that Ermakop geezer, or whoever he is!" He rubbed his shoulder gingerly. "I'm going to blow his nasty little hairy head off."

Peabody studied Smith a moment. His eyes grew smaller as he shook his head slowly. "I swear my man if that bullet had missed your arm and gone in your ear it would have come clean out the other side, no harm done. Do you ever listen? We can't go back to 1918 for another eleven months yet, remember!" He dug the little timer out of his jacket pocket and held it in the air between his index finger and thumb. "This obstinate character won't let us." Frustrated, he banged the little egg timer onto his desk and then stood up suddenly in fright as it produced a blinding, white flash of light. "Oh, go to hell!" cried Peabody, staring at it more alarmed than he appeared to be.

"Blimey boss, we will have forgotten what it is we want to go back for by then!" exclaimed the hapless Smith, taking no notice of the buoyant mood of the timer or his boss.

"Maybe that is part of the reason for this whole yearly thing," said Peabody quietly, almost to himself. He rubbed his chin in thought. He took his seat again behind his desk, and took out a key from his trouser pocket. He unlocked one of the bottom drawers, grasped the white enamelled egg with his long, skinny brown fingers and brought it up to his chest lovingly. "I must make it complete," he said. "Clodius will never know. I'm sure there will be something going on with him and those Bolsheviks in order to secure all those eggs when the time comes. But nobody knows that those parts are missing now and no doubt, will still be missing when it matters. Only us, Mr Smith. Only us, Tatiana Nicolaevna and that coward that she hung around with."

"But didn't Fanny Romanov say she lost it, boss?" cried Smith, still happily warming himself by the fire.

"Who? You idiot!" He set the egg down on his desk, securing it between two paper clips. "Tatiana Nicolaevna *said* she lost it, but I'm not so sure. Hidden somewhere maybe, but lost? No."

Smith grunted softly at the reproach from the master he adored. Suddenly, his face lit up.

"Ooooh boss, I've just had a thought!" he exclaimed

"Be careful, Smith my man," answered Peabody sarcastically, "I may have to make an official announcement!"

"No boss, listen to me," insisted Smith. "Do you think that the little shooting incident we were involved in before you decided to 'rescue' us was 'the end' for her? That she bought it then and there? After all, you told me that they all *do* get it in the end."

Peabody gazed at Smith, his face emotionless.

"As complicated as this sounds, Mr Smith, try to understand." Peabody picked up his gold pen that lay in front of him. He rolled it between his palms. Smith looked down at the floor. He put his two index fingers at the side of each temple in concentration. "We are at present in 1915 and none of these little episodes have happened yet, though as I have already informed you, I am sure our friends at the 'Club' are already busy with their plans. Old Nick trusts them. Hence the little trick he and the Club pulled on us with those fake eggs we 'rescued' from Livadia. Egg was all over me Smith, but that is not going to happen again. As it stands today, the trust old Nick has for Clodius and his pals will lead to his and his country's downfall. For as you know, that little trip we took to the future the other day still stated that they all get murdered in the basement of that house. Obviously, what has been recorded seems to have been manipulated, Charlie boy. For we know for certain the event was a little different from what that history book said. For instance, how can we explain the photos of your friend Ermakov and that Yurovsky character? Their photos in that book and the two hooligans we met in that house just do not match up. That book in the library of 2012 clearly states without any doubt they had also found all their bones, including those of Fanny Dodger, identified by some modern scientific way of testing." Peabody smiled at Smith knowingly. "Apparently, no bodies had ever been found until they made that discovery, prompting rumours that all or at least some of them managed to escape. Do you have the aroma of the 'Masters Club' in your nostrils yet, Mr Smith?" Smith grunted softly but did not look up, nor did he remove his fingers from his temples. "So if things remain as they are and the Club have their way, the fate of old Nick and his family will be just as we read it: a ghastly murder. But more importantly for us, the eggs seem to remain 'lost'." Peabody put down the pen. "Is the smell getting stronger yet, Smith? They try to explain the bodies lying hidden for almost a hundred years due to them chopping them up, pouring acid all over them and then burning them. I mean, Smith, have you any idea what heat is required to burn a human body to ash? You certainly cannot do it with sulphuric acid and a match," Peabody continued.

"But why would they go to all that trouble, boss? I mean, why try to hide what they are going to do to them? Why not rather put it in the newspaper?" said Smith.

Peabody raised both his eyebrows. "You know, Mr Smith, you do surprise me with a bit of intelligent perception sometimes. That is just it! Why didn't they advertise the fact that they had done away with 'Bloody Nicholas? Is the aroma becoming a stench yet, Smith?"

"I really don't know how they could identify them, boss, if they had done all that to them, and only found them all those years later. Was it their fingerprints?" Smith finally brought his hands down from his temples. He rubbed his behind quickly and then spread out his hands palms up and inspected the ends of his cumbersome fingers.

"The miracles of future science, my dear Smith, are going to surpass the fingerprinting craze of today," Peabody informed him philosophically. He poured himself a large brandy from the decanter on his desk while Smith stared forlornly at the other empty glass next to it.

"You can have one, Charles, when you stop warming that great arse of yours!" Peabody declared, holding the empty glass in the air tantalisingly. Without taking his eyes from the bronze-coloured liquid in the decanter, Smith left the fireside and promptly seated himself opposite Peabody in the 'naughty pupil' chair, where his boss much preferred him. He then helped himself to a large brandy.

"So, let's recap," said Peabody in the voice of the dean of Stoneyhurst College. "Our little visit to 1918 seems to have changed nothing so far, but we know that we can change what happens, don't we? If we choose!" Peabody held the crystal glass of brandy in the air in front of him. His eyes grew wide as he imagined Clodius Albertus drowning in it. "Look at that nincompoop, Custer; we both know what we could have done for him, don't we! Thinking about it now, we should perhaps have let him become the president!"

"But we didn't need to, boss," replied Smith, "for we still managed to come back with lots of that nice Black Hills gold,"

Smith sat back contentedly. "But do you really think we can change history, boss, and that it will stay changed?"

"I believe that is one of the reasons I have been given the use of it," said Peabody airily, "to change it for the better, so that the 'Club,' but with *me* at its head, will continue to rule the world and everything in it. Yes, Mr Smith! Fantasy becomes reality when you have one of these," he picked up the egg timer again and balanced it in the palm of his hand, "even if it is an obstinate little sod." He set it down next to the other larger egg on his desk. "As I was saying, here we are in the present able to see the past and the future, and we have control over both. The hopes and dreams of all those romantics and do-gooders away there in the future, Smith, are in *my* hands!"

Smith stared at his boss in admiration, then he raised both his hands and placed his fingers on his temples again.

" Dreams dreamed up by dreamers that can't except bad things can happen to good little girlies," continued Peabody emphatically. "We are in the good old present where nothing particularly nasty has happened to them yet. Just think that at this very moment, Tatiana Nicolaevna is probably having tea with daddy, mummy and sisters in the best china money can buy over there in Russia, while millions of men and women are dying in this war that is all about greed and stupidity, and yet totally oblivious to the fact that it is being manipulated by you know who. Positively *pongy* now, isn't it, Charles?" Peabody smiled at the wonder of it all.

"But why don't we just go back to 1912 or sometime and nick all the eggs when they're not looking, boss?" asked Smith, still grappling to understand the complexity of the situation.

"Because timer or no timer, that family is too well-guarded. Remember, Nicholas is constantly on the lookout for anyone trying to assassinate him or any of his family. Besides, 1912 is not a good year, Smith; we would miss the 1913 Tercentenary egg. No, what we need to do is cause a few transgressions so that consequences will be different."

Smith tried to grasp all that Peabody was trying to explain.

"But does that mean now, in this time, the egg in your hands is missing in Russia as well?" he asked.

"If I knew where the damn thing is supposed to be in say 1916, we could go and check that out!" exclaimed Peabody. "This one is now in our time dimension. What would happen If we took this back and placed it next to itself, if you know what I mean, would be quite interesting," He looked at Smith enthusiastically, and then shook his head slowly. "I can see that your 'brainy' moment has lapsed," he said, watching Smith scratch his large, shiny bald dome, looking very confused. "I will explain it again to you when you have another attack!"

"But what would happen, boss, if we managed to steal that complete egg in exchange for our knickers and bring it back here. Would we have two eggs?" asked Smith, determined to at least try to understand.

Peabody himself had been wondering about that.

"As I said, my man, that remains to be seen," he answered, rubbing his chin. He crossed his legs quickly and scratched his elbow, and then uncrossed his legs again. His mind inexplicably had suddenly become filled with the image of Tatiana and of that coward Arthur Benjamin. Why had they been on his mind so much this last week or so? It was as if he was being forced to think of them, whether he liked it or not.

Smith seemed to guess his thoughts.

"I wonder where Blew Eyes figures in all this?" he said. "Even though he is a wet lettuce, I can't believe he would have let that Fanny Romanov face the music alone."

"Some men just have no honour, Smith, especially those of the future, it seems. I don't think we have to pay any mind to that loser again; the future is where he is going to stay."

"But boss, how are we going to find the whereabouts of those missing egg bits? We don't know where she put them or when she put them there."

Peabody stood up again; the light had grown even dimmer now as the snowflakes swirled around outside the window.

"I wonder," said Peabody quietly. He stared at the little gold-coloured egg timer on his desk. It couldn't have been a coincidence meeting on the Titanic like we did, he thought. The chances of bumping into Tatiana Nicolaevna like that were quite extraordinary. It must be part of some great plan of the timer's; a plan to bring her and the Fabergé eggs to me. There can be no other reason for it. His mind was racing now. He went over to the timer and picked it up. A faint glow of red, silver and gold pulsed slowly from the bottom phial. "We don't have to know," he said out loud, turning to Smith again. "We don't have to do anything! Don't you see? The timer will take us to when and where we need to be. It just needs a little hint for the coordinates every so often."

He opened a draw in his desk and brought out a single golden key. He slid it across the table where it stopped perfectly in front of Smith.

"Smith, old boy, go down to the cellar and bring up Cleopatra's hair pin. I may have found a use for it." He picked up the newspaper again, as Smith sighed heavily and rose from his seat, studying the headlines. A plan had come into his head. "Yes," he said out loud, "I certainly like their style."

*

The Alexander palace at Tsarskoe Selo was named after Alexander I of Russia. It was given to him by his grandmother Catherine II in celebration of his marriage to Elizaveeta Alexeevna. It was considered to be the greatest creation by its architect, Quarenghi, and by world standards was deemed a masterpiece. The main façade consists of a spectacular Corinthian colonnade, complete with two rows of columns. Built in 1792, over the next one hundred and fifty years its many outside features were restored but never altered, as it was considered impossible to improve on its original beauty.

In the early part of the twentieth century, Nicholas II and his wife Alexandra Feodorovna made it their permanent home. Indeed, they were to live here for the last thirteen years of Nicholas's reign as emperor. Their living quarters were situated in the east wing of the palace. The suite on the left contained their bedroom, the Mauve Room and Alexandra's Palisander drawing room. The suite on the right contained the working study and the emperor's dressing room, as well as other service rooms. All the rooms were sumptuously decorated, homely and deeply personal. Later as their family grew, the concert hall that had occupied the full width of the east wing was converted into more private rooms. The architect Silvio Danini was commissioned to create a new study for Nicholas and above this on the first floor, a nursery with bedrooms to accommodate their four daughters and son. Nicholas, Alexandra and their children loved their home, though perhaps the family's favourite room of all was the Maple Room. It was so called due to an abundance of maple wood furniture and wall panelling. It was divided into several cosy sitting areas with richly upholstered chairs, sofas and tables. Scattered on the table tops and mantelpiece were fine Russian and Danish porcelains. The family would gather here for after-dinner coffee or evening tea, and when the children were young they would play board games together. As the girls grew older, it would be the place where they would talk with their mother and among themselves as they sewed and embroidered. She would often sit on the elaborately maple-carved mezzanine floor, also sewing while enjoying looking down proudly on her beautiful daughters. This way she was near to all she loved, for her husband's study was only accessible from the mezzanine. In the spring, the room was filled with the scents of her most loved flowers: violets, gillyflowers and lily of the valley.

It was in this room one balmy summer evening in 1903 that

eight-year-old Vassili Kharitonov, son of one of the imperial cooks, found himself. He had inexplicably been asked to join the family for tea. They had not yet arrived from dinner but he had been shown into the room by one of the footmen, told to wait and not to touch anything. He seated himself in the shadows upon a cane couch within one of the cosy corners. The fruity smell of wood all around him filled his nostrils. There was also a vague perfume of blackcurrant in the air that was unfamiliar to him. Even though he lived in the palace with his father, he had never been to the east wing before, for this was off limits except to the personal guests or retainers of the imperial family. He sat waiting nervously, wondering why on earth he had been summoned. It had never happened before, nor had he heard of anybody else of his standing being summoned in this manner either. He was scared. The enormous grandfather clock ticked vociferously in the opposite corner of the room. However, he studied his surroundings intently. Beneath his feet lay an enormous grey-green luxurious carpet, from which a faint smell of lavender emanated. The carpet covered every inch of the large floor. Upon this were scattered various rugs. One in particular caught his attention: a large brown bear skin complete with fur, head and wide open mouth from which gaped a large pink tongue surrounded by huge yellow fangs. Vassili then wondered again why he had been summoned. I hope I don't end up like this bear, he thought, shuddering. The floor area was divided into several 'cosy corners' complemented by ultramodern, yet elegant furniture, the like of which he had never seen before. The upholstery was of rich green, deep pinks and forest browns. The high walls of the room, which were dusty pink in colour, curved inwards at the top, giving a delightful coving effect. The highest of the coved walls went over the balcony and then over the large window and door which gave access to the mezzanine floor and then to what looked to Vassili like the entrance to another room. A secret room, perhaps? The foot of the staircase that lead up to the mezzanine floor was flanked by a large square, maple wood pillar. The wooden balcony which reached across the whole width of the room was of a dull golden hue; the colour of honey, Vassili thought. He stared up at the ceiling, completely mesmerised by the unique carvings inset with emerald-green coloured glass. As the low light shone through the glass, Vassili saw that each 'cosy corner' was radiated in a low green haze. In the right-hand corner of the room, he noticed a round sofa that seemed to have been built into the wall with the same golden-hued wood panelling. In its centre lay a beautiful maple wood cabinet. Upon this lay an assortment of porcelain and glass busts and statues. Through the leaded glass doors of the cabinet, he could see an arrangement of what looked like large, coloured, egg-shaped ornaments. Their shells were elaborately decorated with tiny jewels or gold inlay. They stood on equally elaborate gold and jewelled stands. Vassili counted them. There were seven. Returning to the surface of the cabinet, Vassili now saw what to him looked a little out of place: A tiny, dark grey metal square box that had been placed directly in front of a bronze statue. This particularly caught his attention. It was the statue of a Russian infantryman from the Napoleonic Wars. His clothes were torn, his sculpted boots were worn and his face looked weary, yet somehow triumphant at the same time, as he held his sabre high above his head.

Vassili loved the history of his people, so he knew the story well: How in 1812 Napoleon had tried to force the then Tsar Alexander I from trading with British merchants by invading Russia. A French army of six hundred and eighty thousand men crossed over the Neman River. A victory at Smolensk followed, forcing the Russians to retreat. Vassili smiled to himself as he thought of how clever his ancestors had been. Instead of engaging the enormous French army directly, they had retreated deep into their own country while their Cossack regiment used the 'scorched earth' tactic so that the French were unable to live off the land. When the two armies finally did meet at Borodino, although the Russians again were defeated, the main body of their army managed to escape. This left the French once again victorious but undersupplied of food and clothing to protect them from the approaching winter.

Vassili's face grew hot at the thought of the severely depleted French army entering Moscow and then grinned again to himself when he remembered that even then, the tsar would not sue for peace. For the Byel-liy Czarina (White Empress) would soon come to the rescue of her people. Playing for time, the Russians deliberately held back from another engagement with the French. Realising there was no decisive victory in sight, Napoleon retreated. As they marched for home, the French army was obliterated by the onslaught of the merciless Russian winter. When they finally crossed over the Berezina River, only twenty seven thousand soldiers remained fit for battle. There are many obstacles to invading my land, he thought proudly. If my people don't get you, the Byel-liy Czarina will.

He looked around quickly; he had a feeling that he was being watched. It seemed he was still alone. He leaned over to the table and picked up the statue. It was lighter than it looked. The details of the face were so fine that he felt he could see the depths of misery and sorrow in its lidless eyes. He turned it upside down and saw with surprise that a cork stopper was sunken into the base. The figure was hollow! He was so lost in his thoughts that he had not noticed a young girl had entered the room and was now standing on the right side of the couch, staring at him inquisitively. He put the statue down quickly with a loud thud. The girl looked a little younger than he; maybe six or seven, he thought. She wore a thoroughly ruffled lilac-coloured skirt, an ivory-coloured blouse with lace at the nape of her neck reaching high up just below her chin. It was soiled with a red sticky substance that looked like jam. Her dark hair was waist length and untidy, her dark grey eyes mischievous and oriental looking. Looking down at her feet, he saw that she was only wearing one white ankle sock and no shoes. Her right fist was clenched into a ball as if holding something very tightly. She quickly looked back over her shoulder at the door. Then she stepped on to her tiptoes and peered up at the mezzanine floor. Seemingly satisfied that they were alone, she tried to smooth down her skirt with both hands, making it even grubbier. Then she faced him squarely. Her eyes now grew wider, her mouth opened a little and then snapped shut. She looked like she urgently needed to tell him something.

"Can you keep a secret?" she finally gasped in a hurried whisper.

Still startled, Vassili made no response. Who was this girl? Was she one of the servant children? She certainly looked the worse for wear. But what was she doing here? Had she also been summoned?

"Cat got your tongue!" she exclaimed in a high pitched voice while shaking her head from side to side theatrically, "can't you speak when you're spoken to?"

"No cat has got my tongue!" he declared. "*See!*" He promptly stuck out his large pink one. "And anyway, I don't know if you are one of the kitchen girls or something, but you'll be in for it if you get caught in here! You see, *I'm* supposed to be here. *I've* been summoned!"

The girl laughed. "I know that, you idiot!" she cried. She then immediately sat down next to him. Vassili edged a little away from her. "Papa wants to speak to you about something."

"Papa?" enquired Vassili, a sudden sinking feeling in his stomach.

"Yes, Papa," she answered. "He, mama, and my sister will be here in a minute or two, so we better be quick."

"Oh," he cried. Although he now noticed that the fabrics of her skirt and blouse were very fine, she certainly didn't look or behave like a grand duchess. He wondered which grand duchess he was talking to and whether he should be bowing or kneeling in front of her. But the girl didn't seem to care about etiquette. She held out her hand directly under his nose and then slowly unclenched her fist. There, on her grubby, sweaty little palm lay a quite remarkable tiny crown. Its tiny diamond stones glistened in the low light. Wrapped around it at its base lay a tiny gold chain from which hung a minute sapphire.

"I need to hide this," she told him simply, "before the others come!"

Still rather taken aback and really not knowing how to respond to her, he pointed steadily at the small metal box that lay on the cabinet next to the soldier. "You could put it there," he stammered awkwardly. She picked it up and opened it.

"This is no good!" she declared. "Mama keeps her thimble in there, so she is bound to find it."

"But what is it?" he asked, his confidence growing due to her simple, down to earth manner.

"It's Papa's crown, you fool!" she answered him rudely, "and I need to hide it."

Unfortunately, Vassili could not contain himself and burst out laughing at the thought of the emperor wearing that little crown on his head. The little girl glared at him, her face growing crimson with annoyance. "Are you making fun of me?" she cried.

Vassili very quickly straightened his face. He picked up the statue of the soldier. "You could put it in the little box and then in here." He suggested quite seriously. He pulled the stopper out of the base of the statue. "I am sorry your Imperial Highness, I did not mean to offend you, but where did you get that beautiful little crown from and why would you want to hide it?"

"Perfect!" the little girl exclaimed in delight, her demeanour changing at once. She promptly removed a silver thimble from the little box. She placed it on the table and then placed the tiny crown and pendant inside. Vassili handed her the statue, which she took, and turning it upside down, she dropped the tiny box inside and then forced the stopper back into place. This she struggled with, so Vassili helped her.

"Now Papa's crown is safe!" she said, satisfied. "I have been having bad dreams that somebody will take away my papa's crown. So when my sister Olga and I opened Grandmama's egg the other day and found it inside, I thought it a good idea to keep it until I found a suitable hiding place. Thank you, young man! Now I know it will be safe."

"Will you tell your sister?" he asked, wondering why Grand Duchess Olga was not in on the 'hiding scheme.'

"No, no I wouldn't want to worry her with such things," she said, displaying a maturity way beyond her years. "Anyway, my sister thinks we lost it, which we did for a short while, but then I found it again." She looked at him thoughtfully. "But now you must make an oath to me, my minion," she said solemnly, "never to tell of the whereabouts of Papa's crown and pendant to *anybody!* Do you understand? Swear to me!"

"I swear!" he answered just as solemnly.

"Now you may kiss my hand, and then the oath is sealed," she said, holding out the back of her hand. Vassili bowed low and taking the back of her hand, kissed it gently.

"I swear on my life," he said, standing straight, his face flushed pink.

"Good!" said the girl. She turned around and was about to leave the room when Vassili called to her.

"Forgive me, your Imperial Highness. I am not sure who I made my oath to. Which grand duchess are you?"

The girl stopped her hand on the door handle.

"Really!" she said. "I am Grand Duchess Tatiana." He mouth broke into a mischievous grin as she disappeared through the door.

About an hour later, Vassili stood before Nicholas II, the emperor of Russia. They were in the 'secret room', which was actually Nicholas's study accessed from the mezzanine. He'd had tea with Nicholas, Alexandra and their two eldest daughters, Olga and Tatiana, in the Maple Room. The three younger children, Alexei, the tsarevich, Marie and Anastasia were asleep in their nursery. He had sat bewildered through most of the light conversation. It had been the empress who had conversed with him the most. She had immediately tried to put him at ease by bidding him to call her 'm'am' and not 'Imperial Royal Highness.' Likewise amazingly, the emperor himself had also instructed him to address him as plain 'sir.' She then proceeded to ask him questions: Was he happy living in the palace at Tsarskoe Selo? Did he see enough of his father? Did he have many friends? He would answer all her questions with a short yes or no, at which she would smile warmly at him. The emperor in the meantime merely observed him silently. Vassili liked the empress. He wondered why she was not popular among the Russian people. She was looked upon by them as being aloof, haughty and unapproachable. But here in her own home she seemed warm, loving and gracious. It was certainly the most peculiar evening in his short life so far. Tatiana, he noticed, had changed into a clean skirt and blouse and was wearing smart black shiny shoes over a pair of pure white ankle socks. She pouted her lips at him when she saw him studying her clean attire. She made no mention at all to their previous meeting, though of course he didn't expect her to. Both she and Olga were quiet through most of the conversation and huddled together on one of the couches, poring over a picture book. They only entered into the conversation when encouraged to do so by their mother. He had never seen any of the children before, even though he had lived in the same palace. In fact he had only seen the emperor and empress on a couple of occasions.

In the quiet moments, as they sipped their tea or, as in the empress's case, coffee, and the great clock ticked away the awkward seconds, he saw Tatiana peering at the bronze statue of the Napoleonic soldier, a smug look on her face.

"You may stand easy, my boy," indicated Nicholas, fully aware of Vassili's apprehension. Nicholas leaned back in his leather chair behind his large ornate desk. "You can relax. You have nothing to fear from me. Have we not made you feel welcome, my boy?"

"Yes sir," he confirmed, "but I am confused, Imperial ... I mean, sir."

"Yes, yes I quite understand. It was necessary for the little tea gathering downstairs as I needed to make doubly sure of something."

Vassili looked even more bemused.

"Come, Vassili Kharitonov! Sit down here, in front of me. Make yourself comfortable, for I am going to tell you a story." The emperor signalled for him to seat himself in the leather chair opposite his desk. He then learned forward and took out a cigarette from a silver box that lay on his desk. He lit it, then leaned back and blew the smoke up towards the ceiling.

"It is necessary to tell you things that I would not normally tell such a young boy," the emperor began. "Indeed, there are parts of this tale which I would not repeat to anyone. But as I have said, it is necessary, and indeed it is only right that you hear it."

Vassili felt incredibly uncomfortable again. Though the evening was becoming like a dream to him, he now decided it was time to become fully awake.

"Please sir, I think you may have got me confused with somebody else! I am only Vassili Kharitonov, the cook's son. I do not want to hear anything that is not meant for my ears," he said.

Nicholas smiled softly. "I have been observing you all your short life, my boy. I know who you are and I can assure you, there is no mistake. It was not by chance that your father was given the job as cook to my family nearly ten years ago. Nor was it by chance that you were allowed to stay with him in his

23

quarters in the service rooms." The emperor now looked at him keenly. "And it is only to your good standing that you make it clear to me that you would not want to hear what is not meant for your ears. You remind me of someone I knew very well long ago. Your uncle, in fact."

"My uncle, sir?" Vassili was confused again. He wasn't aware of any relatives apart from his father. His mother had died in child birth and he had never known any of his grandparents.

"You're father had an older brother," continued the emperor a little sadly, "and he was my friend."

Nicholas lit another cigarette and leaned back again in his chair. He quickly smoked half of it in silence while still looking at the nervous boy in front of him. He then sat up abruptly and leaned forward eagerly, a strange glint in his blue eyes. "I am going to tell you something that must never be repeated. Do you understand?" His face had now become stern. Without waiting for Vassili to answer, he continued: "Very few know *all* the details of the story I am about to tell you. Before I continue, you must swear an oath of secrecy to me."

Vassili's eyes grew wide in disbelief. Two oaths of secrecy in one evening, and both sworn to members of the imperial family!! Without hesitation, he swore the oath of secrecy to his emperor.

"Come, my boy," said Nicholas, seeing his discomfort, "this oath is a bond between us. A bond between two friends. Don't you want to be my friend?"

The young boy looked at the emperor from across the table, his mouth open. The emperor of all Russia, the most powerful man alive in the world, wanted to be his friend! Yet the man sitting across the table from him certainly did not look superhuman; in fact, he looked perfectly normal. Perhaps too normal, even!

"I can see that all this is overwhelming you a little, boy, but I will begin." The emperor stood up, walked across to the other side of the study and looked out of the large window that overlooked the lake. Though it was dark, the moon shimmered upon the ripples that lapped at the roots of a willow tree.

"I first met your uncle when I was nineteen," the emperor began in a level tone, continuing to stare out of the window. "I had joined an exclusive regiment of the Russian army and it was while he and I were serving in the horse artillery that we became sincere friends. In fact, we became inseparable and did all the things that young men do. We got drunk together, we chased the ladies together. We laughed, we quarrelled and we fell down together." The emperor stopped briefly and sighed in reminiscence. "You see, Vassili, like you, my childhood was not an easy one. My father and I were like chalk and cheese, even physically. He was tall; six feet four, and very strong. As you can see I am smaller and slight, though I can give anyone a good arm wrestle when challenged," he continued with a twinkle in his eyes. He went over to the bookcase and took out a deep red, leather-bound book with gold lettering on its spine. He flipped through the pages. "I love literature and books, especially history books. I have studied languages and science. I admit I enjoy the finer things in life: smart clothes, balls, opera, ballets and ceremonies. It was said that my father lacked refinement, Vassili. He fashioned his image on the texture of some of the rougher element of his subjects. He was straight forward, abrupt and even gruff. In short, Vassili, he looked upon me as being a bit of a 'Nancy Boy.' But I am not ashamed to admit it. We all have our own ways of dealing with the monstrous burden of ruling the Russian empire and every minute of fearing for your life and for the lives of those closest to you."

Even though he was very young, Vassili was mature for his ten years. His heart went out to this soft, gentle and honest man.

The emperor stood above him now and leaned forward, peering into his face. "What do you see in these eyes, Vassili? Speak the truth!"

Vassili stared up into his emperor's face. He did not have to look long.

"I see warmth and kindness, your Imperial Highness," he said softly, and then swallowing hard, he continued: "Yet deeper I see sadness, pain and sorrow; like the eyes of the soldier on the cabinet downstairs!"

The emperor raised both his eyebrows in surprise. "You are very observant, Vassili! I pray you learn to perceive as clearly all the eyes that look into yours." He walked back to the bookshelf and replaced the book. "My father's eyes were bright, yet as cold as steel. His burdens were the same as mine are now. Your uncle helped me to understand that my father and I handled our burdens in different ways. No matter how cold those steel eyes seemed, I learned to know that there was love in their depths. He feared that should something happen to him, I would not be ready to rule and alas, it did."

Vassili remembered a recent history lesson he had received giving the details of the previous tsar's death. He had been struck with a severe kidney disease. The then empress Maria Feodorovna's sister in law, Queen Olga of Greece, offered Alexander III her villa on the island of Corfu in which to convalesce. Unfortunately, while journeying there his condition grew worse, forcing them to stay at the palace of Livadia. He died there in his wife's arms, at the age of only forty nine.

"Yes, inseparable we were for over three years, and so when my father decided to send me on a 'Royal Grand Tour,' with my brother George, your uncle Ilya also came along. My father told me that the best form of education is through travel, so that is what we did. Fifty-one thousand kilometres in total around the greater part of the Eurasian continent. We travelled fifteen thousand kilometres by rail and twenty two thousand by sea, the remainder by horse and carriage. We began our trip shortly after I took part in the opening of the Trans-Siberian Railway. We boarded a ship for Port Piraeus where I met and stayed with some of my relatives. Leaving Greece, we travelled to Egypt taking in the wondrous sights of the Sphinx and the pyramids." Vassili was mesmerised as the tsar painted pictures with his words, describing the places he had experienced during his obviously memorable journey. "I distinctly remember the sound of the tinkling glass of the wind chimes," he remarked with melancholy as he continued to peer through the large window. "We were in a market place in Bombay. Transient aromas of spices drifted by on a hot breeze. We escaped the royal bodyguards and wandered as two friends would among the ragged and impoverished traders and their make-shift stalls, who tried to sell us anything from beads to luxurious rugs and carpets. There we gazed upon the white marble of the Taj Mahal, built in similar design to that of some of our own palaces." The emperor suddenly stood up totally straight. He stroked his left temple with his fingers.

"The sight of this mansion creates sorrowing sighs
And the sun and the moon shed tears from their eyes."

He turned to Vassili. His eyes were far away. "Alas, I cannot remember the rest of it. These are some of the words spoken by the emperor Shah Jahan. The beauty of the building and his memories of love lost were clearly on his mind, don't you think?"

Vassili quickly nodded, though he did not understand.

"Did you know that the Golden Temple in Amritsar has four doors through which to enter? They symbolise the openness of the sikhs towards all religions. If I were to redesign all my palaces there would be only one door, Vassili. Do you understand?"

Again, Vassili was not sure what the emperor meant, but again he nodded.

"Next came Ceylon and then Singapore, where the hot humid air averaged 31 deg C in the daytime and only dropped to 26 deg C in the evening. In fact, the temperature never dips below 23 degrees, day or night, winter or summer. We visited Java and the eighth century Buddhist monument at Borobudur.

It is an enormous, multi-tiered structure of dark eerie stone with a bell-shaped monument at the top. All surrounded by smoking volcanoes," he continued dramatically, "and yet it looks down on peaceful, green lush fields. In Bangkok, we saw the 'Grand Palace' and its 'Temple of the emerald Buddha.' Next came the factories and tea plantations in Nanking, China. It was in China that Ilya and I learned to use chopsticks like Chinamen. I seemed to be so free in those days," he sighed loudly. "It was easy to lose the body guards and walk around, the two of us, like normal people. Then in April '91, escorted by six ships of the Imperial Fleet, we arrived at Kagoshima. We visited Nagasaki and Kobe over the next few days. Japan is a very beautiful country and I enjoyed the hospitality. But it was in Kyoto that something happened that I will never forget!"

Vassili looked up, a little startled at the change in tone of the emperor's voice. It had become even more emotional, but was also now infused with anger. The emperor strode across the room to the thick wood-panelled door. He opened it briefly and looked outside. Satisfied, he quietly closed the door and then resumed his place at the window again. He stared through the glass panes and up at the sky. The snow-flakes swirled in manic fashion. The lake was dark.

"We were visiting the Chion-In Temple in Kyoto," Nicholas said quietly, his soft voice now barely audible. "It was an incredibly impressive place. Jodo Buddhism is the most popular sect in Japan mainly due to its simple teachings and applications, which of course appeal to the common people. The founder of the temple, Priest Honnen, taught that one could be reborn by simply reciting 'amida, amida, amida Buddha.' This of course increased his popularity somewhat back in the twelfth century. But as with the other temples, I did not feel comfortable in such a place and so I did not linger too long inside the building. Leaving my brother George and Ilya, I ventured outside into the gardens. It was April and they were filled with bursting cherry blossoms, laughing red and yellow tulips and of course, pink moss. I was kneeling down to pluck a beautiful red tulip when I felt another's presence close by. I turned and there before me was a doll-like figure, almost like porcelain. Her face was buried in her hands and she was weeping. I immediately went to her to ask what the matter was. It was from that moment and for the next three days, that time and my life in it, seemed to become surreal.

"I am sorry, sir," she said. She obviously did not know who I was. "But the sight of you picking that beautiful flower with such love and caring – it must be for someone you care for very deeply. It made the hopelessness of my own life too much to bear."

She then related to me how she had been promised in marriage to one she did not love, but of course, she had no choice in the matter; the wedding was to be in a few weeks' time, at the end of April. I told her that in Russia we have the same expectations for our royal daughters. She then told me that there would be no wedding, for she planned to kill herself that very next evening. I was horrified. She was not at all like the empress, nor like Malechka, my Marinsky ballerina. Her hair and her eyes were black like ebony, her small plump lips like ripened strawberries. I offered her my assistance and I arranged to meet with her that very evening. We met incognito at a small tavern on the outskirts of the inner city. Ilya kept a close watch over our privacy. We talked and talked and it seemed I made her laugh with my 'strange' accent and 'easy' manner. Her name was Akahana. Before we parted, I gave her a small bible that I kept on my person at all times. When she opened it, the red tulip that I had picked that afternoon fell on the ground at her feet. She kneeled down and picked it up, gasping with surprise.

"Do you know what Akahana means?" she asked me as she placed the flower back on the page of the book and then snapped it shut. "It means red, bright flower!"

In the cool night air under a pale yellow moon, amidst the

sound of a copper pheasant calling to his mate, I kissed her. A kiss I will never forget. I vowed to her that I would take her out of Japan and back to Russia and I would marry her. I did have a sinking feeling at the thought of telling this news to my father and mother, though.

Later that evening, Ilya warned me that I was playing with fire; that there was only one way that it would end: heartache for at least one of us. But I wouldn't listen. The next morning I met her at a market in Otsu. Though my bodyguards were watching, we were left to walk freely and nobody bothered us. At a stall I saw a beautiful brooch that I wanted to buy for her. But the trader said he had something even more special for such a beautiful lady; reaching down into a leather bag, he brought out an exquisite hairpin, the clasp of which was the shape of a serpent. At first, though appreciating its beauty, I was repelled by it and did not want to buy it. But when Akahana saw it she gave such a cry of wild child-like excitement that I had to please her. It was very old and so much heavier than it looked. Even the feel of it disturbed me, I handed the trader the money and gave it to her. She laughed with delight as she held it in the palm of her pale white hand. Its black eye was of a stone I had never seen before. Later as we parted, we agreed to meet again that evening. Ilya and I spent the afternoon together. But he was not himself; he was quiet and withdrawn. I tried to cheer him up by suggesting we have a tattoo, but he declined. I, however, was tattooed with the image of a red tulip on my right forearm in tribute to the new love I had found. When we met that evening she was wearing the hair pin. Again, Ilya took the watch as we had dinner in a quiet, discreet little traditional restaurant overlooking the water in the bay at Otsu. It made her laugh, the awkward way I displayed my new-found skill of eating with chopsticks. I fell more and more under her spell. Later, in a dimly lit room I watched her silhouette on the wall. I was entranced as she stood behind the screen and took out the hair pin and watched as her thick hair fell, caressing her pale, finely sculpted naked shoulders."

Vassili blushed at the thought of the scene the emperor had just described. It reminded him of some of the other porcelain statues downstairs in the Maple Room. The emperor was now quiet, deep in thought. He took out another cigarette, lit it and then cleared his throat.

"We made arrangements to meet briefly the next morning in the same market place where I had bought her the hairpin, but she was nowhere to be seen. The trader who had sold me the pin was there, however, and I am not mistaken when I say he watched me keenly the whole time I waited – as if he knew why she had not turned up. I was about to confront the fellow when Ilya pointed out that we could not linger; I was to be taken to Lake Biwa at Otsu for a day trip by my host, Prince Katashirakawa Yoshihisa. I sent Ilya to look for her. My cousin George of Greece and I spent a day at the lake. Just as we were about to depart, Ilya turned up. His face was ashen. He told me that my beloved Akahana was dead. He explained to me that he had gone to her address and had found her in her bedroom where she had fallen upon her own dagger. In shock and heartbreak, I waved him away. I needed to be alone. But the party was leaving and of course, no one knew of our affair so I was compelled to keep my feelings hidden. In the carriage back to Kyoto, I listened as my friend told me more. It had been discovered that the hairpin I had bought her had released a poison into her scalp. I asked what had become of the hairpin, to which he answered that it was nowhere to be found, but that on leaving her apartments he had been unsettled by a vagrant hovering around near the entrance. When I asked him what he looked like, his description matched that of the raggedy trader. In the note that he had found in her hand, she said she had taken her own life so as not to implicate me. For apparently there was one who had been following us and was aware of our love for each other. As the situation between our two countries

31

was already sensitive, a scandal of this kind would seriously have harmed the already strained relations. With tears in his eyes, Ilya told me that she had taken her own life in order to prevent a potential conflict between our two countries, as I could have been implicated in her poisoning. I am not ashamed to tell you that my tears were hot in the back of my eyes; I was silent as we made the journey back to Kyoto. But more tragedy was soon to follow. On the return journey, I was attacked by a Samurai-wielding lunatic. He was actually part of the official Japanese escort accompanying us. He was also Akahana's intended husband, Tsuda Sanzo, who unbeknown to me had been following us the two previous evenings. Having learned of her death, he was set on revenge." Nicholas pushed back the hair from the side of his forehead to reveal a clearly visible blue scar at least nine centimetres long. "It was so quick," Nicholas continued, "that only a reflex reaction by Ilya saved me from certain death. The first blow gave me this scar, but the second was deflected by Ilya with his cane. The assassin was so enraged that he turned his attention fully on Ilya and struck him with a fatal blow. Then, realising that he had been foiled, the attacker bolted down the street, only to be caught a little later by his own countrymen. But alas! Ilya had taken the blow that was intended for me. He lay there, dying in the dirt of an Otsu street; there was nothing I could do for him. All he could say to me was: "My son, my son! I will never know my son." We had always talked together about the dreams we had for our future sons and that they of course would also be great friends. As he lay dying, I made a promise to him underneath that red sun that the next male born in his family would be looked after by me and my household personally. He would be schooled and brought up to know the finer things in life." Nicholas stood up again. He walked around his desk and to the side of the chair where Vassili was seated.

"I am now fulfilling that promise, Vassili!"

As the year 1903 drew to a close and the excitement of Christmas came upon the imperial household, Vassili's life had changed dramatically. Firstly, it was decided that he should be groomed for a future in the same exclusive regiment that the emperor and his uncle had been a part of. But in order for this to happen, Nicholas informed him that he needed to study the 'deep' history of his country. Nicholas himself, when available, would personally oversee this part of his education. He would learn to ride a horse like a nobleman, with back straight and upright, not, as was commented by the equerry when taking his first lesson, like a 'sack of potatoes!' He was taught table manners in the evenings by the two elder grand duchesses. Six-year-old Tatiana took great delight in giving him the *wrong* instructions with regards to which spoon was for soup and which was for dessert. This brought about a sound scolding from the empress when he was invited the following evening for dinner with the family in order to display his new-found table manners. His cheeks burned as the empress said:

"Tatiana, please show our guest which spoon he should be using for the soup. He seems to have got a little confused. Unless of course he would prefer to eat the Zapekanka first!" Nicholas disguised his chuckle with a light cough, while Olga buried her laughter in her serviette. Tatiana meanwhile, perfectly straight-faced, proceeded to show him the opposite of what she had shown him the previous day. The next time he was invited for dinner, immediately after taking his seat, he promptly picked up his fish knife and began to clean his finger nails with it. The empress's eyes grew wide with horror as she looked at her husband, and then severely reprimanded him again. This time, however, Nicholas had noticed Tatiana smirking broadly at her sister just before the incident and had guessed who the real perpetrator was. Later that evening, when his 'deeper' history lesson with the emperor had finished, Nicholas gave him some advice on 'coping' with the 'fairer sex.'

"In order to aim high my boy, you must first gain the respect of the one you are aiming for!"

A few days later, Vassili was asked to join the imperial children for morning tea. It seemed that morning only Tatiana was aware of the invitation. As she watched him stir his tea slowly from side to side with a teaspoon she sighed heavily.

"Really, boy!" she exclaimed. "I thought you would at least know how to stir your tea properly."

Vassili looked up, suspicious that she intended to trick him again. He let go of the spoon and left it in the teacup. Passing both over to Tatiana, he said. "Please, your Imperial Highness, would you show me how a gentleman would do it?"

Tatiana took the cup and saucer, and with a very serious look on her face proceeded to stir the tea at a furious rate in a clockwise direction, spilling the liquid into the saucer. She then showed what a gentleman would do when this happens by lifting the saucer up to her mouth and slurping its contents loudly. Vassili took the cup and saucer from her and then refilled it with scalding hot tea.

"Thank you, Imperial Highness, I will remember that. Do you know how the men of the Cossack Regiment wake each other up for breakfast?" he enquired. Very interested, Tatiana leaned forward eagerly. "No," she said, "please show me. I love the Cossacks!" Vassili took the teaspoon from the hot tea and branded the thin skin on the back of her hand with it.

"Ouch," she cried, and then instead of scolding him or even worse as he expected, she rubbed the back of her hand and laughed. "I didn't know that!" she exclaimed. "I am going to wake up Olga and Marie like that every morning at breakfast time." The next few mornings, when again he had been invited for breakfast tea, he noticed with amusement that all the sisters were sporting angry little red marks on the back of their hands. Indeed, on the one occasion, Marie came to tea with two on her forehead!

Vassili and Tatiana began to spend a lot of time together. Whenever he was invited for breakfast, high tea or dinner, he would always arrive at least half an hour earlier than expected, where he would usually find the little girl waiting for him patiently. Afterwards, when the rest of the family had arrived, he would feel her clear, grey eyes admiring him. He had never really made friends with any of the other servant's children in Tsarskoe Selo, even before he had been given special privileges. He was a deep and sensitive boy who did not make friends easily. But with Tatiana it was different. They seemed to understand each other. Sometimes, each lost in their own thoughts, one would say out loud what the other had been thinking. A very close bond began to develop. The empress soon began to notice.

"I think we may have a little suitor for our little darling Tatiana," she informed Nicholas one evening. They were in the empress's boudoir or Mauve Room as it was known in the palace. It was her favourite room. The walls were covered in an opal-coloured silk known as Lampas Violet Reseda. This had been especially imported from the Charles Berges firm in Paris and had been tremendously expensive. The matching fabric on the furniture from Moscow was similar, though a slightly lighter colour tone. She and Nicholas were seated at the built-in corner sofa. As Nicholas read and she embroidered by the light of the lamp on the table directly in front of them, she observed not for the first time how the beautiful fabric seemed to be infused with an unusual soft glimmer.

"Oh! my love," answered Nicholas matter of factly, while deeply engrossed in the politics of his newspaper.

"Are you listening, huzy?" she said sweetly "I think we may have a love match on our hands."

Nicholas rested the newspaper on his knee and looked up at her. His relationship with his wife was a close and loving one. There were very few secrets between them. He smiled.

"You are talking about young Vassili?" he asked.

"They are spending an awful lot of time together. I'm not

sure that it is good for her. He is, after all, a little rough," the empress replied, placing her embroidery onto the table.

"I would call him a rough diamond, my wifey," Nicholas answered, "he was hardly brought up with the serfs, was he? Anyway, I think our little Tatiana can look after herself a little more than you know."

"Yes, yes Nicky. But I have never seen two such young ones so totally and innocently engrossed with each other. It's so beautiful to see and yet a little disconcerting at the same time." Alexandra leaned over and touched his hand. "You know, my love, that our daughters cannot marry our own, and will more than likely marry a foreign prince. Grandmama Victoria had her eyes on Olga for Edward, if you remember!"

"Olga is eight and Tatiana is six, my pet, and I know in families such as ours it is common place to be betrothed at a young age. But wifey, all that changes with me. Remember the trouble I had with Father trying to convince him to let me marry *you*. He was so opposed to your German background. Dare I say it, if he hadn't died so suddenly we would not have had it so easy. No, my darling, I will not do that to any of my daughters, or son, in fact. They will marry for love and love only."

Alexandra squeezed his hand. "I think you and I would have been like those two little ones if we had met at their age."

"I have no doubt, my wifey," he squeezed her hand back. Then abruptly, he returned to his newspaper again. "I do believe we are finally heading for trouble with Japan," he said.

The hostilities between Russia and Japan had been building for some time. The assassination attempt on the then Tsarevich Nicholas's life had certainly not helped relieve the tension. Later after becoming tsar, Nicholas had ambitions to extend his already massive empire by way of acquiring Manchuria and Korea. Likewise, Japan had similar ambitions. As a compromise, Japan offered to recognise Russian dominance in Manchuria in exchange for Japanese dominance in Korea. Nicholas refused. The

Japanese now considered the Russian threat reason enough to go to war, and on 8 February 1904, their navy attacked the Russian fleet at Port Arthur in Liaotung Province, which was leased to Russia by China, three hours before formally declaring war against Russia. The Japanese had attacked at the very heart of the cause of the conflict, for Russia had been seeking a warm-water port for their navy as well as to expand trading opportunities. Their fleet was only able to use Vladivostok during the summer months, but due to more favourable weather conditions, Port Arthur was able to operate all year round. Though the battle of Port Arthur was indecisive, the attack caused a devastating psychological effect on the Russian military, as they had deemed themselves invincible against their 'far weaker foe.'

The battle also provided the cover Japan needed to land a force near Incheon. They then proceeded to occupy Seoul and the rest of Korea. By the end of April, the Japanese imperial army was ready to cross the Yalu River and into Russian-occupied Manchuria.

Vassili loved Tuesdays; at 6pm he would go to the emperor's study and receive a personal history lesson from Nicholas himself. It was also the evening when afterwards he would be allowed to play board games with the two elder grand duchesses, though lately he had noticed that Olga had now preferred to bury her head in one of her many books, so he and Tatiana were often left to play alone.

The emperor stood in the amber rays of a low sunset that streamed through the window, giving him an almost mystical look.

"This evening, my boy, we are going to study an episode in another great empires' history. It would be very naïve to study only one's own country's history, Vassili; there are many great lessons to learn from around the world." There were two small hardback books on his desk. He handed one to the young, eager-faced boy.

Vassili studied the cover: 'BLACKWOODS EDUCATIONAL SERIES – SHORT STORIES FROM ENGLISH HISTORY'.

"Turn to page eighty," Nicholas instructed him. "The year is 1588, and Philip II of Spain is ready to subdue England and make it part of the Spanish empire. He builds the largest fleet of ships ever seen and takes three years to construct the one hundred and thirty-two vessels. A complete and total victory for the Spanish was expected," he continued, "as the royal navy of England at that time consisted of just thirty-six sailing ships."

Vassili looked at the intricate black and white illustrations of the huge Spanish battle ships compared to the small, dingy English ships.

"But," the emperor said putting his copy of the book down on the desk and turning, his hands behind his back, to face a large portrait of his grandfather that hung on the wall. "The English gentry realised their predicament and rallied around their queen. They eagerly built and fitted out vessels at their own expense, each one with a great number of cannons and large quantities of gun powder. Very soon, they had a fleet of one hundred and ninety-one ships. Though they were much smaller that the Spanish 'Man o' Wars', they were swift and agile; their crews were made up of daring sailors with the confidence of their monarch imprinted in their hearts."

Vassili sat stock still, his face radiant and expectant as he waited to be told the outcome.

"On the evening of 19 July, a party of Royal Naval commanders, Lord Howard, Drake and Hawkins were playing bowls on the green of the Pelican Inn on Plymouth Hoe. As their shadows lengthened in the evening sunlight, an old sailor burst upon their game. He informed them that a Spanish fleet large enough to darken the belly of the sea had been sighted off Lizards Point. It was headed up the Channel; ships like sea castles in a crescent formation measuring seven miles from tip to tip. Lord Howard wanted to leave and engage the enemy at once, but Drake insisted on finishing the game of bowls, saying that there was plenty of time to whip the Spanish."

Nicholas's own shadow had grown long and lean across his desk as he continued:

"Drake had a plan, Vassili. He would not meet the Armada head on, but attacked from the rear, picking off the warships one by one. Being too large and cumbersome, the great Spanish ships were unable to turn sufficiently to defend themselves and so the smaller and much more agile fleet won the day."

Vassili wondered at the humiliation of the Spanish king when hearing about the loss of his great Armada.

"A commander can never afford to underestimate his opponents, Vassili," said the emperor.

"And big is not necessarily better!" exclaimed the boy eagerly.

The emperor laughed. "No, not necessarily," he agreed.

Vassili proceeded to study the pages of the book, but his concentration was interrupted by a soft knocking at the door. A tall army officer entered without waiting for permission. With his cap under his right arm and his left hand gripping a single sheet of white paper, he declared:

"I am sorry, Your Imperial Highness, we have distressing news from the front." Nicholas took the sheet of paper from the officer's hand and slowly read it. As he looked up a few moments later, Vassili could see that his face had sunken with worry and his eyes were deeply troubled.

"Makarov dead?" he said quietly.

"Yes, Imperial Highness," confirmed the officer. "The Petropavlovsk and the Pobeda were struck by mines as they slipped through the blockade at Port Arthur. The Admiral went down with Petropavlovsk."

"And the Pobeda?" asked the emperor gazing steadily at the officer.

"She has been towed back to port for extensive repairs, Imperial Highness," he answered.

The emperor looked at Vassili. He picked up the copy of his book and studied it momentarily. He then placed the open book back on the desk abruptly.

"This history lesson is over," he said and strode out of the room with the officer following closely behind him. Vassili peered at the open page of Nicholas' book. It showed a black and white illustration of a very large ship being attacked and sunk by a very small one.

The war between Russia and Japan continued throughout the year. Russia suffered devastating defeat after devastating defeat, and yet Nicholas believed that ultimately his country would win and chose not to face humiliation and sue for peace. It was also during this time that general unrest among the Russian workers and people intensified.

CHAPTER 2
THE SWASHBUCKLER

Winston Peabody was downcast. Nothing had changed. He had made a trip to the future to see if there had been any adjustments to recorded history concerning the fate of the imperial family or, even more importantly, the fate of the Fabergé eggs. There weren't. It was still recorded in 1992 that the Russian government had declared that the remains of Nicholas and his family had been found in a remote grave in a forest in Siberia. Even though only nine bodies had been found, the Russians and the world now believed that this was proof that the last imperial family had, as rumoured, been murdered in the Ipatiev house, taken to the nearby Koptyaki forest and 'disposed of.' There had also been no change as to when the hostilities between Russia and Japan began, which Peabody believed was the 'spark to the flame' for the revolution. It had not been brought forward, as Peabody had hoped, through the poisoning of the Japanese woman. It was surely not the fact that the family had been murdered that grieved him. It was the whereabouts of the eggs eluding him, and the possibility that they could be lost forever; Peabody had decided this meant that Clodius and his pals had been able to get their thieving hands on them. But if this was true, did they also manage to recover the missing crown and pendant from the Hen Egg?

"Why did that little yellow swine have to kill herself!" he said, banging his fist down on his desk. "It got young Nic out of a sticky situation and out of an early war; absolutely nothing changed in history to enable us to locate those damned eggs. I will have to think of something else now to disrupt things."

Smith sat opposite Peabody in what had come to be known now as 'the naughty chair.'

"But boss, perhaps we *can't* change anything. I mean, who are we to be able to do that?" His piggy eyes squinted at Peabody.

"Don't be any more ridiculous than you already are, you simpleton!" bellowed Peabody, suddenly standing up. Smith cowered down in his seat. "Why else would the timer come to me if I was not able to use it to manipulate time and its events? Look at what we've achieved so far." He slowly turned the large thick platinum signet ring on the middle finger of his left hand. "We have enriched the 'Club' very nicely and dare I say ourselves too, a little," he continued, as he admired a splendid original Monet that hung on the chimney breast over the fireplace. "No, no! We must just persist until something does not get in the way!"

"Do you think it was love, boss?" asked Smith, sitting up smartly to study Peabody's face.

"Love?" answered his boss. "Now that's a word I don't hear very often, Mr Smith, and personally that's exactly what I believe it is. Just a word. Tell me, old chap, what do you think it means?" Smith thought for a moment. Then suddenly his face lit up.

"Well, I used to *love* the pies my old ma used to make me when I was a lad!" he exclaimed.

"Very interesting," said Peabody, "and what about your old ma; did you not love her?"

"Not a chance, boss!" exclaimed poor Smith. "That wasn't all I remember about her. I also remember the hard knocks her boyfriends used to give me when I was a young 'un. In fact, me and my brothers had to all stand together one time and sort out one particular nasty character. She used to bring 'em back home from the 'Black Bull,' drunk as lords they were, and this one was …"

"That's enough, Smith!" said Peabody sternly. "I don't need to hear the sordid details. No Mr Smith, love is just a word that people use to get what they want."

Peabody had been an only child and did not harbour any particular bad memories from his childhood. He also certainly had no feelings whatsoever for his parents. They indulged each other and forgot about him, he concurred.

"In that case, I would *love* some of that brandy, boss!" exclaimed Smith, eying the cut-glass decanter on the desk.

Over the next few days, Peabody devised another plan in which to try his hand at disrupting historical events. In his office late one evening, Peabody opened the round glass door to the grandmother clock that stood in one corner of the room. He peddled both the fingers with his own so that the clock chimed seven times.

"I want to check something," he said as he closed the glass.

They stood in front of Peabody's desk, in the middle of the room. Smith was sweating profusely. The pockets of the enormous trench coat that he was wearing were crammed full of grenades. "I hope one of these don't go off boss, when that thing starts its firework display," he said, his arms splayed out like an over-developed body builder.

"Shut up and pay attention!" said Peabody, ignoring him. "We only need to go back a couple of years." The little egg timer sat in the palm of his hand as he held it at arm's length. Both of them stared at it. "Repeat after me," Peabody continued, "and don't make a mistake. You know what happened last time."

Peabody mouthed the words slowly so that Smith hopefully didn't make any mistakes.

"Sarajevo, 10 a.m., 28 June 1914." Smith repeated the words slowly and clearly. They both looked expectantly at the little golden egg timer. Nothing happened. Peabody repeated the 'co-ordinates.' Again, nothing happened. Not a spark or even a low glow from the timer. "What's wrong with it, boss?" cried Smith, the sweat now dripping off the end of his nose. Red faced, Peabody shook the timer in his hand violently.

"Work, you little cretin!" he demanded. Peabody was more precise this time with the coordinates. "Army barracks, Sarajevo, 10 a.m. on 28 June." But he could now see quite clearly that all the powder was stuck in the top phial; it looked very moist and damp. Peabody wrapped his fingers around it and held it tightly and then with an action reminiscent of a professional bowler in a game of cricket, he flung the timer at the opposite wall. The timer did not work on that occasion for Winston Peabody. Indeed, it did not work again for many years.

*

On 13 June 1932, Clodius Albertus turned eighty years old. To celebrate this momentous occasion, it was announced to the members that a special meeting and later a birthday party was to be held by the 'Masters Club' at his castle in Cornwall. By 1932, the number of members had increased dramatically and the great horse-shoe shaped table had to be increased in size, so much so that it was necessary to build it inside the grand conference room; there was no other way to get the solid piece of wood inside. At the outside perimeter of the shoe-shaped table sat forty-two members, including Clodius Albertus at the head. Down each leg sat the jewel thieves or 'rescuers', as they had now been officially titled. Twelve on either side, making a membership total of sixty-six. Each one was a multi-millionaire. The nearer you were seated to the head of the table, the more status you had within the 'Club.'

"I would like to begin as always, my illustrious brothers, by thanking you all for attending this meeting and of course, my eightieth birthday," Clodius began in his usual slurred manner.

The room erupted with his anticipated applause. He pushed himself back a little in the wheelchair in which he now sat. This had been recommended by his physician who was also, incidentally, a fellow member. Doctor Winter-Bottom had noticed with sincere anxiety that Clodius was becoming very unsteady on his feet, especially, he had noticed recently, towards the end of their meetings at the 'Club.'

"Just think, Viginti Tres Master," the doctor had informed him when presenting him with the wheelchair at the previous meeting. "You will be able to enjoy a few more brandies quite safely now."

Taking a large gulp of brandy from his glass, he glanced to his left and right. The oldest and most distinguished members were closest to him. Sir Thomas, leaning back in his chair, his long white beard cascading down the front of his black dinner jacket, was smiling contentedly. Lionel Featherington still looked the same as always, though he had gained a little weight over the years. He gazed down the length of the table and fixed his eyes on Winston Peabody. Then, as the room quieted down, Clodius returned his gaze upon the men opposite him; his 'rescuers'. The new one, young Frederick Havisham, fresh-faced and eager; then of course the old faithfuls: Jack Hawkins, Henry Trent and Mathew Stanley. All had been tremendously good 'rescuers' in the past. His eyes narrowed as he continued to stare at them. Their feats of 'rescuing' had diminished somewhat over the years. It seemed that nobody had the touch that Peabody had. It was never fully explained to him why Peabody had decided to 'hang up his nickers', a phrase that had been coined at the Club at the time, and he certainly hadn't been happy about it. He had immediately relegated the once-renowned Historical Artefact Rescuer to the bottom of the table, hoping to change his mind. But seventeen years later, Winston Peabody was still sitting there, quite contentedly, it seemed. They'd hardly spoken to each other in the seventeen years that followed. Indeed, if Clodius could have banished him from the Club he would have, but that would have been breaking his own rules: 'Once a member of the Masters' Club, always a member'. The only thing that could break the bond was death itself. Blake Cadbury and Joseph Kingsburg were the only two members to have taken that exit so far. He glanced down the length of the table at Peabody again. He had aged gracefully; damn him. His hair was still thick and shaggy, though now tinted with threads of silver. The hair at his temples was completely grey, giving him an air of wisdom. His seemingly ever-tanned face still had the healthy glow, if not of youth, of contentment. Maybe I should wipe that look off his face, Clodius thought. But then again, I seem to have made a mistake admitting that youngster, Havisham. Perhaps this is a way to replace him with someone of use. Clodius was then struck with another thought as he looked at Lord Louis, and then dismissed it. Too well-connected; his elimination would not go down at all well in certain circles.

"Gentleman, I will come straight to the point." There was a light sigh of relief from everybody, "for I know you are all looking forward to the 'after-meats'," he continued. "Our collection of VIRPS (very important rescued pieces) has not increased for some time due to some quite catastrophic failures by some of our 'rescuers.'" Lord Louis shifted uncomfortably in his seat. Frederick Havisham looked less fresh-faced and eager. "Though, up until now our magnificent reputation has not been damaged with our friends around the globe due to the vast collection that we have already amassed. I must add, however, failure for the appointed 'rescuer' in this instance will not be tolerated. Our membership has reached the appointed number; no other persons will or can be admitted, unless one of our existing members passes away. I certainly don't need to inform you that there are many well-qualified prestigious individuals waiting to join us. The price of failure for the 'rescuer' appointed will be the ultimate." The Grand Hall was silent. Not a person moved. "Failure in this mission will not be part of the member's résumé. I hereby adjust the rules for this assignment. If you transgress, there will be a very unpleasant consequence." Lord Louis looked into space. Frederick Havisham bowed his head. Clodius looked directly at Peabody again. Peabody returned the challenge unblinkingly. Clodius continued: "So, gentlemen, let me come to what we hope will turn out to be the greatest 'rescue' of all, and what a coincidence to be able to announce this on my birthday." Clodius waited for the applause that this time didn't come. "Information has been given to me from my usual reliable source that a certain artefact has been located; that its whereabouts are now known. If this is correct and we as the appointed rescuers manage to recover this artefact, we will govern the hopes of all mankind." The dead silence inside the hall was suddenly invaded by the distant sound of evening church bells, soft but persistent; its resonance seemed to hang in the air. Clodius stopped, irritated. As he lifted his glass to his lips, he examined the windows for any being open but, strangely, they were all shut fast. "Because of the importance of this artefact, its identity will only be revealed to the appointed rescuer. So now I need to ask you to vote for the rescuer. Place your names in the hat, my brothers!"

The black top hat was passed from member to member as they placed their nominated rescuer's name into it. Then the last person who voted brought the hat back up to the head of the table. "Honourable master," said Peabody, as he placed the shiny silk hat down in front of the Viginti Tres Master. As Clodius looked up, Peabody was aware of a peculiar glint in the old man's eyes and a slight curl of his lip. For the next ten minutes or so, the Viginti Tres Master personally counted the votes, while discreetly hiding the names on the small pieces of paper from view. The church bells continued to toll. Then, suddenly, they stopped; in the dead silence, Clodius made the announcement.

"Gentlemen! We have for the first time in many years a unanimous decision." Most of the members nervously shifted in their seats. "The appointed rescuer for the most important historical artefact in the history of mankind will be ... *Winston Peabody!*"

There were a number of sharp intakes of breath from the members as every eye in the room turned to look upon Peabody, who was sitting at the end of one of the inside legs of the table. There was no applause. Though everyone was tremendously relieved, Peabody was the last person each had expected. Who had voted for that useless old goat? This question was running through most of their minds. Peabody himself was just as stunned as everybody else. It had been almost seventeen years since he was nominated. He had officially retired from rescuing. What was Clodius up to?

"It is my eightieth birthday today, Mr Peabody, and it is my and our members' wish that you undertake this mission. Revisit your glory days, *master jewel thief!* Redeem yourself, sir!" Clodius' voice fairly shook around the room with emotion. All the members looked at him with knowing smirks on their faces. Peabody was trapped, of course; there was no way he could refuse on such an occasion.

*

The ancient city of Aquileia lies at the head of the Adriatic, about ten kilometres inland from the ocean. It initially served to protect Rome's faithful allies, the Veneti, during the Illyrian Wars and also against other hostiles such as the warlike Carni and Histri tribes. Though the Romans undoubtedly developed the colony, it is likely that it had previously already been a trade centre of Venetia due to its strategic position aiding the Venetic trade in the importation of amber from the Baltic regions. Due to the discovery of goldfields near to what is known today as Klagenfurt, the settlement grew dramatically around 130 BC. It soon became a place of great importance to the Romans as a centre of trade for products in agriculture and viticulture. In the years that followed, further development was made as Jewish artisans established a flourishing trade in glasswork. Forges were established where metal was processed and exported. The wine trade grew and its famous Pucinum, made using the precious vines the Romans had brought, was also exported. From Proconsular in Africa, oil was imported. A long period of peace was enjoyed by the city and its inhabitants. Then in 167 AD it was attacked by the Marcomanni. Due to its complacency and unlikely chance of being attacked, its fortifications had fallen into disrepair and the city was hard pressed. It only narrowly escaped being sacked by Rome's enemies. This led Marcus Aurelius, co-emperor of Rome with Lucius Versu, who was generally regarded as Rome's last 'good' emperor, to fortify the city and declare it the principal fortress of the empire against the barbarians of the north and east. This was to be the city's finest hour and the population soon grew to over one hundred thousand persons. Indeed, in AD 238, when the city supported the side of the senate against the Emperor Maximinus Thrax, the fortifications were again hastily restored and proved strong enough to withhold the assaults for many months, until Maximinus himself was assassinated. In the fourth century, it was regarded as the ninth most important city in the world behind Rome, Mediolanum, Constantinople, Carthage, Antioch, Alexandria, Trier and Capua. It was during this century that a mint was established and coins were produced, many of bronze, some of silver and a few very special ones of gold.

Their journey had been long and arduous. As they sat now in the foyer of the small hotel in Aquileia, Peabody could see that Smith's face was only just beginning to resume its normal, ruddy pink colour. "I am not made for sitting in uncomfortable French contraptions," he declared. Their journey had begun at the Doncaster aerodrome where, much to Peabody's delight and Smith's unbeknown horror, they were to board an aircraft that Clodius Albertus had arranged for them in order to save time and get them on the continent: Paris, to be precise. Peabody had not informed the acrophobic Smith that their journey was to begin with a flight across the channel, for obvious reasons. As the starting day of their journey coincidently was Smith's birthday, Peabody decided that he would blindfold him and tell him that he had a wonderful 'birthday boy' surprise in store. He had telegrammed the pilot beforehand, informing him of the plan. As Peabody guided the unseeing, excited Smith along the runway, the pilot sat grinning from the raised cockpit of the DH. 83 Fox Moth aeroplane, purposely not starting the engine. As Smith was helped up into the small light aircraft and into one of the three passenger seats, he actually began to giggle with excitement.

"Oh, boss, this is the best birthday ever," he giggled. "I just love surprises!"

"Well, you're certainly going to love this one, my man!" cried Peabody, turning around and banging twice on the roof, which was the signal for the pilot to start up the engine. As the incredibly loud De Havilland Gypsy Major I inline inverted engine rotated to life, Smith suddenly stopped smiling. He placed the middle finger of his right hand up to his temple as he always did when trying to solve a problem of some kind.

"I know boss, I know what the surprise is!" he cried out gleefully. "You've got me one of those Riding Lawn Tractors from the Ideal Power Mower Company in the States! Oh boss I hope it is the 'Triplex!'"

Smith had recently been complaining that now he was getting older, the extensive grass cutting at the college using the hand-pushed mower was becoming too much for him. He had shown Peabody the 'The Macho Mower' magazine which had featured an article on that very machine.

"Yes old boy, and we're both going to test drive it right now," confirmed Peabody as the light biplane passenger aircraft bumped up and down and swayed alarmingly from side to side along the runway.

"Let me see boss, let me see!" cried Smith, bringing both hands up to his thick, black silk blindfold.

"Not yet, Mr Smith!" shouted Peabody over the din of the engine. "Don't be so impatient! This is a special model."

The aircraft built up speed and then rose abruptly into the air, gravitated slightly and then rose up, still swaying from side to side, buffeted by the wind. The pilot smiled to himself as he dipped the plane down abruptly and then brought it up again.

"Ugh! Boss, I feel queer!" shouted Smith.

"Okay, birthday boy!" cried Peabody through wide grinning teeth. "You can look now, but let me warn you, don't look down and don't look up."

Smith tugged at the blindfold. His eyes narrowed at first in confusion and then widened in fright as he took in his surroundings. Through the window at his left side, he saw that he was already ten thousand feet in the air; it steamed up immediately from the screams of one as if suffering excruciating torture. Peabody's grin soon disappeared as he realised that there was nothing he could say or do to calm down the panic-stricken Smith. Even when he informed him of the fact that the fuel tank of the De Havilland had been modified so that it now had a range of 400 miles, more than enough to cover the 356 miles, as long, of course that they didn't get lost, Smith continued to scream. The only person that enjoyed the trip was the pilot, who of course could not hear the shrieking above the sound of the engine as the cockpit was positioned up and behind the passenger compartment. As per initial instructions from Peabody, he proceeded to 'dance' the little light aircraft up and

51

down and from side to side, grinning at the thought of his visit to the Moulin Rouge that evening. Smith was promptly sick.

The next day, it was Peabody's turn to be unhappy. The automobile that had been laid on for them was certainly not up to his standard.

"I don't know what that old drunk was thinking when he organised this for us," he said with disgust as he scrutinised the Voisin C11 Fevel automobile.

"It was probably Mrs Clodius," answered Smith, just as disgusted. "Ever since we said we would find that hoard of 'Jain Bronzes' for her, and couldn't because the timer had stopped working for good; we just didn't have a clue where to look, did we boss?" He had been physically sick on the flight until he could be sick no more, and there was the stench of vomit that emanated from him that no amount of bathing the night before could remove.

"Must you keep on pointing out the obvious, you nincompoop!" declared Peabody, moving out of range from Smith's acrid scent. "And I don't think it helped much when the hoard was found by a bunch of illiterate farmers last year near Chausa in northeast India," he continued.

"It's not even new, boss," said the thick-skinned Smith, moving closer to Peabody.

"Not only is it not new, it is ugly; the green is not the right shade and worse of all, it's *French!*" cried the patriotic Winston Peabody; he had settled down nicely with his British racing green Rolls-Royce Silver Ghost, Piccadilly Roadster that he had bought for himself in 1925. "And don't stand so close to me, Smith; you stink!"

Ugly or not, the car served them well as they travelled to Orleans the first day.

"Do you recognise this place, old boy?" Peabody asked, turning over his shoulder briefly to look at Smith, who had been relegated to the back seat.

Smith looked out the window with renewed interest. He gazed at a series of arches that belonged to a large majestic, cream-coloured building. These finished abruptly and opened into a large square in which stood the statue of a prancing horse upon which sat a woman clad in armour. "Can't say I do, boss."

"Well, little wonder, "answered Peabody, "seeing that it was a few hundred years ago we were last here. This, my man, is the city that the 'French Witch' liberated from our boys back in 1492." Peabody pointed in the direction of the statue at 'Place du Martroi.' "Looks a little different now, wouldn't you say?" he continued, swerving out of the way of an oncoming tram and then expertly overtaking a slow-moving automobile that was blocking his path. "Phew, boss!" exclaimed Smith, his eyes wide as he began to appreciate the sights of a pre second-world war Orleans. "Where is that stinky river?"

"The Loire is over there somewhere, and that bedraggled army of hers. For your information, Smith, I doubt that it is 'stinky' now," Peabody answered, pointing again with his hand. He pulled the automobile over.

"I suppose our friend Alberta Alburtus booked this for us as well," he cried with displeasure, as he stared at the obviously run down 'Historical Hotel' where they were to spend that evening.

"You know, boss," said Smith, his finger still on the side of his temple, "I think it was lucky for the English that we nicked that sword of hers, or she just may have liberated the whole country."

Peabody turned off the engine. "I thought you said we couldn't *change* history, Smith, my good fellow," said Peabody patronisingly, "but if you *are* correct, then our boys would have 'whacked' her anyway, sword or no sword. Which of course, they did!" Peabody whistled the first few bars of 'Rule Britannia' as he got out of the car and stepped onto the sidewalk. "I did wonder though, what she must have thought of those silky black cami-knickers that I tied to her shield after we had made off with it."

"Yes boss, she was quite a looker," gasped Smith, misinterpreting Peabody's comment, as he lifted two heavy suitcases belonging to his boss off the luggage rack. "Though that Fanny Romanov was the best!"

Peabody strode in front of Smith through the entrance to the hotel and into the reception area. As he did so, for some unknown reason a very vivid vision of the face of Tatiana Nicolaevna came into his mind.

Later, Peabody lay looking at the timer on the bedside table. He had for some reason been compelled to bring it along on the trip. As he stared at it in the shadows of his room, he remembered the words that the 'Maid of Orleans' had spoken to her soldiers before the battle for the city. 'I am the star that will point you to the father of light.' As he remembered these words, the vision of Tatiana's face again invaded his mind. He closed his eyes tightly, frantically trying to block the image. Her face faded slowly and was gone. "What drivel!" he said out loud. He turned over to face the wall and fell asleep.

After an early breakfast, they left Orleans and set out on what Peabody estimated to be a seven-hour trip to Lyon. It took ten hours due to the 'pesky' vehicle experiencing three punctures. Still, they both enjoyed the trip along the narrow winding road that cut through the pretty French countryside. The weather had also remained fair with the sun frequently blinking through the thin blanket of cloud. There was not even a hint of rain. Later, that very same sun was drowning in its own blood as the Voison made its way down the main road in Lyon.

The next day they crossed the border into Italy. Tall Cyprus trees began to appear, at first intermittently, then in places they marched on either side of the road as the rays of the sun tried in vain to pierce the dark green dense sprays of foliage.

"Did you know, old man, some of these trees can live to over a thousand years old?" Peabody informed him, replacing the sun visor to it normal position as they sped through the dull tunnel of Cyprus trees. "Just think, some of these could have been here the last time we visited, six hundred years ago."

Smith began to snore loudly.

A few hours later as they approached Turin, Peabody pulled the automobile over to the side of the road to admire the view. The lights of the majestic buildings in the foreground of the city twinkled like garnets in the early twilight. The black silhouette of the Mole Antonelliana was tattooed on the jagged snow-topped teeth of the Alps on the horizon.

"I wonder if they'll ever find out that it's a fake, boss?" said Smith, staring at the beautiful sight before him.

"Well, last year they were still convinced," answered Peabody, smiling broadly. "That wrinkled old, pickle-livered swine has no idea what we went through to pull that one off. I hardly need to remind you of that. That is when the timer first started to give us trouble. We spent six months on the streets of nineteenth century Turin, lugging that damned thing around. It was lucky that I had my watch and jewellery, or we would have starved to death."

"What year was that, boss?" asked Smith, smiling at what was to him a fond memory, and how Peabody had almost become his real friend at that time and not his boss.

"1898, Mr Smith," replied Peabody. "The year that Frenchman took the photograph." Smith remembered how they had stolen the 'old blanket' as he called it, the day after the photograph had been taken. They then took it back to their own time and to Clodius Albertus, as instructed. It had then been decided that the 'shroud' could not just disappear as that would add to the mystery and controversy even more. So he and Peabody took a trip back to the fourteenth century where they located a similar one that had recently been wrapped around the crucified body of a Knight Templar. They took this back to their own time, and waited the required year before returning it to 1898 on the very same day that they had stolen the original one. They then placed the fourteenth-century shroud in its place. It was at this point that the timer had refused to take them back to their own time, or indeed, anywhere! "That was the beginning of the timer not working properly, boss," he pointed out.

"Much to our disadvantage," mused Peabody, jumping back into the driver's seat.

"I never did understand why we had to replace that old blanket with a fake one, and not the usual knickers," Smith said, as he opened the door to the passenger seat.

"No, I don't suppose you would, old boy," muttered Peabody half to himself, "I don't suppose you would."

Two days later, they reached Padua. Peabody took a short detour so as to be able to admire the ancient arches of its university.

"This 'house of instruction' is 800 years old," Peabody exclaimed in his lecturing tone of voice as the car passed beneath its late evening shadow. "Galileo once taught there."

"I like ours better, boss," declared Smith simply. "And one day in the future people will drive past our college and say: 'Did you know that Winston Peabody once taught there?'"

Peabody felt a warm glow inside. Even though Smith really was a halfwit most of the time, he never seemed to fail to come up with some excellent perceptions.

On the evening of the fifth day of their journey, they finally arrived at their hotel in Aquileia. It was small and discreet and comfortable at best. But this time, Peabody did not seem to mind. He took a long, cool bath, changed into his evening suit and met Smith in the small lounge area set to one side of the foyer. Peabody seated himself facing the main entrance to the door.

"You expecting someone, boss?" Smith asked.

"Never you mind, Charlie boy," answered Peabody crossing his legs rapidly and scratching his elbow. "I need you to go down to the river to get us a boat."

"What! At this time, boss?" Smith cried, looking at his watch. It was after seven in the evening. He was hungry and his body ached from sitting in the same position in a very uncomfortable automobile for the last five days. He was also eying the cognac bottle that stood between two fine-looking cognac glasses on the table in front of them.

"Don't be impertinent, Smith! Just do as I say," said Peabody in an icy tone. "It doesn't have to be too big. Just a nice yacht will do."

Smith sighed and rose. Forlornly, he looked at the brandy, and then made his way to the door of the hotel. "Yes boss, no boss, three bags full, boss!" he muttered as he walked out into the warm, still night air.

As he waited, Peabody studied one of the tourist leaflets on the city. Most of the information he of course knew already. As usual, he had thoroughly prepared for his next 'rescue.' He quickly poured himself a cognac and sipped the smooth, warming liquid.

"Mr Peabody, I presume?"

Peabody looked up quickly, surprised by the silent approach of the man suddenly appearing in front of him. He was equally startled by his appearance. His yellow blonde hair was cut short and acute. His large round face was covered with patches of the same stuff, though he certainly did not wear a beard or moustache. His khaki shirt was opened to reveal springy curls of the same colour. Beneath his khaki shorts, his legs were bare. He wore heavy, leather sandals and no socks. His appearance resembled that of an orang-utan, Peabody thought. Recovering quickly, Peabody stood up and offered his hand.

"Ah! Mijnheer Koets, I presume!" he said, offering his hand.

"Plain mister will do. Or just call me Gerri," answered Gerri. The familiarity did not impress Peabody at all.

"Plain Peabody will do, Mr Koets," remarked Peabody stiffly.

"Suit yourself, mijnheer!" answered Koets, unfazed.

They took their seats; Peabody poured a large cognac for his guest, while his glass remained empty.

"Am I supposed to trust a man that doesn't drink, Peabody?" Koets said in a low voice, eying the empty glass. Peabody paused for a moment as if in thought.

"Of course, Koets! Please forgive me. I am just tired from our long journey." He poured himself a small amount of the dark honey-coloured liquid.

They made light conversation for a few minutes, discussing Peabody's journey from Paris and some of the cities they had passed through. Koets nodded at the names of places, as if he knew them well. He seemed to have been well-travelled, informing Peabody that he had in the last year alone visited Morocco, Shanghai, Persia and the Philippines – not in that order, he exclaimed mischievously. Then he tipped up his glass and swallowed the remains of his cognac.

"Have you got the sandal, old chap?" he asked matter-of-factly in the best English – gentleman accent he could muster.

"Have you got the coins, mijnheer?" Peabody replied, with a perfect Hollander accent.

*

In 1932, the once large population of the ancient world city of Aquileia had shrunk to barely three thousand five hundred people. It was quiet and quite deserted as Smith walked along the streets, their emptiness emphasised by the hollow echoes of the heels of his smart brogues. The full moon behind cast a great bulky shadow before him. He stopped abruptly. He put the large cigar back into his mouth and then turned his head to an angle where he could see its shadow clearly. He took it out of his mouth and then laughed with amusement as he tried to watch the same shadow blow smoke up at the stars. He chuckled all the more when he realised he couldn't, then carried on walking towards the river Natiso. There were still traces of the old Roman harbour to his left, but Smith gave it no thought. He wanted to get this job done quickly so that he could get back to a nice dinner and a few of those cognacs. As he turned left into another deserted road, he was startled by a little mongrel dog that seemed to appear from nowhere. It growled briefly at his ankles, then darted away quickly as he aimed a wild kick at it. Smith was not fond of dogs. The old stone buildings were dark on either side of him, no light emanating through the cracks in the closed wooden shutters. This place is almost as dead as Hurst Green, he thought as he made his way further down the road. At the end it veered sharply to his left. Here at last he began to see some signs of life. Gay orange lights streamed from some of the windows, lighting up the cobbles in front of him. He could hear the faint sound of a scratchy record playing Puccini's 'Madame Butterfly,' Cio-Cio San portrayed by Tamaki Miura. He stopped outside the house from where the music came and listened. He could hear talking and laughter as the family inside had dinner together. The sound made him a little sad, though he was not sure why. The sweet peppery smell of oregano, however, aroused his nostrils reminding him of his hunger and he started again on his journey, quickening his stride. In the distance, he could now see the river. It shone silvery in the moonlight. As he reached it, he could see buildings on either side of it. Here again, all seemed deserted and still. As he turned the corner, the shadows of the buildings on his left blacked out the moonlight. He stopped to finish his cigar, wondering which way to go. He could hear the creaking of the boat lines straining against their mooring, the flapping in the breeze laden with the scent of frangipani, of loose canvas broken free from rolled up sails, and the gentle, soft ripple of the water against the stone quayside. There were boats, but all seemed unmanned. He was just about to turn around and explain to Peabody that seven thirty in the evening was not the ideal time in Aquileia to hire a boat, when he heard the unmistakable sound of loud snoring. It had begun suddenly and was coming from the large yacht nearest to him. Smith walked quietly over to the edge of the quay and peered over into the deck. A young man with his hands behind his head lay stretched out. He was grinning broadly in his sleep. Smith decided to complete his task now rather than early in the morning. He had no doubt that Peabody would order him to be up at the break of day to rectify the previous evening's failure. He gingerly climbed aboard the yacht and stood legs astride over what appeared to be a snoring, grinning corpse. He lit another cigar and then bending forward low enough to be able to catch the scent of hard liquor, he purposely blew two large puffs of blue cigar smoke, one after the other into the sleeping man's face. The man mumbled something, screwed his face up and shook it slightly as one might when irritated by a fly, then stretched out one arm as if trying to grab hold of something. As his hand gripped the air and his eyes opened, he levered himself up onto his elbows and stared up at the great bulky figure standing above him.

"G'day, sport! Who are you?" he said with a very slurry Australian twang.

Immediately, Smith did not like the look of the obviously quite drunk young Australian. During his long years of employment with Winston Peabody, he had been taught never to trust a colonial. Also his accent reminded him of 'Blew Eyes', Fanny Dodger's friend, and he certainly was *not* fond of him. He clenched his fist threateningly and growled. With surprising speed, the young man was up on his feet. He looked to his left into the shadows and then bent down and groped for a half-drunk bottle of cognac.

"Fancy a swig, sport?" he said, offering the bottle to Smith, who immediately began to think that the accent was not similar to that South African coward's after all. He took the bottle, pulled out the cork with his teeth and poured down at least half of what was left.

"My name's Fletcher," said the young man, thankful at seemingly appeasing the giant standing before him. He was tall himself but much more on the thinner side. "Fletcher Christian."

"My boss wants to hire your boat for a couple of days," said Smith, ignoring the introduction and taking another gulp from the bottle.

"Hey, steady on old sport!" cried Fletcher. "That stuff is crazy expensive."

"If you let us use your boat for a while, my boss will buy you all the cognac you need," answered Smith.

Fletcher looked on in dismay as Smith gulped the remains of the bottle. "So, what figure would you have in mind for the hiring of this luxurious sailing vessel?" he asked, hiding his annoyance with a sweeping bow.

"Fifty guineas a day," growled Smith, getting ready to punch him.

"I have a partner, sport; make it seventy-five and we have a deal."

Smith looked at the now empty cognac bottle.

"And another bottle on the house!" declared Fletcher.

Smith lifted his finger to his temple and paused in concentration. "One hundred a day and not a penny more!" he growled viciously.

Fletcher spat in the palm of his hand and held it out. "Done!" he said. "Let's start on that bottle straight away. We have a whole stash of them down below. By the way, where are we going?"

*

"You can stick yer fine food like caviar n wine
Fish n mashed potaties on which it's nice to dine
Cos if I told yer that I liked em I'd be tellin yer lies
Cos what I really love is me old ma's pies."

Smith's voice echoed through the dark streets of Aquileia. It was 2 a.m. and he was very drunk. It was something he didn't usually make a habit of, but at that moment any feelings of guilt lay at the bottom of two empty cognac bottles. The cuffs of his shirt sleeves gaped open. He stopped a moment, trying to remember what he had done with his cuff-links. It was at this moment that he also realised that he was jacketless. "Cuff-less, jacket-less and dinner-less!" he exclaimed drunkenly. "Who cares!"

He then proceeded to stagger further up the street.

"You can stick …"

A sash window above him opened abruptly.

"Smith! I'll have your guts for garters for this!" Peabody threatened in the loudest voice he could muster while still trying to whisper. "Get inside and go to your room at once, and stop that infernal singing!"

Smith stopped. He looked up at Peabody hanging out of the window. "Wait for me, boss!" he cried. "You can't do the job without me, you know. I'm the brains." Looking up suddenly made him feel giddy and he collapsed backwards onto the seat of his pants in a roar of laughter.

Peabody looked at him icily. "Imbecile!" he said, then banged the window shut.

The next morning, a sorrowful looking Smith sat across from Winston Peabody at the breakfast table. He had apologised for his previous night's behaviour at least a dozen times during the silent 'treatment' that Peabody was giving him. For when Peabody was really angry, he did not waste 'articulate words' of discipline on him; he simply wasn't worthy of them. Now he would pay for a lengthy course of ill treatment, which would definitely involve no cognac, or even brandy for that matter, for the remainder of the trip. Smith knew this.

"I will say one thing about your behaviour last night, and one thing only," said Peabody with contempt. Smith put his elbows on the table and rested his head in his hands. He groaned silently. "There are consequences for our actions, Mr Smith and yours will be particularly unpleasant when we return; and take your elbows from my breakfast table!"

Smith remembered the last time Peabody had inflicted a punishment of this nature on him. He had been ordered to clean the enormous stone floor of the great hall at the college with a toothbrush. Peabody helped himself to another slice of toast. He spread the butter thinly and then put it back on his plate. "What have you got to say for yourself?"

Smith's eyes were the colour of the Union Jack as he looked up at his boss through the spread fingers of both his hands.

"That Tasmanian Devil can drink, boss!" he said painfully.

"Tasmanian Devil?" exclaimed Peabody.

"The one with the boat! I got us a boat, boss. It's down on the river a short walk from here. But that young Australian wanted more money for the hire of it, so we played a game or two of cards to see what price we could agree on." Peabody knew that Smith was making excuses for his unacceptable behaviour and that at least half of what he had said was untrue.

"I have two problems with that explanation, Mr Smith. Firstly, because you took so long to return, I decided to do the job myself. I have organised a nice yacht which will be ready for us to board at 9 a.m." He looked briefly at his watch and then poured himself another cup of tea. "Secondly, any money with regards to the hiring of any boats is the Club's, and you have no right to gamble with it." Peabody noticed the open cuffs of Smith's shirt. "Any money or anything else you have lost is for your own account, old boy. By the way, those were Prince Albert's cuff links that I gave you last Christmas, Smith," said Peabody, continuing to stare at Smiths gaping cuffs. "If you have lost them, I will be extremely upset."

"Were you down by the river last night too, boss? I didn't see you," answered Smith, trying to change the subject while also deciding to risk a bread roll without butter.

"You wouldn't have been capable of seeing me even if I had," answered Peabody. "No, you drunken imbecile! I met an acquaintance of an acquaintance here in the hotel shortly after you left. Coincidentally, he and his partner are sailing around the seven seas on a large yacht and he has offered their services to me for a couple of days."

About an hour later, Peabody waited in the driver's seat of the C11 as Smith loaded their packing cases onto the luggage rack. He patted the pearl handle of his walking stick that lay on the passenger seat next to him.

"Gosh, boss! What have you got inside your case? It feels twice as heavy as it did before!" cried Smith as he climbed sweating onto the back seat, to which he had been 'demoted' again.

"I made the swop while you were gone last night. We have the first one hundred gold coins ever minted by the Romans in this city in that case, so do be careful with it." Peabody turned and grinned for the first time that morning.

"A hundred gold coins for one smelly old sandal, boss! Now that's what I call a good deal!" replied Smith, trying to butter Peabody up again.

"Especially as it wasn't even the genuine one, old boy," replied Peabody, forgetting that he was still angry with him. "The parcel you collected from Longfell Tannery, remember?"

"Oh yes, of course, boss!" cried Smith. He had collected the parcel the day before they had left and for some reason had forgotten to check the handiwork properly. But he was sure it would be alright. Old Bob had done many jobs for Peabody before. Though he was known for playing practical jokes, he was sure that Bob wouldn't dare play one on Winston Peabody. Anyway, on the quick inspection Smith had managed to give it, it had certainly looked like Julius Caesar's sandal.

"And what's more, Smith my man," continued Peabody unaware of Smiths slight discomfort. "I now know exactly where the other one of the pair is. Our friend is a doctor at the Institute of Archaeology at Groningen. Our next 'rescue', wouldn't you say?"

"I would, boss!" answered Smith, "but I keep getting confused. Do we have the real one or does the 'Club' have it?"

"I would prefer you to stay confused. The more confused you are, the better these days, Mr Smith."

Peabody took a detour on their way to the river. He parked the car briefly to admire the Romanesque-Gothic style of the façade of the Aquileia Cathedral.

"Hey, boss! Look at all those policemen! You don't think they are after us, do you?" Smith whispered loudly while at the same time trying to lower himself from vision in the back of the automobile. A crowd made up of mostly policemen had gathered at the entrance to the cathedral. They seemed to be taking notes and questioning tourists and locals alike.

"If you care to look, Smith," answered Peabody calmly, as he started the engine to the automobile, "you would see that there is a building connected to that façade by a portico. It is the so called 'Church of the Pagans.' In a secret vault behind the nave in that church there used to lie a small chest with one hundred large coins in it. Not any more, it would seem. No, they aren't looking for us, Smith. Though they could quite easily be looking for the thief!"

A little later, Peabody parked the car at the end of the street that lead down to the river. They didn't expect to be more than a day or so, as he had been informed by Koets that their trip was not far down the coast. He grabbed his walking stick from the seat, instructed Smith to load all the luggage onto the backseat and lock all the doors. As he slipped his arm into his sports jacket, he felt a slight weight from the pocket. He dipped his hand into the side pocket where his fingers closed around the familiar shape of the little egg timer. Even though it had been no use to him for years, he found it difficult to leave behind.

"All being well Smith, we will be back here tomorrow, and if that tin can on wheels permits, we'll be back home in just over a week," he informed Smith, pointing at the much maligned automobile with his walking stick. As was the usual 'Peabody policy' when on a 'rescue,' they would never stay in the same hotel on two consecutive nights. Tomorrow they would find another one on the other side of the city. As they approached the yacht, Smith suddenly grabbed his arm. There were at least a dozen Politzia swarming all over the deck, with no sign of Koets.

"Too late, Smith old boy; just keep walking or it will look too suspicious," said Peabody under his breath. As they passed, Smith began to think that he had seen the boat before; his suspicions were confirmed as a familiar voice from somewhere on the deck rang out.

"G'day sport! You're a bit late!" Smith looked down to see the smiling, rather handsome face of Fletcher Christian. "Come on board. Don't mind this lot – they'll be gone in a mo."

Smith turned to Peabody. "That's the Tasmanian, boss! I'll just go and tell him that you have made other arrangements."

Peabody was just about to confirm, when another voice rang out from amidst the melee. "Mr Peabody, I presume! You're right on time." It was Gerrit Koets. He didn't seem at all bothered by the presence of the police and stepped up onto the stone quay with an agility that defied his physique.

"Don't bother about our friends in blue," he said without any discretion. "They are searching all the visiting boats on the river. Apparently, someone made off with some old coins from the basilica last night. Right under their noses, it seems."

Fletcher now also stepped up beside them. "Well, would you believe it, Gerri," he exclaimed. "This is my friend from last night! I guess we now all know each other." He offered his hand to Peabody, who merely stared at it with disdain. Fletcher introduced himself anyway. Turning around to face the police officer who was supervising his men, he said loudly: "You see,

Sergio! I have my alibi right here as promised. I couldn't have got up to any mischief last night. We were practically comatose together."

The Peninsula of Istria is located at the head of the Adriatic, between the Gulf of Trieste and the Bay of Kvaerner. The yacht carved its way through the moderate swell at a steady speed through the transparent blue waters, hugging the coast line.

"That, my big bald friend," said Fletcher, pointing with a chicken drumstick, "is Trieste. By mid-afternoon, we should be in the vicinity shown on your map."

Smith was too hungry to take offence at the nickname given to him and merely continued to devour the enormous rump steak on the plate in front of him.

"Thank you for that information, my alcoholic shipmate," replied Peabody, observing Fletcher take his first sip from his cognac bottle. "I just hope you will still be on your feet when we arrive there."

Koets took the bottle out of Fletcher's hand and hugged it to his chest. "Come on E! I thought we agreed to only drink after 4 p.m. when at sea."

Fletcher threw his hands in the air. "Okay, okay, sport! Nobody will ever have an excuse to call me unprofessional."

"But that doesn't prevent us offering our hosts a gin and tonic," suggested Koets, looking at Peabody where he and Smith had seated themselves in two of the deck chairs at either side of the stern.

"I, Mr Koets," answered Peabody firmly, "never touch gin and tonic, and as you say, it is too early in the day."

For centuries, the sea has enslaved the spirits of sailors and adventurers of this world, from ancient times to modern. Peabody thoroughly disliked Fletcher Christian. His flamboyant, brash and arrogant manner he found as irritating as his open, devilishly handsome face. Then of course, he was an Australian and therefore a *colonial* – in Peabody's mind, a 'pretender.' He was also most likely a liar. Fletcher Christian, indeed! We all need to hide our true identity sometimes, thought Peabody, but does the idiot have to be so obvious! He also claimed to own the actual sword that once belonged to the infamous Fletcher Christian. He proudly presented it to Peabody for him to inspect. But Peabody doubted its authenticity and promptly told Fletcher so. The young man had merely laughed at his conclusion and thrust the blade a couple of inches into the wooden deck beside him as he worked the boom. The gleaming blade flashed in the sun as it quivered for a few seconds. Notwithstanding all this, Peabody could not deny that the young man knew how to sail the small schooner. He watched in admiration as he single-handedly directed it expertly over the increasingly choppy water. The bow rose and fell smoothly like a race horse over a steeple chase. He always seemed to duck beneath the boom just in time as it swung from left to right, whether his eye was on it or not. He could see that this young man had need for the sea and adventure. He hated him for it.

Peabody finished his light lunch of chicken with salad. He pushed back the deck chair from the low table on which he was sitting, and stretched out his legs. Koets surprised him again by suddenly appearing. He had gone into the cabin below a short time before. He carefully placed an empty bottle of cognac on the table in front of Peabody.

"You know, Mr Peabody," said Koets, bending forward and looking at the bottle, "this is genuine cognac. In order for a brandy to be named so, it must be produced in the wine growing region that surrounds the town of Cognac."

"Yes, I am well aware of that fact, Mr Koets," replied Peabody. He quickly stamped out the stub of a cheroot that he had been smoking and sat up. There was a slight edge to the tone of Koet's voice.

"Then you will also know that genuine cognac has to meet stringent French legal requirements," continued Koets, "one being that it is made from Ugni Blanc grapes or Saint Emilion, as the locals of the town of Cognac call them. You will also be fully aware then that it is distilled twice in copper pot stills and then aged for at least two years in French oak barrels from either Limousin or Troncais."

Smith stopped eating.

"And your point, Mr Koets?" declared Peabody, feeling more uncomfortable.

"My point, Mr Peabody, is that any old shop can put a label on a bottle of brandy and call it cognac, but the proof would be in its aroma, then the tasting of it and even the way it looks. Its clarity."

Fletcher crossed his arms and looked out to sea, but he was listening intently while grinning broadly.

"Those polizia back at Aquileia were a little unsettling, don't you think? Even though they found nothing, of course. Still, it could have been a very unpleasant experience. I performed an intricate little job back there in the cathedral, my friend. My contact was paid handsomely, yet it seems for me there are no wages forthcoming."

Smith watched Peabody closely and then slowly rose to his feet.

"No further, my big bald friend!" said Fletcher, dislodging the cutlass from the deck and holding it out in front of him threateningly.

Undeterred, Smith growled and started forward.

"No, Smith my man, stay where you are!" commanded Peabody. "There is no need for any violence. I am sure this is all just a misunderstanding."

Koets continued: "This cognac, my friend is genuine – unlike the sandal you gave me. You see, at first glance it certainly looks to be genuine. It certainly feels genuine; it even has the odour of a two-thousand-year-old sandal. But you see, it is in the clarity that it fails. The closer you look, the more you see it.

For instance, I doubt that the real Julius Caesar's sandal would have JC printed on the inside of the sole."

"But that *was* his name, wasn't it?" cried Smith, relieved that the tanner at last got the name correct.

"You idiot!" shouted Peabody. "I told you to check it!" Then turning to Koets and now to Fletcher, who had joined him, the curved broad cutlass in his hand. "There has obviously been a mistake on our side, and being a man of honour, I will rectify the matter immediately."

"Listen to him, Gerri!" laughed Fletcher. "Rectify the matter, he says. I say let's throw him overboard."

Peabody dug his hand down into his trouser pocket, and brought out a beautiful cut diamond the size of a walnut. Fletcher and Koets stared at it in disbelief. "I will give you this, sir, as security until I can get the correct sandal to you. You are very welcome to check its clarity."

"Not Fanny's diamond, boss!" Smith blurted out, clearly distressed, for he knew how much Tatiana's name-day diamond meant to him.

"Do we have a deal, Mr Koets?" said Peabody, ignoring Smith and handing Koets the exquisite stone.

Koets's eyes widened as he took the diamond. He held it up in the sunlight. "Here, E!" he said, tossing the diamond to his companion. "Take a look at that! You went mining in Papua New Guinea. Tell me what you make of that."

Fletcher caught the diamond smartly, much to Peabody's relief, and then proceeded to inspect it. "Wow, sport!" he said in mock wonder. "I have never seen such a beauty! But I'm sorry, Gerri, I told you a little porky about the diamond mining. I did go mining, but I never actually found any diamonds, so I wouldn't be able to tell you if this is real or not. If you want my expert opinion, I certainly would doubt its authenticity. Knowing these two and looking at the size of it, I would say it's a phony."

"A phony! You imbecile!" screamed Peabody in disbelief. "There is nothing phony about it."

"There is nothing phony about this either, you limey bean pole!" cried Fletcher. He started forward with his sabre. At the same time, Smith sprang across the few meters between him and Koets. He gripped him from behind in an iron-like arm lock around his neck. With one movement, Smith turned the struggling Koets to face Peabody. But Fletcher was just as quick, and before Peabody could grab his walking stick that lay at the side of his chair, he had thrust the blade of the menacing-looking cutlass at Peabody's throat.

"This sword *did* once belong to the *real* Fletcher Christian, my friend! It may not have spilled any blood for the last 145 years or so, but we can soon remedy that." Smith literally howled in anger, but it was hopeless. There was no way he would be able to deal with Koets and then cover the distance between himself and Fletcher before his boss was run through with the cutlass. But there was no need for intervention from Smith. Peabody was a very intuitive person, as well as being of exceptional intelligence. In his mind, he had already summed up Fletcher Christian, 'E' or whoever he was – and he wasn't a murderer. Peabody had come face to face with many of those in the years of time travelling, and had had some very narrow escapes. But this situation felt almost rehearsed, even rather comical. It was as though Fletcher Christian was acting.

"I think it's time you handed that little treasure map over now, don't you?" suggested Fletcher, his eyes flashing at Peabody theatrically.

"Come, come my friend! We've all lost our heads a bit here!" Peabody answered smoothly. "Put that ridiculous-looking sword down so that Mr Smith can put your ridiculous-looking friend down." Both Peabody and Fletcher glanced over to where the powerful Smith in his anxiety for his boss had lifted the unfortunate Koets clean off his feet. His face was slowly turning from crimson to purple; the patches of blonde hair that covered his face looked even more unruly.

"Hand over the map," demanded Fletcher, his voice now filled with uncertainty.

"Smith!" bellowed Peabody. "Stop strangling that orang-utan and put him down. Just keep hold of him."

Reluctantly, Smith slowly released the iron grip he had around Koets's neck until his victims toes touched the deck and then levelled out.

Peabody then produced the small piece of paper that had assumed the role of 'map.' He handed it to Fletcher, who lowered his sword and studied it.

"So where's the wreck, sport?" Fletcher asked. He traced the line of the coast with his finger from Trieste down to Porenzo. "Where is X marks the spot?"

"I don't work like that, Mr Christian," answered Peabody. "All the detailed information is in here." He tapped the side of his silver temple with his finger, "to guard against situations like this one." Fletcher looked closer at the map, turning it this way and that and then even holding it up in the sunlight, hoping to see a water mark or something. Peabody made his move. He sprang cat-like across the few metres where his walking stick lay propped up by the side of his chair. In one swift and skilful movement, he grabbed the walking stick with his left hand and drew the long, thin cruel blade out with his right. Though taken by surprise, Fletcher was quicker and more agile than Peabody anticipated. He immediately brought up the sword and crashed it down onto Peabody's blade.

"No you don't, sport!" he cried. Ordinarily, such a blow from a cutlass would have broken through Peabody's as if it had been a thin piece of plywood. But the blade of the walking stick was special. Peabody had taken part in the research himself with the metallurgist at the college and had been delighted when a correct mixture of chromium, molybdenum, vanadium

72

and of course, iron, had produced a blade that was practically unbreakable. It simply bent out of the way and then sprang back into action, as the heavy cumbersome cutlass continued its trajectory, embedding itself in the wooden deck. This bought Peabody more time. Again, like a cat he sprang across to the other side of Fletcher while running the thin, sharp steel across his adversaries shoulder. A thin red line appeared; it grew rapidly until it saturated the sleeve of Fletcher's white shirt.

"This is no play acting, Mr Christian!" shrilled Peabody, as he started to dance around Fletcher in expert rapier-fencing fashion. But again Fletcher was a quicker and more agile opponent than Peabody had guessed. Though unable to attack due to having to dodge this way and that from Peabody's prodding blade, he was himself able to dance out of harm's way. However, things would have gone ill for the young man when Peabody, with a new move he had recently learned, side-stepped to his left, feigned a swerve to his right and then with a peculiar flick of his wrist was just about to plunge the cruel, thin blade into the side of Fletcher, when he stepped onto the rolling cognac bottle that Koets had dropped when Smith had grabbed hold of him. Peabody lost his footing completely and overbanked dramatically, the momentum of his movements taking him to the side of the yacht. He wavered for a second and then tumbled over the side.

"Man overboard!" yelled Fletcher, but before he could react, Smith let go of his captive, who crumpled to his knees, and flung himself overboard.

"Wow, Gerri! Did you see that?" said Fletcher, standing astride over the groaning Koets, one hand holding the cutlass and the other holding his blood-soaked shoulder. "Did you see the way that guy moved his feet as he fenced? It was like poetry in motion! That is the type of actor I want to learn to be when we get to England. A swashbuckler!"

Koets groaned, and sat up slowly. "Pass me the cognac, Errol!" he said.

C HAPTER 3
THE CROWN HOTEL

The 'Book of Truth,' in which she had recorded her and Arty's time travelling adventures so far, lay open on Tatiana's lap as she sat on the single bed in which she had recently been sleeping. It had only been two weeks since she had first been rescued from captivity from the house, albeit unintentionally by Arty, but perhaps not quite so unintentionally by the timer. They had later of course returned to the Ipatiev House in order to try to rescue the rest of her family – a rescue that would have been in complete contradiction to what the history books of 2014 had recorded. Indeed, the more time she spent in 2014 with Arty, the more she was lead to believe it was most probable her life along with those of her family was cut short in 1918 in that dreadful house. The timer for some reason dictated that its users are unable to return for a year to the same time and place and so, though dreadfully sorrowful, she took heart from the fact that the timer had bestowed on her a gift of time: A year in which she and Arty could travel through time and find out the truth behind certain events in history. Arty had quite rightly pointed out a small amount of time spent in 2014 could run to thousands of years if they wished it to. For when they travelled to another time, no matter how long they spent in that place, when they returned they found that no time at all had gone by. Though she would miss her family terribly and worry about them, she became aware of the fact that nothing would change for them in the time she spent with Arty and the timer, and that their situation would still be the same when they finally did return to the Ipatiev House. Inexplicably too, soon after arriving in 2014 she began to develop an incredibly close bond with Arty, as Harry, Arty's friend informed them would happen; a closeness to another person far beyond anything she had felt before.

Unfortunately, their plans of time-travelling adventures together abruptly ended when attempting to retrieve the other timer from that no good Winston Peabody. On their 'trip' to the last night of the Titanic they had 'chanced' upon this unscrupulous character and had discovered that he was in possession of the timer that had previously been used by their friend Harry. Harry needed the timer back in order to be released from his endless life, for though he lived as a normal person, time for him had ceased to exist; a nightmare for one who longed to die and then be with his adored wife Magda. For on their last trip she had been shot and grievously wounded by none other than that evil highwayman, Dick Turpin. Their crossing back to the present had faltered and they had found themselves at one point somewhere in place and time in England, which is when Harry inexplicably lost the timer, later to be acquired by Winston Peabody. When they finally reached home, Magda died shortly afterwards of her wounds. He had stated that her death and the loss of the timer had all been his fault but he had not explained to them why. Shortly after their return from the Titanic, Harry had passed 'The Book of Truth' on to them, for all their adventures must be recorded in it. Unfortunately, the entries of the timer's previous owner mysteriously disappeared when she had first opened the book, so there was no way that she could find any clue for Harry's self-imposed guilt.

Now, as she sat alone in her bedroom in Arty's small cottage by the sea, a void of immense grief and sorrow gaped in the pit of her stomach. All her pent-up emotions caused by recent events flooded out in the form of great tears streaming down her face. Her hand shook as she tried to write the words describing how her beloved Papa, Nicholas the former tsar of Russia, had been caught in the crossfire of the gunfight in Yurovsky's office. He had taken the bullet that was surely meant for her. Her tears splashed onto the page, yet even in her torment and sadness she was aware that, inexplicably, the page of the book absorbed the moisture immediately, leaving no trace of a mark or a smudge. Oh, dear Papa! What will become of us without you? What will become of dearest Mama? As she stopped writing she looked, her eyes still blurred with tears, through the window that overlooked the Indian Ocean. Unusually, the early evening sky was infused with rays of green, silver and gold. Immediately, the timer filled her mind, or rather its presence. A wild longing engulfed her. The warmth of the sun and a summer breeze melting the last snows of winter filled her heart. She felt stronger!

She recorded how Plant, a mysterious undercover British agent, helped her and Arty escape from the clutches of the Bolshevik executioners and race to the station where her sisters were being held prisoner on a train, in terrible danger of being shot by two hard-line Bolsheviks. She stopped writing briefly again, as the memory came back to her; one of those two assassins had spoken with an American accent. She noted this also, then continued to write of her own emotions and the remorse that she now felt for shooting that very man herself. Her chest heaved again with the weight of her guilt, as another large tear fell onto the page, but again it was miraculously 'swallowed' up. Her hand steadied slightly as she wrote of how she and her sisters had been finally rescued by more undercover British agents who had stopped the train. But who were they working for? Why did they then shoot those poor soldiers who had refused to shoot her sisters when ordered – her own countrymen? So much death, misery and horror! If Plant had not suddenly reappeared, they would even have shot dear Arty! Finally, she wrote of the terrible decision that she had to make: Whether to stay in 1918 with her sisters and hopefully be taken to a place of safety, or with the help of the timer return with Arty, with whom she had developed a strange and inexplicable bond, back to 2014. She had decided to trust the timer to make that decision for her, so here she was, back at Arty's simple cottage by the sea, where the palm trees swayed, the sun shone forever and the humidity made her feel the need to bathe at least three times a day. But what now? What was she doing here? Where had her family been taken to now and would she ever see them again? As she closed the book, her thoughts were disturbed by a single soft knock on the door.

"Are you alright?" she heard Arty ask.

She heaved a great sigh, fighting her emotions. She could not let him see her like this. She was Tatiana Nicolaevna, a grand duchess of Russia. A Romanov! She had lost her father; she had, for the time being it seemed, lost the rest of her family too. There must be a reason for all this. It had something to do with the egg timer.

"Yes Arty, I am just resting," she replied as she put the old, worn leather-bound book back into the chest of drawers.

"We only have two Jammy Dodgers left and no coffee! Would you like to go to Carlo's?" Arty's voice was soft at the other side of the door.

Yes she felt a little better now. Always when she thought of the timer she seemed to be filled with tranquillity; an inner peace. All will be okay, she thought.

"Yes, okay uncle dear!" she answered even a little mischievously, "as today isn't Sunday and if you haven't eaten *both* those Jammy Dodgers, you may take your 'antique' out to dinner."

*

"Where on earth are we?" asked Arty, looking around wildly at their surroundings. "I can't believe nobody seems to notice when this happens!"

They had just returned to the cottage from dinner. In the little kitchen, Arty was looking for the coffee when the timer had quite unexpectedly decided to transport them to who knows where. Indeed, they had just been commenting on how nice it would be to just relax and take things a little easy for a few days while they thought about their next move, when it began its irrepressible display of colour and commotion.

They were now standing in the main entrance of what looked like a very smart hotel. People were walking past them on the pavement, seemingly unperturbed by their sudden appearance. By the shape and style of the cars on the road behind them, their clothes and those of the passersby, Arty concluded that they had arrived in pretty much the same year as they had left – 2014 – which was confusing. But they were certainly not in Africa, Tatiana had declared, hugging the shoulders of her bright blue duffle coat that the timer had very thoughtfully provided. It was a cold day, overhung with a dense blanket of darkening gray clouds. Arty put his hands into the side pockets of his trench coat and looked up at the large golden letters that arched over the entrance to the hotel.

THE CROWN HOTEL

"Why is it that when we come to England it is always bloody cold and just about to bloody snow?" he cried indignantly.

Tatiana ignored him. "Excuse me, madam," she asked with a friendly smile as an elderly woman walked passed them, making her way up the steps to the entrance. "This is *the* Crown Hotel in … ?"

"Yes, young lass," answered the women turning around sharply, "this is Harrogate's finest! Though I'm not so sure about some of the guests these days." She looked at Arty from head to toe, then disappeared into the cosy light that came from inside. Arty, puzzled by the lady's seemingly unprovoked outburst, looked quickly down at the clothes he was wearing. Tatiana squealed with laughter.

"Why does it always do this to *me*?" he cried in disgust, looking down at his shoes – a pair of very smart and shiny brogues, but the left one was black and the right one was brown.

"Where am I going to get one black shoe from?" he cried, as they instinctively linked arms and walked up the steps and into the hotel.

"Or one brown one!" giggled Tatiana.

The Crown Hotel in Low Harrogate was bought from the 'crown' in 1778 by the Thackwray family. By 1784 William Thackwray had made so much money that he was also able to buy the neighbouring Queen Hotel. It was visited in 1806 by none other than the famous Lord Byron, who at that time was still to gain fame as poet, politician and a scandalous philanderer. However, what really put the hotel and the town of Harrogate on the map was the discovery of the sulphur well in 1822. This led to the building of the Crown Hotel Baths and then the creation of the town's spa. By 1840, so many people were visiting the baths for the miraculous healing waters, the hotel was nicknamed 'The Hospital.'

In 1848 the hotel was extensively renovated, revealing the building that Arty and Tatiana had just gazed upon. The long façade of double story, large arched and ballasted bay windows looked over a sidewalk where shiny black, Victorian-style iron street lamps marched. At their top glowed a merry yellow light, brightening an otherwise colourless afternoon.

As they entered the impressive foyer, Arty stopped suddenly. "Wow!" he exclaimed. "Look at this place!"

"Yes, uncle," replied Tatiana a little tersely. "So please remove your hat."

Startled, Arty quickly removed the thick woollen 'Bob Hat' from his head that, in his defence, he had not been aware he was wearing, and gripped it tightly in his clenched fist.

"Yours?" he said, staring at the red felt beret that she had just tilted provocatively to one side.

"Ladies don't need to remove their hats indoors, uncle dear, if they don't want to," she answered playfully, "and besides, I like it."

Feeling rather conspicuous, Arty bent his knees a little as they stood observing their surroundings, hoping that his long, brown trench coat would cover his odd shoes.

The foyer to the hotel was certainly upmarket. The multi-coloured carpet that covered the floor was thick and luxurious. The long, wooden curved reception desk was inlaid with brass. Behind this were the smartly dressed hotel staff, busy either on telephones taking reservation bookings or checking new arrivals into their rooms and suites. A large chandelier hanging from the centre of the ceiling and brass stand lamps with green shades positioned in each corner of the room lit the foyer. They both felt uneasy amidst the low murmur of voices.

"What do you suppose we are doing here?" asked Tatiana.

"I have absolutely no idea, my imperial antique," Arty answered. Then a thought occurred to him. "Perhaps there is a message at the reception for us?"

"Arty!" She said looking at him doubtfully, "perhaps there *is*, but I just hope it is not for me!"

Arty turned to look at her sharply, understanding immediately what she meant.

"Well, we can't just keep standing here like two lost souls," he answered, bending his knees quickly again as somebody walked past them. "Sooner or later, somebody is going to ask us what we are doing here."

They decided to toss a coin for it. Heads, Arty would ask for any messages at the reception and tails, they would leave the hotel altogether and look for a possible reason for their trip somewhere else. Luckily, Arty found a one-pound coin in the pocket of his trench coat. He flipped it high in the air and then stumbled a few steps forward in order to catch it. He apologised to the young couple that he bumped into, who looked at him in mild amusement. He stepped back to where Tatiana stood, the back of his hand covered with his right hand. He turned away and as he placed both his hands under her nose.

"Heads!" she cried.

"I should have known," he said with disdain.

"I will ask for the messages, if you like," she declared boldly.

Arty thought a moment. "No," he said. "You just seat yourself over there on one of those sofas. I'll join you in a minute." He squeezed her hand and then walked across the room to the reception desk. Tatiana made her way to the three chesterfield style, ox-blood-coloured leather sofas arranged into a large square. A single leather chair stood at one side and a large coffee table in the middle. She seated herself at the end of one of the sofas, relieved there was nobody else there. She sat humming a little to herself as she observed the many vases of flowers that she had not noticed before, dotted around this part of the foyer, giving it the feel of a separate enclosure of colours and fragrances. Three yellow tulips gave her the impression that they were smiling and bowing slightly to her over the lip of a tall, long – necked, glossy black vase that seemed to have suddenly appeared in the middle of the table in front of her. She glanced over to where Arty was standing in a short queue, waiting to talk to one of the staff at the reception. She was feeling very warm now. She put her hand up to take off the red felt beret that she had been wearing; what she took hold of did not feel like felt at all, but more of a silky type of material. She removed it and to her astonishment found the hat was the shape of a bell. It was canary yellow and the brim had been flipped up, which is why she obviously hadn't noticed the sudden change. A mid-calf length, thick tweed skirt fitted snugly around her waist and over her hips. It hugged her body so closely that she blushed slightly at the thought of having to stand up. Her shoes, which had previously been knee length black suede boots, were now of brown leather and rounded at the toe, the heels thick but low. She gasped slightly at the rich, deep red carpet beneath her feet. Her cream, silk blouse with puffed sleeves and rounded collar was open at the neck. A jacket of the same colour and material as her skirt lay at her side on the sofa, under which she could see the edge of a soft leather bag. Tatiana was much less anxious than one would expect. She was getting quite used to the timer and its shenanigans and anyway, she trusted it. The music had also changed from the 'modern' style that had been playing as they entered the hotel to what sounded like something Arty had played recently for her. It was what he had called 'brass band' music. She liked it. With no intention of standing up, she sat back quite relaxed, and tapped her foot, waiting for Arty to return so they could see what the timer had in store for them next. A man had seated himself in the single leather chair to her left. At least, she thought it was a man for the head and shoulders were hidden by the newspaper in which he seemed engrossed. The person's legs were crossed and their trousers were raised, revealing a pair of quite shocking multicoloured, striped socks. Curious and very amused, Tatiana saw that his feet wore one smart and highly polished black brogue shoe and one brown one. She was just about to stand up and punch his newspaper, thinking the man in the chair was Arty, when she noticed his hands. Arty had long thin skilful-looking fingers; ideal piano fingers, she had told him. The man in the chair had thicker fingers and what's more, the nails were bitten almost to the quick. But it wasn't the man's hands, socks or odd shoes that made her stare; it was the print on the top right hand corner of his newspaper. She leaned forward and squinted slightly to make sure of the date.

Again, Tatiana wasn't as flummoxed or scared as anyone else in her situation would have been. She was, after all, a time-travelling tourist, as Arty called them both, though she preferred time-travelling gypsy. Yet, she *was* surprised and confused that there had been no sign of glowing or sparks of any kind from the timer. Had the timer just decided to dress her for dinner, perhaps? Was the gentleman just reading a very old newspaper? Where on earth had Arty got to? She was reluctant to stand up in her tight-fitting skirt to look for him, so she decided to wait for his return. As she continued to stare at the back of the newspaper, a headline caught her attention.

EXCLUSIVE REPORT FROM LOCH NESS

FROM LOCH NESS IN SCOTLAND – WHERE THEY MAKE THE STRONGEST WHISKY ON EARTH – TOURISTS AND LOCALS ARE COMING FORWARD WITH AN INCREASE IN SIGHTINGS FOR THE LOCH NESS MONSTER. IT IS DESCRIBED AS A SEA SERPENT ESTIMATED AT FIFTY FEET LONG. THE SECRETARY OF STATE FOR SCOTLAND, SIR GODFREY COLLINS, HAS FORBIDDEN THE CAPTURE OR THE SHOOTING OF IT, HE …

As she leaned forward to try to see more of the report, the newspaper suddenly folded in half with a crisp snap, revealing the head and shoulders of a young, handsome man. His dark blonde hair, though cut short at the sides, was long and thick on top. It was parted smartly down the left side and then 'brylcreemed' to the side. His suddenly widening hazel eyes were bright and lively. His strong jaw jutted forward in interest as he keenly observed the lovely young woman seated on the sofa diagonally across from him. He lowered the newspaper further and then laid it flat on his knees. Caught a little off guard, and not wanting the young man to think she had been staring at him, Tatiana said:

"Excuse me, sir! Would you by any chance know what time dinner is served in the hotel?" She really couldn't think of anything else to say. He looked at her mischievously.

"That, my dear, is a rather roundabout way to ask me to dinner," he said, with an arrogant curl of his lip, "but dinner is at seven, and I accept!"

The sweet tones of Maurice Chevalier singing *All I Want Is Just One Girl* drifted across from a gramophone in the corner of the foyer. As she looked over in the direction of the reception area to see if she could spot Arty, she saw that the lighting had grown dimmer. The room away from the lamp-lit enclosure where she and the young man were sitting was quite dark and shadowy. Through one of the tall, arched windows dotted with rain drops, she could see that the afternoon had closed in to the early darkness of winter. The young man's voice had been soft with a cultured English accent, but there was also a trace of an accent that she couldn't place. In her immediate predicament, it took her a few moments to realise that he had, in fact, been quite rude.

"I beg your pardon," she answered curtly while gathering her wits, "I merely asked you a question!"

"Yes, I know and I accept," he said, quite unperturbed, "though I do think it would be good manners to introduce yourself *before* asking me to dinner!"

Tatiana stood up quickly, bewildered. She had never encountered such impertinence before, even from Arty, and she really was not in the right frame of mind to deal with it at that moment either. She looked towards the reception counter again, hoping to see Arty leaning back on it and laughing at her, but along with 2014, it seemed he had also disappeared. What was going on? What was the timer up to?

"Sir!" she cried in the best grand-duchess voice that she could muster at that moment, "there seems to be a misunderstanding. My uncle is over there organising things and I was merely wondering what time dinner is served, as we've had a very long journey." She sat down on the sofa, then deciding to give the young upstart some of his own medicine, she continued: "We travel through time, you see, and it makes one awfully hungry."

The young man leaned forward and grabbed one of her hands; before she could stop him, he had pulled it to his lips and kissed the back of it. "I know, my love! You have been looking for me forever through the mists of time! And here I was waiting for you in Harrogate in 1934. Personally, I would have preferred you to have found me somewhere else. Paris, maybe. Just think of it! You, me, Hemmingway and Scott-Fitzgerald in the '20s. I'll spot *you* for dinner if you can organise that!" He looked over at the reception counter to see two Mink-fur-coated ladies signing the guest book. "I see," he said knowingly, "which one is your uncle? And can he by any chance box?"

Louis Armstrong began to sing *I confess that I love you*; the stranger grinned broadly and continued to stare at her. Tatiana was at a loss for words. Though she was feeling very much intimidated by this babbling, arrogant, all be it handsome idiot, she was afraid to leave as Arty might suddenly turn up and then wouldn't be able to find her.

"I'm an actor, you know!" he blurted, obviously intending to try to impress her.

"I can see that," she answered coldly, turning away from him to look at the tulips on the table in front of her.

He laughed. "No really," he cried, thinking that she didn't believe him, "though I'm not contracted to a studio yet. I have been working in the theatre for the last few months."

"What? As a clown?" Tatiana couldn't resist the comment, and though she said it in a frosty tone, he couldn't help but chuckle a little as she regained her confidence.

"I got fired, you see. I gave the silly tart a little nudge down the stairwell. Trouble was, she broke her arm. Old Burt saw the little scene and reported me to the boss. There I was, sacked! Just like that, after seven months, and I'd just got my first lead part. But I'm ready now, so who cares."

"Ready?" asked Tatiana. "Ready for what?" She really had no idea what this rumbustious, audacious character was talking about. Pretending to be distracted, she tapped her foot nervously to the music as she looked again for any sign of Arty.

"The studio, of course!" he exclaimed. "Which one do you belong to? Are you one of Alexander Korda's girls?"

Tatiana looked at him. How dare he! A gypsy, yes; Arty's partner in time, yes; but she was certainly not one of Alexander's girls, whoever he was. The empress inside of her decided to reveal herself in quite a frightening manner. She stood up suddenly in anger; conscious of her tight skirt she just as quickly sat down again. But her anger flared afresh, and she rose once more but again, blushing, she seated herself hastily. The wandering and very appreciative eyes of the stranger watched her like she was a jack in a box.

"Listen to me, impudent fool!" she turned, glaring, finally remaining seated. "You are a rude and preposterous person, and if you don't leave me alone immediately I will have you sent to the front. In fact I've a good mind to ..." She ran out of words in exasperation.

The young man was thoroughly taken by surprise by this quite vicious and certainly high and mighty onslaught. Who the hell was this girl? His tried and tested wooing had never been repulsed before! Perhaps she'd escaped from the loony bin?

"Sorry, sorry!" he cried, seemingly apologetic. "I have obviously mistaken you for somebody else!" He raised both his hands defensively. He then glanced at her again briefly. For a moment, she thought she saw a wounded look in his eyes. Then he raised his newspaper and proceeded to read it again, hidden from her view.

Tatiana was getting very worried. There was absolutely no sign of Arty anywhere. Where on earth could he be? For some reason and without any warning whatsoever, the timer had transported them to 1934. Why? As usual, she didn't know. Sometimes she never really could figure out why the timer sent them to the places it did; she just had to trust it. Then, in a flash, a thought came to her. Were *they* in 1934 or just *her*? Did Arty even come with her, or was he still in the foyer of this same hotel, eighty years in the past? But was that possible? How could she travel without the timer? She really didn't know what to do. If she went to look for him they might miss each other and anyway, where was she to look? He was clearly not at the reception desk. She decided to stay where she was a little longer. Then if he still did not turn up, she herself would go to the reception desk to see if there were any messages. After all, that was the start of all this mess! She leaned forward and took the Vogue magazine from the table in front of her. She felt the eyes of the man in the chair watching her again, but ignored him and studied the magazine cover. It was a drawing of a young woman. She wore a long sleeved, ankle length charcoal-coloured dress. Around her tiny waist was a thin scarlet belt; around her neck, a thick woollen scarf was draped, and upon her head was a strawberry-coloured beret, very much like the one Tatiana had been wearing when she and Arty had first entered the hotel. The young woman in the drawing also held aloft a brown unfolded umbrella. Her cheeks were rosy; her eyes and mouth were smiling, and she was on tip toes. Tatiana liked the drawing. She felt she was the girl in the picture, about to be caught by a gust of wind and blown to who knows where. She tapped her foot to the music and began to feel a little better again

"I say," she heard the young man say, "I really am sorry I was rude. I forget myself sometimes."

Tatiana glanced coolly at him. He actually looked quite nice now that the arrogant curl of his lip had disappeared. His eyes even seemed more sincere.

"That's alright," she said softly. "I am sorry too, though you can be quite a pig, you know!" She rubbed the back of her hand as if trying to clean the memory of him kissing it.

"I'm in a pickle, you see," he continued, ignoring the 'pig' comment. "I need to make friends. I've been so dreadfully alone since I left home."

She studied him briefly again. He had a strong rather kind face, without the lip. He was clean shaven. He wore a dark green, woollen sports jacket, an open-necked white shirt and a multi-coloured cravat loosely around his throat. To match his socks no doubt, thought Tatiana with amusement. She couldn't help but stare at his caramel-coloured Oxford bags with the incredibly wide turn ups. She had never seen trousers like that before. She still couldn't place his accent. Feeling a little sorry for him, she asked:

"And where would you call home, sir?"

He leaned forward, folded his newspaper and placed it on the table in front of him.

"Well," he answered, looking at her thoughtfully, "are you familiar with the movies?" he asked, avoiding her question.

"I love them," she answered. "I loved 'Titanic'. The detail of the movie is so close to the real thing."

"Titanic?" he asked, a rather puzzled look on his face. "No, I mean modern talking ones, not that old silent one with Dorothy Gibson in it."

"Dorothy Gibson was in a movie about Titanic?" she cried in disbelief, "but wasn't she on the real ship, in real life?"

"Sure she was," he answered, warming to her apparent movie intellect. "I haven't seen that one myself, but I must admit making that with one of the actual survivors must have been as close to actually being there as you can get."

"Mmmm," agreed Tatiana thoughtfully, not quite grasping the fact that the movie star Dorothy Gibson whom she had met on the ship had actually starred in a silent film of the tragedy that was made shortly after the event. She even wore the same dress for the filming that she had worn on that fateful evening. Tatiana's mind was suddenly filled with a vision of all those people that she and Arty had met on the last night of the actual Titanic's voyage. She swallowed hard, as she tried rather to think of a movie that she had seen with Arty; one he had said was an 'old' one. Obviously it would be a movie made in black and white. She had watched so many of those with him!

"I really enjoyed Casablanca!" she exclaimed hopefully. "Rick is such a sweetie, and Ilsa is very beautiful and a wonderful actress!"

"Rick? Ilsa? Gosh!" he cried, "I don't think I've seen that one either. Have you seen the Wake of the Bounty? Now that's a good movie! Apart from the wig." He continued trying to catch her out as he now thought that she was some sort of movie buff or critic.

Coincidentally, Arty had just shown her a movie that sounded like this one pretty recently.

"Oh yes, I really enjoyed that one. Old Captain Bligh was a bit of a scoundrel, don't you think? I don't remember a wig, though," she said with a light laugh.

"So the fact that you don't recognise me must be that damn wig's fault," he said, quite seriously. "I told Charles that I hated that bloody thing, but it was the only one in Australia so I had to wear it."

"I don't remember seeing you in it," Tatiana replied with honesty, "which part did you play?"

"You saw the movie and you don't remember me in it!" cried the young actor in disbelief.

"Wait a minute," said Tatiana trying to think. "I remember the actors' names. Arty ... I mean my uncle takes great pleasure in telling me their names. Which part did you play?"

The young man stood up. He spread both his arms out theatrically.

"Fletcher Christian, of course!" he declared.

"So you must be Clarke Gable," she said looking up at him, "but you certainly don't look like him."

The young man was just about to protest when he seemed to change his mind.

"Clark Gable at your service, madam," he said and bowed lowly before her, trying to grab hold of her hand. She quickly put her hands by her sides and then promptly sat on them.

"But I thought you said you were on the stage!" Tatiana said, wondering if the person before her really was the actor she had seen in the movie. If so, the wig he had worn had changed his appearance completely.

"I made that movie as a one off just before I left Australia … Errr .. I mean America. I wanted to refine my craft you see, by getting some theatre training. So I decided to leave the movies for a while and sail to England, learn a bit of stage acting and then go back to the movies."

"You sailed to England?" asked Tatiana, now really becoming interested. She loved anything to do with boats and sailing.

"Practically around the world," he informed her proudly.

She looked at him in wonder. He was so young yet he seemed to have done so much.

"You must have been to some interesting places on your travels," she said a little enviously.

His eyes flashed at her as he recollected the memories.

"I've been to the Orient; crossed the Andaman Sea and the Bay of Bengal in a French boat called the D'Artagnan. I had tea in Ceylon and then the hottest curry you can imagine in Madras where I disembarked. After a week of a wandering through the city and the mind – bending images of magnificent temples and the poverty and dung heaps in the street, I caught a train for Calcutta. It was jam-packed full of men, women and at least thirty children. I had to contend with that for five days. Imagine – the train couldn't seem to move any faster than a man leisurely running. Intolerable heat, little water and only rice for food; though the stench of sweat and urine didn't make me feel very hungry, anyway."

Tatiana crinkled her nose and shuddered at the thought. She looked swiftly around, hoping to see Arty.

"I then hopped on another French boat – La Stella – and headed down the Indian coast, through the Gulf of Mannar and then west for Africa.

"You must have met many people on your adventures." Tatiana thought he was exaggerating most of what he was telling her, and she was beginning to lose interest again. She tapped her foot to the music of Cab Calloway and his Cotton Club Orchestra.

"On that particular voyage," he continued, "I slept in steerage and met an exceedingly annoying character that would insist on drooling on me from the bunk above. His saliva would dribble through the wooden slats of the frame and land on my forehead, waking me up in the middle of the night."

Tatiana gasped with horror at the thought. She was beginning to think that travelling was perhaps not so appealing after all. "Agh … ! What did you do? Did you move to better sleeping arrangements?" she asked.

"I told him to spit somewhere else, to which he replied he would spit wherever he wanted. So I threw myself out of bed in a rage and grabbed hold of him. I dragged him out of his cot and onto the floor. But when he stood up I realised what a mistake I had made. He must have been a least seven feet tall and almost as wide."

"Really," said Tatiana, her interest waning again.

"He hit me with one blow which knocked me out for two days. When I finally came to, I told him I was happy for him to spit wherever he liked."

Tatiana was growing impatient. It felt like she had been listening to the constant drone of 'tall tales' from this 'adventurer' for hours; what on earth was she going to do if Arty did not turn up soon. Where would she go? She wouldn't be able to stay here much longer; she had no money with her! How could the timer do this?

"But the strangest couple of characters I met were in the Adriatic," she heard 'Clarke Gable' continue. "We had stopped off in Aquileia for a little something, and when my partner had gone into town for an appointment I was woken by an enormous bald fellow wanting to hire the boat that we had hired! Of course, never one to let an opportunity to make some doe slip, I bargained with him and we came to a suitable arrangement. Then to celebrate we got drunk together, but he got drunker than me and he told me the strangest things."

"Oh yes," said Tatiana, wondering if there was perhaps any money in her bag under the coat beside her. "What things?"

"It was halfway through his second bottle of cognac, very expensive merchandise may I add, that he started to tell me about himself and his boss. Funny enough, he also told me that they used to be time travellers. Maybe you know them?" He smiled sarcastically at her, pleased now that he seemed to have finally got her attention. "They had been able to do this by using an egg timer, would you believe it, that his boss had found in some safe in a house in Yorkshire."

In shock and surprise, Tatiana dropped the handbag onto the floor in front of her. Bending forward, the young man picked it up and laid it on her knees.

"Really strange, I would say. When you are drunk you normally tell the truth. Believe me, I am an expert on the matter. Its only when you're drunk that you decide to cry over that lost love …"

"Never mind about that," Tatiana interrupted sharply, "what else did he say?"

Pleased that he had got her full attention again, he continued:
"Apparently, they had got up to all sorts of mischief stealing

all sorts of priceless things for themselves and some organisation that they belong to; then all of a sudden, the timer (for that is what he called it) stopped working and they hadn't been able to use it for the last seventeen years or so. This bald-headed dope was really worried for his boss, because they had just been given the greatest assignment of their lives; they could not fail or it would be curtains for them." He stopped enjoying the keen, yet puzzled look on her face. "If I ever get time I could write a book about the things he told me. He was so convincing, I am sure he almost believed what he was telling me was true!"

"What had they been assigned to do?" she asked breathlessly.

The young man now leaned forward, feigning that he was sharing a great secret.

"Well, he told me there were two things that worried him and that he was afraid it would kill his boss if they failed. The first, he said, was a crazy obsession for some ornamental eggs and especially for a little crown and necklace that was missing from the centre of one of them."

Tatiana nervously caressed the strap of the leather bag that lay beside her with her thumb and index finger.

"He was afraid this crazy obsession would one day get them both killed," continued the young man, "and when he told me there was a woman involved, I heartily agreed with him. Up until the timer had stopped working, they had been trying to alter events in history so as to be able to locate those eggs, but apparently so far nothing had worked. You really hear some tall tales on your travels, my dear! I actually asked him which brand he was smoking!" The young man sat back in the leather chair and crossed his legs again. He searched through his pockets and then brought out a pipe. He lit the tobacco with a match and his face became engulfed in blue smoke for a few moments. This young man had been with Peabody and Smith and not too long ago by the sound of things, she thought. It made her shiver slightly.

"What was the other assignment?" she asked tentatively, fearing that it could have something to do with her family.

"Well this part, even for one with such an obvious wild imagination, I thought was just a load of old rubbish. Then his boss turned up the next day with a very basic map showing its alleged location. They hired our hired boat to try to find some old parchment for the organisation that his boss belonged to."

Tatiana's mind was spinning. Parchment? What was this fellow talking about? Instantly, she remembered her and Arty's trip to Cyprus and what Arty had told her about Richard the Lionheart and the real reason for his crusade to regain Jerusalem. Surely it could not be the same one?

"But why would you think it more rubbish than the previous wild story?" asked Tatiana, trying to find out more about the parchment.

The young man smirked and the arrogant curl of his lip appeared again. "He told me a load of religious baloney about it having the words of the song that God sang when he created the earth etched on it! Now, stuff like that really makes me scoff."

He covered his mouth with his palm with a mock show of stifling uncontrollable laughter. But Tatiana did not even notice. Peabody was still hot on their trail it seemed, but had been hampered by his timer not working. Yet, somehow he and Smith had heard about the parchment and were desperately trying to locate it. It could only be the parchment that Richard the Lionheart had told Arty about.

"Where were you when you met these two unlikely characters?" she asked, trying to sound like she wasn't too convinced by his story.

"Aquileia!" he repeated. "I know it sounds far-fetched, but I swear this guy told me these things!" he declared.

"So what happened?" she asked, forcing a little chuckle trying to make out as if the whole thing was a joke.

The young man suddenly looked uncomfortable. He

uncrossed his legs, and took the pipe out of his mouth. Obviously hiding something, he said:

"They decided to hire another boat; one a bit larger than ours."

She would have been more relieved if she had known the truth.

The other tales he had told her seemed much more unbelievable to Tatiana. Now that she was pretty sure of the reason for this trip, she tried to relax a little in the knowledge that Arty would be sure to turn up soon and 'collect' her. She acted as if what he had told her about the eggs and the parchment was as unbelievable to her as it was to him. But now she began to notice a change in him. His eyes had become softer; less of a mirror to some far away and most probably mythical event. He seemed to become a little nervous, constantly nibbling at his finger nails. He told her that he had left home, or rather, was thrown out of it by his mother. Tatiana struggled to imagine that. He had always been lured by the sea, so he caught a ship to Papua New Guinea where he intended to make his fortune as a tobacco farmer but ended up as a mining magnate. She noticed a change in his eyes again as he said this. He boasted of the size and quality of the diamonds that he had found. Pointing to the headline in the newspaper about the Loch Ness monster that Tatiana had been reading, he gleefully declared that due to the local 'coconut' juice, most of the islanders had also seen a Loch Ness monster! Being of English, Irish and Scottish descent, the sea was in his blood, he said. He was too young to be tied down so he gave up the fine living of a diamond mining magnate and settled for a new, dubious occupation: gun running. He told her how he spent five years roaming the high seas between New Guinea and Sydney, taking part in many skirmishes with pirates while transporting other forbidden merchandise between the two countries. Whether the truth or not, she had to admit he was a marvellous story teller.

"The weed was so good in New Guinea, that on the journeys back to Oz I almost became a chain smoker," he declared proudly. "Just wait 'till I introduce some of that stuff to Hollywood – they'll make the greatest movies ever! It'll be the golden age of the cinema!" he informed her prophetically. "They won't know what's hit them." It was while lying low in Sydney and due to his claim of being a descendent of the real Fletcher Christian that he was offered the part in the 'Wake of the Bounty.' His eyes now softened again.

"I am not sure which was worse," he said, "my acting or the script! And then of course there was that confounded wig."

Tatiana laughed. He really was rather endearing, though she was still not sure which parts of his tales were true or not. They were quiet now. Tatiana sighed and looked at her shoes, wishing they would turn back to the 'modern' ones she had first arrived in. The man chewed his nails. Then he leaned forward suddenly.

"Would you have dinner with me?" he asked, now rather humbly. The music had changed again. This one she knew, as Arty had played it for her from his vast collection: Ethel Merman and Bing Crosby singing *You're the Top*. She bent her head and continued to look at her shoes, praying silently for a miracle. She avoided his question and invitation.

"I personally met Dorothy Gibson once!" She felt more secure again now that a song that both she and Arty knew was playing. "On the Titanic."

The young man held his pipe halfway to his mouth, then he leaned forward again and placed it carefully on the table in front of them.

"You don't believe a word I have told you, do you?" He sat back chewing his nails again.

Tatiana now realised that he did not believe her. Then again, it would be unlikely that he would. She peered again at the reception for Arty.

"You must write them down one day!" she declared. "Truth or not."

He grinned mischievously at her again, that same faraway look in his eyes.

"I think it is time I finally introduce myself," he said. Standing up and then bowing theatrically, he said: "Lord Byron, my lady, and as you can see my club foot has been miraculously healed by the waters of Harrogate."

"Lord Byron! my foot!" said a familiar voice from behind her. She turned quickly to see Arty standing resplendent in a tweed trilby hat and dark grey Mackintosh. He strode around the side of the sofa and then seated himself on the left side of Tatiana between her and the handsome young man.

"Arty ... Uncle!" she cried with relief, and then turning to the young man, "Uncle dear, this is Clarke Gable or Lord Byron, I am not sure which!" She then whispered furiously in Arty's ear. "Where have you been? Why did you leave me alone so long?"

"This is not Clarke Gable!" declared Arty loudly and ignoring her quiet rebuke. "This is Errol Flynn!"

Errol Flynn stood up immediately, the newspaper falling onto the floor in front of them. He stretched out his hand to Arty. "Hello uncle Arty! Are you a studio scout? If not, can you box sport?"

Arty stared at the soon-to-be worldwide sensation in front of him. He looked more handsome than most of his movies portrayed him. He noticed Tatiana was smiling at him. Hot waves of jealously rushed up the back of his neck, the back of his head and then down his face in a gush of scarlet.

"I'm not her uncle," he answered indignantly, "I am her dearest friend and travelling companion."

Tatiana sensed the tension and impishly grinned at her shoes.

"Yes, sport! I'm sure you are, but can you box?" insisted Flynn.

Arty disliked the actor in everything he did except for three movies: 'Captain Blood', 'The Sea Hawk' and of course, his most famous role as 'Robin Hood.' He was angry; the brute clearly had designs for Tatiana, but boxing certainly wasn't one of his recent hobbies.

"Box? No, I don't box! Can you sword fence?"

Arty was now incredibly protective over his 'very dear travelling companion' and the memory of his expert display of fencing against Sir Guy only a few days previously was still very clear in his mind. He was certainly prepared to repeat the feat if he needed. Then he suddenly remembered who he had just challenged; Errol Flynn was to become perhaps one of the greatest swash-buckling actors ever to grace the silver screen! Indeed, Flynn was to become an accomplished fencer outside of movies as well. But at that moment, Flynn was a little taken aback by Arty's challenge. He cast his mind to a near-death experience he'd had a few months previously with a fencing expert just off the coast of Trieste. He studied Arty, wondering if he could move his feet like that guy. Yet Flynn was never one to shy away from a challenge. He pointed to two pokers in the fire place just behind the sofa. "Ok you're on, sport," he said. "Let's grab those two pokers. At least we'll have similar weapons!"

Arty looked at Tatiana and grit his teeth. He felt the little timer in his pocket. Another nice situation you've got me into, he thought. He closed his hand around the cold metal. As he did so, he felt a slight vibration shoot into his fingers. It travelled quickly up his arm along his shoulder and then ended with a sharp little tap on the side of his temple, making him raise his hand to his head in protest.

"Steady on, steady on, old sport!" he found himself saying quite calmly. "Before we go poker fencing, don't you think you need to answer a few questions first?"

Flynn's brow furrowed heavily. Tatiana picked up her Vogue magazine and began to hum again softly with the music. She stretched out her foot so that the toe of her shoe touched Arty's where he stood, lightly.

"Questions?" answered Flynn, feeling slightly uncomfortable. "About what?"

Arty pressed lightly onto Tatiana's toe and continued.

"Well, should we start with Montague Jeffrey's of Northampton?" Arty clicked his tongue and furrowed his brow in wonder. What was he saying? Where was he getting this information from? "And a certain wool sports jacket, colour green," he continued looking suspiciously at the jacket that Flynn was wearing. "It disappeared from the fitting room, I believe. Very impressive but alas, expensive taste you have, Mr Flynn!"

Flynn grinned sheepishly and then folded his arms defensively. "I was only borrowing the stuff, sport," he admitted. "I was going to return it."

"One black and one brown brogue kept in the same box to discourage theft, but it didn't discourage you, did it?" Arty was beginning to enjoy himself. He looked at the other man's shoes and then comically down at his own. "And then there is the sad case of the female stage manager that mysteriously lost her footing and fell down the stairwell, breaking her arm. That same female stage manager has laid charges against you for assault and battery from her hospital bed in Northampton General Hospital.

"A little tiff sport, that's all," answered Flynn apologetically. "She was sore at me because I wouldn't return her advances."

"You said the same thing about Betty Davis, old man!" cried Arty. "But you didn't throw *her* down the stairwell."

Flynn was beginning to look and feel very uncomfortable. "Betty Davis," he said quietly. "She's way above my league. I've never even met her!"

"You will, sport," cried Arty, "and I'd watch out for her left hook if I were you!" he continued triumphantly.

Flynn was confused and more than a little scared. Who was this guy? FBI? MI1? A private detective? Obviously, that damn shopkeeper had chummed up with the Northampton Theatre Company and had him tailed. Arty then said something that confused himself more than it confused Flynn.

"Then of course, there is the matter of that little thing in your pocket. Something that certainly does not belong to you." Arty strode forward in confrontation. Tatiana now also stood up.

"Look, I don't know who you are," Flynn cried defensively, "but it really wasn't my fault that I ended up with the thing. Its previous owner left rather suddenly, so what was I to do?"

Flynn was beginning to think that that little squirt Peabody had somehow managed to get ashore and had also hired this guy to nail him, obviously thinking that he had gone after that parchment thing as well. Surely he wouldn't have gone to all this trouble for a worthless piece of pretty glass! He pulled Tatiana's name-day diamond out of his trouser pocket. Even though he knew it was fake and had had some fun times impressing the ladies with it, he would be sorry to lose it. Tatiana gasped with surprise. "Yes, my dear," he said looking at Tatiana. "Beautiful, isn't it! Of all the monsters I found as an expert diamond miner in New Guinea, this beats them all." Then, turning to Arty: "Look sport," he said, "this is worth an absolute fortune, but money means nothing to me. I will trade you this for my freedom. You take it in exchange for never having seen me. You can say you found it in a safety deposit box or something."

Arty stared at Tatiana's beautiful name-day diamond. This really was an unexpected turn of events. "It looks fake to me," he said.

Flynn now looked really worried. "No, sport! I tell you I am an expert. This is as genuine as the crown jewels!"

Arty discreetly nudged Tatiana, and then looking down at Flynn's feet, he said: "Tell you what, sport. You give me that fake diamond and that black shoe and you've got a deal."

Looking mightily relieved, Flynn dropped down onto one knee and untied the shoelace of his black brogue. He handed over the diamond and swapped his one black shoe for Arty's brown one. "I consider that a good deal done!" he declared. He took hold of his newspaper from the table, nodded a little tersely to Tatiana and started to make his way towards the reception desk. They watched him as he turned and faced them again. "I never did catch the name of my beautiful young, half-hour host," he said.

Tatiana was about to answer him when Arty interrupted her. "Anne," he said

"*Anne?*" cried Tatiana, looking at Arty questioningly.

"Anne?" cried Flynn as if she certainly didn't look like an 'Anne.'

"Yes," cried Arty again. "This is my very dear friend, Anne Teak!"

As they watched Flynn walk away shaking his head, the dimmed lights became brighter and Al Jolson suddenly turned into Harry Styles.

"Will you please take that hat off, Arty!" Tatiana remarked, looking at the dark woollen Bob Hat that now covered most of Arty's head.

"Perfect," exclaimed Arty ignoring her and looking down at his perfectly matching shoes. Bowing lowly, he handed her the priceless diamond. "Any idea what time dinner is served?" he said. "I think we should stay!"

*

The sea mist rolled in. Arty's cottage was immersed in what Tatiana referred to as 'God's blanket.'

"November can be a little wet and miserable!" exclaimed Arty, pulling on a sweatshirt, "but not usually as cold as this."

For the first time since she had 'arrived' at the cottage

Tatiana, was also a little chilly. Arty lent her his only pair of sports socks. She wiggled her big toes through the holes in the front. It was early afternoon. They had both slept very late through the morning after their trip to Harrogate, but were now seated in the small lounge discussing what they were to do next.

"Did he mention what had happened to Peabody and Smith?" asked Arty. Tatiana had told him what Flynn had said about his drunken conversation with Smith and what had been said about the parchment.

"I was so used to him telling tall tales that I was completely taken by surprise when he started telling what could only be the truth," she answered.

Arty took a gulp from his coffee mug. "I am just wondering, my dear, what you are going to put in the book of truth about our friend Flynn?"

She smiled to herself. He really had been quite charming, though an utter scoundrel.

"I will write that he was somebody who hid behind tall tales and adventures to escape from the hard reality of life," she answered.

"I like the sound of that fine mental analysis, doctor Dodger!" he said grinning broadly.

"He actually was also a very hurt and insecure person, probably caused by the poor relationship he had with his mother," she continued, taking his encouragement seriously. "Did you see how he chewed his nails?"

Arty looked at his own slightly gnawed fingers. He then picked up the beautiful cut diamond from where it stood on the table in front of them. "Well, all I can say is anyone who cannot see that this is a genuine diamond must be a complete idiot," he said, handing it to her.

"Or somebody who is so used to living in his own world of adventure, and constantly searching for another one," answered

Tatiana, "so that when he comes across the *real* adventure, he does not recognise it. He is so blinded by the false adventures that he can't even begin to experience the greatest adventure of all – life as we were intended to live it."

The room was quiet. Sometimes Arty was astounded by some of the things this young girl said to him.

"But anyway, listen Arty," she continued, not wishing to talk about Flynn any longer. "There is something we need to do. I was obviously meant to learn that Peabody and Smith are after the parchment. The eggs we know about. But how do you suppose they have learned of the parchment's existence? I mean, neither you nor I had ever heard of such a thing until King Richard told you about it. Is there anything about it in the history books of today?"

"No," said Arty, "I even checked on the net; there is no mention of a Parchment of Life. But Richard was surely convinced that one existed; it was his main reason for the crusade, remember!"

"Then we must warn him," she said solemnly. "If such a parchment does exist, we must help Richard find it or at least make sure that it is safe in the future from the likes of Peabody and his associates."

"Then our next trip is to 1192 and Jerusalem," confirmed Arty, but he had a sinking feeling in his stomach. Even though he had thoroughly out-fenced Sir Guy, he had after all been using Richard's magical sword at the time and he really would not relish another confrontation with that 'peacock.'

"We have some time for once," she said, taking a sip of coffee from her new porcelain tea cup that Arty had especially bought her. She placed it delicately back onto its saucer. "Flynn told me that Peabody's timer had stopped working."

"Well," said Arty, "I hope that was one of the truthful things he told you. But we must also hope that it never works again for him, or it won't make any difference. Complicated, isn't it?"

They were silent again for a moment. Tatiana had now got

so used to the soft sighing of the waves upon the shore that she almost didn't notice it.

"Where did you get to, anyway?" Tatiana asked. "Are you aware I could have been devoured by that lone wolf you left me with for over an hour?"

Arty stared at her, confused. "What do you mean, an hour or so? It was hardly a minute or two! In fact, I was just about to ask you how you learned so much from him in such short a time."

"Arty!" Tatiana returned his stare. "You were gone for at least an hour."

Arty thought for a moment. "I was on my way to the reception desk to ask for messages when all of a sudden the lights dimmed. Beyoncé metamorphosed into Bing Crosby, and I realised that I'm a Humphrey Bogart look alike. I had a weird feeling that I had lost the timer so I checked that it was still in my pocket; there it was, though it felt unusually light. Obviously worried about you, I immediately made my way back to find you sitting there with Don Juan. It couldn't have been more than two or three minutes from me leaving you to coming back."

*

Later that evening as Tatiana recorded the events of the trip in the Book of Truth, she gazed at what she had written. Who would be the next person after her to write in it? She was a little sad at the thought that her words that recorded her adventures with Arty – *real* adventures – would also simply disappear from the page as leaves in an autumn breeze, just as Harry's had done when she tried to read them. She looked for a moment at the next blank page. What would she write there? One day she hoped to write the words describing that her remaining family were all safe, well and happy. As she gazed at the blank page, a faint image of a face slowly appeared, like a grainy sketch made with a thick soft pencil, very faint at first and then growing clearer. It then grew faint again. She looked closer. As she did so, the image grew clearer again till it was as clear as an old black and white photograph. It was the face of a very young boy. His lips were moving, but she could hear no sound. There was something vaguely familiar about the boy; then she remembered – it was her friend from long ago: Vassili!

CHAPTER 4
JANUS HONS PRIS

Smith heaved the dead weight of his boss up on to the slippery, treacherously smooth, rounded rocks. Against all the odds, he had managed to finally reach them. He had tried to aim for the little sandy cove that he could just make out above the swell of the water in the distance, but no matter how hard he swam, the current pushed him to the left until all that faced him was the immense cliff face. Of course, Peabody had never learned to swim. Why should he? He was a 'cat burglar', and cats hate water! Smith laid him as flat as he could on the rocks. The sea was rapidly rising and caressed the jagged expanse of rock with antagonistic mirth. Smith kneeled and bent over him. He was worried. Peabody's face was pasty, almost colourless, except for his lips that were an unnatural shade of purple. He stood up quickly.

"Boss!" he shouted, trying to make himself heard above the wind that had suddenly begun to howl in his ears. "Wake up!" At that moment, a large wave leapt onto the rocks, drenching him and forcing him to lose his balance. He toppled forward and landed unceremoniously on top of Peabody. The sudden weight of Smith landing on Peabody's chest forced sea water to gush out of his mouth like water from a burst pipe. He coughed, spluttered and opened his eyes, blinking erratically as Smith helped him to his knees. Peabody retched and was promptly sick. Then he lay on his back squinting up at the dark clouds racing to do battle above them. Smith looked down at his boss incredulously. Peabody's dark suit, wet and clinging to his wiry frame, made him look remarkably like a half-drowned cat. Another wave crashed over the rocks, drenching them both and this time almost dislodged Smith from his perch completely.

"Boss!" he screeched, trying to make himself heard over the dreadful din of the wind and sea. "What are we going to do?"

Finally realising the menacing situation they were in, Peabody sat up slowly and leaned on his elbows. This time a mixture of vomit and sea water spewed out of his mouth and onto the sodden, shoeless feet of Smith. Cursing loudly and spitting constantly, Peabody finally came to his senses and scrambled to his feet, swaying from side to side staring at the great jagged cliff wall that towered above them

"Where's that nice sandy beach?" he shouted, glaring at the soaked and bedraggled Smith.

"As much as I tried, boss, I just couldn't seem to get there. The current kept pushing us to the side. It must be around that corner!" Smith shouted in between great gasps of breath, pointing to their right. He was not looking forward to another swim.

Peabody could see well enough the angry surf storming upon them and that the lonely expanse of rock on which they stood was rapidly getting smaller. The sky had become quite dark now and the wind seemed to have lulled momentarily. The ocean had become the colour of slate and swelled menacingly. Both men could smell their own fear.

"We have to get off these rocks, Charles!" cried Peabody, cupping his mouth between his hands. His voice sounded eerie and hollow in the prelude to the dreadful din that was soon sure to begin again. "Follow me!"

Smith watched as Peabody with his usual cat-like agility began to tiptoe across the rocks towards the cliff.

"We will have to go back into the water, boss, to get around to the cove!" Smith shouted, his voice full of melancholy. He would rather die where he was.

Peabody turned sharply. "Follow me, you oaf, and quickly! If we go back in the sea we will be smashed to smithereens, and I don't have a key for old Davy's Locker, so pull yourself together, my man!"

Reluctantly and with no idea what Peabody had in mind, Smith clumsily made his way over the rock as the sea danced madly, ready to grasp them with wet salty claws to drag them down into its belly. The stillness of the air was more menacing than when the wind was howling. For once, Peabody also had no idea where he was going or what he was doing. As the wind paused, he had a strange feeling that if he could just make it to the cliff face everything would be alright. He had become aware of a weight in his jacket pocket. The thought of going back into the water was never contemplated. He picked his moment expertly to dart forward in between the hungry lashes of water; Smith behind him likewise was hit with the waves, yet his bulk kept him upright and on his feet. Both men hoped against hope that as they reached the foot of the cliff they would find some hidden pathway that would lead them to the right and around to the safety of the sandy cove. But now, as they stood at the very foot of the cliff, there was no sign of any miraculously appearing pathway. Peabody felt the cold shadow of the cliff upon him. They had made their way as far as they could to the right. Now, the platform of rock disappeared into the sea. The tide had caught them up and the pounding foaming waters crashed on the rocks to their right and behind them. As the wind drew breath and then expelled with a shriek of furious rage, Peabody knew that it was hopeless. The tide would not turn before the waves smashed them like stringless puppets against the unforgiving rocks. They sat down side by side, staring at the onslaught.

"I could do with one of my ma's pies now!" shouted Smith.

"We are just about to be smashed to bits and drowned!" screamed Peabody, "and all you can think about is food!" He brought his knees up under his chin and shivered. "I could do with a brandy!"

"Well, I was thinkin' of my old ma!" shrieked Smith, "it would have been nice after all to have seen her one last time."

The water roared and crashed all around them; the high-pitched howl of the wind made it impossible to converse with each other as they both hung on, waiting for the end.

"Get off me, Smith!"

Peabody's words were lost to the wind; Smith had grabbed hold of his arm and was tugging it frantically. Peabody could see Smith's purple, snake-like lips moving, but he couldn't hear a word. Smith was frantically pointing like a lunatic at Peabody's jacket pocket. Peabody looked down; to his amazement, the familiar glow of red, silver and gold was seeping through the material of his jacket. He thrust his hand into his pocket. He hadn't even been too conscious of the fact that he had brought the egg timer with him on their journey, but here it was and now, unbelievably, working. He held it up and laughed crazily, dancing like a manic puppet. Smith also started to perform a little jig upon the rock but was rudely interrupted by the most monstrous and vicious wave yet. It flung them both backwards, jarring then both against the foot of the cliff face. Peabody held on to his glowing saviour.

"Take us away from here, you beautiful thing!" he cried. "I swear if you save me I will be good in future; I pledge this oath to you!" But nothing seemed to be happening. Smith tapped on his own ear and then pointed at the timer as if to say, "Perhaps it can't hear you!" Another wave struck them again, jarring them against the cliff wall. Peabody grabbed hold of Smith to steady himself. "Perhaps that wasn't enough!" he screamed. "Okay!" he shrieked as loud as he could, "I am sorry. I am sorry I have misused you; I will do so no more."

In the throes of his very likely savage and watery death, Smith's eyes grew wide with surprise and confusion as he could just make out his boss's admission over the roar of the wind and the crashing of the sea. But still nothing apart from a colourful display of red, silver and golden lights appeared to be happening. In complete desperation, Peabody turned and leaned forward against the cliff face. "Help me!" he screamed as if to the rock of the cliff face. "I am not ready!"

Even above the tremendous din of the sea and the wind, they heard it: the sound of a mountain being split apart from within. As he leaned forward onto the cliff face, Peabody's arms and body began to shake; the shocking vibration made him cling to the rock like a spider paralyzed with fear. Unbelievably, the smooth cliff face was being torn open from within. Peabody closed his eyes and screamed though he could not hear his own wails above the ear-splitting pandemonium. Then, when his long arms could no longer feel the ever widening gap, he fell forward into the sinister black space and onto what felt like a cold, damp sandy floor. He opened his eyes, and then closed them again in exasperation and pain as Smith fell on top of him once again.

They were inside a cave. The only light emanated from the little egg timer that Peabody had placed in front of them on the smooth sandy floor. It was almost quiet here; the din of the raging sea was quite dim in their ears. They both felt a sudden and strange sense of calm even though they could still see the furious, hungry sea clawing madly at the sky and rocks as they looked back through the jagged opening of the cave. With an exclamation, Peabody held the timer up in wonder from where he crouched; by its eerie glow, they could see that the cave was small, barely room enough to fit six persons. The far wall was smooth and as black as coal.

To their left the wall was jagged and uneven and formed shelf-like compartments. He stood up, rubbing the base of his spine painfully as he did so. Picking up the timer, he used its light to illuminate the smooth, dark wall. He felt Smith's breath on the back of his neck as he read the words that had been daubed in a rusty red colour, as if with a finger:

JA NUS HONS PRIS
1192

"No man who is in prison," Peabody translated the words quietly.

"What does it mean, boss?" asked Smith, peering at the strange lettering from behind him.

Peabody ignored the question and repeated the statement 'no man who is in prison' over and over, louder and louder. At last, he exclaimed ecstatically:

"I have a feeling, Mr Smith –a feeling that we may have found our cave after all!"

"But the map was wrong then, boss!" declared Smith.

"Perhaps," agreed Peabody, "or most likely one of those two buffoons on that yacht had dulled his sense of direction with cognac!"

"Then have we found the parchment, boss?" asked Smith hopefully. "Should I start digging?" He began to remove his jacket.

"Wait a minute, Charlie boy!" cried Peabody. He covered his brow with his hand as if deep in thought. "Where do I know those words from?" he said aloud. Then suddenly, " That's it Mr Smith," he continued with glee, "*Ja nus hons pris* is the title to a poem that Richard the Lionheart wrote while being held captive at Castle Dürnstein for his crimes by Leopold of Austria."

"But wasn't Richard the Lionheart a hero, boss?" asked Smith, screwing up his face in consternation.

"To some he was a hero, yes," answered Peabody, sounding like the dean of a very famous college in Lancashire, "but to his captors he was the disloyal prince who rebelled against his dying father. He was the arrogant king that insulted Duke Leopold of Austria at Acre by lowering the latter's standard from the castle walls and raising his own, therefore claiming the total victory himself. He was the aggressive warrior and 'opportunist' who wronged Leopold's kin, Isaac of Cyprus, by conquering the island and then using it as a supply base. Finally, his captors also suspected, and quite rightly in my opinion, that he had been behind the murder of Leopold's cousin, Conrad of Montferrat. Conrad was to be the next Christian king of Jerusalem, remember Smith, whereas Richard was in favour of reinstating Guy of Lusignan."

Smith put his fingers to his temples and then sighed heavily. "No, I don't remember that, boss, but what is the connection to the parchment?"

Again, Peabody ignored the question.

"Perhaps the likelihood of his capture prompted him to write this here in 1192," he said, almost to himself.

Smith, who had heard of Richard the Lionheart, had a vague admiration for the charismatic figure from history, but did not know too much about him.

"Why would anybody want to capture 'good king Richard', boss?" he asked.

"Because, old man, he tweaked a lot of noses on his little failed expedition to recapture Jerusalem back in 1191 and '92. For one, as I have already mentioned, imagine how old Leopold of Austria felt. He laid siege to Acre as part of the Christian crusade for almost a year, costing him men, money and supplies. Then, just as the city is about to fall through hunger anyway, mister high and mighty Lionheart turns up to beat the city into final submission in only a couple of days with his siege engines and fresh soldiers. To top it all, only the three-lion standard was raised on the city walls and the plunder of the city was only shared between himself and his boyfriend, Philip of France."

"Who would believe it, boss," said Smith, thinking of the magnificent stature of a resplendent Richard astride a splendid war horse outside the houses of parliament in London, "no wonder his sword doesn't seem to be very magical."

"Don't babble on so, Smith," said Peabody, turning to him with a sudden look of realisation on his face, "don't you see what this means? The timer itself brought us to this place; it showed us all this and now *there* I believe, you will find our parchment!"

Peabody swung around theatrically and pointed to a dark rectangular shape that was half hidden, lying on one of the irregularly shaped shelves upon the jagged wall. As he drew nearer, the light from the timer clearly lit up the shape of a small wooden, chest-like box.

Smith lifted it down as carefully as his ham-like hands would allow. Peabody himself lifted the lid.

"Those two imbeciles!" screeched Peabody at the top of his voice. He violently tugged the small wooden chest from Smith's grip and lifting it high above his head, flung it against the jagged rock wall. The wooden box disintegrated into small fragments of wood and dust. As Smith looked down in both shock and surprise at his boss's sudden outburst of anger, he could see quite clearly what looked to be a pair of outlandish, used, very pungent pair of size nine trainers.

"Wow, boss!" exclaimed Peabody, "somebody else must have got here before us!" He stared at Arty's black trainers that he had given to the king when he and Tatiana had used the timer to attend his wedding to Berengaria in Cyprus.

"None of this makes sense," cried Peabody in desperation. "You saw how we got into this cave. Nobody else could have got in here. We are meant to be here!"

He looked at the timer as it glowed softly, a brighter light now. He quickly examined the trainers. "The only way into this cave, Mr Smith, is with a timer, and we know who has the other one!" Peabody handed one of the training shoes back to Smith.

"They look a little large to be Fanny Romanov's, boss," said Smith, shaking his head slowly while peering at the large sports shoe in the dim light. He then looked up and smiled at his boss as a thought occurred to him. "But it does mean, boss, that she didn't get it after all in that house, and that she and 'Blew' Eyes are travelling around in time again."

"To their hearts' content, Mr Smith," agreed Peabody, "and it also means that they probably have the parchment, or at the very least know where it is!" He leaned against the jagged rock wall of the cave, deep in thought. The gap in the cliff had only appeared at the same time that the timer had started to glow. He knew now that without the help of the timer, even though they'd been given the coordinates to the cave by Clodius, they would certainly not have been able to find the cave.

"Richard was supposed to have left the golden box here after being shipwrecked on his way back to England," Peabody mused, "so where is it?"

"Do you think that those two have got the parchment as well as the eggs, boss?" cried Smith, truly horrified at the thought. After all, weren't *they* supposed to be the 'cat burglars?'

"I don't think I can take any more of this," said Peabody, collapsing abruptly onto the rock floor, his thin spidery legs spread out before him. Smith joined him. "Today," Peabody continued, "I have almost been beheaded, drowned, smashed to bits on the rocks and then drowned again. On top of that, I lost something very valuable and very dear to me: her diamond!"

Smith knew that one day Peabody had hoped to use the diamond to entice himself into Tatiana's affections, but that was the problem. When! Would they ever be able to use the timer again?

"Then, my little friend, the timer *finds* the cave for us, revealing that Richard the Lionheart and our two dear friends were here," Peabody continued despondently. "By using their timer, no doubt, Benjamin and Tatiana learned of its existence and got here before us. That coward is laughing at us, Mr Smith! That's why he left those smelly old sports shoes. How can I ever explain this to Clodius and the boys?" Peabody laughed again as he held aloft the tiny twinkling egg timer. It was glowing brighter, even brighter than before, but neither he nor Smith seemed to notice. "I retired from rescuing because this little swine stopped working for us," Peabody sighed deeply. "How could I keep up those assignments without its help? It would have been impossible, Mr Smith! Before it came to us we were given easy tasks, like the Ardagh Chalice, Elizabeth Tudor's ring, Sir Walter Raleigh's tobacco leaf, and Julius's crusty old sandal, but then we bewildered and amazed them with the Mona Lisa and I became the most important member of the club. Remember, Smith?" Peabody stared at his ally. His eyes reflected the light of the timer. Quite mesmerized, Smith nodded solemnly. "Don't forget Elizabeth Taylor's ring too, boss," he said, gallantly trying to cheer his boss up. The timer had made it so easy for them to steal anything, in any time, whenever they wanted. "When I have been sent on a mission, Smith, I have *never* failed; this will be the first time. I will be a dead, laughing stock."

Smith, determined to be of some value to his boss amidst this dire circumstance, studied the training shoes closely.

"Boss," he exclaimed excitedly, turning the shoe upside down, "I think you're wrong about Blew Eyes and Fanny Dodger. Look! These shoes belonged to somebody called Mike." He thrust the shoe forward directly under Peabody's nose, "but they spelt it incorrectly!"

Neither of them had noticed up to that point that the timer had been getting steadily brighter and brighter, but now it was unavoidable.

"Boss, what is it doing?" Smith looked wildly at the opening to the cave where the sea still raged outside, expecting it to snap shut at any moment and the timer to extinguish itself and leave them in pitch darkness to die of thirst, hunger and cold. But Peabody had other ideas. He had been the primary handler of the timer and he could see that though it didn't seem to be in the mood to transport them anywhere quite yet, it did at last seem to be doing *something*.

"Take us to the Parchment," he said out loud, staring at the timer, his large liquid brown eyes struggling to reflect any authority. He knew full well he had no control over the little device. "I will do all you command of me to keep it safe until it is *time!*"

"Boss!" cried Smith, "Don't make such a … "

But it was too late. All at once, the opening of the cave crashed shut; they could feel the walls and floor of the cave shudder with the force. Then in less than a blink of an eye the old familiar crashing of sea on rocks and roaring of a hurricane filled their ears. The blackness of the cave disappeared.

*

Peabody had found the seminar given by Magda Ginsburg exceptionally interesting. They had 'arrived' in the foyer of the Rosebank Hotel, and then been inexplicably ushered into the conference room by the doorman. Peabody looked at the timer as to any clue to the year they had been transported to. The numbers pulsed softly along its top rim: 1965.

"If you please, sir," the doorman had said, "there are two places left at the front on the left – hand side. The professor is due to start in a minute or two."

Peabody had never actually used the timer before for anything other than a mission of rescuing and so he was always perfectly aware of his destination and what he was going to do in it. He thrust his clammy hands into his pockets and followed the doorman.

"How do we know we are in the right place, boss?" whispered Smith as they took their seats.

"We don't," answered Peabody irritably, studying the program. "Just shut up and listen!"

As Smith listened to the questions and answers, his mind suddenly realised all the other possibilities that they could have used the timer for apart from just rescuing historical 'artefacts'. "Just think, boss," he whispered to Peabody, "We could have kidnapped Helen of Troy, brought her back and bought Longfell Hall for *her*." Smith chuckled to himself, trying to imagine Helen of Troy locked up in Peabody's vault under his office.

"That can still be arranged, you arse," Peabody whispered back unkindly.

When it came to the asking of more questions, Peabody winked at Smith. "Let's start with this one," he said, and stood up smartly.

"Would you by any chance know where the missing Faberge eggs are?"

All eyes in the room focussed on the wiry, slightly wizened form of Winston Peabody.

"Or the Parchment of Life?" He continued.

As soon as he said these words everybody in the room became overwhelmed with one sensation or another. Some literally felt a little nauseous, some suspicious and began to look around wildly for the unseen eyes watching them. Some on the other hand were almost overcome with a tremendous feeling of love, warmth and affection. All eyes returned to Magda.

"My apologies, I should have introduced myself," Peabody broke the silence again,

"Good evening, Professor Ginsburg. My name is Ambrosia; Professor Ambrosia."

"Good evening, Professor," acknowledged Magda.

"I have a question madam, to which I am sure a lot of people in this room would like to know the answer."

He paused in typical Peabody style. The room suddenly grew very still and tense with anticipation.

"There are eight missing Fabergé eggs. Madam, with all your seemingly un-exhaustible knowledge of seemingly unknown events in history, perhaps you would be able to shed some light on their whereabouts?"

He sat down smartly. "I think, Mr Smith, our ship has finally arrived. I know who she is!"

Magda was caught off guard for a moment; it was a question she least expected. She glanced briefly at Harry, who had the sudden urge to put his timer back in his pocket

"That is a strange question, sir," she answered, "though for obvious reasons I can understand why you asked it," she cleared her throat and steadied herself by holding onto the podium with two hands. "I am afraid, Professor, we are in the business of historical fact finding and not historical financial gain. It has never occurred to me to research their whereabouts." Her voice was quite stern and in order for her answer not to sound too much like an all-out rebuke, she added, "I knew that there would be at least one or two questions that I would not be able to answer, Professor, and I am afraid that is one of them." Her voice feigned the apology.

But Peabody was persistent. "Come now, madam!" he cried, "You have the knowledge of the gods, it seems! Surely you would know where the most famous 'Easter Eggs' are? Perhaps you are in possession of them yourself?"

Harry turned sharply. Who was this strange-looking upstart? The audience erupted in humour. All eyes peered at the wiry academic with the mad hairstyle.

Magda laughed. "I can assure you, sir, I would not be standing here today if they were in my possession. I do not know too much about them, though coincidently, I read the other day that their collective value is worth around one hundred and twenty five million United States Dollars. No, sir, my interest in history goes far beyond gold and treasure." She looked at Harry proudly.

Peabody suddenly wondered about the year they had come to. Of course, he thought; these two have not lost their timer nor have they met Arthur Benjamin or Tatiana Nicolaevna yet.

"Forgive me, Professor," he answered, enjoying the attention. "I did not mean to insult you. Indeed, quite the opposite; I was merely confirming your integrity. May I see you for a few moments after this seminar?"

Peabody's statement didn't make Harry feel any better, though he appreciated it when Magda was shown the respect she deserved. There was something sinister about Professor Ambrosia.

On Sunday evenings, the bar of the Rosebank hotel was usually quiet, and this Sunday evening was no exception. Most of the participants of the seminar had chosen to have dinner in the hotel restaurant, so for the present, Harry, Magda and Peabody found themselves quite alone as they huddled around one of the small highly polished, beaten – copper-topped tables in a shadowy corner of the bar room. Peabody had instructed Smith to sit at the bar where he would be able to keep an eye on things. He had also been instructed by his boss that under no circumstances must he participate in the consuming of any alcoholic beverage.

Sullenly, Smith sat at the bar as the African barman, resplendent in evening suit and bow tie, grinned at the sight of his enormous bald-headed white patron dwarfing the round stool beneath him. There must be some Zulu blood in him somewhere, he thought. Smith glanced around the empty tables and chairs and then at his boss, to see that he was deep in conversation with the professor and her husband. He turned back to survey the many types of liquor bottles on the glass shelves behind the bar. He sighed heavily and took a sip from his lemonade.

"As far as we know," said Magda in a low voice, "the thing you talk of is the stuff of legend and does not actually exist." Their shadows grew longer on the wall as the barman dimmed the lights.

"But you've heard of such a thing?" responded Peabody eagerly. As far as he was concerned, her just knowing of the parchment spelled out that she knew more than she was saying.

"Well, yes," replied Magda uncomfortably. On one of their trips they had met a hermit who had made a reference to such a thing. He had told them that it contained the words of the song that God had sung while creating the world and everything in it, and that one day it would be found and that very same song would be sung again, creating the world anew, banishing all its sins. Though the hermit's story had touched them both at the time, for some reason neither had spoken of it to the other and both in their own minds had simply dismissed it as another religious 'hope,' like the Holy Grail or the 'True Cross.' Anyway, unlike the latter two supposed relics, they had never heard reference to it before or after. But how did professor Ambrosia learn of such a thing?

"May I ask how you would know of its existence?" Peabody asked slyly

The room was warm and cosy in the low reddish light, and Harry seemed to have become engulfed in a hushed calm presence, interrupted occasionally by the low murmur of Smith and the barman's broken chatter. Abruptly, he stirred himself. Even though he had been trying to listen avidly to his wife and professor Ambrosia's conversation with his eyes closed behind his gold-framed glasses, his mind was becoming inexplicably foggy and clouded.

"I may like to ask you the same question," he managed to say, removing his glasses and cleaning the lenses with the handkerchief from the top pocket of his jacket. He leaned forward in his chair. "There are certain secrets from history that we have been blessed with," he said. "History speaks of the past, and most of the truth of it is not presented in the future." As he spoke, he felt the sweat form on his brow; sudden chills swept down his lower spine. Why was he revealing this information? It was as if he could not help himself. Magda stared at her husband, her surprise and concern clearly showing in her eyes. "Unless you can verify why this conversation should continue," Harry continued breathlessly, "I am afraid we must say good evening." A sudden thought had managed to reveal itself in the fog. "For you have approached us sir, for knowledge I presume on its supposed whereabouts, but unless you can tell me how you are aware of its existence we must say good evening to you." Harry gulped the last of his whisky and groggily took hold of Magda's hand. "Come, my dear; it's getting late!"

Peabody was distracted momentarily by a large broad man entering the room. He seated himself at the bar next to Smith.

What was it that Clodius had told him about the parchment? He must remember, and quickly. Magda swallowed the last of her drink and also stood up, holding Harry's hand tightly. Peabody looked up at them with clear unblinking eyes.

"Please, please my friends," he said in a loud whisper, "I did not want to reveal myself yet but it seems you give me no choice," he continued, staring at them steadily." I am of the bloodline," he said simply, "and therefore also blessed with the knowledge of it."

Magda gasped and squeezed Harry's hand even tighter as they sat down heavily, both shocked and surprised. Immediately, they both remembered more of what the hermit had told them.

'It will be found only when it is meant to be found, and it will be found by one of the bloodline, and then passed down to the time of the end.'

How could this man know what the hermit had told them? They knew they themselves had only been able to learn about the existence of the parchment through the use of the timer, and that anyone else knowing of it meant that they were of the bloodline, according to what the hermit had told them. The trip on which they met the hermit had been the previous one, when they had witnessed the martyrdom of Saint George; was there any connection? They had actually forgotten about it and even at the time had thought the hermit quite possibly mad with religious fervour for something made up by some ancient scribe or even the hermit himself. But Harry was now deeply troubled. There was something not quite right about this suntanned, wild-haired skinny little fellow with the wide, watery deceitful eyes who only half an hour previously had been enquiring as to where the priceless lost Fabergé eggs were – not in line with the merit for one claiming to be of this so-called bloodline. Yet, how did he know so much?

"You are of the bloodline?" Harry asked, his voice low and steady, hiding his troubled suspicion.

Peabody was merely repeating what he had learned about the parchment from Clodius: That at the end of time, one from the bloodline would retain the parchment and be able to read the words and music written on it and so sing again the song in order for the world to be reborn. Of course, it was all a load of old tosh, Clodius had informed him in his usual 'know all' way. Yet the word had gone out that such a parchment did exist and would soon be 'found.' "Imagine the power the organization possessing such a thing would wield over the world!" Clodius had declared. The highest echelons of all the religious bodies of the world knew of its physical existence and all knew it was a fake, Clodius had laughed. It was imperative that the club get it first. It was literally a matter of life or death – especially for Peabody. Peabody smiled to himself as he remembered Smith pointing out quite seriously that they would all be in trouble if the parchment was the real thing. Peabody had replied that he would show him how 'real' it was by walloping him over the head with it when he got his hands on it.

"Yes, I am of the chosen bloodline," he answered, blinking

with false pride, "I have been assigned to find it," he continued truthfully, " and then to keep it safe until the time comes."

"The time?" asked Magda.

"The end of Time," answered Peabody as seriously as the situation demanded.

Harry and Magda looked at each other. Harry nodded to her.

"I would like to ask you professor Ambrosia, what made you think that I would know where the parchment is to be found?" asked Magda, again feeling uncomfortable.

"You are my only hope," answered Peabody, "you claim to know what other historians do not."

Harry replaced his glasses.

"But surely, if the parchment is ready to be found, and you are qualified, you will find it without our help," he said.

"I am the one to find it," answered Peabody, suddenly gaining a soft and yet emotionally charged tone in his voice, "but I can only find it through love. Love between all brothers and sisters will bring about the finding of the parchment and the beginning of the renewing of all." He could barely keep his face straight as he remembered the laughter from Clodius when he had informed him of this rubbish.

Harry almost lost his temper; he bent down and took hold of Peabody's tie and began to push the knot tighter until Peabody could barely breathe. "You still have not told us how you came to hear about the parchment, bloodline or no bloodline!" Harry's uncharacteristic behaviour shocked Magda, but she simply stared, rooted to the spot, as Peabody glanced hopefully over to where Smith was deep in some sort of conversation at the bar with the large, broad gentleman. There would be no help from there.

"W-w-w-w – weeders," Peabody managed to croak, as his faced began to turn a deep shade of red. Harry released his grip slightly.

"Weeders?"

"Its existence is known to my government," replied Peabody quite truthfully, for Clodius had informed him of this. Harry relaxed his grip further. "Papers were discovered in some old military intelligence files that were due to be released for public consumption. Of course, this sort of information cannot be made public, so our friend the 'weeder' handed it to the Lord Chancellor's office, who then made the decision to inform me, for he knows of my heritage, and then destroy the file." Half of this was true and half of this was a lie. Harry suspected as much but he now released his grip completely from the much-relieved Peabody's throat.

Magda took hold of Harry's hand. A tear rolled down her cheek. She cleared her throat.

"Many years ago when we were still blessed," she said, "we learned of the existence of the parchment. We were neither charged with any duty to perform nor any secret to keep, and we have never been inclined to talk about it, even among ourselves. As strange as it may seem to you, I personally have ne ver been inclined to believe or disbelieve its existence, but one thing I will never forget are the words that were spoken:

> *"In Leather I am formed*
> *In maple I am laid*
> *When the egg is opened*
> *All will be remade."*

"You say somebody recited this to you?" Peabody asked, trying to catch Magda out.

"No, we read it," interrupted Harry, "on a parchment," he added.

"That is all we can say that we know about it," said Magda.

Peabody repeated the words in his head, making sure that he would remember the verse clearly.

As Magda and Harry got up to leave, Magda held out her hand. "I am not sure of your motives, professor, or whether we have done the right thing by telling you the little we know, but do remember one thing about us: From love we were sent and to love we will return."

Peabody watched them disappear out of the bar room. He shook his head. Love, he thought, feeling his throat delicately, how can you go back to love, if love sent you away in the first place? That sounds like the same sort of old tosh as this damned parchment codswallop. He sat down at the table and spun the words of the rhyme over in his mind. He took out the timer from his pocket, stood it on the table and leaned protectively over it. Well, my friend, he thought, we cannot go back to Clodius empty handed and you certainly brought us here for some reason. As he thought again about the rhyme, a vivid vision of Tatiana Nicolaevna formed in his mind. "She is connected to all this, or Smith isn't an imbecile!" he said out loud as he passed Smith, who was still sitting on his minute stool, conversing merrily with the large gentleman at the bar. "Stay off the booze, Smith," he said, and then realising that the rather large gentleman with the rather large glass of beer in front of him was a potential drinking pal, he continued, "and don't cause any trouble!"

As he slipped out into the foyer, his mind was racing; he was also quite conscious of the fact that Smith had not followed him. That blockhead had better not get up to any mischief, he cursed under his breath. He was still smarting and was extremely angry that Smith had not come to his aid when he was being manhandled by that oaf, the professor's husband. He is going to pay for that!

"Drrink yor beer, boikie!"

Smith looked at the man sitting next to him. He really was trying to be as good and inconspicuous as possible. If only Peabody had not imposed the drinking ban upon him he was sure that he and this very large fellow would have got along quite amicably, even though Smith was having immense difficulty understanding what the fellow was actually saying. It was obviously a colonial accent, he thought, but he had no idea of its origin. This also suddenly made him realise that he had no idea where the timer had brought himself and Peabody to! It was unlikely that they were in England, considering his surroundings. He looked at the barman. Perhaps they were in America, he thought. He glanced sideways at the man sitting next to him. He was indeed a very large specimen with a neck like that of a bull. Indeed, the short dark curly hair on his head enhanced the likeness and Smith grinned broadly at him. On his travels, he had occasionally come across farmers from Devon and Cornwall and had great trouble making sense out of what they said, never mind some of the people he had met further north and in such places as Glasgow and the like. Smith's usual line of defence was to revert back to his native, thick Lancashire accent. Peabody had over the years tried to 'cultivate' as he called it, his syllables and Smith had spent many hours, at the insistence of his boss, in elocution lessons. Smith, though, had never forgotten his roots and had absolutely no trouble in reverting back to his 'common' tongue whenever it suited him.

" 'Av a beer, ma boikie!" the man declared loudly in his ear, grinning back at him. He signalled to the barman, who was by now also grinning broadly, to open Smith a bottle of beer. The barman placed it next to an empty glass on the bar in front of him. Smith ignored him while he tried to work out what the fellow had just said to him and took another sip from his lemonade. He looked at the beer bottle in front of him, sighing again. He suppressed a deep throated growl and then turning to the giant sitting by his side, as he finally put two and two together, he began his attack by way of defence.

"Ahrate lad," he said, plunging down for the baritone notes of his voice box, "thanks fot laaga, but no thanks, me boss'll kill me."

126

Smith's potential drinking partner gave him a quizzical look as he worked out what Smith had just said to him.

"Come, ma boet," said the man, now standing up, "dent moind abet im ay."

Smith looked quickly down at the floor, scowling. He couldn't help but think that the man had called him a rather rude name, but struggled gallantly to keep his temper under control as he remembered Peabody's strict instructions. He managed to swallow the growls that threatened to explode out of his mouth.

"Ah dawnt want nowt me auld cock, a'll just stick wi it!" Smith managed to say, pointing at his lemonade, desperately trying to keep the peace, "'Ere, av a laaga on me!"

The large Afrikaans gentleman had never in his life heard such a language and now concluded that Smith was definitely the foreigner he suspected him to be, most likely Danish or Finnish, though from Smith's mannerisms, he clearly recognised that he was being offered a drink himself.

"Dankie bud, I'll hev a Klippies! By the way, ma name es Vander Merver, not Koch, boet!"

Smith raised his eyebrows at his new companion, whose eyes grew wide as he observed Smith's face turn an angry shade of purple. What did he just say to me? Smith fumed, placing both his palms to the side of his head. He then exploded.

"I've gotta 'angover! Yuno, sore 'ed! Stupid git. Bugga off!"

The barman, who had been grinning at their unusual conversation so far, suddenly lost his grin and decided it was time to evacuate.

"Ah, you got a babalaas, bru! 'Ave a Klippies 'n coke!" the man sympathised, the grin quickly returning to his face.

At the reception desk, Peabody booked two rooms for the evening: a luxury double suite for himself and a standard single one for Smith. Thankfully, he had found plenty of the local cash in his pockets. Ah, he thought, his face beaming at the young female receptionist, just like the old times: the timer is providing.

He showered quickly and then rang reception to ask someone to inform Smith of his room number and to come to him at once. He slipped into the bathrobe that was provided and sat in one of the armchairs. He rolled the words of the rhyme over and over in his mind. His thoughts were disturbed by the sudden burst of the door opening as Smith appeared, looking highly agitated and a little worse for wear, sporting a swollen cheek. His left eye seemed to turn from a cross red to a furious purple as Peabody gazed at his accomplice. He chuckled in disbelief. "What on earth happened to you?" he asked.

"You should see the other guy, boss! They just wheeled him out on a stretcher!" answered Smith, suddenly sheepish.

"I hope we are not going to get a visit from the local blue brigade Smith, because if we do I am going to let them take you away!" Peabody said this in a way that Smith couldn't tell if he was serious or not.

"Don't worry, boss," said Smith, "the two that *did* turn up have also been wheeled out on stretchers. I couldn't understand a word they were saying to me, except that they just kept calling me a backside."

Peabody shook his head slowly from side to side; the comical nature of the situation prevented him from being angry, for the time being at least. He could see there was more to the story than Smith was revealing. "Sit down, Mr Smith," he said, sighing as one of great patience would sigh. "Pour me a drink and let's start at the beginning."

Smith sat in the armchair opposite Peabody. He emptied two miniature bottles of whisky into two tumblers. Peabody pretended not to notice.

"It all started, boss, because I couldn't have a drink at the bar," he said, gulping the whisky down in one.

"Is that so?" replied Peabody. "Are you telling me all this is my fault?"

"No, boss! You see, this big guy comes up and sits next to me and starts being abusive. He kept calling me a backside. I tried to take no notice boss, honest I did. I even offered to buy him a lager but ..."

"That's my man, Smith," interrupted Peabody. "Tolerance is a virtue in a hotel bar!" Peabody's eyes were bright now with humour. Life would just not be the same without old Smith.

"Try telling that to him, boss. I offered to buy him a drink and he called me a donkey's backside!" replied Smith incredulously, still hardly able to believe the manners of the man.

"A what?" cried Peabody.

"Yes, boss! But the final straw came when he called me a bobble arse. I mean, I don't have to take that from no one!" Smith eyed another miniature bottle hopefully.

"No, Smith my man," answered Peabody. "I quite agree; nobody should have to take such abuse. So what did you do to him?"

"I gave him the old jockey's whip with me elbow, boss, but he was quicker than I thought and he managed to get an old-fashioned left hook in. Then I got really mad! You know how to make a Venetian Blind, don't you boss!" (Echoing a private joke they had between them.)

"But he wasn't from Venice, Smith you fool, was he?" Peabody's wrath finally exploded. He sprang out of his chair like a scalded tom cat. "I also doubt very much either that he was being abusive to you!" Peabody picked up a newspaper that was lying on the table in front of them. "We are in Johannesburg, you idiot!" he said, pointing to the image on the front page of a black man being arrested. "The man with whom you were conversing so nicely was no doubt an Afrikaans gentleman; not my favourites, but not a bad lot and I doubt very much he was being rude." Peabody glared down at the hapless Smith.

"While you were playing 'scrabble' with Jan Smuts, I was getting throttled, you useless rubbish!"

Smith gazed up at his boss. "I … I … I didn't see that, Mr Peabody! You know I would never let anything happen to you, you know …"

"I know nothing of the sort these days Smith, but what I do know is that you have become slow, soft and even more stupid. What I also know is that if you don't get your act together now that the timer is working for me again, you are not going to last very long. Do you understand?"

Downcast and looking truly heartbroken, Smith's great bald head lolled forward in shame.

"No time to cry, you great baby!" exclaimed Peabody unkindly. "You do realise the local law will be looking for you and could quite possibly be on their way up here as we speak."

Smith clenched both his fists again. "I ain't going nowhere!" he cried defiantly.

"No, Mr Smith, you are *not* going anywhere," confirmed Peabody, "but remind me to send you on a refresher course of elocution lessons when we get home; you seem to be reverting back to your old habits again." He emptied the remaining two miniature bottles of whisky into the two empty glasses. "Talking of home, you do realise we are unable to return there until we have the parchment?"

"We can go on the run, boss! I know lots of places we could hide." Smith said. "Or I could fix *them* for you, boss," he continued, clenching his fists again.

Peabody shook his head and glared at Smith. "Sawdust and straw!" he exclaimed, "is all you have in that big fat head; enough to cover the floor of a Saxon dining hall! We can't hide from them any more than anybody else can, and don't even think of trying to fix even the lowliest of their members, Smith, or you will see us involved in some mysterious and very nasty 'accident' before you can say Louis Mountbatten. No, Smith, when we go home we will have the parchment with us, and if I am not mistaken, the Fabergé eggs as well."

"Do you know where they are, boss?" asked Smith, looking at the door. A loud babble of voices could be heard in the hallway outside.

"I do," confirmed Peabody, "and listening to that I think *you* have overstayed our welcome, and we should be on our way immediately."

Much to Smith's and indeed Peabody's relief, the timer was already glowing as Peabody took it out of his pocket. They both stared at the little egg timer; the sparks began to spew from all sides as a loud banging was heard on the door of the suite.

"Dis is de sef effrican poolees! Owpen dis dawrrr!" a loud voice shouted from the other side.

The sparks multiplied ferociously from the little egg timer as it stood balancing on the palm of Peabody's outstretched hand. Smith's smiling face turned to a look of incredulousness as Peabody shouted out the 'coordinates.'

"Where are we going, boss?" he shouted above the din.

Peabody answered with his large, deceitful, liquid brown eyes.

When the lock finally capitulated and the door burst open, four very angry South African policemen fell through it on top of one another. The room was empty. There was no sign of the large bald suspect or his wiry little friend.

"Tjeck de window, Fraanz! Bowf dees armchairs eez still warm! Dey can't hiv gone verrry farrr."

The officer took off his peaked cap and scratched his head in confusion.

CHAPTER 5
CLOCKS

The Jammy Dodger packet lay half opened on top of the granite breakfast nook. They were silent, each lost in their own thoughts. Tatiana was thinking about a friend she had known long ago and was trying to figure out why now all of a sudden the book of truth had showed her his image. She was going to mention it to Arty but for some reason he was grumpy this morning. Cantankerous and sullen were not words she would normally have used to describe him. When she had asked him if he would like coffee (which he usually made anyway but he hadn't even filled the kettle with water this morning) he had answered with a grunt. She took the grunt as a yes. He had grunted again very rudely when she had filled his plate with biscuits and had placed it very nicely in front of him. Was he sick, perhaps? He hadn't even looked at the coffee she had made him. Tatiana had not slept at all well the night before. The wind had been blowing and wailing like a scolded witch around the cottage and had only relented as the sun began to make its appearance on the horizon. The beautiful sun! Ever since she arrived at the cottage, the sight of it slowly emerging from the ocean horizon up into the cloudless sky like a great orange balloon filled her with the hope of a new day. But this morning as she gazed at it, shielding her eyes from the brightness, something was deeply troubling her, yet still she struggled to believe it.

"Arty," she said.

"Uh," he replied gloomily, looking through the dining room, and on through the large picture window of the little sun lounge. Seagulls drifted aimlessly on the breeze. The blue ocean lapped the shore with wide, grinning waves.

"We are in South Africa, right?" she asked him.

"I believe so," he answered, still deep in grumpiness.

"Which is in the southern hemisphere?"

"The last time I looked, yes," he answered. "What did they used to teach them in the olden days?"

Ignoring his sarcasm, Tatiana continued: "And the water spins anti-clockwise when it disappears down the hole of a wash basin or a bath, where as in Russia it disappears with a clockwise motion?"

"I believe I did inform you of that phenomenon," he answered, screwing up his eyes in distaste as he finally tasted the coffee that Tatiana had made for him.

"So does the sun also rise in the east like it does in Russia?" she asked.

Her words suddenly jolted him to attention.

"Yes," he answered, looking into the troubled depths of her eyes. His own were pools of confusion. "But unlike Russia, it seems all of a sudden in South Africa the sun has now begun to *set* in the east as well!"

"Arty," she said, "I think we need to go and see Harry!"

*

On the last occasion that they had seen him, Harry had given them his home address in case of an emergency. It was further away than Arty had expected, and in the direction of Port

133

Edward, another thirty or so kilometres south of Arty's cottage. The powerful engine of Arty's black Jaguar growled as it came to a halt at the four-way stop. Arty took the turning to the right and then wound up the narrow lane amidst the deep, lush green vegetation. The road forged a tunnel through the overhanging tees on either side. At the T-junction, they took the turn to their left. Tatiana looked at Arty disapprovingly. Cursing under his breath as they headed down the narrow dirt track of the coffee plantation, he desperately tried to dodge the pot holes that were a serious threat to the wellbeing of the Jaguar's very expensive low profile tyres.

"No wonder he doesn't get many visitors!" Arty exclaimed, gritting his teeth as one of the front wheels slammed into a gaping hole in the road. The dirt track eventually became wider as they saw a large, wooden cabin at the top of the hill. The small cottage-pane windows made it look cheery and welcoming. At the front of the cabin, the driveway came to an abrupt end by way of a large turning circle. In the centre of the circle stood a tall, four-sided, tapered stone monument. As she stepped out of the car, Tatiana noticed what looked like hieroglyphics carved around its base, but she didn't have much time to study them, for Harry came bounding out of the front door, obviously pleased to see them.

"This is a most welcome surprise!" he cried, shaking Arty's hand vigorously and bowing respectfully to Tatiana as she beamed at him. "The fact that you are back and in one piece is all I need to know for now. Would you like a beer, Arthur?"

Arty looked at his wristwatch. It was 8:30 a.m. "No," he answered, "but a nice cup of coffee would be great."

They looked at each other with slightly puzzled expressions as they followed Harry through the front door. This wasn't the placid, mild-mannered Harry that they were accustomed to!

Harry did not own the cabin but rented the property from the owner of the coffee plantation. "I live in a time that is not my own," he explained to them, "So I'd rather spend the time I haven't got these days in a house I don't own." He laughed, beaming at them mischievously. "Let me know if you ever figure that one out!" he said. "I'd be interested to know what it means myself."

"I love the smell of wood!" Tatiana declared as she entered the large open-plan room that served as the kitchen, lounge and dining room. The walls of the cabin were of bare timber. The floor was parquet and the ceiling was also covered in wood panelling, but what really amazed and interested her was that the room was inundated with clocks of all shapes and sizes. The whole room resonated with the sound of their workings. Some ticked away time with light, fast movements, others with slow, heavy cumbersome ones. She could imagine herself reading one of her favourite books, Ivanhoe or Anna Karenina, in one of the comfy armchairs in the corner of this room, the homely scent of wood in her nose as the ticks and tocks reverberated off the walls. A few egg timers sat as ornaments on bookshelves (there were lots of these) and on the mantelpiece. Two in particular caught her attention, as they were almost as tall as the chairs she and Arty were sitting on. Their frames were made of rich and highly polished wood – one of light oak, the other of dark oak. Their phials were so huge that the white granules inside them were almost the size of small sugar lumps. Upon each stood an empty, seven-branched candlestick. Quite clearly, she thought, these large egg timers were not being used as anything else but rather beautiful little tables. But she looked at the others suspiciously.

"No, no my dear!" cried Harry as he watched her study the small assortment of egg timers apprehensively. "There really are only two with magical powers in this world."

Tatiana smiled at Harry and sighed with relief. Then she noticed the two large grandfather clocks, one in each corner of the room. It was Harry's turn to smile as he appreciated her obvious admiration of them.

"I see you are capable of acknowledging stunningly gorgeous and ravishingly handsome time mechanisms," he gushed. "Well, may I also enlighten you of the fact that the first pendulum clock was made by Christiaan Huygens, who was a Dutch scientist and not, as the history books record, by Galileo Galilei." Tatiana grinned at Arty as they took their seats, ready for the story. "Although Galileo's design preceded Christiaan's by seventy-four years," Harry continued, "its accuracy would never have been good enough to actually tell the time by and of course, I told him so. His design was never used during his lifetime, whereas Christiaan's in 1656 only lost a minute per day. I might whisper you the reason for that accuracy and then again, I might not." He grinned happily at some past memory. "His design just needed a little tweaking here and there." He winked at them.

"Well, would you mind tweaking this?" cried Arty in mild disgust, brandishing his modern wristwatch. "It seems to lose about five minutes per day since I bought it."

Harry laughed as he opened his beer can. "Ah!" he continued, laughing. "A Swiss watch made no doubt in ... "

"Yes," interrupted Arty, "just like the chocolate."

"What are you two talking about?" cried Tatiana, suddenly remembering the reason for their visit.

Harry looked at them and studied their faces.

"I can see you are both troubled," he said, as he took his first gulp of beer for the day.

"Yes you could say th ... " Arty began, but was interrupted by an enthusiastic Harry.

"But before you tell me all about it, let me tell you about time."

"That's exactly what we came to talk to you about, Harry!" Arty blurted out, now clearly agitated.

"I used to love time!" Harry continued, pretending not to notice Arty's irritation, "and the instruments that record it, even though I'm not part of it these days." He turned expectantly to face the mass of timepieces on one of the walls as they all chimed eight forty-five in perfect harmony. Like a choir of clocks, Tatiana thought. She even thought she could hear the sound of a cuckoo from somewhere. The sound of the ticking and the chiming seemed to be taking all her cares away. Indeed, she almost forget the reason for their visit again. But Arty was becoming annoyed with Harry's unusual disposition. He seemed unusually happy this morning, Arty thought. Was he just obviously relieved and happy to see his friends, as he had said? Or had something else happened? There was also something different about the look in his eyes. It was as if the shadow of deep sorrow had been lifted.

"Did you know?" Harry asked them both, his face beaming, "that the term 'grandfather clock' came from a song written by the American, Henry Clay Work, in 1875, called 'My Grandfather's Clock.'"

"No, I didn't," cried Arty, trying to disguise his rapidly rising bad temper, but failing. Though he was very pleased that his friend was in such seemingly good spirits, he had something extremely urgent to discuss. "I suppose we just must be happy he didn't call the song 'My Stepfather's Clock,' shouldn't we? I mean, it just wouldn't have had the same ring, or *chime* to it, should I say," he continued, relieving his annoyance a little with his usual sarcasm. Tatiana glared at him. She was also impatient for answers but there was no need to be rude. The wonderful calm that had immersed her as she listened to the sound of the clocks was all at once replaced with dreadful apprehension. She leant forward and rubbed the muscles in the back of her long, slim neck. She tried to close her eyes as she sat back on the sofa. Harry's voice sounded as if it was coming from a long ago, almost forgotten dream. A *dream*! Surely it was all just a *dream*. The timer; Arty; his lovely cottage! None of it really existed. She would wake up just now back in that dreadful Ipatiev house with her family. But at least dear papa would still be alive! She was suddenly dreadfully tired. Oh, dear papa! She cried silently as the claws of grief began to tear away at her deep down inside. She gazed wildly at the clock faces. Everyone uncomfortably reminded her of a face she detested. Each one stared back at her with a knowing, arrogant smile. Accusing her, the fingers on their faces appeared to move quicker than they should, until the hour hand moved quicker than that of the minute. The more she stared, the faster the fingers rotated and the ticking became louder and louder. Somewhere in the back of her mind she could still hear Harry's voice but it had become like a dead echo from the far end of a tunnel. She felt her forehead. It was cold and clammy.

Arty, however, was listening attentively to Harry.

"The obelisk in the middle of the driveway, the one you passed as you arrived, is an example of probably one of the first clocks ever devised. It comes from Egypt; 3497 BC, to be precise. I guess we would call it a sun clock today. As you can guess, it is quite authentic," Harry continued. "I've also got a water clock out back from Greece dated 322 BC, also very authentic, I may add." Unfortunately for Arty and Tatiana, time pieces of any kind were Harry's passion, and he had very little opportunity to share that passion. He looked up and around at his prized possessions again.

"Okay, people!" he cried, his arms spread out like some mad musical conductors, "block your ears!"

Two loud ticks counted in an orchestra of dings, dongs, chimes, rings, bells and now cuckoos as 9 a.m. was ceremoniously announced. Harry stood beaming, his eyes wide with pride as he counted the chimes. It was on the eighth chime that Tatiana finally stood up shakily, her hands desperately covering her ears. Then, all at once she collapsed to her knees, her face in her hands, sobbing. Arty dashed across and down to her side to comfort her. Harry finally noticed what was happening and horrified, he threw his arms in the air and then also knelt down next to her.

"My dear, my dear," he cried guiltily, "Please forgive this selfish old man! What is the matter?"

"It's their faces," she cried desperately, "his *face* in every one of the clocks. It's all too much, too much," Tatiana sobbed, "I'm in a place I don't belong, in a time I don't belong. I should be with my family!"

Arty and Harry stared at each other. "Whose face, my dear?" asked Harry, his voice now full of concern.

Tatiana took her hands from her face. Her beautiful grey eyes were illuminated in tears; her lips quivered as she whispered:

"Peabody!"

*

Arty helped Tatiana back onto the sofa. Her chest heaved with silent sobs as she looked down at her fingers fumbling with the material of her skirt. Strands of her hair had curled against her damp brow. He wanted to hold her forever, tell her that it will be alright, but he couldn't lie to her or himself. He stood up abruptly and with angry emotion, he related to Harry the events at the Ipatiev house, now paying particular attention to Peabody's part in the matter. "How could history have got what happened so incorrect?" he declared. "Was it by mistake or for a purpose, and if so, why?" Though the tsar had indeed been shot and killed, it was certainly not by a firing squad, and he had been the only one of the family to suffer that fate in the house. He related how her three sisters, Olga, Marie and Anastasia, had finally been rescued by a British Intelligence officer and that they were to be taken to Odessa to meet up with their mother, the tsarina, and brother, the tsarevich. He related how he had tried to say goodbye to Tatiana just after the rescue, thinking that their purpose together had been fulfilled, but even though she had indicated that she needed to stay with her family, the timer still brought her back to 2014 with him. Tatiana looked up

139

at Arty; her face streamed again with tears. "I am so confused, Arty!" she said.

"I know, Tanechka," he answered, "so am I."

Harry gazed silently at each of them. More than anything that Arty had told him, the term of endearment concerned him the most.

"So," continued Arty, "even though when we left, most of them had been saved; we still don't know what became of them, and we certainly can't rely on the history books for information." He knelt down again by Tatiana's side and took her hands in his. "It must be absolute torture."

"And for you?" asked Harry, searching Arty's face.

Arty let go of Tatiana's hands and looked away. "For me also," he sighed emotionally, "it is almost as if I left my own family back there, Harry. How can I have become so involved?"

Harry shook his head in bewilderment. "Is there more?" he asked, looking down first at Arty and then at Tatiana who was blowing her nose with the only handkerchief that could be found in Arty's cottage. (Arty had inherited it from his grandmother along with the Royal Albert).

"No, no!" exclaimed Arty, "nothing like that." He knew he wasn't convincing Harry any more than he was convincing himself. Harry looked at Arty thoughtfully.

"Do you have the timer with you, Arthur?" he asked.

Arty took it out of his trouser pocket and balanced it in the outstretched palm of his hand. Immediately, a raucous din of clock movements filled their ears. The sound of the beautiful timepieces had become very unpleasant, not as before – soft, yet full and harmonious. The sound was rough and harsh as if the cogs in the workings were not aligned correctly and the teeth of those cogs were splitting and breaking. Arty snapped his hand shut and replaced the timer in his pocket. Instantly the din abated and the soft, smooth harmonious sound of the clocks returned.

"The timer was not made in time and does not exist in it," Harry tried to explain to them. "It comes from a place where all days are present and the present lasts for eternity. The movement of time is certainly not part of its makeup. Time itself tries to rebel against it. Have you noticed at home, Arthur, that your wall clock, if you have one, ticks louder since you have acquired the egg timer?"

Arty nodded. He had grown pale. He was dumbfounded. He looked at his wrist watch again; it was at least five minutes slow already, even though he had set it at the correct time the evening before. Come to think of it, it had only been playing up these last two or three weeks since he had bought the timer from Harry.

"So, the fact that the sun doesn't know how to behave properly any more is also the timer's fault, I presume," Tatiana blurted out. "What do you mean?" Harry asked, looking down at her, a shadow of worry on his face.

"Just what she says," cried Arty, "The sun is getting up and going to bed in the same place – the *east!*"

"And *you* witnessed this?" Harry asked.

Arty nodded.

Harry walked over to the double-door fridge. "I need a beer," he said. He snapped the tab of the can open and then gulped down at least half of it before wiping his mouth with the back of his wrist.

"I cannot believe what is happening," he said clutching the top of the open fridge door with his left hand, steadying himself. "Where you two are concerned, nothing seems to happening as it should!"

"Tatiana, tell him where you saw the sun set last night!" Arty cried in desperation.

Before Tatiana could answer, Harry cut in.

"For Tatiana it will be so, just as it is for me, for when she is in any other time but her own, time will cease to be. It will

141

seem that the days begin and the days end but, as you have noticed, it is with a strange difference. But for you Arthur, this is impossible. I cannot understand what the timer is up to. As I told you, the fact that Tatiana is here at all is breaking its own rules. Believe me, I should know. What else has happened?"

Arty then told him that even though they had barely returned from their ordeal at the Ipatiev house, the timer sent them off on one of its own missions.

"Another trip to England again; can you believe it?" said Arty, "Some place called Harrogate actually, and to cut a long story short, Tatiana bumped into Errol Flynn of all people, who told her that Peabody and Smith are very much at large and are, were or whatever, searching for the parchment."

The empty can of beer slipped through Harry's fingers and fell on the floor boards with a hollow thud. "The parchment!" he said in a low voice, "and did you meet up with this Peabody character again?"

"No," said Tatiana, shaking her head, "but Clarke Flynn had met him."

Arty was then forced to explain how during Tatiana's conversation with *Errol* Flynn she had learned that Peabody had been assigned by 'The Masters Club' to find the 'parchment' and it sounded like the very same 'parchment' that King Richard himself had mentioned.

"And did they find this 'parchment'?" Harry asked anxiously.

"I don't know!" answered Tatiana, "but they were searching the coast of … mmm… let me think; what was the name of that place?"

"Aquileia!" cried Arty, "by the Adriatic, or that's what you told me."

Harry put his beer down on the counter top. He strode across the room purposefully until he stood directly in front of them.

"I don't know what is going on with you two," he said almost apologetically, "but I do know that if Peabody did find the parchment and if it is in the possession of his friends, we and many others in this world are in grave danger. I am afraid that I have met your Mr Peabody!"

Arty and Tatiana gasped with surprise. "Yes, I'm afraid so," Harry continued, "but he introduced himself to us by a different name, no doubt intending to put us off his trail and it has worked until now. It was a long time ago and upon which rung of the timer's ladder, I am not sure."

Arty looked at Harry again. This time his face screwed up in confusion. "You talk in riddles, my friend," he said, exasperated.

"You will understand the terminology one day," answered Harry with equal exasperation. Tatiana rolled her eyes at Arty and refolded her arms. She turned her face away again as she sighed heavily.

"I suspect he was trying to intercept the intended sequence of events planned out for the parchment by using *his* timer," said Harry.

"There you go again," said Arty quietly shaking his head.

"In other words, he is bent on actually trying to change the course of history," continued Harry.

"But I thought you said that was not possible," declared Arty, "and anyway, we know what happened in the Crusades, don't we? At least, I do!"

"Do you?" said Harry, looking sternly at Arty over the rims of his spectacles. "In which time did you read that history? The time you used to live in or the time you exist in now?"

The realisation of what Harry had just said struck Arty.

"Yes Arthur," said Harry, "the Book of Truth is the only real history book and the one that will be read at the end! But there is something else I need to tell you. After our little altercation with Peabody, Magda and I decided we needed to find out more about this parchment, whether it actually exists or not."

"Obviously, you found out that it was all a load of

codswallop!" cried Arty, chuckling, "like the rest of that sort of stuff."

Tatiana glared at him again. "Some people are just blind, no matter how much is shown to them," she said, her voice quivering with emotion, "and even if Harry was to say now that he did find out that it was the stuff of legend, I would still *want* it to be real anyway, not like you."

She turned her face away from him again to stare with moist blinking eyes through the window.

"You needn't fear, my dear," said Harry calmly, "the parchment exists alright."

Tatiana did not move, though Arty noticed her knuckles whiten as she gripped the arms of her chair. He sighed rather dramatically, shaking his head slightly.

"You've seen it?" he asked

"No," Harry answered abruptly.

Arty raised his eyebrows.

"We asked for guidance as to its whereabouts," Harry continued, "and we were whisked away and onto a ship at the port of Constanta."

"Constanta!" Tatiana exclaimed with surprise. "Why, we were there during that long hot summer just before the war!"

Both men looked at her enquiringly.

"We had travelled as usual to beloved Livadia in April, the year the war started," she continued, reminiscing with undisguised excitement, "Oh, the sea, the sun, the trees the flowers!" her voice softened to the notes of sadness. "That was the last time Olga and I attended a ball in the Crimea. I remember dancing with Prince Jean Woroniecki for simply hours and hours," she continued dreamily.

"Is there a point to this wonderful story?" said Arty, the annoyance in his voice quite evident.

"There just might be," said Harry, again looking hard at Arty. "Please carry on, my dear."

"Olga made it quite plain to both mama and papa that she had no intention of marrying anybody that might cause her to leave Russia, but for the benefit of protocol we made the voyage in 'the Standart' across the Black sea from Yalta to Constanta in order to see about a possible match for her with Prince Carol of Romania, but of course, nothing came of it." Tatiana crossed her legs and smiled sweetly at Arty.

"And?" exclaimed Arty, ignoring her and looking enquiringly at Harry. "Do we have a connection?"

"As I was saying," Harry continued, ignoring Arty for the time being at least, "we landed on a very pleasant little sailing ship and from its design I would say somewhere around the thirteenth century. The ship, strangely enough, was bound for Yalta!" He looked curiously first at Tatiana and then Arty. "But on this ship, as they were loading it with supplies, we were approached by one of the sailors who informed us he was working for his passage. He enquired as to where we were headed. It never crossed my mind that the question was quite impertinent, as we were in the guise of a rich nobleman and – woman (courtesy of the timer, of course) and he had the look of one of lowly stature. Yet, there was an air about him that defied his appearance. "Like a king who has lost his crown," was how Magda described him. For some reason he seemed drawn to us, and I remember clearly the timer becoming unbelievably heavy in the pocket of my inner tunic. That evening he joined us up on the poop deck as we were watching the sun settle on the sea's horizon. We were labouring with the reason why we were there and what the timer was up to. But we had no reason to wonder for much longer, for the man brought with him something that looked heavy, wrapped in old sack cloth. He put the bundle down upon the deck and unwrapped it; there stood the most beautiful golden box. On the lid were inscribed strange letters, the like I have never seen before. Yet the strangest thing was that he wanted to give it to us. He explained that inside was a leather parchment that contained a strange and unreadable script similar to the letters on the lid, and that he was prompted for some reason to give it to us."

"The parchment?" asked Tatiana, "so *you* have the parchment!"

"No," answered Harry, "I asked him how he opened the lid, for I could see no way to do this, and he informed me that the letters changed in such a way that he could read them. When he did so it opened, revealing the parchment. There was no change in the letters when either I or Magda tried to read them. I knew then for sure what it was. I told him. I also told him that for whatever reason he was meant to keep it and that he had a role to play."

"So what happened to it?" asked Arty, "where did the guy take it?"

"I do not know," answered Harry, "for at that very moment the timer brought us back; it was as if our purpose was to inform the man what he carried, and of course it to be revealed to us that there was such a thing in the world."

"But who was the man?" asked Tatiana. "Did he not give his name?"

"Alas, no," said Harry. He looked searchingly at Tatiana. "But I cannot help thinking that you, my dear, are connected to all this."

All the clocks ticked quietly and steadily as one.

"Well, it's time to be on our way," exclaimed Arty. He abruptly rose from his chair and looked expectantly at Tatiana.

"You got an idea?" she asked.

"Only that I think it's time we joined the Third Crusade," he answered, without a trace of humour.

"But why would you want to do that?" asked Harry.

"Well, actually, we made a promise," said Tatiana. She remained in her seat as if reluctant to leave for the time being. Again, she fumbled nervously with the fabric of her skirt.

Harry stared at her with unblinking eyes. "A promise?"

"Yes, yes," interrupted Arty, "we promised that we would return to the Third Crusade and to King Richard. He seemed to like us, you see." Arty certainly did not want to tell Harry that he had promised to return to the Holy Land in 1192 with a ship load of Nike training shoes for King Richard's army. He struggled with the idea himself.

"That, I think, in this case will happen only if the timer were to oblige," Harry said thoughtfully. He walked over to where Tatiana was sitting. He could see she was pensive, and knelt down beside her.

"There is not much I can say to you by way of comfort, my dear, except we must trust the timer," he said.

Tatiana put her hands on her lap; her eyes suddenly filled again. "I know," she answered quietly, "but it is just so *difficult*."

Harry touched her hand softly. "Hope," he said quietly, "there is always hope." He sighed and then stood up. A shadow had returned to his eyes again. "Now it seems to make a little sense," he said again almost to himself. He thought a moment. Obviously, he was much more troubled than he looked.

"And the *impudent* sun?" asked Arty, mimicking a word used often by Tatiana.

"Perhaps you should have a beer after all, Arthur," Harry answered a little wearily. Arty shook his head but seated himself in his chair. "The clocks stopped ticking years ago for me," Harry continued, "as I have already told you, after Magda was taken. But I don't understand why you, Arthur, would find yourself in our position; it just doesn't make sense." He looked down again at Tatiana, his eyes full of pity and then down at the wooden floor boards, deep in thought. When he raised his head, his eyes were pools of tears. "In all the years since she was taken from me, no matter how hard I tried, I have never been able to dream about my darling Magda, but last night she came to me. It was so real that at first I thought somehow you had managed to retrieve the other timer and that she had finally come for me.

I felt her touch my hand as she sat on the side of my bed, just as she always used to when I was ill occasionally. I could smell her hair and her perfume. I made to jump out of bed to get ready to go with her, but she held up her hand and told me that it was not yet time. She told me that the timers are finally split; that the world is spinning faster now to its destiny. Then she said the last thing I expected," he cleared his throat. "That somehow I must find the boy. That the boy must go back. I must undo the wrong and then my labour here will be over."

Arty scratched his head. Tatiana stared at Harry with wide shining eyes.

"Hang on a minute," said Arty, "before we get to this 'boy' bit, are you trying to tell me that the clocks have stopped ticking for us now as well; that no time is passing?"

Harry nodded. "Not in the way you would know it to, no," he answered, "The sun rises and *sets* in the east for me also; for no one else on this earth, just us three. For Tatiana it makes sense, but for you, Arty ... " Harry shook his head in confusion.

"What about Peabody?" asked Tatiana.

"I suspect the sun rises and sets as normal for him and his friend, Smith," Harry answered, "just as it used to for me before Magda was taken. It's only when they travel to other times that they will be in no time at all."

"So we are in no time at all here, *and* when we travel," Arty blurted out. "So what does it mean? Are we ghosts or something?"

"I don't think so," answered Harry quite seriously, "I mean, she certainly does not look or feel like a ghost, does she?" he bent over and touched Tatiana's hand comfortingly, "and neither do you, most of the time."

"I sort of understand this 'no time at all' while I'm here," said Tatiana, "But why would Arty be experiencing the same thing? Did he also do something wrong?"

Harry threw his hands in the air again, this time in

exasperation. "When I thought about you being here which, as I said, according to the timer's own rules should not have happened, I suspected that indeed no time would pass for you in the real sense. Though as you say the sun comes up every day and every evening you watch it sink back down again. Yet no time at all has passed for you. If you were to stay in 2014, Tatiana, you would never get a day older. The fact that your destiny was not fulfilled in the Ipatiev house and forgive me for saying this, that you or your sisters, brother and mother were not murdered there as history records, means that the timer is still 'busy' with you all. Why it has allowed you to spend time here with old Arthur I really cannot imagine. But you *will* go back, for your destiny is there, Tatiana, in 1918 – and you will go back to fulfil that destiny sooner or later. Through the timer, I have learned that every second of our lives in time is all part of the great scheme of things and how we fit into the magnificent puzzle. But where you figure in all this, Arthur, completely beats me. It's as if you are stuck in the same vacuum, limbo even, as I. It really doesn't make sense!"

"Very comforting, my friend," said Arty dryly. "You are telling me that I don't actually belong anywhere or in any time, and the fact that Tatiana is here as well, the same applies to her. Well, my friend, the timer it seems has organised us to be thrown off your 'great scheme of things.' My next book should be interesting!"

Harry looked uncomfortable. He didn't want to comment too much on what he himself didn't fully understand. "It would appear so," he said stiffly, "but I am afraid I don't have all the answers." He gulped more beer. "Tell me all *you* know of this parchment!"

Arty related the story of how Richard the Lionheart had told them of its existence when, through the timer, they had attended his wedding to Berengaria in Cyprus. That he believed through a dream he had had and on seeing a hermit he was destined to

149

find it, for it was hidden in the bowels of the Holy Sepulchre in Jerusalem. That was his real reason for his crusade to reclaim the city from the Saracens. Arty then remembered something.

"It was strange, Harry," he said enthusiastically, "he mentioned that in his dream he had seen the timer, or one of them at least, and that it was by the light of the timer's glow that he saw the parchment lying on a table; a table that had been laid as if for a great feast. Yet when he was about to pick up the parchment, a voice commanded him to stop. The voice recited a rhyme of some sort that I can't remember. But whatever the voice said, Richard then tried to become worthy of the parchment. His first step was to marry Berengaria."

Both Harry and Tatiana listened, fascinated.

"You didn't tell me all that, Arty!" Tatiana declared. "That should have been written in the book of truth."

"I have only just remembered it now, "he replied edgily, "a lot has happened in between, your Imperial Highness."

Harry walked as if in a trance to his own armchair. He collapsed in it once again, deep in thought.

"I have often wondered," he said, "how Peabody found me and Magda. Obviously, we didn't know who we were talking to at the time, but somehow he certainly knew it was us."

Tatiana looked at Arty quickly. They remembered the conversation that they had had with Peabody and Smith at Stoneyhurst College when they had tried to retrieve Harry's timer, but instead had become ensnared by the wily Peabody; how Arty in desperation had told Peabody everything so far up to that point, and how he had come by the timer in the first place.

"I am afraid it was probably my fault," Arty admitted.

"All things happen for a reason, Arthur. Remember, there are no mistakes where the timer is concerned. We must take comfort from that."

Harry went on to tell them of his and Magda's conversation

at the Rosebank Hotel shortly after Magda's seminar and how Peabody had also duped them by claiming to be of the 'bloodline,' so they had told him the rhyme that had been recited to them by the hermit on one of their trips.

"Was it the very same hermit, do you think?" asked Tatiana.

"It was," answered Harry.

The room seemed to have become almost silent now. There was only a very faint, almost an echo of ticking.

"It slowly seems to be making some sort of sense," he said, looking first at Arty and then Tatiana. "For there is something that we did not tell that wily old owl face. The reason Peabody did not find it from the directions on his map is because it had already been removed. The hermit told us that Richard did indeed find and remove the parchment from the sepulchre. He and a few of his most trustworthy knights slipped into the city unseen one evening when his army had camped at a distance, deciding whether to attack and lay siege to it or not. For Richard's army had been severely depleted when his so-called ally, Phillip of France, had deserted him and gone home. Under the cover of darkness and with guidance from a map also given to him by the hermit, they found the secret tunnel that led beneath the city walls and straight down to the belly of the old temple. But when he brought it back to his camp, he found that he was unable to open it, for neither he nor any of his trusted knights could decipher the lettering that was carved into the lid of the golden box in which it lay. But the fact that he had possession of it was good enough for him. His mission was accomplished, which is the real reason he and his army did not lay siege to the city. You know Richard; sheer numbers would not have deterred him if he had really wanted to capture Jerusalem and anyway, I would think Richard would think its capture now irrelevant. Instead, he came to an agreement with his foe Saladin who, remember, had no idea that the parchment had been found and indeed removed from the city under his very nose. The truce stated that certain territories like Jaffa, Caesarea, Haifa and Acre would remain under the control of the Christians. Ramla, Lydda, Yubna, Majdal Yaba and Nazareth would remain under Saladin. But most importantly and what stood out as a real victory for Richard, apart from unknowingly taking possession of the parchment, Christians would in future be allowed to visit the holy city and pay homage to their holy sites. Considering that Richard was in a hurry to leave the holy land, as he was also under major threat from losing his Kingdom of England to his loathsome brother John, and his other territories to his equally fiendish 'friend' Philip of France, I think he bartered rather well, don't you?"

Both Tatiana and Arty remembered the king with fondness. Both had agreed that he had been very misunderstood by recent history books.

"So what did he do with the parchment?" asked Tatiana.

"On his way home and of course, to captivity, his ship was wrecked off the Istrian coast somewhere between Aquileia and Venice. He and a few of his knights managed to get ashore where they found a cave. Fearing for their safety as he knew that they had landed on potentially hostile land and that they would now have to travel by foot, they disguised themselves as pilgrims. Richard also decided to leave the box with the parchment inside in the cave, intending one day to retrieve it. He must have felt better when on leaving the cave, its opening snapped shut, leaving no trace of any entrance."

Arty knew the rest of the story well; how his 'friend' the king would then be apprehended in Vienna by the Duke of Austria's men. He was, apparently, hiding in a poor man's dwelling while preparing food for himself and his small band of companions. He was then imprisoned in castle Dürnstein, which was built high up on a rocky slope overlooking the Danube. He was to stay in captivity for a year while his mother Eleanor arranged for the astronomical ransom that was demanded for his release.

In the meantime, his crusader 'ally,' Philip of France, did indeed take possession of most of his lands on the continent.

"I rather think your trip to meet Richard was somehow more for your benefit than his, Arthur," observed Harry, seeing that he had become rather crestfallen.

"So, what became of the parchment in the end?" asked Tatiana.

"The hermit told us that it would be found by one of the bloodline. Those were his words. I still do not understand which 'bloodline' he means. Then this person would take it with him to a land his descendants eventually would conquer and then rule. The parchment would become the rock of their dynasty and as long as it was kept safe, their house would never fall. Indeed, it was implied that that country would become the strongest empire; it would not be cruel and violent like those preceding it, but would rule through love, hope and faith in God."

"So the sailor you met on the ship was of this 'bloodline,'" Tatiana confirmed.

"Would that be the Americas?" asked Arty a little doubtfully.

"Do you really think so, Arthur?" answered Harry shaking his head.

"Okay, the Chinese, the Spanish, the French, the Ottoman, the Russian, and the British all had mighty empires, but which one could you honestly say would rely on such a thing as the parchment as it's rock, as you call it?"

They were silent. The room was silent. Neither Arty nor Tatiana noticed that the ticking of clocks had ceased completely.

"So Richard did leave it in a cave on the Istrian coast," said Tatiana trying get to grips with what Harry had told them, "But then it was found, as prophesied by the hermit, by someone else whose descendants would eventually rule the world in God's name. Do you think Richard ever went back to try to retrieve it?"

Harry shook his head. "No," he said. "Again, it was Richard's

153

part to do just what he did. To take it from the Holy Sepulchre where it had lain for thousands of years and then leave it in that cave; anyway, even if he had returned to the cave I doubt he would have been able to find the entrance again. His part was meant to be no more or no less than that."

"Then we don't need to go and warn Richard after all," cried Arty, thoroughly relieved, "because the parchment is on its path of destiny anyway."

"Destined," confirmed Harry. "We are all *destined* for a purpose. For the time being at least on the timer's ladder rung it seems that the destiny of the parchment is on track, but when people like Peabody, and myself for that matter, interfere with destinies, things start to get muddled and all hell breaks loose."

"You!" cried Tatiana, "But how have you interfered with someone's destiny?"

CHAPTER 6
IN THE EYES OF THE ANGEL

The history lesson this morning was going to be a little different, the emperor had informed Vassili. He had waited for the tsar as usual in the Maple Room, taking tea with the two elder grand duchesses and the tsarina. He noticed this morning that Tatiana was not herself and that she seemed a little upset. At five minutes to ten, the girls and their mother had left him alone to wait for the emperor to arrive. He and the emperor would then walk up the staircase together and into Nicholas's study where the lesson would take place as usual. The last year or so had been the happiest so far in the young boy's life. He was now looked upon as almost a member of the imperial family. He took breakfast with them two times per week, dinner weekly and tea almost every day. The tsarina had become a mother figure to him and he looked forward to her warmth and smile when he would meet with them. He and Tatiana were inseparable whenever they met, even though they teased one another and even fought occasionally. Many times, Vassili would attend his history lesson sporting an angry red whelp on the back of his hand or his cheek where she had caught him unaware with her scalding hot teaspoon. Likewise her mother would ask her with

155

concern what had happened to her ear lobe or forehead when he had justifiably retaliated. He had shown her how to ride her first two-wheeled bicycle, and had helped her up again when she had fallen off. He was also there to witness her first pony riding lesson and had whispered encouragement to her as her father watched. Their love for each other was as innocent as their youth but, as Tatiana remembered in later years, they had been like two lovebirds nestled in a gilded cage while the wolves outside prowled ferociously waiting to devour them.

Nicholas was so pleased with his progress in general that he was asked to accompany them on their Royal Yacht, the Standart, in the summer of 1904. Under the guidance of one of the ship's officers, he had learned the basics of how to calculate tides and understand nautical charts. He was shown the procedures of docking and undocking, anchoring and mooring. He also learned about safety on board ship and about the life boats. The sailors were especially impressed at how soon he learned to tie the special knots required of a sailor. He had felt immensely proud when the emperor himself had presented him with a sailor's uniform which he wore for the rest of the holiday. Tatiana would often hide behind or even in one of the life boats and watch him admiringly as he was tutored.

But the warm summer days passed and then autumn spread its blankets of red, gold and brown upon the cultured lawns of the Alexander Palace. Then the skies grew heavy, and as the weeks slipped by the light faded and the green blankets turned to white. The sound of bells filled the cold crisp air as winter and Christmas came upon them. As January 7 – Christmas Day (Julian Calendar) – approached, Vassili became apprehensive and uneasy. He earned a little pocket money from the emperor but what on earth could he buy that would be worthy of his beautiful grand duchess? When Christmas morning arrived in the Mauve Room, Tatiana presented to him on behalf of the imperial family a Louis Lowendall violin. Her smile had been radiant, her eyes dazzling as he unwrapped the beautiful instrument. The emperor himself had noticed how Vassili loved music and he informed him that his next task would be violin lessons. His face had burned with delight as he received the handsome gift, but he was now even more nervous about what he was about to give Tatiana. He knew that it was unthinkable that he would be expected to give any of the imperial family a gift but he wanted more than anything to show her that she was very special to him. Later in the day, as they sat alone in one of the cosy corners in the Maple Room, he finally plucked up the courage to awkwardly give her the small, flat rather grubby looking little package that he had wrapped in plain brown paper. In her enthusiasm to open the little parcel, it fell from its wrappings onto the floor at her feet. Vassili turned away in embarrassment but Tatiana squealed with delight at the charming, highly polished leather book mark. He had made it from an old unused saddle that he had found in the stables. In each face of the leather he had carved perfectly and very intricately and neatly the words to the Lord's Prayer. Tatiana was so pleased with the gift that she began to read even more books!

Christmas and New Year had now passed. The dark, cold evenings of mid-January looked even gloomier than usual.

No sooner had the girls and their mother left him alone to wait for the emperor, when the door opened again and in crept Tatiana, her finger to her lips, shushing him to be quiet. The little girl looked worried and apprehensive. With concern, Vassili immediately got up from his seat and they met in the middle of the large room.

"It's papa's crown," she said, but she was almost in tears, "I had another awful dream last night that it had been taken from him. That some bad men made him give it to them."

He stood directly in front of her and put his hands on her shoulders, comforting her. "Don't worry, Tanechka," he said. "I am sure it is safe in its hiding place. Come, let's see."

As he started towards the large maple cabinet on which the statue still stood, they heard the door to the room open again and in strode the emperor, his startling blue eyes studying them fondly.

"Come, Tanechka," he said smiling, "the boy has work to do, and I heard mama calling for you."

She looked hopefully at Vassili, who winked back at her.

The familiar smell of leather, wood and tobacco filled his nostrils as he sat in his usual chair opposite the emperor. There was only the usual array of many framed photographs of Nicolas's beloved family on his highly polished desk, but not the usual history book in front of him. Vassili wondered what it was that he would be studying. Nicholas watched him keenly as he looked at the empty space on the desk in front of the emperor.

"There are no books that have recorded fully what you are to learn today, my boy. The story I am about to tell you has been handed down from generation to generation," said Nicholas, looking at the boy keenly.

Vassili sat up straighter in his chair. It sounded as if Nicholas was going to teach him some more of the 'secret' history of Russia.

"It is time for you to hear another story," declared the emperor, "though there will be no need to make an oath of secrecy to me this time, Vassili. This time your promise of secrecy I pray will be made to another."

Vassili was a little puzzled; not uncommon during his many lessons with the emperor, but he was still very eager to hear the story. Nicholas continued to stare at him with clear, unblinking eyes, searching his face. Vassili returned the gaze.

"Yes my boy, I think you are ready!" the emperor declared. He cleared his throat. "In 1275 AD there lived a Prussian prince whose name was Glanda Kambila. During that year his country came under attack from invading Teutonic forces

– forces we would now call German. Much of this time in history is shaded in shadow, but what we do know is that he fled his country, fearing for his life. We are not sure of what his intentions were, for first he travelled south through Austria, down through northwest Italy until eventually he came to the shores of the Adriatic where he sought refuge for a while at the lagoons of what is now called Venice. He had now become so poor that his only source of food was the fish from the sea. It was while he was fishing one day that he discovered a mysterious cave, and inside this cave he came upon a curious sight: two boxes. One was made of wood and really was nothing to behold, but the other gleamed golden orange from the evening sun that peeked through the small entrance to the cave. It was obviously made of gold. Being of an unassuming and modest character, Glanda investigated the wooden box first and on opening it, he discovered a strange pair of black shoes, so light it was as if they were made of air itself. But as humble as his new circumstances had made him, his eyes were drawn to the golden box. It was about the length of a man's forearm and half that in width. Struggling with his curiosity, he again returned to the wooden box and decided to try on the shoes. Although the box seemed to be very old and worn, the shoes were incredibly well preserved – as if they had only been left there recently. Unfortunately, the condition of the shoes were tarnished somewhat by a rather bad odour. They were also a little large and did not fit him. His attention was irresistibly drawn again to the other box. His suspicion that it was made of pure gold was confirmed when he lifted it, for it was heavy. It had the shape as if topped with a lid, though there were no hinges or seal line. Still, he was inclined to try to open it to see what was inside, but he could not. As he looked at his bedraggled reflection in the highly polished lid, he saw that there were strange letters carved upon it; letters the likes of which he had never seen before. As he looked closer, the letters began to move and distort into one another until he found that he could understand what was written.

In flesh I am formed
In maple I am laid
When the egg is opened
All will be remade.

His eyes grew wide with the miracle that had taken place before him and he read the words aloud. Immediately, the hidden hinges operated and the lid sprang open.

"What was inside?" Vassili asked, quite mesmerised with the story so far.

The emperor stared at him, his blue eyes intense and searching. He ignored the question and continued.

"He gently closed the lid, and as he did so the letters again distorted, back to their original unreadable formation. Glanda left the shoes inside the wooden box upon one of the jagged rock shelves but he took the golden box with him. As soon as he stepped out of the cave, there was an almighty crash and a boom; looking behind him, he saw that the narrow cave entrance had completely closed shut, leaving not even a hairline crack. Immediately, his fortune seemed to change, at least for a while, and he was able to secure his passage on a ship that was bound for the Black Sea. He left the ship at Yalta and from there he journeyed by land to Russia. It is here that we lose track of his affairs except that his son, Andrei Kobyla, rose to prominence in 1347 as a boyar under Semyon 1 of Moscow, and that on his death bed, Glanda gave to Andrei the beautiful golden box that he had kept safe through his years of hardship and toil, never once thinking to sell it to relieve the strain of poverty. He told Andrei what lay inside the box, and made him swear an oath that he would keep it secret and never part with it. Andrei took it in wonder for he was baffled that his father had been in possession of such a beautiful and obviously valuable item, yet for most of his life had remained in poverty. Andrei Kobyla, however, became very wealthy; he married and had many sons and daughters. But he never forgot the words of his father and it seemed to him now that the box was part of his family and must be handed down accordingly to the son most worthy to possess it. He therefore entrusted the golden box to his youngest son Feodor, instructing him to always keep it secret and safe and then pass it on to his most worthy of sons."

Vassili was fascinated. This was much more interesting than his 'conventional' history lessons, where he would learn about some of the old tsars like Peter the Great or Ivan the Terrible. Nicholas seemed unusually animated too, as if he was immensely proud to be telling him this story. The emperor lit a cigarette and blew out the smoke as he continued.

"Feodor was nicknamed Koshka, which means cat. Eventually, as traditionally happened in our country, over the years his descendants took the surname Koshkin. This changed again to Zakharin. Always, the box was handed down to the son deemed most worthy of it. Then somehow the secret of the golden box was discovered, though it was never confirmed, for no one could ever read the strange letters on its lid. A rift in the family then occurred, causing them to split into two branches. They now renamed themselves Yakovlev and Yuriev. After giving land to the Yakovlevs, the Yurievs kept the box.

Nicholas put his cigarette down and stubbed it out prematurely in the small glass ash tray on his desk. "I suppose you wonder what this is all about?" he said a slight smile on his face. "All families come from somewhere, Vassili. Some rise to greatness and wealth; others are destined for greatness in other ways. The line of Yuriev continued to be affluent and the grandchildren of Roman Yuriev, due to his immense influence and their love for him, changed their name to Romanov."

Vassili's mouth opened and his eyes grew wide as he suddenly realised that Nicholas was telling him the history of the ancestry of the House of Romanov; but where did this golden box fit into all this?

"So now the keeper of the box is a Romanov." He smiled again at Vassili's eager yet slightly puzzled face. "It was at this time, in 1547 actually, that the Romanov's fortunes changed again for the better. Roman's daughter Anastasia married the Rukrid grand prince of Moscow, Ivan IV, who incidentally was the first to assume the title of tsar. Anastasia therefore became the first tsarina. It was during their son Feodor's reign that his right to rule was contested by his brother-in-law, Boris Godunov and by his Romanov cousins. When he died childless, the seven-hundred-year old Rurik Dynasty came to an end, but on his death bed, suspecting that Boris Godunov would be victorious in his fight for the crown, the gentle and pious Feodor gave the box to Feodor Nikitich Romanov, who he favoured for the tsardom. A bitter fight now ensued for the crown between Godunov and the Romanovs and when Godunov won the battle and was elected tsar in 1599, his wrath upon the Romanovs was terrible. He had heard about the beautiful golden box and the wonder of what was rumoured to be kept within. He deemed that as tsar it should belong to him. Of course, the Romanovs were not willing to give it up to him. So he banished them all to the cold uninhabitable lands of northern Russia, where most of them died of hunger. The box was not lost, however, for it was still in the possession of Feodor Nikitich Romanov, who had become the family leader. He was forced to take refuge in the Antoniev Siysky Monastery. But Feodor never lost hope. He was compelled to reveal the golden box to the priest of the monastery, who declared that the box was indeed of great religious importance and with his help the whereabouts of the box was kept secret and safe. It was this priest who suggested that perhaps the words engraved on the lid were the key to opening it, and that when the words could be understood it would miraculously open. But no amount of study or research they performed could decipher those letters. It was also this priest that suggested that this golden box and its precious contents were to become the foundation of our country. So in order to keep the box and its keeper hidden, Feodor Romanov changed his identity and he now became known as Feodor Filaret."

Vassili held his breath while the emperor told him what happened next.

"Feodor knew that the box had been entrusted to the Romanovs and that at the right time the box would open and its contents would be revealed. I am sure he must have wondered, as I do, why we had been given this tremendous gift, for we deserve it no more than any other family. We try to live up to its expectations, Vassili, but just like every other family, we fail."

Vassili knew that he had been told something enormously important, and that he was incredibly privileged to be part of the emperor's inner circle. He felt an immense love for the kind, gentle man sitting across from him, even though he had not specifically told him what the box contained. The emperor continued:

"Then, with the fall of the Gordunov dynasty in the June of 1604, our beloved country entered the 'Time of Troubles,' and along came the 'imposter tsars.' Demetrius I claimed to be the youngest son of Ivan the Terrible, but his real name was Grigory Otrepyev. Fortunately for Russia, his reign only lasted a year. Then another imposter, Dimitri II, came to the throne; he also claimed to be that same son of Ivan the Terrible. Unfortunately for him, it was discovered that the real son Dimitri had been assassinated in 1591. However, during the reign of these imposters, Feodor Romanov was given the recognition for who he was and he was able to come out of hiding; indeed, Dimitri II raised him to the dignity of Patriarch. On the death of Dimitri II and finally seeing the need to revert back to the 'old bloodline' in 1612, the Zemsky Sobor (Assembly of Land) offered the crown to several of the still surviving Rurik princes, but they all declined it. Feodor was now living with his sixteen – year-old son Mikhail at Ipatiev Monastery in Kostroma when the crown was offered to Mikhail. At first Mikhail burst into tears, for he did not want the dreadful burden of ruling Russia. But then his father showed him the box and explained to him that it had been passed down through the years; that it was said to contain the parchment of life on which is inscribed the very song that God sang while creating the earth and that each keeper of the box had risen in strength and was able to overcome all their trials. The box was now his, for he believed that this was the very purpose for which the box had been found. Mikhail gained strength from this knowledge and accepted the crown of Russia. He was a good and noble ruler. He established close ties with the Ruriks and took the advice from the Zemsky Sobor on all important issues. He was considered a good tsar. Every Romanov ruler since, including Mikhail Romanov, has taken strength from the golden box in their own 'times of trouble.' They all made many mistakes, as we are all inclined to, for it is our form, but we know that as long as the box is in our possession, our dynasty shall not fail."

Nicholas stood and strode over to the large arched window. The pale sun filtered through the gray clouds in insipid tones of yellow. Ice coated with a heavy frost was spread across the lake. The old willow was sad, gray, cold and bare. "We have unrest among our own people even as I speak," he said, "but I take strength from God and from what is his."

Vassili was well aware of the wave of strikes that had engulfed the city of St Petersburg. The Assembly of Russian Working Men, with Father Gapon at their head, were due to march to the square and the Winter Palace tomorrow in a mass demonstration, where they would hand their petitions and air their grievances to the tsar himself. But Nicholas, under advice from his security police, had moved from the Winter Palace where he stayed occasionally to be nearer to the city, back to the Alexander Palace and the less threatened Tsarskoe Selo.

"Only I, the empress, and now you, Vassili, know of the secret of the golden box. It has been laid on my heart to tell you of it; for what reason, only time will tell. At all costs, the box must be kept safe. As long as it is, the house of Romanov will not fall."

The lesson was over. He could sense that the emperor had grown pensive and troubled as he had talked about the forthcoming march. He was also troubled himself, as if a great burden had suddenly been placed upon his shoulders. He wondered why the emperor had trusted him with such knowledge. After being dismissed, he left Nicholas in his study and trotted down the stairs and into the Maple Room. It was empty. He swiftly strode over to the cabinet where the statue of the Napoleonic soldier stood as always. He lifted it; grasping the cork at its base, he gave it a mighty pull. It came out with a pop. He shook the statue from side to side and out fell the little heavy, dark gray metal box. He lifted the lid quickly with his thumb nail and was relieved, as much for himself as he was for Tatiana, that the tiny replica of the tsar's crown along with the tiny sapphire pendant still lay inside. He quickly dropped it back into the statue and placed the statue back into its place on the cabinet. It was then that he noticed, through the glass door of the cabinet, the beautiful egg-shaped ornaments arranged in an oval circle around something else; a box of some sort. But the cabinet was dark inside and he could not quite make out what it was. He tried the door of the cabinet, fully expecting it to be locked. It opened quite easily with a low creak. Light filled the cabinet. The beautiful ornamental eggs surrounded a long, low, gold-coloured box. He peered closer and could just see faint letters or runes carved into the lid of the box. Was this the very box that the emperor had just told him about? He stepped back in shock and surprise. At that moment, he heard the sound of the main door to the Maple Room open. He pushed the door of the cabinet shut quickly.

"Hello, Vassili!" cried the empress. "Has your lesson finished?" She walked over to him, smiling; her face changed to concern as she saw the guilty look on Vassili's face. She stopped. "What were you doing in the cabinet, Vassili?" she asked.

Vassili backed away from the cabinet, "Err… nothing m'am!" Even though he had been accepted as part of the family, he was pretty sure he had over stepped the boundaries by opening the cabinet door in which the parchment was hidden.

But the empress made light of the situation. "I have no doubt that you have learned by now that there are some things you are allowed to touch and some things that you are not allowed; the contents of that cabinet are definitely of the latter."

"Errr … I am sorry, m'am!" answered Vassili, not knowing what to say.

"Well, run along boy, before you are tempted to open any other forbidden doors!" The empress's tone was forceful but without malice. She was sure she had caught the young boy merely snooping with curiosity at the Fabergé eggs.

"Yes m'am!" said Vassili sheepishly as he disappeared through the door. The empress looked at the cabinet thoughtfully. As she did so, its door slowly swung open again with a creak. She bent down to look at the eggs. It is so important to keep them safe, she thought. We really should have a lock fitted. Then her eye caught the golden box. "I will speak to Nicholas," she said out loud and then mounted the stairs to have tea with her husband.

*

The war with Japan was to be both a humiliation and an utter disaster for Nicholas and for the Russian people. After the loss of the charismatic Admiral Makarov, who had been perhaps the most single effective naval strategist of the war, the shame and embarrassment of the siege of Port Arthur continued. Learning quickly from their adversaries, the Russians soon employed their own tactics of offensive mine laying and on 15 May, they took heart when two Japanese battleships, the Yashima and the Hatsuse, struck at least two mines each. The Hatsuse sank within minutes, taking the lives of four hundred and fifty sailors with her. The Yashima sank a little later while being towed to Korea for repairs. But the Russian fleet was still trapped in the harbour, unable to break through the blockade imposed by the Japanese. In mid-April, another attempt was made to break through under the new command of Admiral Vilgelm Vitgift, but it failed again to the effect that by the end of the month the Russian fleet was in serious threat of being obliterated by the shells that the Japanese had now started firing into the harbour. The siege was to continue for the rest of the year and the situation deteriorated further for the Russians when the Japanese captured the key hilltop bastion in December, enabling them to fire their long range artillery down into the harbour and wreak havoc upon the exposed Russian squadron, whose retaliation was completely ineffective. Unable to break through the blockade and to defend itself against the bombardment from the precise shelling from the overlooking hills, the remainder of the squadron was doomed. Before long, four Russian battleships and two cruisers had been sunk, causing further carnage and loss of lives. The fifth battleship made a final attempt to escape and miraculously finally succeeded in slipping through the blockade to head home as the sole survivor of the once proud and impregnable Russian Pacific Fleet.

On land, the war was not going much better either for Nicholas. The attempt to relieve the besieged city of Port Arthur also failed at the battle of Liaoyang in late August of 1904. When Stessel, the commander of the Northern Russian force, saw that the fleet had all but been destroyed, he withdrew his troops and retreated to Shenyang. Stessel now believed that the reason to defend the city had been lost. The loss of Russian lives throughout the conflict had been terribly high due to the ceaseless, persistent bombardment of the Japanese guns. So on 2 January 1905, he made the decision to surrender. However this decision was taken without first consulting Nicholas, who disagreed vehemently. What had been unthinkable for the Russians at the outset of the war had now taken place – the harbour and the city of Port Arthur lay in the hands of the Japanese. (In 1908, Stessel was court-martialled and sentenced to death for disobeying orders, but Nicholas later pardoned him.)

*

The Empress Alexandra sipped her coffee thoughtfully as she sat in the emperor's study. Her husband stood before her in full military regalia. He had just returned from a meeting to discuss the latest crisis to hit his country.

"The Stachka (Strike) is upon Saint Petersburg, Alix," he warned her. "The people are in revolt. Grandfather's emancipation has only brought higher expectations and in these times those expectations cannot be fulfilled. This disastrous war is depleting our resources and putting even more pressure on our people. We must change things, Alix. We *have* to make changes."

"But you are their emperor, Nikky! You have God's given right to rule; what changes could you possibly be referring to?" Alexandra asked. She put her cup down, uncharacteristically clattering it against the saucer, spilling some of the coffee.

Ignoring her question, Nicholas continued, "Gapon at this very minute is organising a demonstration. He wants to present me with a petition at the Narva Gate. They just want me to be aware of their plight, Alix, but I will not even be there to receive it. I am advised that like a thief in the night I must steal away to the safety of the Alexander Palace here in Tsarskoe Selo."

"Don't worry, my darling," the empress answered soothingly, "Grand Duke Vladimir will take care of the situation." She looked at him with her steady blue eyes. "You cannot take the blame for incompetent admirals and generals, hubby. This dreadful war has not been your fault."

"But I should have been there, Alix," he cried with frustration and rested his hand on the hilt of his sword, "I should have been leading the armies myself, just as I should be facing my own people tomorrow morning and accepting their petition and listening to their grievances. Uncle Vladimir, as usual, informs me that I am not needed and he will take care of the problem. Am I not the leader of the people?"

"Calm down, my darling," said the empress picking up her cup again, "it will all blow over. It always does."

Nicholas strode across the room, unconvinced. He loved his wife very much but sometimes he felt patronised a little by her. It was enough that he had to deal with Grand Duke Vladimir!

"Alix!" he said firmly standing behind his desk, "this march tomorrow comes from the heart of the people, our people. They are not coming to kill us or to harm us. They are merely making sure that we know of their unhappiness so that we can act and do what we can to change it. This is not a march organised by the Bolsheviks, Mensheviks or Social Democrats; in fact, I am told that they even disapprove of the march as the petition's demands are not political."

Alexandra flipped through her small personal bible that rested on her lap. She carried it with her most times during the day. Nicholas himself had given it to her when they had first made the Alexander Palace their home. She found the passage she had been looking for.

"*In thee, O Lord, do I put my trust,*
Let me never be ashamed;

Deliver me in thy righteousness;
Bow down thine ear to me, deliver me speedily.
Be thou my strong rock,
For a house of defence, to save me.
For thou art my rock and my fortress,
Therefore for thy name's sake lead me and guide me.'"

(Psalm 31)

The emperor listened intently as he always did when she read to him from her bible. He stroked his beard thoughtfully. "I must trust in the Lord to guide me in this task I have been given," he said, "and perhaps not so much in the often ill advice given by my uncles."

She looked up at him again with calm, steady, deep-blue eyes. "All is still safe, my darling," she said, seeking to comfort him further. "I looked upon it this very morning. Though I do think we ought to at least put a lock or something on the cabinet, Nicky. Do you know I caught that young scoundrel Vassili looking in our cupboards downstairs?" She chuckled again at the thought of Vassili's very guilty face when she had caught him.

"You mean the box?" he asked.

She nodded. "As you imply Nicky, times are perhaps changing, so perhaps we do need to be a little more vigilant with something that is so important to our house."

Nicholas studied his wife a moment. How he valued her love and support!

"Alix, it is something that has always been there. Father kept it at Livadia, grandfather at Peterhof. It is our time now and we keep here with us, for we have made this our home. But strangely enough, I have never felt the need to have it guarded. For to all except us, it is merely a beautiful golden box, in monetary value probably worth less than say the eggs or most of the other

170

jewels. But now you mention it, I would feel easier if it were guarded. I will speak to Master Hercules."(Her Ku Luss) Then, as if a weight had been taken from him, he smiled. "Vassili has come along nicely, don't you think?" he said.

Alexandra pursed her lips. Though the wood burning in the fireplace gave off quite adequate heat to warm the room, she shivered slightly and covered her shoulders with the woollen shawl that rested on the arm of her chair. "You still think that he is right for one of the girls?" she asked. "He is not even a distant relative!"

"His bloodline is noble, Alix," the emperor answered stiffly. "He would make an excellent choice for one of the girls if they decide that they want to stay in Russia and not marry a foreign prince."

The empress chose her words carefully. She was quite aware of her husband's affection towards the young boy.

"He just seems so uncommunicative," she answered him. "I really struggle to draw him out of his shell. He barely says two words to anyone. You are never quite sure what is really going on in that head of his; what he is really thinking!"

The emperor was not perturbed. "We must give him time, Alix. He lost his mother at birth; time with his father has been very limited. The one who could really have helped him along was also taken. Though I do know what you mean about his uneasiness with people: perhaps it is more shyness than slyness and I think a lack of trust?" Nicholas picked up the 'Short Stories from History' book that he had first read to Vassili. He stared at it thoughtfully. "Yes," he said seeming to make his mind up, "I think that he struggles to trust people apart from you and me."

"And of course, Tatiana!" declared the empress, smiling at her husband with only her mouth.

"And Tatiana," agreed Nicholas, returning her smile.

*

171

In the freezing predawn hours, men, women and their children began to gather in the industrial areas on the outskirts of St Petersburg. Their fatigued, pale faces were emphasised all the more by the darkness that surrounded them for there was no light from the empty starless sky above. Most had eyes that were puffy and red through lack of sleep. It was an icy winter's morning, and all were wrapped in their warmest garments. Steel barrels stood on the street corners, filled with whatever fuel was available to burn. Groups huddled around them in an effort to stave off the searching, icy fingers of a Russian winter wind. Mothers kept their children close to them. There was no laughter and very little chatter. The mood was sullen, though not without hope, for they had brought along with them their holy icons and pictures of the tsar. As they waited patiently, a beautiful deep, lone voice began to sing. Then a woman's voice harmonised and soon the breath from the mouths of three thousand souls formed a literal white mist as the mood changed and they enthusiastically sang hymns, including 'God Save the Tsar.' For this gathering was not revolutionary, or a rebellion of any kind, for that matter. If anything, the march was anti – revolutionary. For their leader, Father Gapon, had instilled in his movement the traditional conservative values of orthodoxy and faith in the autocratic tsar. Obviously 'our little father' was unaware of their plight. The line of communication must have been broken somewhere between the factory managers and him – those same abusive, power-drunken factory managers that enforced long working hours, squalid working environments and horrific safety conditions. It was generally felt among the working class that it had been better to work under the noble landowners prior to their emancipation of 1861 under Alexander II. Surely if the tsar knew of their plight he would help them! For after all, he was appointed by God and therefore obligated to do what was right for his people. Slowly, the singing faltered and then stopped altogether. A commotion had begun. They looked up from the fires; their heavily gloved hands thudded together as they stamped their feet to fend off the cold. A voice cried out in dismay. "The emperor is not home. Our little father is not at the palace to receive our grievances!" The mood of the people changed again to one of foreboding. An ominous expectation hung in the hollow predawn air as they waited in silence for their leader.

*

The petition had been prepared at Father Gapon's headquarters, 'Gapon Hall' on the Shlisselburg Tract in Saint Petersburg. It detailed clearly their demands for improved working conditions, higher wages, and a reduction in working hours of no more than eight hours daily. It also sanctioned an end to the 'needless' and very costly war with Japan.

Georgi Apollonovich Gapon set his pen down carefully on the desk in front of him. He sighed deeply. His long wavy hair cascaded over his shoulders and halfway down his back. He was a distinguished and charismatic leader. Though having been born to a lowly family of peasants in the Crimea, he showed promise in the studies of religion at a young age and was educated in a theological seminary. Later he graduated from the Saint Petersburg Theological Academy while being employed as a religious teacher at the Saint Olga orphanage. It was here that he became passionately involved with the poor, the destitute and particularly with the factory workers. His ambitions and contacts brought him financial aid from Colonel Motojiro Akashi of the Japanese Imperial Army to form the 'Assembly of Russian Factory and Mill Workers of Saint Petersburg'. The purpose of this assembly was not only to defend its member's rights as workers but to also educate them in moral and religious issues. However, the organisation was soon infiltrated by Nicholas's Okhrana (secret police) in order to make sure that the body did not become one of political intent with revolutionary tendencies.

Indeed, at first the political parties such as the Bolsheviks and the Mensheviks *despised* Gapon for his lack of political intent.

Gapon had also decreed that all members had to be of the Russian Orthodox denomination but this certainly did not prevent the Assembly from rapidly growing into twelve branches and gaining eight thousand members in total.

Father Gapon reread the last lines of the petition, memorising it. Then he stood up as if practicing a speech. "And if thou dost not so order and does not respond to our pleas," he cried passionately, "we will die here in this square before thy gate." He spoke the words very loudly and forcefully, as his great, long beard wagged in shadow on the wall. Satisfied, he sat down again. "Pinchas!" he shouted again. A young man, looking worried and apprehensive, immediately appeared in the doorway. "Take this copy to the Ministry of the Interior, along with 'the intention to march'!" Gapon handed the two documents to the young man, who quickly looked at the petition, and read it briefly. "I hope these last lines do not become prophetic, Father," he said gravely, "we know how hot-headed the Imperial guards can be."

Father Gapon smiled. "The emperor knows what must to be done, Pinchas. He is fully aware that when he receives the petition and acts upon it, the credit will be for his account and not for one of the political parties. It is in his interest to support us. This war with Japan and his unwavering determination to try to win it no matter the cost is playing perfectly into the hands of the revolutionists. If he shows us support, the people will be more forgiving of the hardships thrust upon them and will love him more." He leaned forward and with both hands lifted his kamelaukion (tall cylindrical hat worn by Russian Orthodox priests) from the desk and placed it carefully upon his head. "I will hand the petition to the emperor myself!" he declared.

Pinchas looked away awkwardly. "You do not know Holy Father?" He asked.

Gapon looked at him quizzically.

"The emperor left the Winter Palace yesterday! He has returned to the Alexander Palace at Tsarskoe Selo to be with his family," Pinchas said.

Father Gapon quickly stood up again, clearly shocked. "Is the emperor mad, stupid, or just plain indifferent!" he cried. He snatched the petition back from Pinchas' grasp and banged it down flat with the palm of his hand onto the desk again. "Surely his uncle, Grand Duke Vladimir, *must* have informed him of the march and the consequences for not at least listening to his people's grievances. The duke is the head of the Secret Police; he is certainly fully aware of the situation."

"It is he, I am told Holy Father, that will receive the petition in the emperor's absence," answered Pinchas, his own voice cracking with emotion.

Father Gapon spread his hands wide upon his desk, studying the petition again.

"So, once again Nicholas plays the game of hiding behind one of his uncles," said Gapon, rubbing his beard in agitation, "no doubt this is a ploy to get us to cancel the march! But that is not going to happen, Pinchas!" He picked up the petition again, and folded it neatly. "They are waiting for me and I will not disappoint them. Nicholas can play his games, but the petition *will* be delivered."

*

Grand Duke Vladimir was one of Nicholas's four paternal uncles. In 1894, when Nicholas had attended the wedding of Alexandra's brother, Ernest Duke of Hesse, he also had a proposal for her hand in marriage on his lips, and he welcomed the support and accompaniment of his stalwart uncle. The occasion would be intimidating to say the least, for the wedding was also to be attended by Europe's finest royalty, including the seventy-five year old Queen Victoria, her son

Edward the Prince of Wales and her nephew, Kaiser Wilhelm ll of Germany. Not long after the acceptance by Alexandra of his proposal, Nicholas's father had died, leaving him totally unprepared to carry the weight of the crown of Russia. Vladimir and his brothers fully intended to help him carry the burden. Vladimir's meddling began with his insistence that Nicholas marry his new bride in public and not in private at Livadia, as both Nicholas and Alexandra had wanted. Out of respect, Nicholas relented to his demand. Unfortunately, the respect for his uncle led Nicholas to a very unpopular decision very soon after his wedding and coronation, when a disaster occurred at Khodynka Meadow. Thousands of Muscovites gathered in an open field that had previously been used for army manoeuvres and was therefore riddled with trenches. They were eager to get their first glimpse of the handsome new tsar and his beautiful tsarina. Unfortunately, a rumour spread that the promised free food and beer was about to run out. This caused a stampede of catastrophic consequences, culminating in hundreds of people being crushed to death, and thousands injured and hospitalised. The French government meanwhile had planned to hold a French ball in honour of the new tsar and his bride, for Russia was France's only European ally. This had been planned in advance to take place, unfortunately, the day after the tragedy; enormous expense had been borne by the French government in organising the ball. Nicholas's first reaction, however, was to retreat to a place of prayer and to mourn for the dead and injured. Afraid that Nicholas and Alexandra's absence from the ball would seriously offend the French, Vladimir advised and indeed insisted that Nicholas attend with his new bride. Nicholas, being inexperienced in the affairs of state, took the ill advice. This show of apparent indifference did not go down well with the Russian people. Over the next ten years, the mild-mannered Nicholas would be intimidated and bullied into doing what his father's brothers wanted him to do. For instance, if one of their favourite generals needed a special favour from the tsar, it would be granted. If a Russian ballet in Paris was wanted by one of his uncle's favourite Russian ballerinas, permission for the Paris season would be granted by the tsar. For the next ten years, the indecisive Nicholas was also to lose face and respect from many of his own aristocracy. Most recently, when Nicholas could see that his army and navy were demoralised during the war with Japan, against his own good conscience he did not make the trip to the front in order to boost the morale of his armed forces, but instead stayed at home with his family.

Ironically, on Sunday, 22 January 1905, Grand Duke Vladimir had, at the last minute, decided to take the same advice that he had given to Nicholas and not to be present at the Winter Palace during the handing in of the petition. He had given the responsibility of handling the demonstration to one of his favoured generals.

Commander Prince Vasilchikov sat upon his great dappled charger. He was seemingly alone in the vast, empty Palace Square. His horse's hooves clattered on the cobbled paving, echoing in the freezing stillness, as he trotted around the gigantic column that stood in the centre of the square. He gazed up at the forty-seven-and-a-half meter red granite column to its summit where the angel carried the cross. It was said that the face of the angel bore a striking similarity to the face of Alexander I. He stared proudly at the magnificent monument. It had been erected in recognition of the Russian victory in the war with Napoleon's France and had been named after the then Tsar Alexander I. It had taken three thousand men to erect it in less than two hours, even though it weighed over six hundred tons. His eyes traced the column again from top to bottom and then fixed on the engraving at the base on one of the four sides: 'To Alexander I from a grateful Russia.' The palace opposite was dark and deserted; he shivered slightly as the gust of an icy breeze blew around him. Suddenly, red rays of light streamed down from the awakening sky and lit up himself and the column. He blinked and squinted up at the rising sun, shadowing his face with his hand. He then looked down towards the Nevsky Prospekt. The sound was unmistakable – the deep-throated resonance of Russian voices singing 'God Save the Tsar.' The sun gave no warmth and he shivered a little. Then, drawing his sabre, he saluted the statue and reined his horse to the left, signalling to the orderly lines of silent troops that were standing to attention at the far end of the square. His orders were that under no circumstances were the crowd to enter the square. The lines of the troops moved quickly to block the access from the Prospekt to the Palace Square. He had recently been informed by a member of the Okhrana of rumours that Gapon was cooperating with certain individuals whose intention it was to end the autocracy of the tsar and to set up a Duma. "Russia has run for centuries under the God-given right of the tsar and it will continue to do so for many more," he had told the informer. "If Gapon wants to use the people as puppets for his real purpose, let him do so. We will deal with him."

*

Father Gapon arrived on the outskirts of the city of Saint Petersburg on a wooden cart drawn by an old farm horse. When the crowd saw him, it surged forward to greet him. He climbed up onto the back of the cart as the people massed around him.

"Fellow workers!" he cried. The mass of people stood silently listening, reaching out for any thread of hope that the Holy Father might have brought. The cry of a baby echoed in the cold stillness. "I have just learned, my friends that 'our little father' is not at home to listen to our grievances. Once again, it seems that he would prefer to hide away and ignore the hardships of his faithful people. We all know it was tradition in Mother Russia for two hundred years to bring a chelobitnaya (petition) to our tsar, so as to communicate our grievances in order to make sure he was aware of our hardships; to submit it to the Prikaz office in Moscow."

Suddenly, a loud distinct voice interrupted him.

"But that tradition was abolished, my friends! Abolished by the house of Romanov!"

There was a ripple of disquiet through the demonstrators. This was true. It was the ancestors of Nicholas Romanov that had abolished this tradition.

"In those days, my fellow workers," Gapon continued, looking blindly at the multitude of faces, trying to see who it was that had spoken, "our tsar would make an appearance outside the Winter Palace and the people would give the petition to him, even talk to him."

"Yes!" cried the voice. "That was when the tsar cared for his people; when he loved his people. This tsar does not care for us or love us; he only cares for his fabulous jewels and his spoiled brat children and wife!"

Father Gapon looked out in the direction of the voice for its owner, but still could not make out clearly where it came from. The crowd were now beginning to become angry. "Yes! Gold and diamonds is all he cares for!" shouted an old woman.

"Friends!" continued Father Gapon, "We must not lose sight of our intention today! It is the contents of the petition that we are concerned with, nothing more."

"What about his Easter Eggs!" shouted the voice again, "What about his priceless Fabergé eggs that he keeps as nothing more than eye candy for himself and his family, while his people starve."

Father Gapon again tried to pick out the voice in the crowd, but again he could not see who it was that had spoken.

The crowd had become much more emotional. A sense of volatility hung in the air. Father Gapon was uneasy. He remembered the last few words of the petition that he had specifically composed for the heart strings of the tsar himself. The situation was possibly getting out of his control.

"We have nothing but misery," came the voice again, "Barely enough cloth on our backs to protect us from the cold, barely enough dinner in our belly's to stop us thinking about breakfast while our so-called little father eats trifles from a golden spoon just for the taste."

"Who is that devil?" cried Father Gapon, turning to Pinchas.

But the crowd had had enough. Without waiting for Father Gapon to lead them, they started the long walk through the cold grey streets of Saint Petersburg towards the Palace Square. Their singing began again. But it was mournful and forlorn. On the horizon, a hint of a blood red sun began to appear. Father Gapon quickly jumped down from the wooden cart and with Pinchas Rutenburg tailing him, he ran after the crowd.

*

Vassili could not sleep. Earlier it had been one of the evenings when he'd had after-dinner coffee with the family in the Maple Room. But Tatiana had not been herself. They had stolen away into one of the cosy corners while the empress was showing Olga how to embroider. She was clearly distraught and her little hand held his tightly under the pink woollen blanket that was spread across her lap, as she told him that the previous evening again she'd had the dream where someone had stolen her papa's crown.

"We need to take it away, Vassili. We need to hide it somewhere where they will never find it!" she said almost tearfully.

Vassili looked over to where the empress and Olga sat huddled together, engrossed in the embroidery lesson. He gazed across to the staircase that led to the mezzanine and on to the emperor's study.

"I think we should tell your father," he said, "I think he should know if somebody is trying to take his crown away."

Tatiana looked at him in horror. "No!" she whispered, as loudly as she dare, "my papa has enough worries with the war and our poor little ill brother; we mustn't worry him anymore!"

Vassili raised both eyebrows in surprise. "The heir is ill?" he asked.

"I am not supposed to say anything, but both mama and papa are dreadfully worried about him," she answered, her eyes beginning to water.

"What is wrong with him?" he asked. He had never seen the six-month-old boy. But like everyone else in the household and in the whole of Russia, he had been mightily pleased when the tsar and tsarina had finally been blessed with a male heir.

"Every time he takes a knock or a tumble, a large blue swelling appears. In fact, yesterday he banged his face only ever so slightly; the swelling was so bad that both his eyes have now shut." As she finished speaking, Tatiana buried her face in her hands. Vassili wanted to hug her and comfort her and tell her that all would be right, but he knew that would never be allowed.

"I will hide the statue somewhere else," he said simply, "where no one will ever find it."

Or perhaps, he thought to himself, I should put the crown and pendant back where they belong!

Tatiana took her hands from her face. It was red and wet with tears. "Oh, please Vassili; please do that!" Then she looked at him thoughtfully, "But of course, you will show me where you have hidden it."

"I will take it tonight and hide it and then tomorrow I will show you where," he answered. He would tell Tatiana tomorrow what he had done. Surely the emperor would be pleased if he found that the little crown was back where it was supposed to be. Perhaps Tatiana would then stop worrying. He really thought that her dreams were more to do with the guilt of her having hidden it in the first place. He would fix things and make everybody happy!

"Do it early in the morning," she said, nipping the thin skin on the back of his hand and sighing softly, "then you can tell me where you put it at breakfast time."

Vassili stifled a yelp, but still managed to smile at her. It lifted his heart to think he could do something to make her happy.

The Maple Room was cold, dark and quiet when Peabody and Smith arrived there just before dawn on Sunday, 22 January 1905. The candle that the timer had provided them seemed only bright enough to cast eerie shadows on the wall; the room around them was very dim.

"Phew, boss! We got out of that place just in time. Things were getting a little heated. I certainly didn't like the look of those Russian soldiers looking at *us*," said Smith, his voice echoing around the cavernous room. "Why it didn't send us to that nice hot and sandy place like you asked it too, I don't know, boss. Do you think it enjoys messing us around?"

"Shhh, you nincompoop!" Peabody whispered furiously at him, "or we'll have plenty more of those Russian hooligans looking at us!" He looked over to the door of the room where a dim light seeped from underneath it. "The timer didn't send us to Richard the ding bat and his third crusade," he continued, whispering as loud as he dared, "because there was no need for it *obviously*; and stop clicking those blasted heels of yours on the floor! There could be a guard on the other side of that door!" Smith looked down at his smart leather shoes sheepishly while Peabody peered around the rest of the room until his eyes became accustomed to the dim light. "Yet you are right, Smith my man, I think my ventriloquism worked a treat, so we had better be quick because I suspect that the mob will not just be stopping off at the Winter Palace. I suspect I might have succeeded in antagonising them to come here, and they won't be calling for tea! When we get home, Smith, I expect to check the history books to find that old Nic was done away with a little earlier, which means I might get my hands on that blasted egg after all!"

"You were brilliant, boss, especially when you told that cavalry commander or whatever he was that Father Gapon was now working for the Bolshies. That really put the cat among the pigeons!" Smith whispered, hardly able to contain his adoration. It was just like the good old days, now that the timer was working again!

"Yes, yes, but never mind about that now, Smith my man! Let's focus on the task at hand," he whispered back. "'In Maple I am laid, In Maple I am laid.'" He thought to himself as he slowly scanned the room. They both began to explore its contents, starting along the perimeter and slowly working their way in.

"Stop crowding me, you oaf!" cried Peabody when Smith had bumped into him to avoid knocking over a chair. "In fact, you just stand still there where you are! That way you will not cause any mishaps!" commanded Peabody.

Smith stood stock still. He put both his hands in his pockets and whistled softly under his breath. Peabody turned and glared at him. "And stop that infernal racket!" he whispered furiously, "I need peace and quiet when I work."

Smith watched Peabody's dark silhouette silently move around the room, studying every shelf, every cabinet, and occasionally disappear as he moved stealthily into the shadowy cosy corners. He studied each wall looking for any sign of a secret panel. He cautiously moved to one side each and every painting, expecting to see some sort of compartment where the safe would be, but he found none. He scratched his head thoughtfully. "In maple I am laid," he whispered aloud. "But this is the Maple Room! Perhaps this is not going to be as easy as I expected!"

Smith blew hot breath onto his large, cold stiff fingers. The ticking of that damn clock was starting to eat away at his nerves.

He could no longer see his boss but he could make out his

shadow on the wall. Abruptly it stopped and bent down, as if looking at something. "Get yourself over here, Smith, and bring that candle with you."

Smith could just make out the dark shape of his boss to one side of a wide black expanse, which was possibly a staircase. He crept over to him, careful not to knock any of the porcelains from where they stood and onto the floor. The flame of the candle flickered alarmingly as the candle dripped welcomed hot wax onto the back of his cold, thick skinned, blue hand.

"What have we here?" Peabody whispered excitedly. He took the candle from Smith and rested it on the top of the cabinet next to the statue of the Napoleonic soldier. He bent down to look through its leaded glass doors. Smith knelt down behind him and peered over his shoulder.

"Bingo, boss!" he cried, unable to conceal his own excitement as he saw quite clearly, seven Fabergé eggs sitting upon their stands inside. Peabody looked at the key hole in the door. There was no locking mechanism visible. He stepped to one side of the cabinet and felt the smooth polished surface of the wood with his long skinny fingers. There was no catch or secret button that would release the door. He felt the other side, but there was nothing that would resemble a secret locking mechanism. He lay down on his back between the four legs of the sturdy cabinet. He felt as far as he could underneath and then up the back panels with the palm of his hands. He crawled out, and then sat on his haunches, deep in thought, flummoxed.

"Gosh, boss, the real ones are so much heavier. Have you felt the weight of this?"

Peabody looked up. His look of agitation turned to one of amazement as he saw one cabinet door wide open and the enormous dark shape of Smith with a very plain-looking egg almost smothered between the palms of his hands. He leapt to his feet. "How did you open the door, Smith?" he asked with a mixture of anger and suspicion.

"I just pulled that latch and it opened!" cried Smith, still holding the egg and pointing with his eyes to a perfect gold-coloured latch that was fixed on the door next to the key hole.

"You mean it wasn't even locked?" whispered Peabody astonished, and no less annoyed. "Old Nic is really going to be in for a nasty surprise in the morning. Give me that egg. Heavier? You idiot! It's the same one that we have at home!"

Scratching his head and looking extremely confused, Smith handed him the egg. Peabody could barely conceal his excitement. His hands shook as he took hold of the top of the opaque white, enamelled egg and lifted it. There inside was the perfect yellow golden yolk. With the tips of his delicate fingers he opened this to reveal the small golden hen. Smith took the candle from the cabinet and held it above their heads to give the revealing of Peabody's desire the wondrous sense of occasion it deserved. Peabody was breathing heavily and Smith eyes were wide with anticipation as he delicately opened up the hollow hen. Smith was so dumfounded that he almost dropped the candle as he stared at the tiny empty chamber. Peabody's eyes grew wide at first with astonishment and then anger. He took hold of the egg, snapping each compartment shut, and made as if to fling it to the other side of the room. Just in time, he managed to control himself.

"When did that little brat lose the bloody thing?" he whispered manically. "I'm beginning to wonder if this so-called tiny crown of Russia exists at all!"

"But boss, didn't Clodius tell you about it, and didn't he say that the egg is virtually worthless without it?"

For pointing out the obvious, Peabody finally did lose his temper now. With silent indignation, he promptly stamped on Smith's toe with the heel of his shoe, while at the same time he slapped the palm of his hand across Smith's mouth to stifle any sound that his poor accomplice had been inclined to make.

"Don't squeal like a girl, my friend!" he whispered, looking into the watery eyes of Smith menacingly, "I *will* find it one day!" He bent down and replaced the egg. As he did so, he caught sight of the long gold-coloured box that lay amidst the other Fabergé eggs. "Smith, you fool! The box is there! Now *that* is what I call *bingo!*" He reached inside and carefully placed the eggs to one side so that he could lift it out. It was heavy. He could not believe how heavy. "Here, Smith; help me with this!"

Smith knelt down gingerly beside his boss, careful not to put any weight onto his damaged big toe. Together they managed to pull the box forward to the edge of the shelf and then lift it out. They laid it on the thick carpet in front of them. "Don't bother about it now, Smith," said Peabody, noticing that Smith was looking in wonder at the strange runes carved into the surface of the lid. "We will inspect it properly when we get it home. Let's get the rest of the eggs at least."

"It's a pity, boss," whispered Smith as they systematically brought out the eggs from the cabinet and laid them on the carpet next to the golden box, "that we don't have any cami-knickers with us."

Peabody put the last egg on the floor in front of him and then scowled up at Smith. "Remember that draughty, nasty palace by the sea that Nicholas and his brood seemed to love so much? Remember that old Nic knew about our knicker-leaving shenanigans then, didn't he! Well, you idiot, if we *did* have any to leave, he will know by 1912 who left them and who stole his eggs and box. You imbecile!"

Smith thought a moment. "Yes, boss, but if we steal the eggs now, that would mean we wouldn't have a reason to go there anyway, would we?" answered Smith in one of his rare perceptive moments.

Peabody looked up, immediately grasping the significance of what Smith had just said. "I swear," he whispered, "If you showed those rare glimpses of intelligence just a little more often, you might one day pass your eleven plus, but as it is shut up, and take off one of your socks."

*

Vassili hid behind the pillar. He had not been aware that during the early morning hours the room was guarded. He peered around the pillar cautiously and down the hallway at the magnificent looking figure standing to one side of the door to the maple room.

Jim Hercules was a Nubian guard. He was often referred to as the 'Ethiopian,' but he was actually an American Negro. He had begun his service in the Russian Imperial family under Nicholas' father, Alexander III, and though often looked upon as a 'servant' by some of the ignorant visitors, he was bound only by his loyalty to the family. His relationship to them had become so close that on returning from a vacation to his native land he would present the children with jars of delicious guava jelly.

Vassili cursed his luck. If it had been any other of the guards, he was quite confident enough now to order the guard aside and enter the room to go about whatever business he had inside, middle of the night or not! But the mere presence of this enormous, ebony-coloured giant quite frightened him, notwithstanding the fact that he was sure he had seen disapproving looks from the 'brute' when he had first started to become acquainted with the tsar and his family. Now he merely did not look at him at all, but Vassili felt the whites of his eyes burning into the back of his neck when he walked passed him. He imagined he could see the guard's black nostrils flaring with annoyance even from behind the pillar. Jim Hercules (Herr Ku luss) was at least six feet five inches tall. His shoulders were so wide and his neck so thick that Vassili thought he looked rather like a bull with a head like a large, shiny black cannon ball. Upon this head he wore a golden cap of steel in the centre of which

187

protruded a twirled spike. His robe and cloak were of scarlet as were his patent leather slipper-like shoes, the toes curling up and back towards him. Into his immense and magnificent red, embroidered golden sash were buried two cruel looking curved scimitars. One midnight-black, densely muscled arm was laid across the front of his torso; the hand gripped the hilt of one of the swords. The other, held slightly aloft, gripped an impressive spear ornamented with spheres and a broad shaft. To Vassili, the spear looked to be twice his own height. He was just about to turn around and go back to his quarters; then he remembered Tatiana's distraught and tear-stained face. Though he had no doubt that she really had nothing to fear with regards to the little crown or big crown for that matter being taken from her father, a promise was a promise. He remembered Nicholas's words about gaining respect from the one in your heart. Well, this would surely impress her, he thought. He crept back into the shadow of the pillar. The guard stood stock still. Vassili could not even see the rise and fall of his great breathing chest. He looked closer; he couldn't even see the whites of his eyes! This was strange because though the distance from the pillar to the Nubian Guard was about twenty meters, he was sure that he would be able to see the contrast of his eyes against his black skin. He tried to look closer. Could it be possible that his eyes were shut? Then another thought occurred to him, for he had heard of such things before – that the guard was asleep on his feet. He had left his slippers behind in his quarters and his bare feet were now cold but at least they made no sound on the black and white tiled floor as he decided with bated breath to edge down the wall to the next pillar. Still the guard did not move. He was less than ten meters away now and could see clearly that the guard's eyes were indeed fast shut. He certainly *seemed* to be asleep. Silently, Vassili edged again to the next pillar, his heart in his mouth; if the guard was suddenly to awaken, he would be looking straight at Vassili. He made it to the next pillar and stood directly opposite the immense and splendid figure. From where he now stood, Vassili could see that Jim Hercules virtually filled the space of the entrance to the Maple Room. The gas lights had been turned down so that there was a low, yellow glow down the length of the hallway; as he studied the giant 'Ethiopian,' he was sure that the unthinkable had occurred and that the famous Nubian guard had fallen asleep on his feet. Putting one foot slowly in front of the other he started the longest walk of his life towards the doorway. He could barely breathe. The nearer he got, the bigger the hands and the muscles of the guard became. He decided to try not to look at the immense 'sculpture' and to concentrate his eyes on the round gold-coloured handle of the door. His knees were weak when he finally gripped it. He froze suddenly with the horrible thought that it may be locked. With his heart now in his stomach, he turned it slowly. The door swung silently inwards.

"Can I help you, Master Vassili Kharitonov?"

The voice was deep, dark and chocolaty. Vassili froze in shock and fright. He slowly turned his head to look up at the guard, who to his surprise remained facing forwards with his eyes still seemingly closed.

"I... I... I forgot something. I just need to go in and get it," he stammered, fully expecting the guard to suddenly turn on him and lift him up by the scruff of his neck. But still the guard remained with his eyes closed, standing as still as stone, facing the front.

"I will guard you while you get it," he said simply.

Feeling only slightly relieved, Vassili walked into the darkened Maple Room. He closed the door behind him. He decided not to turn on the light. It would not take him long to do what he had to do. Instinctively, he made his way over to where he knew the statue stood upon the cabinet. As he reached for the statue he stubbed his bare toes painfully on something hard and obviously quite heavy on the floor just in front of the cabinet. He looked down; to his astonishment, two of the richly jewelled eggs that he had seen the morning before were lying loosely on the carpet next to the golden box. But before he could cry out, a very large, rough hand covered his mouth from behind; at the same time, an elbow was forced into the lower half of his back. In pain, he fell to his knees.

"Don't make a sound, you little rat," hissed a voice in his ear, "if you ever want to make a sound again, that is!"

Vassili had no choice. The hand was pressed so firmly across his mouth that he could not utter a sound.

"Time to go, Smith!" he heard a voice whisper hoarsely. "Just pick up those last two eggs."

Thieves in the Maple Room! But how did they get in with the guard outside? His mouth and back hurt terribly; perhaps if he lay still, they would leave him and jump out of the window or something!

"Damn!" he heard the same voice, "It's not doing anything. Isn't this just typical!"

"What are we going to do now, boss?" He heard another thicker voice utter lowly. There were a couple of curses, as if one of the men was struggling with something.

"Shake it again, boss!" whispered the same 'thick' voice.

"Ah... Something's happening!" the first voice again exclaimed. An eerie glow of red, silver and gold seemed to spring up from nowhere, like some sort of strange firework.

"What should I do with the boy, boss?" asked the thicker voice.

There was a moment's hesitation. "I don't care what you do with him!" was the agitated reply. "Throw him through the window if you must, but just get rid of him!"

With a strength so far unimaginable, Vassili was 'bear hugged' and lifted to his feet and beyond as if he were a paper doll. Luckily for him, he had managed to keep one arm free from the iron-like grip, and though he felt all the air being rapidly forced out of his lungs, he just managed to catch hold of the

Napoleonic statue as his assailant started across the room for the window. In one movement, Vassili caught hold of it and then levered it backwards over his shoulder with all his might. He felt the statue give way and break into pieces as it hit something extremely hard. He heard an agonising howl and without further ado, he was dropped to the floor in a heap.

The door of the Maple Room suddenly swung open and in strode Jim Hercules. As the light from the hallway seeped in and sought out the dark shadows of the room, Vassili could see around him. A large bald man dressed in the garb of one of the palace footmen stood before him, holding his head with both of his tennis racquet-sized hands. The seven eggs had all tumbled from the inside of the scarlet coat and lay on the carpet at his feet. Behind him stood another man, also dressed as a footman. In his hand was an incredibly bright, glowing object. It looked like a tiny hour glass. Jim Hercules began to cross the floor with the intention of collecting the intruders and taking them to the palace guard house. He suddenly stopped in astonishment at the incredible display of colour and sparks that seemed to be emanating from one of the intruder's hands. The glow was getting brighter and brighter, so bright in fact that he was forced to shield his eyes from it. But Vassili, who was shielded from the incredible glow by the shadow of the almost prostrated Smith, could see that the shadowy figures of the two intruders amazingly began to fade. He could also see that the thin scrawny one held the golden box in his hands.

"No!" he shouted, and lunged forward, trying to take hold of the box himself. "No! You cannot take it away!" But the sound of his own voice seemed vague and distant until all he could hear was the cascading uproar of an avalanche. His shouts burst into screams; he could not hear himself at all now, only the roaring of a hurricane and the crashing of a furious sea. The Maple Room faded and was gone.

*

Three thousand demonstrators lead by Father Gapon marched down the Nevsky Prospekt towards Palace Square. Some of the upper floors of the houses that lined the road on either side suddenly burst into light as shutters and balcony doors opened, and people came out to stare down on the procession below. Some were quiet and thoughtful; others jeered and teased. Up ahead of him, Father Gapon could see the way to the square was blocked with soldiers. He quickly instructed the women and children to come up to the front beside him. About fifty metres from the soldiers and the entrance to the Palace Square, Gapon and the members of his 'Assembly' stopped in silence. The soldiers stood facing them with bayoneted rifles. Then slowly, the lines of the guard began to make way for a tall figure on a horse, the sabre in his hand reflecting the red rays of the sun. All was silent.

"They will not shoot with the women and children at the front," said Gapon in a low voice to Pinchas. "We shall proceed to the Narva Gate."

"The figure on the horse is not the Grand Duke Vladimir," answered Pinchas with surprise, "I don't understand."

"In the rays of the sun we will march for our cause," answered Father Gapon, "their indifference today is the greatest insult possible to the people of Russia." Then, turning to face the dense mass of people behind him, he said: "Friends and fellow workers. It is with regret that I inform you that it seems our little father has been misinformed and that he is unaware of the seriousness of our plight. His trusted relatives underestimate our resolve, for none of them are here to receive our petition. This day, the fate of mother Russia will be changed forever for if they will not listen, or do not choose to hear, we will force them. There are words of blood upon these pages." Father Gapon held up the petition in his hands. "We cannot stop here now! We must march to the palace and if no one will receive it, I will it nail to the palace door myself. To the palace! To the gate!"

The women and children ran out in front as instructed, carrying their icons as well as portraits of Nicholas II. The singing started again as the demonstrators surged forward towards the solid line of soldiers.

"Fix bayonets!" cried Vasilchikov. "Remember men! No one must be allowed to enter the square!"

*

As Vassili 'landed,' he grazed both his knees on the cobbled paving at the entrance from the Nevsky Prospekt to the Palace Square. His right hand was wet and sticky. As he unfolded his clenched fist, he could see the decapitated head of the statue of the Napoleonic soldier. The sharp edges of its 'neck' had cut into the palm of his hand; blood had seeped out between his fingers and was running down between his knuckles. As if in a dream, the delicately sculptured eyes of the soldier stared up at him, instantly reminding him of the emperor. But then suddenly, as if a radio playing horrendously loud heavy metal music had been turned on, he became aware of his horrific surroundings. Gun fire, shouting, screaming, wailing and crying engulfed his ears with a sudden barrage of sound. He looked around wildly at the confusion. Hundreds of people were running around uncontrollably, shouting and screaming in a panic while the soldiers of the Imperial Guard took pot shots at them with their rifles. Some were stabbing people with their bayonets as they lay on the ground already injured. Then he remembered the box and the two intruders. He tried to get to his feet, but as he did so, a soldier of the Imperial guard saw him. He single-mindedly strode forward. The butt of his rifle crashed into the side of his head; Vassili collapsed onto the ground and knew no more.

*

The members of the 'Assembly of Russian Factory and Mill Workers' dropped their icons and their portraits of the tsar and tried to flee from the terrible onslaught. In hysterical terror, they scattered as best they could as the soldiers shot indiscriminately at men, women and children. As they fell, they either lay there groaning before one of the soldiers finished them off with their bayonets. Their cold hands clawed in their own warm blood on the ground in the agony of death. Prince Vasilchikov had, it seemed, obeyed his orders, for not one of those poor souls made it to the palace gates.

The commander had slowly ridden forward with the intention of confronting Father Gapon and of ordering him to disperse his supporters and to turn around, as there was no one available to accept their petition or to listen to their grievances. Obviously, there had been a misunderstanding and they must march again another day. In the meantime, the Okhrana would then have time to investigate the rumours of his recent revolutionary tendencies and if confirmed, he would be arrested – a quick solution to a minor incident. As the hooves of his horse clattered upon the hard ground in the hollow morning silence that hung over the two masses of people, the same voice that Father Gapon had heard an hour or so earlier rang out again. This time, the voice was shrill with alarm.

"They are armed, they are armed!" it shouted. "Protect yourselves, and protect his Imperial Highness. Shoot them! Shoot to kill! Forward! Attack! Attack!"

At first the soldiers were confused as to who was giving them such an order. They looked in front at their commander upon his horse who was also now peering over his shoulder at them, wondering who had given such a command. The people in front surely were not armed; that would be unthinkable. They were carrying religious banners and portraits of the tsar. For a brief moment, Prince Vasilchikov thought that Grand Duke Vladimir had decided to appear after all and that it was him shouting out the incredible orders.

"Shoot them!" the voice shouted out again, even more urgently. "They are armed and plan to over throw our tsar! Shoot them! Forward! Attack!"

A shockingly loud bang then exploded from the left side; immediately, one of the frontline soldiers fell to his knees. He wavered there briefly, his face a picture of grimacing shock, pain and horror. He then fell forward onto the ground. Deep-red blood and pink and white brain tissue oozed from his head to fill the contours between the cobble stones.

There were no more orders needed now for the soldiers to attack. With rifles lowered and bayonets fixed, they started to shoot into the crowd in front of them as they began to run forward. The crowd was unable to immediately disperse and retreat, as they were packed tightly across the width of the Prospekt. Many of them were uncontrollably projected forward and into the direct firing line of the soldiers. Most of these were shot dead and those that were wounded were finished off with bayonets. Soon, the blood of men, women and children ran like a river down the drainage at the side of the Prospekt. Prince Vasilchikov himself was bewildered and panic stricken. He could not decide whether to try to help the poor people in front of him or to try to override the mysterious orders that had been given to the Imperial soldiers. Instead, he did nothing and merely watched the macabre scene unfold before his eyes.

If the eyes of the angel at the top of the Alexander I column had been the eyes of a living being, they would have seen that as the lines of soldiers moved forward, three lone figures were left behind. Two were standing and one was lying on the ground. Then suddenly, between two of the figures, a red, silver and gold glow sprouted to life. The glow became brighter and brighter until it was so luminous that no human eyes would be able to stare at it directly. Then amazingly, two of the figures disappeared, leaving behind the one lying upon the ground. As they did so, the incredibly bright light was extinguished abruptly. Then just as suddenly as the two had disappeared, two different figures appeared a little to the left from where the first two had vanished. This time, there was an incredible glow of green, silver and gold. The two figures looked bewildered and clearly shocked at the scene in which they suddenly found themselves. They ran across behind the lines of the soldiers until they reached where the figure lay. One knelt down and then looked up at the other. There was a shaking of heads and some sort of disagreement ensued. If the eyes of the angel had been living, they would then have seen that a group of soldiers with rifles lowered, started towards them. Whatever disagreement there had been between two of the figures seemed to be resolved very quickly, for they huddled over the one on the ground in what looked like a protective embrace. But before the soldiers reached them, the incredible luminous glow of green, silver and gold began again; in an instant, the two figures were gone, including the one lying on the ground. The light immediately extinguished; the advancing soldiers suddenly stopped in their tracks, looking at the empty space where the figures had been. They then stared at each other, scratching their heads cursing and swearing in bewilderment. If at that moment any eyes from below could have seen the face of the angel at the top of the Alexander Column, they would have seen what looked like a brief smile cross its face. If those eyes looked closer, they would then have seen the eyes of the angel fill with tears that overflowed and ran down its face one after the other, eventually splashing onto the cross that it carried.

*

The little girl missed her friend dearly. So much so that at first she refused to eat anything. She even forgot about the tiny crown and pendant and her great need to hide them from the bad men that wanted to take them away. Not even Olga, her closest sister, could console her. Her mama told her that unfortunately they had been wrong about Vassili and he was a deceitful and bad person. He had taken advantage of their love, kindness and generosity and had used it against them; he had become involved with thieves and most likely, the revolutionaries. Together, they had masterminded a plan by which they had succeeded in stealing something that was the very heart of their ancestry. The days that followed were the worst of her young life so far. The palace became cold and empty to her, as if a light had been extinguished, never to be rekindled. A shadow had fallen. Indeed, she only began to eat again when her papa had come to her bedside with an indescribable haunted look in his eyes. From the time that Vassili disappeared, it seemed to Tatiana her father was never quite the same again. Her once warm and jolly mama now became frequently ill. Her heart ached, she would say. Now she never smiled, not even when her photograph was taken with her beloved family.

Her father also informed her while she was recuperating, that the tiny crown and pendant had miraculously been found on the floor of the maple room amid the broken pieces of what could only have been the missing Napoleonic statue. It had been picked up by one of the cleaners in the aftermath of the robbery. He squeezed her hand as he told her that she needn't feel guilty anymore for having lost it and that it was now back where it belonged. When she was well enough to take tea with the family again in the Maple Room, her mother would notice her staring at the empty space on the cabinet where the statue had once stood. When she was alone, she quickly checked the Hen Egg to see if the crown was inside. As she opened the little hen and stared at the tiny crown inside, a tear fell from her eyes upon it. At that moment, she knew there had been a mistake; something was not right, for her Vassili would never trade anything for their friendship. Many mornings, when she awoke, her pillow was soaked with tears. But slowly as time passed, time healed and his memory faded a little.

One year later she dreamed once again that her papa lost his crown to the bad men of Russia. She again decided that she must keep it 'safe.' So one evening, just before after-dinner coffee, she stole into the Maple Room before anybody else had arrived and took the tiny crown and pendant from the Hen Egg. She then found the little platinum thimble box that had been put back in her mother's sewing basket. She once again placed the crown and pendant inside the box, and then wrapped it inside her handkerchief. She would hide them again. This time, somewhere where nobody would ever find them, not even her friend, if he ever returned!

Jim Hercules was not punished for what was at first considered a serious lapse of guard duty. In a personal interview with the tsar, he described exactly what had happened; that obviously the two footmen had infiltrated the palace, and had no doubt been in league with Vassili. They had hidden in the Maple Room on the night of the robbery, waiting for him to arrive in the early hours when he was to show them where the treasure was and then obviously the best way to escape out of the palace undetected. No doubt, young Vassili planned to carry on with his high lifestyle as if nothing had happened afterwards. Jim Hercules explained that when he had heard the noise and had entered the room, he had been blinded temporarily by some sort of explosive device. It was then that they had somehow managed to slip past him and out the palace, which was rather baffling, as all the guards were called within seconds of them disappearing from the room. Nicholas informed Jim Hercules that the whole of St Petersburg was on the alert; he was sure that they would be found and that the thing most dear to them would be returned shortly.

Another thing that left all who investigated the robbery thoroughly perplexed, from the Palace Guard to the Okhrana, was the mysterious appearance of a man's rather smelly size twelve sock that had been left in the cabinet exactly where the golden box had once been.

CHAPTER 7
"THECLUB"

The silence was obtrusive. Tatiana and Arty gazed up at the wall behind Harry where he sat facing them on the sofa. Each clock read exactly 9:55 a.m; not a single tick could they hear nor could they remember hearing a chime or a cuckoo for the past hour.

"So, you and Magda *also* brought somebody back to the present!" exclaimed Arty. How many other people were aimlessly hanging around in a time they were not born in? Harry guessed what he was thinking.

"No," Harry answered, "Tatiana and he are the only souls ever to have been brought back to the present from the past by the timer. Or should I rephrase that: you, Tatiana, are the only one that the timer has ever brought back by its *own* will. The boy, I fear, was *allowed* to be brought back through my persistence. We knew it was wrong to try to bring him back, as we learned in the episode with the little girl. Indeed, I have no doubt that the timer stopped working for a time because of it. This time, it allowed us to make our own choice, and of course, for the choices we make there are consequences. When he lay there injured on that cold ground amidst all that carnage and terror, Magda screamed at me hysterically to leave him; I knew she was

199

fighting against her instincts, for her eyes were streaming with tears. Like me, she wanted to get the poor thing out of there but *she* had finally succumbed to the will of the timer and to trust it, forfeiting any wants or needs of her own. But at that time, I was still heedless to its identity and would not listen. As the soldiers came towards us, I bent over him and took hold of him around his shoulders with every intention of getting him out of there as soon as possible. Magda knelt next to us, pleading with me to leave the boy. As the soldiers were about to apprehend us, or worse, the timer took us. In a flash, we were in our apartment with a young boy of no more than ten or twelve. Magda immediately forgot her distress of defying the timer; he had a nasty gash in the palm of his right hand and a nice egg-sized bump on the side of his head."

Harry grew silent as the memory filled his mind. Then without warning, Arty and Tatiana were suddenly startled by chimes reverberating from the large Grandfather clock in the corner of the room to their right. At first, it struck each chime alone; but then with each calamitous stroke the other clocks began to join in so that when it finally struck ten, the choir, it seemed, had regrouped, including the cuckoo clock. The clamorous ticking of the clocks that followed was much less obtrusive than the silence.

"Just a noise," Harry said, turning to face them, his face sad and drawn. "Just a beautiful noise with no meaning or purpose!"

Arty gazed at one clock and then the next. Though he understood what Harry's words implied, he was struggling to accept it.

"What happened to the poor boy?" asked Tatiana, her voice high and slightly shaky above the ticking. "Did he go back when the danger was over?"

"Of course we tried to take him back," Harry answered, "I knew immediately when I looked upon him there in our time, in our own home, that I had done the wrong thing. He was simply out of place. Though he had lost his shoes and socks, his clothes, strangely, were of a fine quality; not of one you would expect to have been caught up in such a scene. He also didn't seem frightened or even fazed, for that matter. His English was perfect without any hint of an accent, but he had absolutely no idea who he was, where he was or where he had been. It was like he had amnesia or something. At first we thought that the blow on the side of his head had probably caused it, but as the days passed, his memory did not return. As I told you, he had a nasty deep cut in the palm of his hand, caused by something sharp that he still grasped. In fact, we really struggled to take it out of his hand. It was as if his attachment to his own time was in that little object and he desperately wanted to hang on to it. It was just a piece of porcelain or something and I eventually succeeded in taking it from him. I kept it. Now I wonder where I put it." Harry pondered the thought, as if all of a sudden it could be of great importance.

"Do you know from which year you brought the boy back from?" asked Arty suddenly, rousing himself from his discomfort, "and the riotous event you witnessed?"

"Oh, yes!" cried Harry, staring directly at Tatiana. "We landed slap bang in the middle of what the Russians call 'Bloody Sunday.' That fateful day of Sunday 22 January 1905 – the day on which, I fear, the trouble for you and your family started. We put two and two together, you see; cold, Alexander column, Russian voices, Russian soldiers!"

Tatiana gasped. "Why on earth would the timer take you there?"

"Why indeed," whispered Arty to himself. Why would two people be allowed to be brought back from the troubles in Russia? He couldn't help but think that there was a strange connection in all this.

"I have no idea; only that it was a test that I utterly failed," answered Harry, "it would not let us take the boy back either, though strangely enough Magda and I did seem to be transported partly. We both remembered hovering over the scene of the massacre and looking down on it from above, as if in a silent helicopter. It was so harrowing a sight that I am unable to speak of the things I saw." Harry broke off, his voice thick with emotion. Tatiana swallowed hard and grew pale. "But I feel I must also tell you something else." Harry slowly continued, "Directly at the place here the boy had lain, one of the Imperial guards appeared to be searching on the ground and looking in all directions, bewildered, as if he was meant to do something there, but was unable to do it. It was the strangest thing to see."

"He was looking for the boy who he was meant to either kill or help, but could do neither because you had taken him away," cried Arty with sudden realisation, but without any accusation in his voice. "Will that not unbalance things?"

"Precisely," answered Harry, again with a look of shame upon on his face, "that I believe, is the reason Magda died, and the reason the timer disowned me." He put his head in his hands, "It is over forty years of time ago, but for me it was yesterday and it *feels* like yesterday!"

"But what *happened* to the boy?" insisted Tatiana.

Harry cleared his throat again and stood up. He strode over to the fridge, took out another can of beer and opened it.

"After the funeral, a silence and a shadow came upon the apartment. You must know the boy, when Magda died, had only been with us a few days. I could not stay in our home; the memories were too painful. Thankfully, it sold quickly, for just looking at the boy brought home to me my dreadful guilt. I had let my wife and the timer down and now both were gone. I had to try to move on with my life." Harry stopped, clearly distressed again. "So I gave him to the authorities!"

Arty looked quickly at Tatiana.

"Wow, Harry!" cried Arty, "that was a bit harsh! You bring him back here, he doesn't know any …"

"I think Harry knows what he did, Arty!" Tatiana cried, glaring at him. She had seen the anguished look on Harry's face and understood that he could not cope with the terrible events of his life at that time. Though he had taken the easy way out, he was still feeling the terrible guilt almost forty years later.

"Okay, Harry," Arty said, "but where do we begin to look? For instance, will he still be a boy? For if he's in a time that's not his. He will still be ten or eleven years of age, which would have been very disconcerting, to say the least, for his new parents." He chuckled at his own pitiful attempt at humour, trying to lighten the atmosphere a little.

But Tatiana was not amused at all. "But that is exactly what would have happened, Arty! Don't you see what a terrible thing it was to happen? I am sorry Harry, but the boy, if he is still alive, would have been living in a nightmare! Believe me, I can imagine what it would have been like!"

"I know, my dear," Harry answered, "but the situation was different to yours. The timer itself orchestrated you being here. You have suffered no memory loss. You know who you are, where you are and where you come from. But the boy knew nothing. No, I think that he would have gone on to live a normal life in the time sense of things. Besides, I think sooner or later we would have read some sort of world headlines to the effect of:

PETER PAN REALLY EXISTS –
BOY OF TWELVE FOREVER YOUNG!

I don't seem to recall any massive news story like that!" Harry threw up his hands.

"So, how old would he be now?" asked Arty.

"Magda died in 1972," Harry answered quickly, "which would put him in his early forties today."

Arty rose from his chair. He looked down at Tatiana where

she sat on the sofa. She looked pensive and pale. I need to talk to her, he thought – alone.

"I can't help thinking all this is connected somehow, Harry. I mean, Tatiana is from Imperial Russia. The boy you brought back was also from Imperial Russia. Could it be that her being here has something to do with the boy?"

"I don't know," said Harry finishing the last of his beer, "I only know that we will get nearer to the answers if we find him and then somehow get him back there."

*

One week later, the Jaguar purred contentedly as it sped up the hill. The sun was low. The road carved a tunnel of yellow, green and bronze through the embracing trees spreading their early evening blanket across the road in front of her. She peered upwards through the windscreen. An insipid, speckled sunlight just managed to seep through the leaves here and there. Pressing her foot a little firmer on the accelerator pedal, she felt the engine gasp slightly as it selected a lower gear. The big V8 roared as the 'motor wagon,' as she called it, surged forward gleefully. She glanced wistfully to her left as she passed the crocodile farm. Arty had told her that if they were to visit in the early afternoon, they could watch the ferocious creatures being fed as well as being able to view and even hold some baby crocs. He had told her that it was incredible holding the tiny lizard-like baby crocodile; one could only gasp in wonder at what they would become when 'grown up.' He had promised to take her there, but so far they hadn't made the visit. She sighed, as did the big black Jaguar as the road levelled out past S'khumba where, Arty told her, the most exquisite leather sandals and boots were handmade; the leather of which literally moulded to the shape of your feet with wear. She had looked forward to trying on a pair of boots, of which she was quite partial, but they hadn't made that visit either!

On her right, the banana plantation was beginning to fade in the twilight. The plastic bags tied to the leaves were still clearly visible. Arty had informed her that they were there to scare away the monkeys. She thought about that; maybe it was something to do with the luminous blue colour? She sometimes couldn't tell if he was being serious or not!

Reluctantly, she eased her foot off the accelerator as the car sped past a sign indicating 60 km/hr. Arty had warned her not to break the speed limit, for not only were the roads in the area perilous with pot holes, far more treacherous than that was the presence of many an opportunist 'traffic policeman.' She marvelled again at this 'modern motor wagon' as she felt the engine gear down smoothly to select the correct gear and then carry on indifferently up the hill towards the figure standing in the middle of the road; a figure with one arm reaching up into the still, dense air, indicating for her to stop.

It had taken Arty only a few days to teach her to drive the 'motor wagon contraption,' which she would insist on calling it, much to his annoyance. It was, after all, an automatic model. When she had watched him drive while sitting next to him in the passenger seat, she observed with unwavering concentration that all she had to do was, 'learn how to make it go forward, and point it in the right direction.' Arty had wholeheartedly agreed, except that she had missed out a couple of minor details, like how to reverse and then of course much more importantly, how to make the 'rocket' (as he liked to call it) stop!

"This car is the beast of all saloon cars," he told her when she sat in the driver's seat for the first time. "If you lose control of it, you, me and the car will be chasing the vervets through the trees, *and* catching them!"

Once she felt the brutal power of the thing in the palm of her hands, he had quite expected her to have become scared of the car. Unfortunately however, she had inherited her father's fearless passion for speed as well as an incredibly quick and methodical understanding of how to drive it. Amazingly, within two days she was quite capable of driving down all the little back roads of South View while Arty gripped the edges of his seat with two sets of whitened knuckles. On their second outing, when returning to the cottage at what Arty referred to as an 'unacceptable' speed – Tatiana had indeed been going too fast – she had for a brief moment forgotten how to stop the 'rocket motor wagon!' The car began to sway alarmingly as she tried to navigate it down the narrow driveway that led to the garage. Arty's bulging white knuckles almost broke through the skin and his eyes grew to the size of saucers as she somehow avoided colliding with the rose bushes on the left and the marching conifers on the right. The car screeched to a halt as her right foot suddenly remembered where the brakes were. The front left wheel had narrowly missed the tail of a bewildered vervet monkey that had frantically been trying to guess which way she would go. (The same vervet monkey had recently been visiting their kitchen through an open window and had discovered where their Jammy Dodgers were kept). As she just managed to stop in time in front of the closed garage door, the bold little plunderer screeched back at them and then scampered up onto the wall of the courtyard. Holding its tail protectively with one paw, it raised its eyebrows, grinned with mock humour and then gnashed its teeth, staring down at them as they got out of the car. Arty recovered himself magnificently, grinned back at it and pointed:

"Serves you right, you little thief!" he cried.

The little black face raised its eyebrows at him as if it understood every word he said and then with a loud blast from its rear end, the scamp shot up onto the roof where it stared down at them again, chattering silently, from a higher place of safety.

"Oh! You really are a disgusting little creature, aren't you now!" cried Tatiana, a look of distaste on her face, "no *wonder* you're an orphan!"

Arty had shrieked with laughter.

The car slowed down smoothly and then stopped in front of the blue-uniformed patrolman. There was something vaguely familiar about him. The patrolman jumped quickly to the side and then made his way smartly to her open window.

"Where are you going in such a hurry, Mevrou?" the traffic officer said, as he leaned into her side window, uncomfortably close; she could see her own reflection in his dark glasses. The fingers that gripped the inside of her door looked soft and well-manicured. "Pull over to the side, quickly!" His manner seemed neither hostile nor friendly as he pointed over to the hard shoulder. Tatiana felt that she had been undressed by the eyes behind the shades. There was something familiar in the tone of his voice, yet the accent was strongly South African – an accent she was now getting used to. Should she inform this impudent officer of whom he had just lusted at? Confidently, she pulled the car over onto the side of the road, while the officer walked slowly back to his own car parked just to the left amidst a clearing, hidden from view by bushes. Just as slowly, he returned, clutching a clipboard with an official looking document upon it. He leaned in again and rested the clipboard on the ledge of the window.

"That clock, or whatever it is, there!" exclaimed Tatiana pointing to the speedometer, "that finger thing, showed that I was travelling at exactly sixty, which I believe is the speed limit, is it not?" she imitated her mother's manner perfectly – the manner of an empress certainly not amused. Though his mouth smiled, Tatiana sensed that the traffic officer was also not amused. He sighed heavily and put one hand on the roof of the car, his resentment at this young haughty woman clear as he leaned further into the car. His breath smelled heavily of garlic, but there was also another smell, again somehow familiar – the policeman's cologne! Tatiana was beginning to feel very uncomfortable again under the gaze of those hidden eyes. The officer's mobile phone began to play 'Mama Mia.' He pulled himself from the window and answered it. Tatiana strained her ears to listen to the one-sided conversation.

"Yes," she heard him say. He then lowered his voice, almost mumbling into the little device. He had turned to face away from her. Tatiana released her seat belt and leaned out of her window as far as possible, trying to catch what he said. "Yes, yes! It's all going to plan!" She could now hear him clearly.

But she was unnerved. This man reminded her of the leering soldiers in the Ipatiev house, where she and her sisters had been taunted by them with sexual innuendo and lewd remarks. Some of them had even daubed obscene pictures of their mother in various sexual poses with Grigori Rasputin on the inside walls of the toilet, upsetting them all and especially their father. She felt the colour drain from her face at the memory.

"I will handle it," she thought she heard the officer mumble into his mobile phone, "don't worry! I've got it all under control, Quad Master."

Who was he talking to? There was something vaguely familiar about what he had just said. His accent had become 'smartly' British as he talked on the little 'telephone.' His voice lowered even further so that she could not make out anything. She strained a little more to catch some of the conversation.

"Yes I know, Quad Master," she now heard him clearly, lowering his voice a little. She just made out the words: "She must be *unspoiled*." Just in time, she quickly dropped back into the driver's seat as he replaced the phone into his trouser pocket and, slightly flustered, he turned and walked back to the car. He leaned upon the open window again, though this time not quite so threateningly.

"Mevrou! If you care to view the camera I can show you that you were travelling at over eighty, and that means a fine of one thousand Rrrrrand (Rand). Perhaps the lady would like to come and check the camera?" He indicated with his thumb towards the parked police vehicle. Tatiana felt a cold prickling sensation at the back of her neck.

"I will do no such thing!" she cried, suddenly wishing Arty was with her and that she hadn't ventured out so far alone.

All at once and quite unexpectedly, the expression on the policeman's face miraculously changed into one of projected merriment. He stood back a little and grinned boyishly, a blond strand of hair escaped the confines of his peak cap. With a gasp, she finally recognised him.

"I am not an unreasonable chap!" he exclaimed swaggeringly, whilst also momentarily forgetting to speak with a stronger South African accent. "In fact, most people, I would say think I'm a lekker guy," he continued, suddenly remembering to keep up the pretence. He again leaned into the window, far enough for Tatiana to crinkle her nose at the mixture of garlic and cologne. Yet again, she felt his eyes wander and caress the contours of her body. She wanted to hit him. What was he up to? Suddenly, he become tense; he was staring at her opera bag that lay on the passenger seat. She glanced quickly from the corner of her eye at the red engine start button in the middle of the centre console. "What have you got in your purse?" he asked, as if already knowing the answer. A little relieved that his attention had been diverted from her to her purse, but no less alarmed, Tatiana pursed her lips and stared silently straight ahead through the windscreen. Arty had warned her about the antics of some of the South African traffic department, and to just give them what they wanted, which was usually whatever one had in one's wallet or purse. That she might have coped with, but this was something different. This was no ordinary traffic policeman. Her mind raced. Obviously, he hadn't noticed that she had recognised him. It was tremendously important that she keep it that way. Somehow, she had to get away and get away quickly, back to Arty, to warn him.

"Errr... nothing," she answered, quite dishonestly.

Irritated, and sighing with mild distaste, the officer straightened up. He placed both his hands on his hips. Tatiana could see the soft, pasty skin of his belly through the gaps in between the buttons of the slightly strained fabric of his shirt. The buckle of his trouser belt caught the glow of the dying sun, as did a rather large ring that encircled his wedding finger. But this was no wedding ring, for it bore an emblem that she, with a gasp, immediately recognised. She struggled again not to give herself away, but this time she sensed that he had noticed. Clearly, he had made a mistake, for he immediately removed the offending hand from the edge of the door and quickly drove it into his trouser pocket. Tatiana grew hot, yet goose bumps formed on her arms and shoulders. The smile disappeared from the officer's face. He caressed the holster to his service pistol with his free hand, in contemplation. She discretely rested her left hand upon the centre console, as she gripped the leather-clad steering wheel tightly with her right. The officer bent forward again, his full solid round face almost touching hers. He reached inside and covered her hand on the wheel with his own. It was clammy and rather limp. The smell of his breath and skin had become repugnant and almost overwhelmed her. She gritted her teeth.

"Let me see your license," he said softly.

Tatiana had promised Arty that she would stick to the back roads of South View and only drive to the village store. That way, he had informed her, the chances of bumping into a member of the police were practically zero. Unfortunately, the store had been closed and so, unperturbed, she had decided to drive to the larger convenience store which was ten kilometres away down the main road at Ramshead. Yet even so, she was a prominent member of the Russian Imperial family! Why should she need a license to drive this 'motor wagon?'

"I am sorry, officer," she said without hesitation, and still looking straight ahead. "But I don't need one."

The police officer sighed again, even more dramatically.

"I am afraid that will be another fine, Mevrou, for forgetting the license," he said in the soft silky voice that she couldn't believe she hadn't recognised until now.

Tatiana turned to face him. His face for a moment, due to the oval black lenses, gave her the impression of a fly. A disease-spreading, filthy fly!

"I haven't forgotten it," she said sternly, "I said, I don't *need* one!"

"Eish," cried the policemen, now mocking the local African native dialect, "then just give me a thousand Rrrrand," he said, his unseen eyes gazing longingly at the passenger seat where her opera bag lay, "and you can be on your way."

The fingers of her left hand crawled agonisingly slowly up the centre console so that now she could almost touch the engine start button.

"If you would let go of my hand," she answered, returning to her blind gaze through the windscreen, "I will see what I have in my purse."

The officer slowly removed his hand from hers, but he remained where he was, leaning in through the window. Tatiana quickly reached over to the passenger seat where her bag lay. But with surprising speed, the officer grabbed it roughly from her as she screamed at him in both anger and fright. At the same time, her forefinger pressed upon the start button and the engine roared into life. With racing-driver speed and precision, she selected the drive position on the automatic gear box and rammed her foot down on the accelerator. The car sped forward with such brute force that the policeman did not have time to clear himself from the window. As the car gathered speed, he somehow managed to grip the strap of the opera bag between his teeth and then cling on to the edge of the window frame with both hands. His feet, knees and thighs meanwhile, kicked, banged and bumped against the side of Arty's beloved 'beast of all saloon cars.' Tatiana's screams were soon lost to the roar of the wind through the open window and the ear-splitting growl from the exhaust pipes. The car hurtled forward at zero to one hundred kilometres per hour in 4,5 seconds – its manufacturer's specifications (Arty would have been extremely pleased). Tatiana had never imagined that anything in the world could go so fast and so quickly. Her mouth and eyes grew wider and her screams became louder and more erratic. Meanwhile, the flailing police officer was in a similar mood, except that he could not scream for fear of losing the precious opera bag that he still gripped zealously between his teeth. As the car flew up the hill, a little band of vervet monkeys that were crossing the road scattered in all directions, screaming (almost as loud as Tatiana) and screeching in rage, narrowly escaping the front wheels of the big Jaguar. Things would have gone rather ill for both Tatiana and the policeman if it hadn't been for the long bend in the road at the top of the hill which Tatiana somehow managed to navigate, though not quite as expertly as usual. Unfortunately though for the policeman, the momentum caused his legs to trail behind him at an almost impossible angle, placing his gripping (and by now quite numb) fingers under tremendous pressure. Timing as usual played its part; just as his grip gave out in the very heart of the bend, he flew headlong through the air and into a soft, fresh load of horse manure that was being transported on the trailer of a slow-moving tractor. The driver was half asleep and noticed neither the roaring vehicle that narrowly missed him, causing his instant awakening from a laid back existence, nor the distress signals from a beautiful young woman or the flying policeman. Two of the vervets with raised eyebrows and grinning mouths scampered after the old vehicle with glee as it wound its way up the narrow lane, back to the farm.

The unwanted passenger had vacated the vehicle. Tatiana stopped screaming, but then started again; for all her inherited driving expertise, she truly had lost control of the car. The traffic lights in front of her were glowing red (Arty had insisted that she knew what a red traffic light meant) and even if she had remembered where the brakes were in that instant, she would not have had time to stop. The car hurtled through the intersection, narrowly missing the front bumper of a minibus taxi that hurtled through from her left. In fact, when she relayed the story to Arty later, she could not believe how large and how white the African driver's eyes and teeth became at the prospect of the collision. Luck or fate then played its part, for the road immediately after the junction rose to a sharp incline, giving Tatiana time to gather her wits and to remember where the brakes were. Breathing hard and shaking like a leaf, she finally brought the car to a screeching halt.

Meanwhile, one very dirty and smelly alias traffic policeman rolled unceremoniously off the back of a manure trailer, much to the delight of the following vervet monkeys. Strangely, at that moment he seemed quite unperturbed. He stood up; straw and filth stuck to his hair, face and clothes, giving him the look of a much-neglected scarecrow. He unhooked the opera bag strap that was incredibly still stuck between his teeth. His hungry fingers searched inside it. The vervets watched and chattered amongst themselves as he groaned loudly and held up to the sky a single glinting, beautifully cut diamond, the size of a large raspberry. He drew back his arm and, howling in rage, flung it with all his might into the lush, green vegetation. As he walked dejectedly back to his vehicle, the vervet monkeys dived silently, one after the other, into the bush to search for the discarded treasure.

*

The couple in the photo was so obviously in love. The dark eyed, olive-skinned handsome young man in uniform leaned affectionately to his left so very close to the lovely young nurse

213

seated beside him on the comfortable lilac sofa. Even though as far as he could see, they weren't quite holding hands, the 'soldier boy' might as well have had his arm around her, for the chemistry between them leapt out and inflicted his face with a hot flush of jealousy. They even looked as if they were in *his* quarters, for behind them suspended from the ceiling hung what looked like a man's shirt, or even worse: a man's *night* shirt! His only comfort was that at least there had obviously been a third person in the room to take the photograph. Yes, there had actually been two recent occurrences in his life that had deeply upset him. One, of course, was the issue with the sun (enough to make anybody grumpy) and now this. He had first discovered the photograph on the night of their return from Harrogate. For the last couple of weeks, he had been struggling to get to sleep (not surprisingly, he thought) and while deciding to read as much as he could about Russia and its history (especially the Romanov dynasty) he had once again opened the book that he had been reading the night all his troubles began: 'The Assassination of the Romanovs', and had come across this very disconcerting image. He was quite sure he had seen it before, but quite probably had hardly even noticed its subject on the right, never mind the one on the left. Now it was different. He was in love with her, and he hated the feeling. He wondered if the man was 'Dimitri', the young man with whom she had sneaked a kiss in the hospital where she helped out as a nurse. He then found out by searching on in other books that Dimitri Malama had been killed while fighting for the 'White Army' against the Bolsheviks, the year following the supposed Ipatiev house massacre. Arty lightly touched Tatiana's face in the photograph with the tip of his forefinger. She was so beautiful, he thought; so lovely. This wasn't careless love; it was real. It plunged down to the depths of his soul. But how could he feel like this? So soon!

He wondered if Dimitri really was killed, or whether there was another story for her to write in the book of truth. Would he be waiting for her when she finally returned to her own time? Was *he* her destiny? What part was he, Arty to play in all this? He looked at the photograph again and then immediately wished he hadn't. It was as if his heart had been pierced with a thousand bayonets. His distress at seeing his Tanechka so seemingly happy with another almost made him wish he was blind. He snapped the book shut. Immediately, he heard the front door down stairs slam with a loud bang.

"Arty! Arty!" Her voice, urgent and alarmed, grew louder as she bounded up the stairs and burst through the door into his room. Her hair was a mass of tangles, her eyes clear and bright with fright. "It's Alex, Arty! He's one of *them*."

They sat downstairs at their usual place at the breakfast nook. He had managed to calm her down considerably, though her hands still shook as she sipped the hot coffee and nibbled on a Jammy Dodger.

"I warned you about speeding, Imperial Highness," Arty said, patronisingly, "the cops here are something else! And anyway, what the hell were you doing all the way down there? Did you visit the hairdresser?" He smirked at her wind-blown hair. She glared back at him. "You promised me you would only use the back roads." His condescending tone brought about the necessary change that was needed for Tatiana; her fright and upset were now replaced with anger.

"Listen to me, you fool!" she flared at him, "I know who I saw just now. I know that voice, and though I haven't said anything before as he is your *friend,* but I am also fully aware of the uncomfortable feeling he gives me sometimes when he looks at me. He is not the friend you think he is my *minion,* and anyway, he had the ring on."

Arty stopped smiling, and slowly put his cup down on the hard granite surface, still managing to clatter it a little. "He made a pass at you?" Tatiana brushed the question away with her hand.

"That's not important right now, though it does add fuel

to the fire. Didn't you hear what I said? He had a ring on his wedding finger – a ring exactly like papa used to wear!"

"Ring? What ring are you babbling about? What is so unusual about that"? Arty was just beginning to feel a little uncomfortable. Maybe she hadn't just been given a fright from a member of the local 'friendly' traffic police department after all!

"Papa used to wear a large signet ring on his wedding finger. He was rather proud of it. It was embossed with the shape of a red dragon. I asked him one day why he wore it for I knew it was not the sort of thing mama would give him; indeed, she detested it. He told me that it was the emblem of a 'Club' that he belonged to; a very powerful body of people."

"What sort of 'Club' would the tsar of the mighty Russian empire belong to?" asked Arty incredulously.

"He wouldn't say too much about it, but I do know there were some of our family members in it, and not just Russian family members either, but members from Europe, Denmark, Greece, Germany and England!"

Arty stared at her. A sudden thought had come into his mind. "How do you know that other members of your family were in this Club?"

Tatiana was just about to answer and then stopped. She raised her eyebrows at a sudden memory. "Oh, Arty!" she exclaimed, "I have just remembered something, something rather peculiar." She swallowed. "A couple of years ago, Uncle Ernest, mama's brother the Grand Duke of Hesse, came to visit us at home in ...'"

"Just a minute," Arty interrupted. His knowledge of this period in history was exceptional. "I think you are mistaken, Grand Duchess. Your uncle Ernie was fighting on the side of the Germans. I doubt very much he would, or even *could* have visited your father who was, technically at least, his enemy during the war."

"It was him, I tell you!" Tatiana was adamant. "And what's more, I remember the conversation clearly, for I was sitting in the shadows of the Maple Room one evening with my memories, when my father and uncle came into the room. My uncle said he had been sent by brother Willi to advise my father that it was time to make peace; all had been accomplished. I remember it word for word, for at the time I did not understand what he meant."

"Did anyone else see him?" asked Arty eagerly. Could it be that this was the pebble that caused the avalanche?

"No," she answered him, "Nobody knew about his visit, except one or two of the secret police and my immediate family."

Arty stood up abruptly. "Can you guess who the 'brother Willi' was that he was referring too?" he asked, clearly becoming excited.

"Well," answered Tatiana slowly, "as far as I know, Uncle Ernest or mama didn't have a brother called Willi."

"Bingo," cried Arty, "That's because 'brother Willi' wasn't a brother in the relative sense at all. He was a 'brother' in the 'Club' sense."

Tatiana's eyes flashed at him again.

"As I was saying, mister 'know everything," she retorted, "I noticed that Uncle Ernest also wore a ring like my father's ..."

"Yes, and what's more," interrupted Arty bombastically, "you can bet your bottom dollar, that 'brother Willi also wore one ...'"

"What are you saying?" Tatiana asked, but as she looked at him the same notion that Arty was obviously feeling dawned upon her. "The kaiser!" She exclaimed, "No it's not possible, is it?"

"Tatiana, the mission your uncle was on proved fruitless, did it not, for the war continued, and so other methods were needed to try to get your father to submit."

"I did notice that soon after the visit from my uncle, Papa stopped wearing the ring, as if he had become disillusioned in some way."

Arty stared at her. His mouth dropped open. The pieces of the puzzle finally formed a picture.

"Do you realise what this could mean?" he said, as much

to himself as to her, "That your father belonged to some world-controlling body, and the ring was the symbol of membership. My theories all seem to be coming true!" He exclaimed. "I have always thought that there was and most probably still is, some higher 'secret society,' for want of better words, that the world's leaders, kings, queens, presidents, prime ministers, yes and tsars all belong to – a body of people that rule the world if you like, and dictate world events behind the scenes."

Tatiana looked doubtful. "But Arty," she cried, "do you really think that the world's leaders would be any good all in the same club? I mean, they are all very powerful people in their own right. Surely they would never be able to agree on anything! They would just squabble!"

"They would," Arty agreed, "they did, and they do, but the decisions I suspect would be made by an elected one. Elected by its members to be the leader of the club: the High King or High Tsar, if you like."

Tatiana looked doubtful. She shook her head slowly.

"You mean, this person would be *voted* in charge? Meaning he wouldn't rule through divine right?"

"It's the way of this world," Arty answered, "these days, you rule a country or organisation because you are put there by its members, or that is the way it is supposed to be. There are quite a few exceptions to the rule though, especially here in Africa. There is a certain individual north of the border who rules his country, whether his people like it or not!"

"Probably because he is being allowed to!" Tatiana cried, the realisation suddenly hitting her, "because that is what the Club desires, for one reason or another."

"You are getting there, Tanechka," Arty beamed. Her insight astounded him sometimes. "The club would have a very good reason for keeping a despot in power here in Africa. Just think of that country's mineral wealth and the cheap labour that could be or rather is exploited."

"But that is not democratic at all," she said quietly, "they would be better off with a leader chosen by God."

"Since the beginning it has been so," Arty answered, "democracy these days has come in many guises and the form most widely used is the least democratic." As he pondered his own reasoning, he was beginning to feel a little light-headed. In his distraction, he leaned a little too far and almost fell backwards off his stool. "I guess the club turned against him," he continued, somehow managing to stay upright, "or at the very least, just abandoned him when he needed them the most; when his country was in turmoil." He stopped again; a shadow had covered his face. "That's if that bloody Club didn't of course orchestrate the turmoil in the first place!"

"Who, Arty?" cried Tatiana. "Who are you referring to?" She coughed lightly and cleared her throat. She also felt a little queasy.

Arty stared into the depths of his empty coffee mug. "Your father," he answered slowly, "the emperor of Russia."

He reached across to touch her hand, but Tatiana stood up quickly, brushing it away, "I remember so clearly the words he spoke when he came home to the palace. So pale, gaunt and tired just after they had forced him to abdicate 'All is cowardice, deceit and lies,' he said. He was broken, Arty." A solitary tear rolled down her cheek. Though Arty felt incredibly sorry for her, he could not help himself.

"They *forced* him to abdicate?" he cried.

"Yes. Why?" she answered, brushing away the tear with a finger.

"Because history tells us that he volunteered to give up the throne for the good of Russia!" Arty exclaimed.

"If father truly thought that giving up the throne would have been good for Russia, he would have done so," she answered, "but he knows his people. The Russian people are God-fearing and they need a God-fearing leader to lead them."

"So *did* he abdicate?" Arty persisted.

"Not officially," she answered. "He wouldn't sign the document; the one they brought to him in that train carriage at Pskov. He told us afterwards that Ruzsky tried to copy his signature; it was even forged in pencil! Are you saying that *history* has accepted that he abdicated freely, that he abandoned Russia and his people?" She stared at him in disbelief. Arty turned away from her, his discomfort answering her question.

"It seems we finally know who distorts the facts, and why. They control everything." Arty once again spoke the words quietly, as if he could hardly believe them himself. He looked up through the archway that led to the lounge. The clock upon the wall was silent. His mind seemed fuzzy and unclear.

"But why on earth would they want to destroy my country?" Tatiana asked. "Surely the leader of such a powerful country would have a big part to play in the affairs of the world?"

"That was just it," he said, "Russia was and still is a very powerful country, so therefore its leader or leaders need to be controlled. Let me tell you, Grand Duchess, your people have been a pretty sad lot since 1917 and the 'abdication.' They certainly haven't been any happier without a tsar. In fact, I read recently a poll showed that they would actually favour the return of a constitutional monarchy. But back to 1917 and the war; Russia was broken through lack of supplies, mainly food. Its people were hungry and no population is very happy when they are starving. The more I think about all this, the more I suspect the situation was incited, for no country will stand fast if it is divided. No, I suspect that the 'Club' secretly feared your father and Russia itself. They feared of what might transpire ..."

"But Arty, as you say my country was ..." Tatiana's attempt to interrupt him was unsuccessful.

"I was fishing around the other night in some of my rather obscure history books," he continued, "books that haven't sold very well and therefore their authors are not very well known. In fact, I suspect they were probably suppressed."

"How on earth did *you* get hold of them?" Tatiana asked

"Alex gave most of them to me," Arty replied with a look of consternation, "just give me a moment." He left the kitchen, muttering to himself and walking a little unsteadily. He returned shortly with a slim wad of papers that looked like a list of statistics that he had made. "I want you to listen to this, though you may know most of it anyway. Yet, if you could compare these facts with today's, as I can, I think you would be just as amazed as I am." He paused briefly to gulp some coffee from his mug. Tatiana decided to be patient, even though she knew she shouldn't. She also felt a little light headed. Did Alex notice that she had recognised him? Clearly vexed, she leaned forward and folded her arms on the hard cold surface of the kitchen top while resting her chin on her wrists. She peered up at him through long lashes.

"Your country, Tatiana, during the latter part of your father's reign, was at its peak. It had never been as powerful before or after. Its military was perhaps the strongest in the world at that time. The army possessed one of the best rifles in the world, the Mosin-Nagent, and of course, its own version of the Maxim machine gun: the Pulemyot Maxima." Tatiana sighed forcefully. "Please, bear with me, your Imperial Highness," Arty pleaded, looking up from his papers briefly. "I promise that you *will* find this interesting!" Tatiana gazed at him coolly. She could not believe that he wanted to talk about guns at a time like this. A thought had just occurred to her. What if Alex *had* realised that she had recognised him? He would know that she would obviously tell Arty. Perhaps then Alex wouldn't be as sly next time when trying to get whatever it was that he wanted! Perhaps Alex wouldn't care now whether Arty knew about him or not! Perhaps he was busy organising some very nasty visit to the cottage at that very moment with some of his very nasty friends!

She bit her thumb nail and shifted position on the stool but remained staring up at him as patiently as possible.

"The air force, though only originating in 1910, soon developed into the largest in the world. Its navy was also still recognised as one of the best. Your country also had the largest gold reserves in the world at that time. In fact, your father, the emperor, deposited four million gold roubles into the Bank of England on the outbreak of the war. Imagine what that would be worth today, for the rouble then was one of the strongest currencies in the world ..."

"Of course it is, or was ... why not anymore?" Tatiana blurted out irritably.

"You don't want to know, duchess," Arty answered coyly. He changed the subject quickly. "To cut a long story short," he continued, "the Russian Empire was becoming the envy of the world. Your father introduced compulsory primary education in 1908 a full ten years before the Fisher Act in England. Before that in 1898 he introduced tax-free medical care while also authorising the building of shelters for the homeless, maternity homes, orphanages and kindergartens." He nodded his approval as he continued to read out the statistics. Tatiana gazed steadily back at him with dark grey eyes. "Arty," she said steadily interrupting him again, "I am fully aware of all this." He placed the papers onto the nook surface. "That is because you were there, Tatiana, but almost a hundred years have passed now and most of the good that the emperor of Russia, your father did, seems to have been conveniently forgotten. Why?" Tatiana shivered a little. Her eyes became sad and sorrowful. "So how does history portray my father, Arty?"

"We'll get to that and perhaps the reason for it, in a moment. But firstly, I need you to understand why he was brought down and by whom." Arty picked up the papers again and continued with the statistics. "When Russian industry during your father's reign really began to flourish, the alarm bells, I suspect, began to ring long and loud in the high halls of the Club. Just listen to this! From 1890 to 1913, the Russian GDP increased by four hundred per cent. During those years, the production of coal increased by five times, copper and manganese by the same and iron and steel production grew four times. Imagine the 'Club' members' envy when their respective countries were in economic decline during the downturn of 1911 and 1912, while Russia was positively flourishing! Russia was the world leader in growth of national income and productivity. The American president Taft stated 'The Russian emperor has created such a perfect labour law, no other democratic state can boast.' His successor, I suspect, didn't feel quite the same way!" Arty placed the papers down on the hard surface again. "But what I find utterly astounding is how religious and God-fearing the Russian empire was. There were sixty-seven thousand churches and over one thousand monasteries in Russia in the early part of the twentieth century. The influence of the Russian Orthodox Church spread far and wide from the Holy Land itself, across Europe, Asia and even here in Africa. Are you beginning to get my gist?" Tatiana sat up with renewed interest. "A people's belief in God is a powerful thing, Arty," she said assertively, "it binds people together."

"Yes!" he agreed, "and the proposed new regime would not want that, would they? 'Divide and conquer' would be their plan of action."

The room was silent except for the sound of the sea, a sound that Tatiana at that moment likened to God breathing life upon her timeless days; timelessness that was clearly making her feel rather strange.

'He has stolen something that is the very heart of our ancestry.'

The memory of her father's words so long ago was suddenly vivid in her mind. Again, she saw the face of the one who had stolen her heart all those years ago.

"Do you remember what Harry said about the parchment?"

she whispered, "That it would be held by one of 'the bloodline' who would rule the country with the parchment as its rock, and that country would become a great empire. Its ruler would not be violent and cruel like such a ruler usually is, or becomes, but would rule with 'love, hope and faith in God.'"

Arty looked over the brim of his papers, his eyes shining as he anticipated her next sentence, "and that empire was the Russian Empire whose ruler, the one of the 'blood line', was your father," he said quietly but firmly, "and somehow the parchment was lost or even stolen!"

"An onslaught of evil," she cried in dismay, "an onslaught of evil has besieged my country."

Her father's words again rang in her ears, "Arty," she said quietly, "If my father *was* in possession of the parchment, which I truly think was quite possible, it was *stolen*, and what's more, I know who stole it." Her eyes were now also drawn to the silent clock upon the lounge wall.

"Peabody?" he asked.

"As much as I would like to think it was, no. It was somebody else and he was very …'"

Aloud crash made her look up suddenly. Arty had again leaned too far backwards on his stool and this time, had toppled completely over. He stood up, rubbing the back of his head. "I've just had a terrible thought," he said, "though I feel a little queer; what if *Peabody* is a member of the 'Club'?" His words were enough to distract her attention from the clock. They now stared at each other.

"*Peabody is a member!*" They blurted out the words in shocking unison. The consequences were unthinkable. But how? Peabody certainly wasn't the leader of a country or anything, though he certainly belonged to that idiotic Club that collected or stole historical artefacts in order to keep them 'safe.' She remembered the spectacle she and Arty had witnessed through the large picture window of the Sherwell Arms on Christmas

Eve in 1915. There was Peabody, preening like a peacock over his collection of stolen goods – stolen goods that he thought included a very rare collection of imperial Fabergé eggs. What satisfaction it would have given her to see his conceited face melt into astonished dismay when Arty had informed him that they were fake. Yet the fact that her father had purposely given Peabody *fake* eggs to take to his masters was the real start of their troubles with old 'Meebody.' For, ever since, he had been obsessed with trying to steal the real Fabergé eggs, in particular the Hen Egg, or to be more precise, it's missing contents. She smiled to herself at her new hiding place for the little platinum box and its tiny contents, the sapphire pendent and the minute replica of the Russian crown; a place even Arty was not aware of!

"Perhaps Peabody's nasty little 'Club' is merely a branch of the even nastier big one," reasoned Arty. "Imagine the chaos they would order him to cause if they knew what he possessed."

"Arty, I think that he is quite capable of causing enough chaos all by himself, yet a chaos for the sole purpose of the wants of Mister Meebody. It is my guess that if he is a member, he would never let his masters know about the timer!"

"Still," said Arty, "I can't help but think that Peabody is involved in the plight of your family somehow."

"A plight that up till now has still not been realised," Tatiana said sadly. "I pray the timer will send us soon!"

Arty was quiet. His attention was suddenly drawn to the clock on the wall; again, a feeling of light-headed queasiness came over him. He fought it.

"I think it is quite possible that the 'Old Farts Club' that Peabody is involved with, has much more sinister intentions than merely collecting valuables, though imagine the monetary aspect of it." Arty stood up to make more coffee. Perhaps he was merely over-tired; he certainly hadn't been sleeping very well!

"Monetary aspect?" Tatiana asked.

"Well, imagine this scenario. The Louvre has on display the world famous Mona Lisa, and of course there are millions of admirers wishing to pay good money to view it. Except that the one in the Louvre is not the real one at all. The *real* one is stashed away under Peabody's bed, or wherever. So the 'Club' informs The Louvre that they require fifty per cént or more of the revenue generated from the public viewing the fake, otherwise they will make the announcement that the real one has been stolen, which would result not only in an international outcry but also no revenue at all being generated."

"Mammon!" mused Tatiana.

"Precisely!" cried Arty, a little unkindly as he considered Tatiana's fantastically wealthy background. Tatiana ignored his smirk.

"When thinking of that collection at the Sherwell Arms, which I guess is certainly not all they have, the 'revenue' they are generating from such a vile scheme would be enormous!" Tatiana exclaimed.

"Precisely!" repeated Arty, this time without the smirk, "And enough to fund most of their more sinister projects that they have, and doubtless still are busy with!"

"But I still think old 'Meebody' would keep his timer secret, don't you?" Tatiana asked, "Just *knowing* the sort of person he is, greedy and power hungry, I doubt that he would relinquish such a thing to his masters."

"Thankfully, I agree," said Arty, "for what such an organisation could get up to if they possessed such a thing!"

"Peabody is quite enough on his own, Arty," Tatiana almost whispered. "He has created enough havoc already! After listening to Harry's story, do you think he could have had anything to do with the parchment being stolen from papa?"

"It's certainly possible," said Arty. He looked at Tatiana. A change had come over her, as if she was withholding something from him. "In fact, considering what Harry has told us, and though we really don't want to believe it, we must admit that it is highly likely. Why? Is there something you know?"

"A very dear friend of mine was definitely involved with its disappearance," she answered, "could it be that he was working together with Peabody? That is why he befriended me in the first place?"

Arty's face flushed again at the memory of the photo he had been studying. "Dimitri, I suppose," he said indignantly.

Tatiana stared at him in disbelief. She had mentioned Dimitri only once to him, when she had drunk a little too much wine; was he going to hold her 'little' confession against her now?

"As a matter of fact, you idiot!" Tatiana cried almost losing her temper, "The parchment was stolen from us many years before I ever laid eyes on Dimitri. What is wrong with you?"

Arty looked away sullenly. Who the hell was this young woman that had stolen his heart so effortlessly? Of course, he knew *who* she was, but why did he feel so close to her from almost the very moment he met her? It certainly wasn't normal or natural!

"I saw a photo once," he muttered, "a long time ago," he lied, "but I remember it clearly. You were all smug and close-up to some soldier boy on a very nice and comfortable sofa and you were in *his* room. In fact, he even had his arm around you!"

Tatiana concentrated, trying to think of what he was talking about.

"Why, mister impudent jealous britches!" she cried, "I know the very photo you are talking about! My sister Marie even added colour to it!"

"It was black and white," Arty muttered sullenly, rolling his eyes. Once again, his attention was drawn to the clock on the wall of the lounge. Its hands seemed to have stuck at six o' clock.

"That was not Dimitri at all, you oaf! That was Vladimir!"

Arty groaned. Not *another* one!

"I really don't understand why I should have to explain a

silly little photo to you at a time like this, but if it will make you happy, I will. Vladimir was due to go back to the front the next day, Arty! He requested a photo with either me or Olga, just so that he could boast to his officer friends. It was all a joke really. Olga took the photograph!"

Arty coughed lightly and ignored her.

"Anyway," he continued still staring at the clock. Even that 'damn' photo was beginning to become unimportant, "so they destabilised Russia by inciting a revolution, ultimately through Lenin's most effective tool: the press. Lurid stories of your mother's relationship with Rasputin were published and from peasant huts to ballrooms the whispers echoed loudly." He stopped as he dragged his face from the clock to see the anguished look upon Tatiana's pale face, "I'm sorry," he said simply, "But you want to know what history says? Well, it basically says the same as those blasted newspapers in 1917. Your father was a weak ruler and was influenced by your mother and her lover to make stupid decisions that had apparent disastrous effects on your country. Obviously, this incited members of the Russian aristocracy, some of his own family members – note that – and much more importantly, his own generals against him. When the starving population finally rebelled, he could no longer rely on his army to put down the revolt, hence his downfall. But who, we have to ask ourselves, was behind the likes of Lenin and his political aspirations. Who was funding it all?"

Tatiana covered her face with her hands. Arty had not been quite as tactful as he might usually have been with her when sharing such 'uncomfortable' information, partly because he was still cross with her about Dimitri and now Vladimir, and partly because he really needed to get his point across to her. Now he felt sorry. Her face had flushed pink behind her perfect, pale, long slim fingers.

"All is cowardice, deceit and lies," she said removing her hands from her face and staring at him with wide, moist, sorrowful eyes. The words of her father – even more poignant.

"This world is rotten, I'm afraid," Arty said, turning away from her, again glancing at the clock, "everything in it adds up to one big lie!"

"Not everything, Arty," Tatiana answered quietly, "There is still good in this world; you just have to look a little harder for it!"

Tatiana had become very aware of the sound of the 'breath' upon the shore. Her memories began to play in her mind like one of Arty's old black and white movies. She watched as her father summoned Rasputin and then after a brief altercation, banishes him from Saint Petersburg in order to try to quash the vicious rumours. She witnessed her mother's displeasure and tiff with her father because he had done so. She watched the lithe form of Olga walking towards her in the hospital ward to say that she didn't think Rasputin himself had done enough to quell the ridiculous rumours, and that she even suspected he was enjoying the attention. She witnessed again the haunted frightened look in Olga's eyes as her older sister had told her that she thought that it would be better if something 'happened' to the mystic, and that it was most probably going to, and pretty soon. The breath on the shore grew louder.

Somehow in tune with her thoughts, Arty continued: "By the time Rasputin was murdered, it was too late," he said, "the die had been cast!"

Tatiana felt the black expanse of despair beginning to feed on her very soul.

"Oh, Arty!" she cried, "What is all this about? What are we really supposed to be doing? Anything? We don't seem to have any purpose at all. We are merely at the beck and call of the timer. It really does seem that we are just two people discovered by a magical device that sends us any place any time at its own whim. *It* knows our destiny, yet *we* don't!"

Her outburst certainly didn't make her feel any better.

Indeed, she felt a hollowness in the pit of her stomach, as if she had abandoned something so dear to her that she couldn't do without it, yet at the same time she couldn't help herself. Then the hollowness seemed to transform into a great weight, heavy upon the back of her head. So heavy and real did it feel to her that her chin touched the cold granite surface of the kitchen top. Unless she fought it, she thought, it would keep her bowed, keep her at its mercy. She breathed in deeply. It was as if she inhaled the very breath upon the shore. She slowly straightened her back and sat upright. Her eyes were closed beneath a determined brow. Arty stared at her in confusion. Then she stood up abruptly and held out her chin in defiance at both the weight that had tried to crush her and the considerably lesser threatening Arty.

"I know that policeman was your so-called friend," she said, her voice steady and even, "and what's more, I know that he is involved with Peabody."

Relieved that she hadn't fainted or anything, though clearly taken aback at Tatiana's unusual behaviour, Arty chuckled nervously with anxious trepidation. "How?" he asked. He looked down. His own hands were shaking.

"Because he spoke to somebody on his little telephone thing, somebody he addressed as 'Quad Master.'"

Instantly, Arty remembered the night at the Sherwell Arms when they unwittingly witnessed a meeting of 'The Masters Club.' The leader of the club at that time was the 'Tri Master.' If the 'Masters' were elected or whatever in sequence, 'Quad Master' would mean that Clodius Albertus had either died or been ousted. But by whom?

"That," she informed him, "is a certainty!"

"I used to think there were only three *certain* Ts," he answered, solemnly, and then inexplicably, he broke into a smile.

"Certainties?" Tatiana asked, wondering what on earth he was going on about now.

"No, certain Ts," he repeated, "Time, which we now don't

have, and Taxes; how can they tax me when I don't have any money!"

"And the third one," she asked, also beginning to smile. Only Arty could make a joke, and succeed in making her laugh at a time like this!

"Thieving pervert monkeys!" he cried, finally bursting into laughter.

Tatiana immediately hooted and joined him in an almost helpless bout of laughter. As they laughed together, they reached for each other's hands and held on tightly. As Arty stared at Tatiana's guffawing face, its form began to change. The distance from the defined bridge of her nose to the top of her forehead became shorter. Her hair grew all at once down to the small of her back. (The only way Arty could describe it later was like watching the 'quickened up' growth of a mass of plants on some nature program on television). Now her nose shortened and turned up slightly at the tip. Her pale hollow cheeks filled out and became a glow with the colour of rosy red apples. Through twinkling innocent eyes, she laughed with him; or was it at him? Eyes that had not yet witnessed the cruelty of the world; eyes that had only witnessed love and kindness. As he looked at her, he had no time to be alarmed, for his whole body begin to tremble. He looked down at his hands; they were shaking with the same momentum that his face was. The little girl was laughing uncontrollably at him now. In fact she was almost bent double in mirth. He tried to become angry at her but found he couldn't, for he had begun to laugh with her again – a laugh that seemed to emanate from the centre of his whole being so full of happiness and merriment that he began to feel light, as if he was almost floating. It was as if he had never laughed before, and that this was the real thing. In the distance, there was loud banging. Tatiana stopped and turned her head to listen. It was probably somebody breaking down the front door. They both looked into each other's eyes again and once more burst into laughter. He held out his shaking hand and there in his palm, inexplicably, sat the beautiful little timer. Both of them stared at it, laughing uncontrollably as the sparks and light display began. The banging became louder. Suddenly, they were also aware of another sound. A tremendously loud ticking noise had suddenly begun, but it was quicker and more urgent than the seconds of time. In unison, they both looked up at the clock upon the lounge wall as the hour hand jerked one last time to hit upon six o clock; the sea roared in their ears and upon the fury of the hurricane, they were thrust into the will of the timer.

CHAPTER 8
THE NEAR CAVES

The air in the room was hot. The paddle fan hung lifeless from the mottled, stained ceiling. It was broken, he concluded. Broken like 'old Nic's' Imperial Russia. He smiled at the thought, temporarily relieved from his clammy discomfort. He dabbed at his forehead with a soiled handkerchief as he lay on his back in the middle of a crumpled, grubby eiderdown. The room reeked of stale sweat and camphor. Peabody had over the years of time travelling with Smith almost got used to the pungent stench of his accomplice's feet, but the combination of the Rosemary-like scent and the rancid 'pong' made his nose twitch uncontrollably. Adding to this, he had intended getting some much needed sleep but had been unable to due to the smell and the incredibly hard and lumpy mattress on which he was lying. He held his nose and breathed through his mouth as he looked around the room, listening to the 'wild boar' snoring of Smith who was sprawled out upon the floor, covered inexplicably by his great trench coat. No wonder he stinks, Peabody thought. He watched as a droplet of sweat, the size of a substantial pearl, formed upon Smith's great bulbous brow and then slide like a rollercoaster down the side of his face to splash onto the wooden floor boards. The sensation must have disturbed him, for Smith suddenly stopped snoring and blinked erratically.

"Are you awake, you great lump?" Peabody enquired. In response, Smith began to snore again. Peabody sighed. Smith really was getting harder and harder to put up with these days. He had thought about replacing him, but then again that would be a little difficult; he knew far too much. He could only be replaced when he was lying in his pine box! That could be arranged easily enough though, Peabody thought as he stared again with distaste at the great comatose bulk, stinking, grunting and snorting, like something that would be more at home in a farmyard! He turned his attention quickly to the picture on the wall again. Yes, it did look like *her*. In fact, all the pictures of young women that he saw these days seemed to hold a resemblance. Indeed, the evening before last he had taken his usual trip down to the vault beneath his office in the college just to take a peek at one or two of the 'rescued' works of art that he had been entrusted with; to his horror, even the Mona Lisa leered at him with the full lips and eyes of Tatiana Nicolaevna. His dreams also, which were usually always in black and white, were know coloured with her face, form and figure. Those dark gray eyes mocked him as she held out the long white palm of her hand, so obviously teasing him, with the tiny sapphire pendant and the tiny crown. There was no mistaking that she detested him, but that really didn't worry him for there was plenty of time to woo her when he had 'rescued' the 'Hen Egg's Surprise' from her. Her ice would then surly melt, he thought, smiling to himself. For very soon now he would have it, or at least know of its whereabouts. Smith had impertinently informed him that he was either mad or obsessed; Peabody new well enough that he was both. He turned his gaze to the slightly mangled wooden blinds through whose slats the late evening sun of Russian summertime lit up the rising dust particles. This place is filthy, he thought.

The things I have had to put up with lately! But not for much longer! He sat up abruptly.

"What is the time, Smith?" he bellowed, so loudly that the stuttering rhythm of Smith's cacophony of 'blissful sleep' abruptly ceased.

"Time for supper, I hope," came Smith's groggy reply. He then began chuckling to himself, no doubt still thinking he was dreaming. Peabody leaned over the side of the bed and fixed the hapless Smith with his forbidding 'Dean of the College' stare.

"Mr Smith," he said icily, "I asked you a question with regards to time, and *time* I think is very important to us, wouldn't you say? I don't think it appropriate that you answer my 'time' question in such a flippant manner!" He stopped. His voice had risen somewhat, surprising even himself. "As I said," he continued struggling to speak quietly and calmly, "I asked you the time of that moment, not the time of your pathetic needs or wants. Now answer me immediately or I will kick you in the pendulum!" Smith opened his eyes in alarm. He immediately raised himself up onto his elbows, thoroughly concerned at the high pitched tone of his boss's voice and what it threatened. In the last few weeks since they had given the 'Golden Box' to the Masters' Club, Peabody had not been himself. He had become even more agitated than usual and much more quickly.

"Six thirty, boss," he answered sheepishly. He certainly did not want to be kicked in the pendulum, wherever that was!

Peabody roused himself and sat on the edge of the bed looking down at Smith, who remained prone on his back looking up at the broken ceiling fan. He wiped some of the sweat from his forehead with the back of his hand.

"Phew, boss!" he exclaimed dramatically, "six thirty and still hot! I thought Russia was a cold country."

"Anywhere for anybody would be hot with that great coat laid over them," answered Peabody impatiently, "no wonder you stink!"

As was usual when Smith was under threat of verbal abuse or worse from Peabody, he changed to the subject of simple gratification of his boss.

"You know, boss, I've been thinking," he said.

"Well, please don't," answered Peabody unkindly.

"No, boss," Smith persisted, "I've been thinking that when you get Fanny and the little crown perhaps we can retire, you know, go and live in some palace; somewhere nice, like that place we once went to, what was it called, Lavato ..."

"If you are talking about Livadia, you imbecile, that would be the last place I would live. I hated its conspiring, whispering walls," Peabody interrupted. "Anyway, why would I want to retire just when I have acquired a beauty for my arm? Indeed, just think how I will be envied and talked about when I turn up with *her* as 'Grand Master' and his lady to one of our social gatherings."

"She certainly makes Bertha look like the dragon she is, boss," agreed Smith, "a queen fit for a king!"

"That's just what I aim to be," replied Peabody quite seriously, "and sooner than you think!" He spread his hands out, palms down, in front of him. He stroked the length of his wedding finger between the forefinger and thumb of his right hand. "Clodius's trinket will one day be mine, Smith. I saw genuine fear in his eyes when I presented him with that box; surprise and fear. Do you know, I am not even sure he was aware that the box even existed in the first place! I think that in his mind we had been sent on an impossible mission, one bound to fail, but little does he know I have the power!" He delved one hand into his side jacket pocket and brought out the little egg timer, dull and lifeless. "This is *mine*!" he exclaimed, his voice rising again almost to a shrill, "With all its power, who or what can stand against me?"

Smith raised himself up onto his elbows again, squinting through the haze of red sunlight. Though his boss's recent behaviour was certainly beginning to worry him, for his own comfort, he played along.

"Yes, boss!" he cried emphatically, "old Clodius is certainly scared of you, and so he should be. If only he knew what power you possessed."

"If only, indeed," remarked Peabody, "but he will never know *where* my power comes from. This is a secret, Mr Smith! Do you understand?" Peabody stared at the timer with the eyes of a reptile, cold and blank. "I have moved mountains for that lot, Smith," he continued, "I have marked Clodius's cards many times, but now it is pay-back time, and *he will* pay for that last little stunt that he pulled!"

Smith wondered if Peabody had travelled to the future without him again, to see what becomes of the Masters' Club. Could he possibly have observed himself as the next 'Master'? Peabody had indeed on a number of times used the timer to look into the future but had found to his constant annoyance and dismay that the timer had been very selective on what it would show him. So far, anything regarding the Masters' Club, Tatiana Nicolaevna, the Hen Egg's contents, or even that Benjamin character seemed to have been off limits. Wherever his own desires were concerned, the timer's co – operation recently had proved to be rather stubborn! Even though he led Smith to believe that the timer was his and that he wielded its power at will, he had a gnawing, nagging concern that this was not actually so. Still, it obliged most of his needs and wants. They were here after all on the trail of the escaped Romanov women, a fact that he had only just learned. Of course, when the timer had allowed him into the future to see what happened to them, all the history books were in unanimous agreement. All the imperial family and their retainers were murdered in the basement of the Ipatiev house. But Peabody had learnt enough recently not to trust what the history books said. Anyway, he had to find the missing Hen Egg's contents! The history books did confirm indeed that they were still missing as late as 2014. But he had been at a loss on how to accomplish this. What is the use of having a time device if you don't know what time to go to, he declared to Smith in his office in the college one wintery afternoon in 1934. The timer had immediately burst into life as if in response to his frustration, and *whoosh!* A second or two later, they had found themselves in an office. Peabody as usual looked around for clues as to where and 'when' they were! He didn't have to look very far, for upon the desk in front of them lay a diary. It was opened at 23 July 1918 — only six days after they had last visited that year and the events that they had witnessed at the Ipatiev house! Thrilled at the prospect that they were finally on the trail, he searched the walls for clues as to *where* they had 'landed'. It was obviously a monarchist's stronghold, for there was a portrait of Nicholas II in all his military splendour, facing them. The soft, warm and slightly vulnerable eyes stared, it seemed, straight at Peabody, who scowled back at the portrait. He looked at the wall to the left and there hung another picture. It looked like a newly built cathedral. Its beauty was fully appreciated by Peabody who gazed with keen interest at its distinct Gothic style with its pair of gorgeous needle towers. "Saint Nicolas Catholic Cathedral," Peabody read the inscription underneath the image. "Could it be that we are in Kiev?" He began to move around the room, instructing Smith to do likewise for more clues. Apart from the deep, rich, red leather chairs and couches, the walls of the room were pastel shades of greens, creams and browns. But he had no time to study his surroundings for long; the old stand-up telephone on the desk to their left began to ring urgently. Smith turned around abruptly, knocking over the brass and wooden stand-up ash tray that stood to his right with a crash. Peabody glared at him as he lifted the receiver.

"Bezak?" demanded a voice.

"Yes!" Peabody answered instinctively.

"Alvensleben."

238

Peabody was silent as his mind raced; 23 July 1918; possibly Kiev! Who was on the other end of the telephone line?

"*Count* Alvensleben!" the caller obliged abruptly, with the accent of German aristocracy. Quickly gathering his wits, Peabody responded as calmly as he could.

"Yes, Count, I have been expecting your call."

"Yes?" was the surprised reply, "then you will know," the count continued, " that you and Dolgorukov need to meet me urgently, for I have vital information in regards to the benefit of our cause."

"Dolgorukov?" Peabody responded spinning around to face the still flustered and by now, profusely sweating Mister Smith.

"Three sharp, this afternoon in the Monastery of the Caves."

The caller rang off abruptly. Peabody stared at the unsightly Smith.

"I think you had better bathe!" he declared.

'Bezak and Dolgorukov' cautiously approached the imposing walls of the monastery, leaving the tranquil waters of the Dnieper River behind them.

"Will you please refrain from unpacking your trunk, Mr Smith!" Peabody demanded with utter distaste. He scowled at Smith, who slowly removed the chubby, guilty finger from his large and bulbous nose. "You do know that you are supposed to be a prince, you oaf!" Peabody continued, "Prince Alexander Dolgorukov!"

"Oh, so are you a *king* then, boss?" asked Smith rather slyly. Peabody stopped and turned to face his accomplice squarely. "My name is Fyodor Bezak, or that is what it said in the hotel register, and it was just a matter of timing, you great clown!"

Smith raised his eyebrows, pretending to be confused. "If *you* had answered the phone Smith, you would have been me and I would have been you," Peabody continued with obvious annoyance, "But as it is, we will just have to put up with a nose-picking prince!" He strode off indignantly with Smith bounding after him, wondering how on earth his boss always seemed to know the way.

"Sorry, boss," Smith cried, finally catching up with Peabody. "I think something flew up it!"

"Well, if it did," Peabody responded continuing his manic walk, "It will clearly never be seen again. For no doubt it will soon get lost in those great empty corridors and halls of your head!"

He stopped abruptly. Smith bumped into him almost pushing him over. "Thinking about it," he said raising an eyebrow, "I will do all the talking, understand? Remember, we are monarchists! We are supposed to be on the side of 'Bloody Nicholas', and we are in favour of reinstalling his little arse back upon his little throne. Have you got that?"

"Yes, boss," Smith answered, "But I thought we didn't like 'old Nic,' so why are we helping to put him back there?"

"Whatever it takes, my dear fool, whatever it takes!" answered Peabody, clearly with no time or patience to explain the complexities to his accomplice.

Smith still thought that his boss was angry at him for the 'mix up' with their new identities.

"If you'd rather be this prince guy, Mr Peabody, I don't mind."

Peabody looked up at the sky, which was coincidentally the colour of his mood. "I know that, I know that," he said between great gasps for air, "But he heard my voice as being Bezak, you imbecile!" He drew the smart gold-coloured pocket watch from his waistcoat' expertly, he held it in the palm of his right hand as he flipped open its lid with his thumb nail. "Now come on and don't dawdle, or we'll be late!"

Smith grunted and followed his boss down the gentle slope to the 'Near Caves of Saint Anthony.' The Near Caves are in fact not natural caves at all but were literally dug out of the earth by a monk named Anthony when, in AD 1057, Varlaam was appointed as the first Abbot of the Kiev Pechersk Lavra. Anthony himself withdrew from the monastery and made his new home in the caves which eventually became a new underground cell. When 'Fyodor Bezak and 'Prince Alexander Dolgorukov' met Count Hans Bodo van Alvensleben there, the caves contained three churches: The Church of Saint Anthony, the Church of the Entry of the Mother of God, and the Saint Varlaam Church. Also within the caves were seventy-nine graves, and a note discretely sent to their hotel that morning indicated the meeting was to take place at the site of one of these graves. The air was hot and dense. The thick columns and arches threw ominous shadows all around them as they stood by the incorrupt relic of the holy martyr Kuksha.

"Who was this guy, boss?" asked Smith, as he peered gingerly into the open casket-like wooden box, the bottom of which was covered with a rich tapestry of gold and green. At what Smith presumed to be the top sat a velvet, burgundy cushion upon which was embroidered a deep golden cross of cloth of gold.

"That, my nose-picking prince, is another example of a pitiful Christian who was martyred for his shameful behaviour!" Peabody answered with a sneer. "He lost his noggin because he couldn't keep his ridiculous beliefs to himself and insisted on trying to convert the Viatichi tribe (a tribe of west Slavs) who no doubt were keeping themselves to themselves. Well, he paid nicely for sticking his nose where it didn't belong. When he actually succeeded in converting some of them with his monstrous rubbish and lies, they began to destroy their own images of worship, which if you ask me were probably much more authentic than what he had just 'sold' to them! The leaders or priests of the tribe were quite furious with him, so they promptly chopped his head off. Well within their rights too, if I may say so." He flicked open the lid of his pocket watch again and peered at it in the gloom. "Where is that fellow?"

"Oooo," Smith replied enthusiastically. "So I guess that's

why there is that nice comfy cushion in place of where his head should be. Or do you think it might be hiding underneath?" He was in the process of bending down into the box in order to lift the cushion to see if he would make his grisly discovery when he was smacked smartly across his right ear by Peabody.

"Come out of there, you clown!" he cried and then felt the presence of somebody approaching them from behind.

Peabody swung around in fright as Smith growled under his breath at the dark, imposing figure that had appeared silently. Clearly, the man had an air of authority about him.

"Gentlemen," he said, his voice now a full baritone of German aristocracy, "we meet at last, face to face. Which one of you is Bezak?"

Highly relieved, Peabody stepped forward and held out his hand. "Count, how good to meet you." The count shook Peabody's hand with an iron-like grip, almost lifting the wiry 'cat burglar' off his feet. "And this," Peabody winced, "Is Prince Dolgorukov. Unfortunately, he is quite ill and has lost his voice, but not his dedication to our cause, as you can see."

The count stared at Smith impassively, one cold blue eye magnified and framed by a monocle. "Nothing will deter us from our task; only death," he said.

Sensing that Smith was about to reply in some way, Peabody responded quickly. "There is no need to doubt our loyalty to the cause, Count Alvensleben," he said quickly, "the fire of the dragon will fuel our desire."

The count smiled as he acknowledged the 'password.' He held out his left hand and offered the back of it to Peabody, who immediately, much to the surprise and consternation of Smith, kneeled on one knee and kissed the emblem of Alvensleben's ring. He then straightened up, flicking the dust from the sandy floor off his knees with the back of his hand.

"Do you know why 'The Master' allowed alcohol in this world, Bezak?" the count asked, peering at Peabody and then up at the silent, brooding Smith, who Peabody discreetly elbowed in the ribs — a warning to keep quiet. "No, Count," he answered, "I cannot say that I do."

"To prevent the Russians from ruling it," he said, without even a hint of humour. Peabody stared blankly at Alvensleben, hoping against hope that a spark didn't suddenly light up Smith's peanut-sized brain. Then, without warning, the count slapped Peabody on his back with surprising power, forcing the breath to escape out of his mouth with a loud gasp. He then burst into loud bombastic laughter as he leaned heavily upon his cane with two hands. "You see, if they hadn't been spending all their time at balls and in drinking houses, the Russian aristocracy just might have seen all this coming," he said between pelts of laughter. "Their noble minds were numbed in the haze of fine cigar smoke, French champagne and vodka."

Peabody was confused. Was the Count happy about the 'unfortunate' events that had taken place in 1917 and then even more dramatically in 1918 Russia? Wasn't he supposed to be on the side of the monarchy?

Then, just as quickly as the count had begun to laugh, he stopped. His face was now stern as he twirled the end of his 'Tsar Nicolai' beard between thumb and forefinger. "Nicholas is dead," he said simply and quietly, "his widow, the ex-empress, is as we speak being escorted back to Perm after an unsuccessful attempt by the British to get her out of Russia. At the same time, the body of the heir Alexei, who finally succumbed to the 'Royal Disease,' is being transported to an undisclosed location for burial. So as you can see, though they were both due to be executed on the evening of the sixteenth, we didn't have to do anything; fate played its part!"

'Old Nic' dead, thought Peabody. There really was no surprise in that news! The boy too! Well, history was right in a round-about way. But the mother? Wasn't she also supposed to have been executed along with the daughters? He had many times tried to 'persuade' the timer to send them to Russia just *before* the Ipatiev house debacle, but it would insist on sending them to a time *it* decided upon these days, landing them in many an uncomfortable situation! Peabody again imagined the pale white hand holding the tiny pendant and crown. A vision of her mocking face again flashed before him.

"And the daughters?" he asked nonchalantly. The count must not suspect any other motive he may have in mind.

"That is the bad news," Alvensleben answered, "and where you must now act. The British attempt to get them *all* out wasn't entirely *unsuccessful* either. Brother George acted on his own with this one. He let his devotion to his relatives get in the way of his loyalty to the purpose. No doubt the 'Master' will make him answer one way or another. A special agent of MI1 has managed so far to help them escape from the Bolsheviks and three of them are on their way to Odessa. We have been monitoring the situation, you see, but we as brothers do not want to upset George too much. So that is where you two come in. Russian monarchists are hell bent on saving the heirs of Nicolai. You must intercept them, kill the agent and any of his companions and then escort them to Perm. We have already intercepted the ex-empress who will be waiting for their arrival in a 'strong house.' There is a detachment of the Cheka at your disposal to help you with this task."

"You mentioned that only three of the daughters have been abducted," Peabody cried diplomatically, but also eagerly, "which one is missing, and what *happened* to her?"

The Count whistled softly. "It is a strange case," he answered softly, "that of Tatiana Nicolaevna. It was reported that she had fallen in love with a Red Guard as early as the 'Tobolsk' part of the imperial family's imprisonment, and that they had run away together. But it seems our inside information was incorrect, for it was confirmed that she did indeed travel to the Ipatiev house with her sisters and brother to meet their parents there last May.

Then there was the report of her incredible disappearance from the house at the beginning of July. That was why Avdeyev and most of his men were dismissed and replaced with the loyal Yurovsky. How she got out nobody knows. We don't even know if she is dead or alive, for there have been no sightings of her since. Again, the only logical explanation would be that she was smuggled out by a lover; even one of the Red Guards, perhaps."

Peabody breathed a sigh of relief. Then the timer had finally brought them to the right time, after all! Even though she wasn't hanging around right now, she was sure to turn up. The outcome at the Ipatiev house was certainly not the same as what history recorded. Peabody smiled to himself at the count's observation as Yurovsky being loyal for he knew from the events that he himself had witnessed at the Ipatiev house that Yurovsky would have sold his own mother for a Fabergé Egg! So Tatiana must have got away with that loser Benjamin, but she would never abandon her family. Idiot though she is, she will at least want to know what happens to them. She will turn up alright, with her 'loser' friend; he had no doubt about that. But what was going on here? Which side was this German on? Obviously, he was a 'big wig' from the 'Grand Masters' Club,' which was certainly putting a different perspective on things. Was Clodius behind this? He thought briefly as he studied the well – dressed 'gentleman' in front of him. He had removed his trilby hat to reveal a balding cranium with tufts of mousy brown hair scattered irregularly upon its surface. His nose, long and straight, was troubled with the mottled effect of its owner enjoying perhaps a little too much of the hard spirits. His eyes were Germanic blue and cold. His 'tsar' like beard was flecked with gray, though. Peabody guessed quite correctly that the count was no older than thirty-five.

"We are hoping," the count continued, "that when you and the men bring them in, one of her sisters can shed some light on Tatiana's whereabouts. We have very special plans for her, you know."

The count's words wrenched Peabody from his thoughts. "Plans?" he asked. "Aren't the plans the same for all the girls? Like you have just informed us: to restore them to their previous titles with a new tsar as their head?"

"Don't be so naïve, Bezak," the count answered imperiously, "Brother Willi doesn't trust them or his cousin, their mother. He fears they have spent far too much time under the influence of their arrogant father to bow to his will. No, in return for their eventual freedom, they will *appear* to support the new tsar. Seeing this, we feel the majority of the Russian people will also give him their blessing. Then, one by one they will be married off to their new husbands."

"Fascinating, fascinating," cried Peabody. Obviously the Bezak character he was impersonating was not a true monarchist at all but a supporter of some scheme to install a puppet tsar on behalf of the Kaiser-led Germany onto the throne of the 'new' Russia. He was beginning to wonder what they would find in 1934 if they ever got back there. "Is it still the one that was agreed upon?" Peabody asked slyly.

"Ernest, yes," the Count answered, "In fact the Grand Duke is on his way to Perm this very moment so that he can discuss the situation with his sister, the former empress."

"Do you think that haughty old hag will go along with it?" Peabody asked, and then immediately regretted his rather rude reference to Alexander Feodorovna. But he needn't have feared, for the count merely chuckled. "Apparently, she really is not as bad as people say," he said, "much of her arrogant manner, they say, is due to her introverted nature; she detests large social gatherings and ceremonies. A poor choice of a wife, if you ask me, if one day you are going to be the tsar of all the Russias. He paid the ultimate price for it in the end. But in answer to your question, she, like her daughters, will have no choice. The *final* signing of the Brest Litovsk treaty will take place very soon." Alvensleben now lowered his voice. "They say," he said, his voice suddenly strained and hoarse, "that the 'Ultimate Master' is soon to be set free." Peabody felt the cold ice cubes of dread slide down his spine.

"But that is not possible!" he cried. "Surely we are not at that stage already?" The count looked equally uncomfortable.

"It is a rumour among the circles of the wise," he answered, "but I believe it to be more than just a rumour, and he promised Brother Willi the victory in this war. Then Germany will place one of its own citizens, Grand Duke Ernst of Hesse, and legitimate heir to the Russian throne, as leader of what is left of the once mighty Russian Empire. Being the ex-tsarina's brother, I am sure he will manage to 'persuade' her to toe the line. Then Russia and all its resources will effectively belong to the Fatherland. Things are falling into place rather quickly, don't you think?"

Peabody was shocked. If this came off, there would be a great possibility that Germany and not England and her allies would win the First World War. He delved his hand quickly into his jacket side pocket and with relief felt the cold heavy metal object in the palm of his hand. Yet, if I, Winston Peabody, help them with their little scheme, he thought, then I will surely be elevated through the ranks of the Masters' Club, depose Clodius and then with the power I wield, even the 'Ultimate Master' himself! A showdown with The 'Ultimate Master' was something Peabody had not counted on at least for another hundred years or so, but if that was where the world time now stood, he would make sure he was ready. The timer suddenly felt heavy in his pocket.

With regards to the more immediate future, he would have to declare that it was he, Winston Peabody, and not Fyodor Bezak who had apprehended the 'baggage,' but he would tackle that when the time called for it.

"Forgive me Count, for my persistence," he asked, "but I have a rather special interest in the subject of Tatiana Nicolaevna; I made a 'fire promise' concerning her honour. I am sure you understand."

The count understood clearly enough. "Brother or no brother, my friend, the oath you made to your fellow brother in this case cannot stand. It will be over-ruled by the 'Ultimate Master' himself. There is a certain, let's say, *establishment* in Constantinople. Its owner and fellow brother are in great favour of the 'Ultimate Master' and it is to him she will be sent."

But not before I get what is mine from her, Peabody thought to himself. At that moment both men were suddenly aware of a low persistent wheezing, a strange sort of heavy breathing sound. They both looked at Smith and realised that he was laughing.

"If there was no alcohol in Russia, the Russians would rule the world! Ha Ha Ha!" Smith's face was ruddy and creased with humour. Peabody promptly drove the heel of his smart leather boot down onto the soft, patent-leather-clad big toe of Prince Dolgorukov. "Glad to see you're feeling better, Your er … Highness," he said.

This had happened less than a week ago. News had come in on Plant's whereabouts and it was time to act. Peabody rose from the bed, stepping not too carefully over Smith. He filled the white porcelain basin with cold water and rinsed his face. He looked into the mirror at his own reflection. His temples were greying, but his hair was still thick and full. There were a few more lines on his rather long lean face that he thought gave him a dashing, rugged look and even enhanced his air of wisdom.

"Smith," he said, "Inform the men that we leave at eight." He returned to the reflection in the mirror. I guess my next impersonation, he thought, will be that of a certain '*establishment*' owner in Constantinople.

CHAPTER 9
THE HORSEMAN

Plant looked over his shoulder again. The horseman that had been following them at a steady gallop had disappeared around the bend in the road. So far, he had only noticed one horseman, but he knew it was unlikely that he was alone. Others would be following the 'scout' at a safe distance. Was the rider from the Red Army, or maybe from the slightly more friendly Czech army? He was certainly in uniform, but Plant could not see *which* uniform from that distance.

Thankfully, the rain had stopped, and Tudor had finally managed to fall asleep again in the passenger seat. His head lolled backwards and forwards with the motion of the truck. He would awaken occasionally when the vehicle took a violent jolt as Plant tried to navigate over the fish-pond-size pot holes. He would open his eyes briefly, groan and then fall back to sleep, scowling. Plant smiled to himself ruefully. A little different from the feather down and mattress he is used to in the officer's quarters, he thought. He will learn to sleep on his feet like the rest of us, before all this is over. The feeble, yellow headlights only succeeded in illuminating the rear tires of the truck in front and the watery sludge that was propelled and splattered on to their own bonnet and windshield. The wipers were quite insufficient and merely glazed the two-piece windshield with mud and grime, forcing Plant to stop the vehicle to wipe down the glass as he aimed obscenities at the sleeping angel face of young Tudor. "Damn mummy's boy!" he said, " I wonder, apart from shooting 'dead ducks,' have you seen any real action?" In response, Tudor blew a saliva bubble from his mouth and then began to snore lightly. Plant shook his head as he climbed back into the vehicle. "They don't make 'em like they used to," he said, gritting his teeth. The road straightened out again. He peered over his shoulder. Sure enough, he could just make out the shadowy shape of the rider as he appeared again some thirty meters behind them. Dusk was rapidly closing in but he could see that the rider was gaining steadily. They had the disadvantage of having to follow a road, he thought. The rider, on the other hand, could quite easily cut across when the opportunity arose and cut them off. He nudged Tudor roughly, in order to awaken the young officer. The road snaked into another bend.

"Take the wheel, son!" Plant bellowed patronisingly. He had leaned over to his left and to within an inch of Tudor's right ear. The young officer reacted abruptly and in groggy astonishment, watched as his companion released the driver's door and in one fluid movement, using his legs as a spring board, flung himself out of the vehicle and was gone. Tudor frantically caught hold of the steering wheel with his right hand and just in time managed to slide himself across the bench seat and into the driver's position without losing control of the vehicle or even losing the momentum of its speed. He looked ahead at the truck still moving steadily in front. Neither of its two occupants had noticed Plant's sudden exit.

"The crazy fool!" Tudor exclaimed, as he instinctively looked over his shoulder to see the lone horseman about twenty meters behind suddenly assailed by a dark figure that pounced like a leopard from the trees on the left. He rammed his foot down hard on the brake pedal as he frantically hooted the horn three times. The truck in front slowed to a stop. Tudor signalled to the three figures dressed as soldiers on the back of the truck to stay where they were. He lifted the .455 Webley out of its holster and stealthily made his way back along the muddy road. But Reginald Plant was in no need of any help. When Tudor reached him he was sitting astride his unfortunate victim, holding the point of his 'Bowie' knife to the throat of the rider whose horse had thankfully bolted into the woods at the side of the road.

"Obviously you have a death wish, my *comrade*!" Plant hissed through gritted teeth. He slowly pressed the point of the blade until it broke the skin, and a tiny ball of blood appeared to swiftly speed down the side of the horseman's neck. He was fully aware that any sudden movement would mean certain death. "Yes, you are quite right, my friend," Plant hissed again, observing with relish the terror in his enemies eyes, "one move and you'll be drinking your own blood before you have time to blink your eyes!" The rider lay as still as his nerve endings would allow and stared at Plant, not even daring to blink.

"You won't get anything out of him with that stuck in his throat!" observed Tudor practically.

Plant sighed and shifted his weight. He relaxed the point of the knife a little as he looked up and down the road quickly. It was still empty. Then much to his victim's relief, he stood up and sheathed his knife.

"English?" Plant demanded looking down at the still prone horseman.

The man rubbed his throat painfully as he got to his feet.

Ca…Ca…Ca…Captain Jones?" he wheezed. He raised one hand to his throat protectively and rubbed the base of his spine with the other. Warily he glanced into the trees for any sign of his runaway horse. Plant meanwhile seemed unperturbed at the recognition. "Alias Ca…Ca… Ca…Captain Jones to you Ca… Ca…Ca…*Comrade*." Plant followed the horseman's gaze into the woods.

"I am Gorshkov, Captain Gorshkov," the horseman confirmed trying to retain some dignity," and as I am sure you are aware, I have been trying to catch up with you for the last four hours; I have news from Preston."

Plant continued to stare into the woods. "The place or the person?" he asked indifferently. He turned quickly to look at his fellow officer.

"Tudor," he cried, adrenalin again beginning to forge through his veins, "train your Webley right between his eyes. If he moves an inch, blow the top of his skull off."

Then like a large graceful tiger he leapt from the road and into the shadows of the trees on their left and once again was gone.

"What the hell ... !" cried Tudor, staring at Gorshkov in disbelief. But Gorshkov turned again to face the thicket that Plant had disappeared into, for he heard the sound of a long low whistle. Tudor glanced over his shoulder quickly to see the two occupants of the truck they had been following cowering on either side of their vehicle pointing revolvers in his direction. Very comforting, thought Tudor sarcastically. He returned his gaze to Gorshkov, who had now raised both his arms in the air. The night breeze gently shook the leaves on either side of the road. Then again, both men quite distinctly heard another long, low whistle. Tudor shook his head in frustration and sighed heavily. What was 'Samson' up to now? But he did as he had been ordered and trained the barrel of his pistol at the bridge of Gorshkov's nose. The breeze died down. Gorshkov stared beyond Tudor at the three huddled soldier-like figures in the back of the truck. He could not see their faces for they huddled together very closely – unnaturally close, he thought, and their heads were covered by peak caps. The whistle came no more. The large yellow moon hung in the sky like a Halloween pumpkin. Tudor's arm was steady; he would not miss from that range. He glanced uneasily into the woods. If this 'Gorshkov' was part of a larger detachment that was following them, and if they had done Plant in, then he at least would get his man before *he* was silenced. Gorshkov took his gaze from the back of the truck and stared into the trees beyond at the other side of the road. The leaves rustled again. "Look at me," Tudor demanded, his tension rising rapidly, "and only me!" Gorshkov raised his chin proudly at the young officer. Just a boy, he thought, no more than twenty-one or – two! But when he caught the direct stare of Tudor's eyes he averted his own and looked down at his feet. All was now still; even the light breeze seemed to have abated. It was so quiet that Tudor could almost hear his own heartbeat. He was aware that his own breathing had become loud and tense and against the sudden silence of the night, his breathing sounded to him as loud as someone urgently sawing wood. The tension was unbearable. Tudor's finger pressed a little more on the trigger. I will get him before they get me, he reasoned to himself. He knew they were all sitting ducks; there was no doubt about that. It was all Plant's fault! Him and his heroics! He also knew that the .455 Webley Auto MK1, with its .454 inch bullet really would blow the top of his victims skull clean off from that range. The taut wire of tension was finally released with an anticipated but still, when it finally came, shocking movement from the trees on their left as a horse and rider leapt out as from some cavernous black hole. Both men were rooted to the ground as they gazed in awe at what looked for a split second like a great shining horse larger than either had ever seen before and its rider seemed to exude a light as if he was wearing armour; the highly polished metal reflected a dazzling white moon into their eyes. Then the moment passed and the quite normal but highly spirited horse placed itself in between Gorshkov and Tudor. Towering above them, the coal black mare stamped one hoof on the ground impatiently, and champed the bit between her teeth as steam escaped from her flaring nostrils. Tudor stepped back quickly regaining his composure, but could not shoot his prisoner for he could no longer see him. Instinctively, he stared from the corner of his eye at his two companions in the other truck, and saw them start forward. Uncertain, Tudor couldn't make up his mind whether to shoot the rider on the horse or try for the prisoner. But before he could make his mind up, he realized, chillingly, that he was suddenly staring down the barrel of a rather large pistol himself – the barrel of a 9mm automatic to be precise and it was inches from the centre of the bridge of his nose. The rider, gripping the horse between his knees, had also trained the pistol in his left hand onto the temple of the prisoner.

"A riderless horse creates attention, old chap," said the man on the horse, "it usually means a *missing* rider," Plant grinned down at Tudor, "we don't want more of these guys on our tail, do we?"

"You ... you ... blithering idiot! I could have shot you!" cried Tudor angrily, though at the same time thoroughly relieved, "In fact, I should have!"

Plant grinned broadly at him.

"You couldn't even shoot the unarmed prisoner, never mind a crazy, mad, couldn't care less, fully armed freak like me!" Plant replied, dismounting from the horse. The grin was still on his mouth, but no longer in his eyes. "A second's hesitation can cost you your life, sonny boy! You were lucky it was me on the horse and not another of these guys." He pointed at Gorshkov accusingly.

"No, no, you've have got it all wrong!" cried the prisoner desperately. This individual is a crazy man, and Gorshkov was wondering what he would do next, "as I said, I have been sent to warn you!"

"Then explain yourself," demanded Plant. He searched the saddle bags for any clue as to the identity of the rider, but of course found none. "Having no papers in times like these," he said to Gorshkov, "is as good as declaring yourself an enemy to anyone you meet."

Gorshkov quickly explained that he was an operative for the advancing White Army. His task had been to scout out the Bolshevik defences at Ekaterinburg before their final assault. He was also under orders to try and find out if the Imperial family were still alive and where they were being held. Of course, everybody knew that they had been imprisoned in the Ipatiev house, but then after the night of 16 July they seemed to have just disappeared, though it was rumoured, and indeed it had been officially announced a couple of days ago that the emperor had indeed been shot. He himself had been there in the city theatre on 20 July when Commissar Goloshchokin made the announcement.

"The puppets of the British and French have almost surrounded the city, comrades!" Gorshkov recited Goloshchokin's very words to them, explaining that he didn't even attempt to deny that the city was about to fall into enemy hands. "The White Army is made up of Czechs, Cossacks and old Imperialist Generals that think that they will get their tsar back, but they never will, for we have shot him!" Gorshkov described to Plant and Tudor how there had been no cheers of celebration, as the speaker had expected, but rather an ominous silence. It was then that somebody passed Gorshkov a note written on British Consul paper. "Typical!" exclaimed Plant at what he termed as either incredibly lax or incredibly arrogant behaviour by Thomas Preston. The note, explained Gorschkov, stated that though the tsar was indeed dead the rest of the family had escaped. The tsarina and the tsarevich, with the help of Preston himself, had boarded a train bound for Odessa. "Soon after, though, the heir died, apparently in his sleep," Gorshkov informed them rather coldly.

"Show me the note," demanded Plant.

Gorshkov produced a grubby piece of paper that had been folded many times and handed it to Plant, who quickly read it. He then put it in his own pocket.

"Okay, you sonofabitch," hissed Plant, "keep your voice down. We are aware of the heir's death, but they are not," he pointed discretely over to the back of the truck where the three figures still sat huddled together, "and I would like to keep it that way, for the time being at least." The memory of the pale, frail barely fourteen-year-old boy with the translucent skin was still vivid in his mind. He had done nobody any harm. He had lived much of his life under the dreadful shadow of his illness, many times suffering spasms of agony caused by the blood seeping into his joints resulting in chronic bruising and disfiguring swellings. Plant placed his pistol back in its holster and sighed. "Or at the very least, until we get them to Odessa and the reunion with their mother!"

"But that is why I was ordered to find you," said Gorshkov, "the tsarina is no longer on the train to Odessa! The train was stopped and she has been arrested. They have taken her to Perm!"

Tudor visibly paled and cursed under his breath. "Then what is it that we are supposed to do now?" he asked, looking directly at Plant.

Plant shifted his feet irritably. "I can tell you what they *want* us to do, sonny boy," he answered, looking up at the starless sky. "They want us to go to Perm as well! Is that correct, Goatsfoot, or whatever your name is?"

"Your orders are to double back to Perm, yes," answered Gorshkov, ignoring the sarcastic remark, "You must rescue the tsarina at all costs."

"Let me see those orders?" asked Plant, himself now quite dismayed and bewildered. He knew that such a task meant almost certain suicide for him and his men. He also knew full well that orders like that would never be committed to paper.

The two men's obvious discomfort had become so evident that Gorshkov's confidence had grown in leaps and bounds. He raised his eyebrows and smirked smugly.

Tudor lit a cigarette. He blew the smoke out of his mouth high into the air as he chuckled quietly. "Perm is a big place, my friend," he said. "Where do we begin to look? The county jail, perhaps?"

Gorshkov seemed pleased at the reaction his news was having on both men. "There will be no need for that," he answered. "One of our agents has infiltrated the top echelons of Lenin's command. She is to be housed at Berezin Rooms on Obvinskaya Street, not far from the Cheka headquarters, you'll be happy to know!" Gorshkov could barely hide his glee. "And," he continued, "let me inform you, the Cheka is already hot on your trail. They had been ordered by Lenin himself to at all costs apprehend the missing 'baggage' and to restore it to its rightful owners."

"Rightful owners!" exclaimed Tudor with contempt.

"They are angry," continued Gorshkov, staring at Tudor, returning the contempt. "I don't know what you did back there in Ekaterinburg, but they are baying for your blood. We are not too sure what they intend to do should they catch up with you, but we are very afraid for the grand duchesses."

Plant coolly scrutinised the wooded area that surrounded them. His cold, steady steel-blue eyes surveyed the silent trees. Nothing would happen to the grand duchesses if he could prevent it. But how on earth can they be expected to attempt another rescue mission while still in possession of the 'baggage' from the first one? There was also something beginning to niggle at him about the rider. If he was on their side, how did he know so much about their enemy? Had British Intelligence really grown so much?

"They are particularly interested in capturing the one who calls himself Colonel Abromovich," continued Gorshkov, staring expectantly at first Plant and then Tudor. "Lenin himself would like to have a few words with him." He continued scrutinising Plant a little longer. "It seems you are known by many names!"

He stepped backwards with mock awe. "But I have to confess, I do like your style, agent Plant!"

It was a mistake. With one swift, powerful movement Plant had him by the throat. "Listen, you slimy pipsqueak! I'm not quite sure who is pulling your strings, but I can tell you something – if it is that Kraut puppet Lenin, we won't be taking tea with him anytime soon!" He released his grip again. Gorshkov's face was now pained and purple. "You know we carry no papers, agent Plant," he spluttered, once again holding his own throat. "You will just have to trust that I am who I say I am."

Tudor strode forward. "Leave him alone, Reg," he said, "I believe him. Why else would he even be talking to us? If he was the enemy, he would rather be *shooting* at us."

Plant smirked at Tudor and shook his head slowly. He then turned to Gorshkov.

"What else can you tell us, my bringer of glad tidings?" he asked with undisguised sarcasm.

Gorshkov informed them that if the duchesses were not recaptured by the Bolsheviks soon, Lenin would have no alternative than to explain to the Germans that the family's disappearance was due to a secret rescue attempt launched privately by the king of England himself.

"Ah!" responded Plant, "so just because Lenin couldn't complete his own nasty little bit of sport with them, he intends to tell Kaiser Bill a few stories!" Plant laughed as he said this, but he knew that such a revelation could have serious repercussions for the king if the Kaiser made it public, for George had launched his own private rescue against the advice of his prime minister, Lloyd George, who had steadfastly stated that no such rescue was to take place. Being a constitutional monarch, George was bound to obey the will of his parliament. Plant himself knew and all on the inside knew that Lenin had intended to hoodwink the kaiser by murdering all of them in Ekaterinburg anyway, and had actually given the order to do so. He had intended to play for time, for he was well aware of the recent German misfortunes on the western front.

"That is not all," answered Gorshkov, unable to help himself, it seemed, "the Germans were in on the plan to one way or another eliminate the tsar and the tsarevich. I am sure you know that the succession law in Russia only recognises the males and with Nicholas and Alexei out of the way, there would be no immediate rallying point for the anti – revolutionaries. But for some reason, they were demanding that the tsarina and her daughters were to be kept from harm. Perhaps it is because Alexandre is the kaiser's cousin."

"If he knows what's good for him, Lenin needs them alive for bargaining chips," Plant concluded, "But he is mad with his intense hatred for Nicholas, and I suspect for all the Romanov family. He holds them personally liable for the hanging of his brother."

"Perhaps it would be *better* for them to be recaptured!" exclaimed Tudor, "Lenin will dare not do them any harm, at least while negotiations are still on the table. In fact, it is imperative that the Germans are informed that the women folk are safe and that nothing 'unforeseen' by Lenin has indeed happened to them."

All three men glanced over to where the three young women, now clearly visible, sat cross legged and huddled together in a quiet conversation of their own on the grassy glade. They had been joined by Sergeant Mc Alistair and Trooper Yates. Tudor sighed loudly, shrugged his shoulders and loped off to offer each of them a cigarette. Plant watched them. McAlistair and Yates had been hand-picked and were the best available. Plant had insisted that the party to help escort any of the family rescued be as small as possible, for it was going to be a dangerous trek to Odessa. So far so good, but the news that Gorshkov had brought changed everything. He now wished he had *fewer* men.

"There is something else," said Gorshkov quietly. "The

259

Whites are grinding out propaganda in order to incite hatred towards the Bolsheviks."

"Oh yes!" answered Plant just as quietly but with a little more venom, "do they really need to make anything up?"

"They are spreading rumours that all the women of the imperial family were horribly abused; you know, raped and the like, before they were shot," continued Gorshkov.

"Is that so?" answered Plant, continuing to look at the three girls. "Well, it was close for one of them at least, my friend!" The crazy-eyed face of the wild-haired Ermakov came to mind.

"And that they were decapitated and that their heads have been sent to Lenin in a wooden box," exclaimed Gorshkov – a little too eagerly for Plant's liking.

"Well, if that is the case, I'd love to know how he would explain the row of skulls to Kaiser Bill," hissed Plant, his left hand holding the handle of his knife. "With all the crap being spread it really won't be difficult for them to disappear would it, if they could just get the chance? In fact, maybe we should all just disappear." He looked now particularly at Olga. Her sad, pretty face looked up at the stars dreamily.

"So you see," continued Gorshkov hurriedly, "they are going to be dreadfully embarrassed if you guys do manage to get them out at least, but they will never stop hunting you, or them."

"Well, as you say," said Plant coolly, "I have new orders."

Gorshkov looked surprised "But surely you don't mean to obey them? Perm is the last Bolshevik stronghold. It would be suicide for you and for them." He pointed in the direction of the little gathering on the grass.

"My guess is it would take us two days to get to Perm from here," reasoned Plant, as if to himself. "This Obvinskaya Street, where is it?"

Gorshkov seemed surprised by the question and found himself answering correctly. "The Berezin Rooms on Obvinskaya Street are a short walk from both the train station and the Kama

River." He stopped himself abruptly. "I can quite easily report back and say that I was unable to find you; that you had all disappeared." His words came out in a stutter.

"Now, why on earth would you want to do such an honourable thing like that for the likes of me?" asked Plant, looking at Gorshkov keenly.

"Well, not for you," Gorshkov blurted, "for them, and for the others that have already been caught up in this blasted mess."

"Others?" asked Tudor, who had joined them again. "You know, Reg, I've been wondering how the Bolshies knew that the empress was on that train? Didn't she board a Red Cross for that very reason, in order to travel undetected and wasn't your pal the *real* Jonesy with her?"

Plant nodded at Tudor and then looked expectantly at Gorshkov. There was something not quite right about this so called Czech operative who was mysteriously taking orders from Thomas Preston, the British Consul for Ekaterinburg. Why hadn't he been informed about him?

"The Red Cross train that the empress was travelling on was stopped by the Bolsheviks. Her 'travelling companion,' Captain Digby Jones, was killed. As I said: she has been taken back to Perm," Gorshkov answered awkwardly.

Plant was silent. How *did* the Bolshies know that she was on that Red Cross Train? Digby Jones was a good man, one of the best in the organisation. He had travelled with Charles Digby Jones himself under the name of Reed. They had journeyed from Murmansk to Ekaterinburg together as part of the initial rescue plan. Due to the immense sensitivity of the mission, it had been decided he would travel under an alias. He smiled when he remembered that it was the Welsh Captain that had suggested the name Reed, noticing how Plant engrossed himself in his book 'Herodotus: Histories,' whenever he got the chance as they made the arduous journey from India to Russia together. There were not many men that Plant trusted or particularly liked, but

Captain Digby Jones had been one of them. Could their own organisation have been infiltrated? He glanced quickly again over to the grand duchesses, who were startled by a sudden rustle of leaves and an apparent flap of wings close by as the dark shape of a large bird, probably a purple heron, swooped up into the air. He smiled momentarily as all three girls marvelled when it flew majestically, its neck retracted, up and away. If only they had wings, he thought. All at once, his and their situation seemed hopeless. Whether he obeyed or disobeyed the orders, there was no way out.

"The ship will not now be waiting for us at Odessa, my friend," he said quietly to Tudor. He turned and faced Gorshkov, staring blankly at the 'operative.' "The only hope we have now is to *obey* orders!"

So their rescue plans were now in tatters. The tsar himself had been killed in the Ipatiev house; now the tsarina had been recaptured and was being held prisoner in Perm by those that hated her the most. Her only hope now was a negotiated compromise between the Russians and the Germans; a compromise her husband would never have agreed to –another reason why Kaiser Bill would have sanctioned his execution. Was this Gorshkov some sort of elaborate trap? But, as Tudor had implied, why the need for dialogue? Did the empress really need his help now, anyway? Surely she will be sent to Germany as part of the agreement. He disagreed with what Tudor had implied, for surely it would be less antagonising for Lenin if the girls were not captured. But then again, if, as Gorshkov had said, the kaiser were to make public that the king had launched a private rescue mission, it could quite possibly lead to major civil unrest in old Blighty. He sucked hard on the Gauloise. It would certainly be better for him and his brave little band of 'merry men' if they were to ignore the new orders and get them all out of there. But how on earth was he to accomplish that with absolutely no support? For the first time in his life, Plant was completely undecided.

For the first time in his life, his obligation to his superiors was being questioned deeply by his own conscience. To hell with the 'little' king, he thought. After all, I would be doing him a favour. But what of the incredible disappearing Grand Duchess Tatiana Nicolaevna and her mysterious friend? Where on earth had they gotten to? His mind grew foggy with unanswered questions. He looked across again at the three young women sitting on the grass. There was also another little problem that he knew he had to deal with. He gazed fleetingly again at the perfect nose and high forehead profile of Olga, the eldest sister. There was no doubt that he was physically attracted to her. Her beautiful blue eyes were so clear and yet brimming with exhausted tragedy and sadness. He could still feel her touch on his wrist as he was just about to set to work on shaving her head with his cut throat razor in order to disguise them as soldiers; playful words in the midst of her sorrow. "Oh, golly! You are going to discover that my ears stick out almost as much as yours!"

"Tudor," he said quietly, finally making up his mind, "we make for Odessa."

Gorshkov seemed pleased, but Tudor stood squarely facing Plant, both his hands on his hips.

"What are you saying, Plant?" he demanded. "Orders are orders and I understood that we are to go to Perm!"

"They are my orders Captain Tudor, not yours," Plant answered quietly.

"But Reg!" Tudor protested, "Don't you see what that would mean?"

"Yes, I know exactly what it would mean!" Plant turned on Tudor angrily. "It would mean that you and your little club won't get their own way for once."

"Have you any idea who you are putting yourself up against, you fool?" Tudor challenged him.

"So you would risk three young lives in order to try to save one, would you?" Plant retaliated, "Even though the empress herself would be horrified at those orders. I am positive she would want us to get them out of Russia and if she knew, get them away from any plans that you and your mob have in store for them."

"It's not for you to make that call, old man," Tudor persisted, "I do things by the book, and if I have to enforce it, I will."

Plant had made up his mind, but whatever he planned to do in that instance was abruptly interrupted. The shot that rang out was shocking, not only it's sound in the low murmuring, breathless evening, but also the aftermath.

Seeing that the conversation was becoming a little more heated than usual between Plant and Tudor, Sergeant Albert McAlistair quietly excused himself from the presence of the three grand duchesses, made his way across the short clearing and onto the road. He held his peak cap in his hand and at the very moment that he placed it on his head, the deafening blast rang out from the wooded area on their left. His cap was catapulted high up and to one side into the air. It would almost have looked comical except for the ghastly hole that spewed blood and tissue protruding from the soldiers left temple. He balanced on one leg for a second or two aiding the 'comical' macabre show and then crashed to the ground face first with a sickening sound of crunching cartilage as his nose took most of the impact.

The confused silence that followed was quickly made intelligible by a piercing scream from one of the girls and Plant watched in another rare moment of indecision as the shortest of the young 'soldiers' bolted in the direction of the woods on the other side of the road. He clenched his fists willing her to make it, but alas she was bundled to the ground by a burly Red Guard, who appeared suddenly from the trees on the left. They were obviously surrounded, and had been quite possibly for some time, thought Plant. The ten or so seconds of Anastasia's escape attempt had almost played out in slow motion, but as soon as she hit the ground and the air filled with the sound of more gunshots,

Plant was jolted back to reality. He dropped low and darted for the truck. Tudor meanwhile had plans of his own. He immediately drew his pistol and pointed it at point blank range to the temple of Gorshkov, guessing that Gorshkov had been part of the ambush. Another shot rang out and the pistol flew from Tudor's hand; two of the fingers bent back in a hopeless position and broken. High-pitched screams, gunshots and shouts now filled the air, but Plant was oblivious; his training dictated his single mindedness. He had to reach the truck. Bullets flew passed his head like angry wasps, some burying themselves deep into the trunks of the trees to his right, others more dangerously ricocheting up off the stony ground and relaunching themselves in all directions. He had been in situations like this before and just as out-numbered, but now he had a strange feeling in his heart; was it fear? Fear that his life would end there, that night, in the middle of a Russian wilderness? More to the point: who would then protect Olga if it did? He grit his teeth as he darted forward, dodging this way and that, miraculously somehow still unharmed. Out of the corner of his eye, he saw a shadowy figure advance from the woods and come up behind Trooper Yates, who was still rooted in horror where he stood, and place a loop of wire over his head and then pull it tightly around his neck. The cheese wire bit deeply into his throat and he fell silently to his knees. His eyes glazed over in a blank stare as his attacker pushed him indifferently forward and onto his face. He didn't move again. Almost simultaneously, he saw another of the 'soldiers' bolt from behind the truck. She was caught unceremoniously by the coat tails just as she was about to disappear into the same woods her sister had made for. She lay on her belly on the grass verge, breathing heavily, a muddied boot imprinted on the side of her shaven head. It was, of course, impossible that Plant would not be hit. He had been shot twice before, and he immediately recognised the numbing almost 'dead' pain as his left forearm was flung out sideways from the impact. As before, there was no pain and he wondered briefly how bad it was. As he reached the truck, he flung himself headlong onto the back of it next to where the last 'soldier' lay upon the flat bed, cowering and shivering in fright. He knew it was Olga. He held his 9mm automatic ruthlessly up against the back of her head.

"I suggest you cease firing, you bastards!" he screamed, "or you'll have one less chip to bargain with!"

Immediately, there was a high, shrill shout from Plant's right side. Then silence again, except for the groans of agony from Tudor where he kneeled, nursing his broken hand.

"There, there my dear Reginald," came the voice that Plant least expected to hear, "Why *are* you so uncooperative?"

The clipped English accent of Winston Peabody whined in the eerie silence.

"You should know me, old boy," replied Plant, looking down at his left forearm and the shredded material of his coat on both sides. Thankfully, the bullet had passed clean through. Just as thankfully, his pulsating adrenalin had prevented him from as yet experiencing the pain, but he knew it wouldn't be long. Olga began to scream. "Quiet, you little idiot!" Plant hissed as low as he could. "I will not harm you." Olga whimpered in reply.

"Oh yes, we *all* know you, Colonel Abromovich," answered Peabody, "Or is that Reginald Abromovich?" he continued laughing. "Now that would be a contradiction of names, if ever there was one."

"Yes, yes!" answered Plant, the blood dripping from his wrist onto the pale white, outstretched hand of Olga that lay upon the flat bed. She looked up at him. Her eyes for a moment made him feel hopeless. "Almost as big a contradiction as Winston Pibodikov, I should say," he answered, but he couldn't return the laughter.

"I like your humour, inspector," said Peabody, stepping forward into the light of the ivory moon that had just reappeared from behind a cloud. A large, shadowy figure stood close behind him.

"You two really do turn up in the weirdest of places," Plant continued. "You should get a wife, Winston. People are beginning to talk!"

As he spoke, Plant surveyed the perimeter of the woods around him. He could see quite clearly that the whole area was filled with shadowy figures and everyone held a rifle.

"Well now, you're a fine one to talk, inspector," retorted Peabody. "Yes, that is a fine statement to make from someone who has no friends at all, who never has had any friends and unless something quite miraculous happens, never *will* have any either. Oh, unless we discount Boris, of course."

Plant looked at Olga. For some reason it bothered him that she had heard what Peabody had just said. But how the hell *did* he know?

"I'll tell you what," continued Peabody, "My friend Gorshkov over there has got his nice-looking revolver pointing right at your brother officer's head. Whether that bothers you or not, I'm not sure, because no doubt he is not a *friend* of yours. Perhaps for the first time in your life, you can show a little compassion for somebody else apart from yourself."

"That really is a case of the kettle calling the pot wouldn't you say, you old goat!" Plant shouted back but his heart sank, for he knew what Peabody was about to threaten.

"As I was saying, before you very rudely interrupted me," Peabody persisted, "If I wink rather seductively at him he will pull his trigger, if you know what I mean." Plant glanced quickly over to Tudor who was now kneeling and bending forward over his hand, looking into the ground silently. "On the other hand, Colonel Abromovich," Peabody continued, "If you send that bald-headed little duchess over here I will ask my friend Gorshkov to be a nice and tolerant little man and look the other way while your friend makes a dash for the woods."

Plant looked at Olga and finally made up his mind. There was no other way.

"Why don't you wink rather seductively at that great big bald-headed wife you have for a body guard?" he shouted. "Who knows what might happen next."

The silence that followed was broken by heavy breathing and what sounded to Plant like growling.

"My, my," called Plant, "she's getting excited! I think we should all leave so that you two can be alone."

"I am waiting, inspector!" Peabody called, totally immune to the accusations.

"What about all *your* friends?" asked Plant, looking from side to side at the shadowy figures.

Peabody shouted out a command in Russian. Immediately, all the soldiers standing in the shadows of the trees strode forward and stood to attention with their rifles by their sides.

"Just because you have amused us with your little bit of warped humour," Peabody said slyly, "and even though you are quite the talk of the town at the moment and my good friend Vladimir Lenin so desperately longs to meet you, I will let you *both* make a dash for it. At least give you a *chance* to bugger off."

Plant sighed heavily. The pain was beginning to throb nicely in his arm now. Pain always made him more than a little irritated. He looked down again at Olga. Her cap had fallen to one side beside her. The side of her face rested on her own forearm in complete hopelessness. She no longer gazed at him but had closed her eyes. Her fingers twitched nervously. Plant rose painfully, dragging the limp Olga to her feet. She shivered uncontrollably. But Plant grit his teeth.

"Tell you what, Winnie," Plant shouted loud and clear. There was a brief sound of laughter from the soldiers, "me and the bald duchess here are going to walk ever so slowly towards that thicket over there. He pointed gingerly with his maimed arm, causing more blood to spill, this time onto the deck of the truck, "then we are going to disappear ever so nicely into those woods, never to be seen again by either you or your men. In return,

I won't blow her brains out for you or all your nice Russian soldiers to witness. I mean a report on that incident getting back to old Vladimir's mates in Germany is really not going to go down very well, is it now?"

There was a moment of uncertain silence. Smith growled again.

"And the officer?" enquired Peabody not quite as silkily, pointing to when the silent Tudor still knelt.

"Oh, you can blow *his* brains out. As you say, he's no friend of mine. I don't have any friends, remember!" answered Plant. He glanced at Tudor, who flinched slightly but remained silently staring at the ground.

Peabody knew Plant would not hesitate to do what he had threatened. It was well known in the 'club' that Reginald Plant was a 'lost case;' that his reason for exceptional bravery was because he didn't care if he lived or died. He would have to let him and the girl go on this occasion, but there would be time to get them before they made their way back to Perm. Olga he knew could quite easily also know where the hidden 'Hen Egg' surprise was.

"Your ruthlessness is as impressive as always, inspector, but let me warn you, one day you are going to find a friend, dare I say someone even more than a friend, and then your life will be finished. For then you will care whether you live or die and then when you are threatened you will cry like a baby. Just remember, I was the one that told you that," Peabody answered.

Something hot and wet rolled down Plants cheek. He looked at the back of Olga's shaven head. If only Peabody knew that that day had already arrived.

"But I my friend can be just as ruthless," Peabody continued. "Before you leave, I would like you to witness a little spectacle." He made way for Smith to come forward from behind him. "Put that person over there out of his misery, Mr Smith," he said, pointing to where Tudor knelt. Gorshkov stood back quickly as

Smith took his position behind Tudor. Anastasia, who was being held tightly by the big burly Red Guard, tried to cry out but was silenced with a sharp smack from the powerful soldier across her right ear. She fell to the ground, whimpering and sobbing.

Plant had not counted on this reaction from Peabody. They would surely want Tudor alive for questioning. He spoke quickly.

"I have heard that Lenin would like to meet all those involved with the nasty end bestowed upon his chambermaids Ermakov and Yurovsky. Have I heard incorrectly?" Plant's tone was light but insistent.

Peabody gritted his teeth in frustration. His men looked at each other in agreement. Lenin must be obeyed. "So, it wasn't only you that pulled that little trick?" Peabody asked.

Plant smiled apologetically. "Even the best need help," he acknowledged, knowing that his words had hit their mark and that Tudor would be taken prisoner and kept alive at least for the time being.

"Let the fool pass!" Peabody commanded his men.

Smith looked at his boss expectantly. "Can I give him the 'Smith neck twist' now, boss?" he asked, placing a large powerful hand on either side of Tudors head.

"Do you ever pay attention, you imbecile?" cried Peabody, watching Plant help Olga from the back of the truck. Plant kept his pistol hard up against the back of her head as they tentatively passed by the soldiers on the left and then disappeared into the shadows of the trees.

"Can I just shoot him then?" asked Smith.

CHAPTER 10
THE SOKOLOV FILE

It was January 1919; Winston Peabody sat behind a desk in an office in the city of Perm in Russia. In front of him lay a great wad of papers making up the investigation into the murder of the imperial family. It described in detail how they were led down to the basement of the Ipatiev house on the night of 16 July under the pretence that they were to be moved to a place of safety; that after they were all assembled in the basement, Yakob Yurovsky read out a sentence condemning them to death. They were all then subsequently shot. The file described in gruesome detail how, after the first volley of shots, only the tsar and tsarina lay dead. The rest had to be finished off with more gunshots, and the tsar's daughters were bayoneted as the bullets merely ricocheted off their jewel-encrusted corsets. All four were eventually finished off with mercy shots to the head. The tsarevich was also shot in the head when found to be groaning and still alive, even after the daughters were dead. Peabody smiled. Perfect! Just as the history books will say it happened. He read a little further. The report then outlined how Yurovsky, Ermakov and their men loaded the corpses onto a truck and took them out to the Four Brothers Mine, a place that had already been scouted for suitability by Yurovsky. All the bodies were stripped of clothing and jewellery and then thrown down into the mine shaft. It was only when Yurovsky realised that the water in the shaft was not actually very deep and that the bodies were not fully immersed that he decided to bring them all back to the surface, burn them to avoid any recognition and then bury them. Again Peabody smiled. It was a little stupid leaving a clear trace of jewels, clothing and the like at the scene if they were supposed to be trying to keep their gruesome task secret. Obviously, the belongings were *meant* to be found in order to authenticate the report. Indeed, also in front of him on the desk lay the corset stays for six females, but with no damage whatsoever from bullets or bayonets. These Bolsheviks, he concluded, drink too much Vodka to plan anything properly. There was also an arrangement of spent bullet cartridges totalling twenty-one in number. Also not enough if they want to authenticate a massacre of eleven victims mowed down by random fire. He shook his head slowly; the things I have to put right these days! Last but not least was the grisliest of the murder remnants. A finger, cut off just below the knuckle. That's quite convincing, he agreed, as if somebody needed to cut it off in order to remove a ring. The report in the file described it as that of a middle-aged woman with long tapering fingers that had been well-manicured. The owner was identified as the tsarina. Peabody thought about that for a little while. A bit risky, he thought, especially in this age of the diabolical finger-printing procedure. Surely prints would only need to be tested and it would disprove the file's claim? But then again, were the tsarina's ever taken? He doubted it. He suspected the finger to be a fake anyway, and wondered briefly who the real owner was, or rather, had been. This Nikolai Sokolov, whom he was now impersonating, was a bit of a dummy if he thought this was going to fool the future history sceptics. Still, he could certainly put his weight behind the contents of the file. After all, he was wielding the power of the timer. But impersonating this person had proved to be rather tiresome so far. There had been so many people coming forward claiming to have the identity of one or another of the family. There had been many Anastasias, a few Olgas and Maries, a particularly ridiculous Alexie and of course, the ragamuffin from Moscow who had claimed to be Tatiana Nicolaevna. He had told the astonished imposter that she no more looked like the duchess than he did. He tapped his finger impatiently as he listened to the clock tick away the tedious seconds. Someone else had requested an interview with him, claiming they had information concerning the whereabouts of the female members of the imperial family. Now this was more interesting. It seemed the timer was finally coming to the party when it propelled them into 1918 this time. As Nikolai Sokolov, the official investigator into the murder, he would be able to get access to the Ipatiev house itself. In fact, the papers giving him the authorisation would be issued any day now, he had been told. His recent thoughts had constantly been on that great chest of jewels and the Romanov riches that had been brought into the house by that mad man Ermakov on the very night history says the family were murdered. Indeed, it was because of those jewels that the fight broke out and the timer whisked him and Smith away to safety just in time. No history book had ever mentioned that or the chest of jewels. Could it be possible that it was still in that house, hidden somewhere?

There was a knock on the door and Smith entered, followed by a young fair-haired woman. She stood directly in front of Peabody's desk. Her eyes searched the room nervously.

"Thank you, Smith." Peabody spoke without bothering to stand or even look up from his file. He pointed to the door with his pen. Smith muttered something unintelligible under his breath and closed the door behind him.

"What is your name?" he asked her, twirling the pen between his index and forefinger. His manner was light, but it didn't relax the young woman in front of him. He turned another page of the file and stared at the photograph. It was of a British bulldog and it sat very arrogantly, he thought, in the lap of Tatiana Nicolaevna. At the top of the picture someone had written in a large bold script: MISSING.

"Natalya Mutnykh," she answered softly.

"Age?"

"Twenty-six."

"Occupation?"

"Nurse."

Peabody sighed heavily. He turned a page, looked briefly at its contents, sighed heavily again and then closed the file with a snap. He reached across the desk for a note pad and wrote down the information.

"Now, my dear," said Peabody, finally looking up at the young woman in front of him, his voice silky smooth. "I believe you have some information for my investigation on the murder of the tsar and his family?"

The young woman was still very nervous as she stood swaying slightly and repeatedly pushed the blonde strands of hair that straggled the side of her face, behind her ears with the tips of her fingers.

"Yes, Mr Sokolov," she stuttered slightly, "but that is what I came to tell you; not all of them *were* murdered."

This was *very* interesting. Though her voice was trembling a little, her tone was honest and adamant. But it was imperative that the world and the Russian people in particular were led to believe that all the family were exterminated – a term he liked to use when referring to their murder. It was also imperative that she herself was gently persuaded that she had been mistaken.

"Is that so, my dear?" he answered her smoothly. "I do know how you feel. I too am so anguished that the dear family are no longer with us that I also wish them back, but I am afraid that it is not so. They *were* all murdered back in July; look at the evidence." He spread his hands over the pathetic remnants on his desk. "The proof lies here before us."

"But sir, it is not true." The young woman struggled to contain her excitement. "For with my own eyes I have seen them."

"Where?" asked Peabody abruptly, and now not quite so smoothly, "and how?"

She took a deep breath and then spoke quickly in a steady, soft voice.

"My brother Vladimir is the secretary to the Ural Regional Soviet," she began. "One evening, I overheard a conversation between him and comrades Safarov and Beloborodov. They were discussing the imperial family."

"You were eavesdropping?" Peabody said, with a hint of intimidation.

"No, sir!" she answered firmly. "I said I *overheard* their conversation."

"What did you hear?" he asked, his voice resuming its silkiness.

"That the emperor had been shot and killed in Ekaterinburg and the heir had also died from a disease he had had since birth; the ex-tsarina and her daughters had disappeared for a while but had then turned up suddenly in Perm."

"Your brother *told* you this?" said Peabody accusingly.

"No, sir! I overheard a conversation he was having with ..."

"I see, I see," Peabody interrupted. "What else did you hear?"

"Nothing, sir! After that, I acted on my own initiative. I have always been enthralled with the imperial family, you see, so a couple of weeks ago I went to see my brother's fiancée, Anna Kostina, who is the secretary to Comrade Zinoviev at present commanding in Perm ... "

"Yes, yes," Peabody interrupted impatiently, "I know Zinoviev, but get to the point!"

"Well, Anna and I went to see him at the Regional Soviet,

but we were told he was not there as he was on guard duty at Berezin's rooms on Obvinskaya Street. When we saw him, he told us that the imperial family were there, in the basement. I asked him to show me, as I didn't believe him. He secretly took us both down there. I will never forget the pale tired faces of those once great women!" She looked down at her feet; her lips quivered slightly. "I cannot tell how many exactly there were but the conditions they were living in were very poor. They were sleeping on wooden pallets on the floor and without any bedding."

Peabody shook his head as if in disbelief. But the young woman continued her story:

"The only light in the room came from a yellow candle, but I could see that they were all in a terrible state. One of them, Anastasia I think, was sitting on the floor and softly whistling. I know that she was always the naughty one. I would have loved to have spoken to her, but my brother knew what he had done was forbidden and he led us away quickly. Being interested in the family and with Anna so well connected, I soon learned that the family had first been brought to Perm at the end of August. The ex-tsarina had arrived alone and had been housed in the building of the Excise Office at the corner of Obvinskaya and Pokrovskaya streets where she and her daughters, who arrived a little later, were kept in good conditions. But then one of the daughters tried to escape. Some say it was Tatiana and that she *did* get away; others say it was Anastasia and that they beat her and brought her back. After this, they were moved to the Berezin rooms."

The young woman stopped speaking and again looked down at her feet. "Some say that they beat her so badly that she has died."

Peabody ignored the remark. "And where are they now, my dear?"

"They are still there, as far as I know," she answered, almost whispering.

Peabody rose from his chair and came around the desk. He put a fatherly arm around the young woman.

"I am going to tell you a secret that you must guard with your life, my dear," he said, staring at her with unblinking eyes. "Do you understand what I mean by that?"

"Yes, Comrade Sokolov," she answered.

Later, after the young woman had left his office, Peabody read again the sworn testimony that Natalya Mutnykh had signed. I wonder why this was never mentioned in the history books, he said aloud. He smiled broadly as he fumbled inside his jacket pocket for the small box of matches. He struck one and then held up the two page testimony in his left hand. "I wonder indeed," he said again as the small flame grew larger and then slowly devoured the sworn testimony.

*

On 25 July 1918, just over a week after the mysterious disappearance of the Russian imperial family, the city of Ekaterinburg fell to the advancing White Siberian Army and Vladimir Sokolov was appointed as the Official Investigator to the 'murder' of the Romanovs. Even though his appointment was only made official on 7 February the following year, he decided, seeing he was in the area anyway, to begin his investigation a little earlier.

The train journey from Perm to Ekaterinburg had been quite uneventful, though Smith would keep whistling annoying Christmas carols as he stared out the window at the 'Winter Wonderland.' It was late January. The imbecile, Peabody thought irritably to himself.

"You ought to have been a trumpet player, Mr Smith," said Peabody, crossing and then uncrossing his legs in quick succession, as was his habit when displeased or nervous. "Though nobody in the world would have been able to guess what you were playing," he continued, his face creased in mild anguish at the tuneless tones of a destroyed 'Hark the Herald Angels Sing.'

Smith stopped whistling immediately. "I like that idea, boss!" he exclaimed eagerly. "I think I'll ask Father Christmas for one."

"I think, Mr Smith, you would perform a better tune after eating a plate of beans!" Peabody replied, and then chuckled quietly at his rare attempt at humour. Smith put his fingers to his temples. He stared in concentration at his own shoes. "Oh, okay boss!" he answered, "I'll ask old Santa for a tin of beans, then." He returned his mournful gaze to the window. Peabody looked across the compartment at his fellow time traveller. He shook his head. "I must admit, your new name suits you, don't you think, Heinz?" he observed, this time without a trace of humour.

"I don't know why I have to be a bloody Herman, boss," Smith answered, still looking blankly at the glass pane, the sarcasm from his boss, as usual going completely over his head.

"Herman?" cried Peabody incredulously ."How many times have I told you *my* name and *your* name, you imbecile! I cannot believe how suited you are to it, Herr Dimkop!"

Smith looked puzzled and then began to shake with laughter. "I meant 'Herman' as in 'Herman the German,' boss," he said between bouts of girlish giggles, "I quite like my new name though: Heinz Dimkop."

"Yes," agreed Peabody, "rather debonair, isn't it?"

Peabody looked out the window; the train was beginning to slow down. "This is our stop, Dimkop!" he said, looking up at the baggage rack. "Get the bags."

The jagged-toothed top of the wooden perimeter fence that had been erected especially in honour of its special guests nine months previously came into sight against the background of a purple, snow-laden sky. There were two guards on either side of the arched entrance. Sokolov and Dimkop were allowed to pass after showing their papers and the front door key.

"It is very creepy in there," said one of the guards to Peabody. "The whole place has an odour of blood, flesh and bone. There is a shadow behind every pillar, every curtain."

The two men made their way to the front door. As Peabody turned the large iron key in the lock and the door swung open silently, Smith lingered behind him.

"I don't like ghosts, Mr Peabody," he said, looking over his shoulder at the inviting front entrance.

"There are no ghosts in here, you big ninny!" answered Peabody, striding forward through the doorway. "Just a big black leather trunk full of Fabergé Eggs and other goodies, and I mean to find it!

Peabody strode up the staircase to the first floor. Broken pieces of pottery lay in a small heap upon the landing. He knelt down and picked up a badly chipped saucer. "Look at this, Mr Smith!" he said, lifting a gold-leafed saucer up into the light so that he could see the last Russian emperor's monogram on the underside. "Makes Royal Dalton look a bit like your old tin cup, wouldn't you say?" Not waiting for a ridiculous answer from his accomplice, he opened the door to the dining room and went inside. "Stay here!" he commanded, sighing heavily over his shoulder. Slightly relieved, Smith stopped abruptly at the door to the dining room and then turned to face the wide open staircase. "Just scream if you need me, boss!" he said.

Peabody gazed quickly around the room, his eyes surveying the heavy, cumbersome furniture. It was rumoured amongst the elite few that agent Plant had somehow managed to get the tsarina and the tsarevich out of the house without being seen, which Peabody found quite perplexing, for he knew there had been a guard of over two hundred men inside, outside and around the perimeter fence. It was impossible to have gotten them out the front door, so to speak, or even the back door, for that matter. No, thought Peabody, there must have been another way. He remembered a trip he had taken into the future and to one of the history books that he had flipped through on the 'murder,' and had been more than a little surprised and indeed dismayed to learn that this very house was torn down in 1977. A strange thing to do, he thought, considering its status. Unless, of course, its destruction would hide forever any trace of a rescue! Traces, perhaps of a *tunnel!* He turned right and walked carefully through an open doorway and into a long dim, open-plan passage. There were two open rooms on his right. At the end of the passage was a closed door. He walked even more carefully towards it, painfully aware of the creaking floorboards underfoot. He felt an overwhelming sense that the quietness in the house should not be disturbed, *must* not be disturbed. He shook his head in bewilderment. "Fool!" he said aloud to himself. "You're becoming like Smith!" The narrow door at the end of the passage opened and creaked loudly as he swung it open. It was the bathroom. The lewd graffiti scrawled on the walls he found mildly amusing, but what lay on the floor he found a lot more interesting. Three filthy pillow slips were strewn across the white porcelain tiles. On looking closer, he was surprised to see that each one seemed to have been stuffed with hair. Obviously, the hair in each slip belonged to different owners. One pillow bore a light brown, almost blonde colour, another a little darker colour brown, and the third, darker still. The strands of the hair were not very long, maybe two or three inches at most. It looks like our duchesses were, at the very least, preparing to be rescued, he thought. It was quite obvious to him that it was their hair in the pillow slips. At the far end of the bathroom, on the floor, lay a large, soiled, white, crumpled bath towel, inscribed with gold letters 'T.N.' 1911. He picked it up and held it to his nose. It was dank and musty. Not at all like Tatiana Nicolaevna, he thought to himself wistfully. He gave a knowing smile now as he looked again at the hair in the slips on the floor. The colour dark brown, lightly tinged with auburn, was also missing. The watery sunlight melting through the window caught the glint of something on the floor, catching his eye. He bent down to look closely at the single, solitary pearl earring, quite beautiful in its simplicity. He pocketed it without hesitation and then scrutinised the room even more closely for something else he might have missed. There was nothing else and certainly no sign of a tunnel. He quickly walked back through the passage and into the dining room again. The great grandfather clock had stopped at three minutes to ten. That fact seemed to embellish the silence. I'll be smelling perfume next, he thought to himself. There were no windows in this room, so the only light that entered came from the lounge, to his left and behind him. The clock flung its shadow forward onto the toes of his patent leather shoes. He had no idea *why* he should feel such a tremendous presence of calmness in this room, for though the light made it eerie and the shadows a little spooky, strangely it gave him an uplifting feeling one gets when one has gone through a tremendous time of grief and sadness but then the next morning, awakes to a beautiful blood red sky; a new dawn, as if the blood of grief the night before had been spilt for a reason. But the blood still there in the morning was now one's hope. He shivered slightly as if to shake off the feeling, for the calm stillness was now beginning to needle his senses. What sort of new beginning could have happened in this room? Immensely irritated, he thrust his hands into his pockets and stared around its perimeter at the rather dull wallpaper. A bottle of wine marked 'Court Wine Cellar' stood on the top of the tall heavy server. He wondered briefly what such a wine would taste like. It was then that he heard it again. It hadn't alarmed him at first; for some reason, he hadn't noticed it as being odd, really. But now here in this room, the sound was more noticeable and intrusive and couldn't just be explained away as a figment of his imagination or perhaps even a strange noise emanating from Smith, who was still standing guard at the top of the stairs. Silence, he thought, can be full of strange noises if you listen hard enough! But now he clearly heard the snuffle, wheezy breathing sort of noise. It only lasted a moment or two. He stood stock still, looking at the clock and wishing that it was working so that he could at least blame the 'other-worldly' noise in the otherwise silent house on some misdemeanour of its inner workings. There it went again. It sounded both far off and yet just around the corner at the same time, almost as if the noise was bouncing off the walls of the very foundations of the house. Or off the walls of the *tunnel!* The hairs on the back of his neck sprang to attention. Perhaps this was the reason that they demolished the place, he thought. Then, just as quickly as the nameless fear had enveloped him, his thoughts of the jewels and goodies brought forth a resounding resilience to it. He stood still and as straight as a poker, his defined chin pointing towards the door. "Pull yourself together, Master Peabody," he said aloud, "remember, you're a well – bred Englishman, and a supreme cat burglar." Then, all at once his new found courage abated as he was suddenly very aware of something behind him. He could feel hot steam on the back of his neck. Was it some sort of ghostly animal? But then he caught the strong aroma of stale cigars and 'Jasmine de vodka.' He swung around abruptly to find himself almost rubbing noses with Mr Smith.

"I don't like ghosts," said Smith in a voice totally at odds with his height, bulk and general appearance.

"There are no such things as ghosts, you nincompoop!" whispered Peabody loudly, pretending to be thoroughly irritated when meanwhile, he was thoroughly relieved and very pleased with Smith's presence.

"Then what do you suppose that *ghostly* sound *is*, boss?" asked Smith, standing a little closer to Peabody than Peabody, even under the circumstances, was comfortable with.

"Will you please stand in your *own* shoes, Mr Smith!" he cried, retrieving his wits. "There is a perfectly simple explanation for all noises, weird or otherwise. It seems to be coming from that direction," he observed, boldly pointing to his right. "Follow me!" Jewels and the possibility of the missing Fabergé Eggs were winning the day again!

Reluctantly, Smith followed Peabody as he strode across the room to the dark wood-panelled door on their right. "That was the maid's room," said Peabody, pointing to the door adjacent to the one he was now opening. "I have studied the plans to this house," he declared, "I know it better than my own." He walked through the doorway, followed very closely by Smith. It brought them out onto a long landing with bare floors. A banister bordered the stairway on their right that led down to the ground floor. "That is the way down and outside," he informed Smith. "Whoever *was* murdered that night according to the history books, took their last flight of steps down there and ... What the ...! "

He was interrupted as Smith roughly grabbed his bony shoulder. "There it goes again, boss!" he cried hoarsely. "It sounds like a pig!"

Peabody froze as he listened to the unnerving sound. Smith was right. It did sound like a pig, though this pig seemed to be suffering from an advanced case of asthma. He looked across the length of the landing, "It seems to be coming from that direction," he said, and slowly began to edge his way to the other side of the room.

"Oh, let's go, Mr Peabody!" whispered Smith loudly, "I don't like it. It sounds like the 'beast.'" Peabody stopped abruptly and turned to look sternly over his shoulder at Smith, clearly annoyed. "'Beast?'" he asked, raising both his eyebrows questioningly, "What 'beast' would that be?"

"You know!" Smith answered uncomfortably, "Mister... D."

Peabody now looked bemused. "Mister D?" he said. He began to think of any scary type animal beginning with the letter 'D' that Smith could be referring to.

"You know, Mister D. E. Vil," answered the red-faced Smith, even more uncomfortably.

"Oh, *him*!" answered Peabody, finally understanding. "No, I don't think so," he continued flippantly, "I should imagine he left this place back in July last year; no need for him to return now!"

Peabody's answer didn't make Smith feel any better at all. He looked around wildly as the sweat of terror began to drip from his forehead onto the wooden floor. The snuffle sounded again, louder now, and there was no mistaking that there was definitely a grunt or two in between the heavy erratic asthmatic breathing.

"It sounds like it's coming from inside here," exclaimed Peabody. He reached down to the handle of a low cupboard door, the type you might find in an old house under the stairs.

"Oh, don't, boss!" wailed Smith, his eyes wide with fright. "You might let something out that shouldn't *be* let out!" Peabody grit his teeth. Since leaving the dining room he had, for some reason, been filled with a sense of calm and peace, a feeling very foreign to him. But it also filled him with new vigour and he was even now beginning to enjoy himself. After all, there was no way he would be confronting the owner of the grunting snuffle. That was what he had Smith for. He pulled at the small round handle of the door. It opened quite easily and silently. Both men felt a cold draft on their faces. But there was no sign of a pig, or a demon, for that matter.

*

Ortino the 'first' was a small, black French bulldog with pointy ears. He was given as a present to Grand Duchess Tatiana Nicolaevna by her friend, the equerry to the court at Tsarskoe Selo, Dimitri Malama, in early September 1914. Unfortunately, Ortino the 'first' was rather a sickly little specimen and succumbed, sadly, to some unknown doggy disease less than a year later. Shortcomings or not, the little canine had been dearly loved by his mistress and indeed by all the imperial family. So, on hearing of his death, Dimitri promptly delivered another bulldog, but this time of the English variety. Ortino the 'second' was evidently made of much tougher stuff than Ortino the 'first'. Within weeks, the little puppy was rocketing like an express train through the halls and passages of the Alexander Palace, his paws clattering upon the mirror-polished parquet floors, usually in pursuit of some imaginary prey, possibly a cat, or even a mouse, and usually hot in pursuit of him was Jim Hercules.

"That dog should rather be called 'Torpedo,' your Imperial Highness!" the giant guard exclaimed after a particular exhausting chase one afternoon. Tatiana had just returned from her duties in the hospital and was on her way to luncheon with her mother when the familiar commotion had broken out. They both laughed as they watched the tiny scamp slither and slide as he attempted to change direction on seeing his beloved mistress. His four legs rotated at twice the normal speed as the soft pads of his paws fought frantically to connect with the polished floor. As was his habit, he flung himself into the arms of Tatiana, his pink tongue lavishing sloppy, salivating kisses on both of her cheeks. "*And* he has no respect, Tatiana Nicolaevna," continued Jim Hercules as sternly as he could while trying to hide a grin behind the palm of his hand.

"I will teach him to bow, Mr Hercules," she answered, also grinning broadly. "I will teach him the manners of a prince," she continued," so that when this ghastly war is over and things are back to normal he will be able to hold his head up high in the company of any Royal visitor!"

But of course, 'things' never did get 'back to normal' for Tatiana and her family, and when they were all placed under 'house arrest' in the Alexander Palace in March 1917 shortly after the emperor had 'abdicated,' Ortino was also 'arrested' but allowed to stay with Tatiana. Indeed, due to the compassion shown to the imperial family by Kerensky, the Prime Minister of the new provincial government, he was also allowed to follow his mistress to her confinement at Tobolsk and then finally to Ekaterinburg. Although Ortino was a little perturbed at the obvious change in his mistress's circumstances, as long as he was in her general vicinity and she gave him the odd scratch behind his left ear, he was in general a happy and contented dog. It was only on 1 July 1918 that Ortino became deeply upset and depressed, for his mistress had disappeared. Not just for an hour or so as she walked in the garden with her father and sisters in the afternoon (Ortino was forbidden to accompany her on these occasions, for when one of the guards had made a rather nasty and sarcastic remark to Tatiana, something about the beautiful pearl earrings she was wearing, the plucky bulldog promptly bit the impertinent soldier on the boot heel, creating quite a commotion. Fearing for the dog's safety in case of a repeat, his mistress decided it was better to leave him indoors with their mother), but a complete and apparently unexplainable disappearance? The night before she had gone to bed as usual with her sisters, yet the next morning when the family awoke, she was gone. That Ortino noticed was when his life took a turn for the worse, for though the existing rather rude and very disrespectful house guard was replaced, it was by a much more sinister and brooding guard led by that menacing dark – haired human with the peculiar odour. It was a scent that made his tail stand on end in morbid apprehension. Everybody he noticed had now become almost as miserable as himself. Where was his mistress? He missed lying on her long slim feet as she embroidered something (he often hoped it was a winter coat for himself). That familiar scratch behind his ear ... But most of all, he missed the sound of her voice, for it always made him want to leap into her arms. There was certainly no other voice left in his pitiless world that made him want to do that. His days now were dreary and dull and he would lie in the corner of the dining room where the imperial family were usually congregated, his stubby snout resting upon his paws, pretending to be asleep. His left eye slightly open (for any possible sighting of his mistress) and his right ear cocked (for any possible sound of her).

It was on the morning of 16 July over two weeks after his mistress had disappeared that things changed even more for the worse for Ortino. On this particular morning, he was lying at the feet of the tsar under the dining room table as the family ate breakfast. He had taken to being as close as possible to the tsar for he, it seemed, had the closest scent to that of his mistress. He lay as usual with one eye open and one ear cocked and didn't move a whisker as the door to the dining room was abruptly opened. His one eye observed the striding boots belonging to the 'sinister-smelling human.' The boots squeaked rather annoyingly and then stopped as their owner stood in the centre of the room. The sinister-smelling human was silent as he obviously surveyed the scene of the family at breakfast. Ortino's eyes followed keenly as the boots squeaked threateningly down one side of the table. They stopped abruptly just to the left of the emperor's well-worn, brown leather boots. Ortino issued a low threatening growl as he heard the loud, gruff voice of the owner of the boots and the sinister pong, demand:

"Move over, Citizen Romanov! I would also like some breakfast!"

The boots had come so close now that they almost stood on the toes of the emperor. It was obvious to Ortino that the menacing pong was threatening the exquisite smelling emperor, if not even manhandling him. Anybody with a scent remotely like Ortino's mistress being threatened let alone being roughed up would have he, Ortino, to deal with! His attack was precise, without a sound and with the speed of the nickname given to him by Jim Hercules. His strong sharp teeth bit easily through the soft supple leather of the boot and into the calf muscle of the foul-smelling perpetrator. With a surprisingly high pitched yelp and shriek of surprise, the owner of the boots began to shake his leg like a footballer in a tantrum. Ortino, meanwhile, had no choice but to hang on, for his jaw had now locked around the lower leg of his unfortunate victim. The initial outcry from the family at what injustice the menacing one had done to the emperor now gave way to a burst of laughter from Anastasia (Ortino knew that sound very well) as Jacob Yurovsky hopped around the room desperately trying to dislodge a 'crazy' dog from his leg. The sight soon made the whole family titter uncontrollably, including the emperor. But before too long there were many pairs of boots entering the room trying to detach poor Ortino, who was still swinging merrily through the air on the end of the frantically shaking boot. It was soon agreed amongst the guards that the only action to be taken was a good solid blow on the side of the animals head with a hard solid rifle butt. Immediately, Ortino released his vice-like grip and fell onto his side, both his eyes rolling backwards in their sockets. His tongue lolled out to one side. Two of his bottom teeth were still stuck in the supple leather of Yurovsky's boot.

Toothache alone for anyone is usually very unpleasant, but toothache, a blinding headache and a black eye was positively excruciating for Ortino as he awoke in pitch black darkness. He gave a long low soft moan. His misery now was at its utmost worst. He struggled to stand up. When he eventually succeeded, he was dizzy and disorientated. He fell over on his side and back into the blackness of more painful disturbing dreams where his mistress's horse continually clattered it's hooves upon his head. When he came to again, it was still dark and by the feeling in his little belly at least a day or so had passed. This time, when he clambered onto all four paws, he remained in a standing position, not least because miraculously and very invitingly in this complete blackness, his highly sensitive snout picked up the aroma of cooked meat. His snuffling nostrils twitched excitedly. He gave a low howl of glee and tottered forward on his short stubby legs in the direction of the wonderful smell. It was so dark though, and he was so eager to find the food that he fell head first in to what could only have been a large metal dish of some sort of meat stew. As he began to guzzle and slurp hungrily, a thin yellow light appeared above him. It grew larger until Ortino, while taking a snuffly breather from his meal, looked up and discovered that he was in some sort of underground tunnel, and there high above him he could clearly see a woman descending a pair of stepladders. But he had more important things on his mind for the time being and he returned his attention back to what was left of the meat. As he licked the steel dish clean, he felt a cold hand on the back of his head.

"There, my strong boy," a voice said. "We won't let those nasty Bolsheviks hurt you again, will we?" The hand continued to stroke his head and flanks, patting him lightly. "When Evdokiya and I come back again tomorrow to wash the floors, I will bring you some more food, my pet."

After being unceremoniously bludgeoned by a soldier of the guard, Ortino's limp and lifeless body had been removed from the dining room, much to the horror and dismay of the imperial family, for Yurovsky, while peeling the boot off his damaged leg, screamed for it to be bayoneted to death if it wasn't dead already. As the guard who received the order carried the dog towards the backstairs that would lead down to the back courtyard and garden where he would carry out the 'execution,' he took pity on the young bulldog. He had admired it since arriving at the house and so, instead of killing it, he secretly gave him to one of the cleaning women who had been assigned to clean the house. He asked her to hide him for a few days, for it wouldn't be long now and their assignment of guarding the prisoners would be over. He would take the dog home and back to his own family.

On that very same night, Ortino the 'second' was oblivious to the sensational 'goings on' in the house. He was literally out cold and lay in a secret tunnel where the cleaning woman had laid him. She had been the cleaner for the owner, Ipatiev himself, so of course she knew about the old subterranean passage. It had been built for the convenience of the original owner so that his servants could make their way to the chemist and not have to brave the severe Russian winter weather while ill. It had not been used now for many years. By chance, while taking a smoking break in the little cupboard on the landing to the back stairs, she had found it again and thought it a good idea to keep it secret for it would be a perfect place for her and her friend Evdokiya to hide when the marauding 'White Army' invaded the town.

Thankfully, not an eye was hooked nor an ear cocked as the events of the evening of 16 July played out. Nor was the bulldog noticed by Reginald Plant and Arthur Benjamin as they relinquished the chest of priceless imperial jewels onto the cold damp floor of the tunnel less than ten meters from where the unconscious dog lay. Nor was he noticed by his mistress's mother, the empress, or her son, the tsarevich, as they were helped into the tunnel again by Plant and a young woman as they made their escape via the British consul. He was alone, forgotten and miserable. But then the light above appeared and along with it came the woman who brought food with her. It seemed to him that the woman only smelled of food, so he soon began to like her immensely. Each day she would nurse him and pet him and speak kind words to him. She told him that strange things had happened in the house above and that all the family had disappeared. He whined mournfully at that. She also told him that all the soldiers had now gone and that they had been asked to leave as well. But they had nowhere to go. They would probably soon move in, she told him. For many weeks, the woman appeared at the same time, always bringing with her some delicious food and a bowl of water. Obviously though, she and her friend never did move in, for he was never invited back upstairs into the house. Still, though he was very lonely, at least his belly was full and of course, he knew his mistress would not forget him. Soon he began to explore his surroundings and he found that the tunnel wound this way and that and he tottered many times for at least an hour or so. He found that the tunnel eventually came to an abrupt end at a large iron door. It was fast shut and no amount of whining, howling or scratching could persuade whoever was inside to open it. So he returned to the bottom of the ladder and waited for the delicious-smelling woman with the food, and the promise that his mistress just may one day come with her. But his mistress did not come. Indeed, the visits from the woman suddenly began to become less frequent. When she did turn up, she would speak about how sorry she was for him and that she couldn't take him out of the tunnel for fear that it would be discovered that she had hidden an imperial pet. The gap between her visits now became every other day; then, only once every three days. Lately, her visits had only been twice a week. She gave him pitiful excuses about how the White Army had captured the city and were terrorising the locals just as much as the Bolsheviks had; that food was really scarce and that he should be thankful that she came at all. Now, she only brought a large bowl of oats and two large loaves of bread. She told him she was frightened for her own safety, for the Whites knew that she had been cleaning the house when the imperial family had occupied it. They were certain that she must know what had happened to them. They were looking for her for questioning. It was in the middle of the dreadful Russian winter that her visits ceased altogether. He had taken neither food nor water now for two days. He had developed a nasty cold and he shivered mournfully as his bloodshot eyes looked longingly upwards for the light that had ceased to come. But still he would venture down the tunnel, for he still hung on to the hope that his mistress would come to look for him and one day find him. She will not forget me, he thought. But she did not come. Nobody did. Later that day, he became so hungry and cold that he could not lie still. He ran up and down the tunnel, breathing even more heavily than usual due to his cold. Now he began to get angry, not at his mistress, but at the sinister-smelling human. He felt the gaps of his two missing front fangs with his parched, dry tongue. He began to growl and grunt in positive annoyance. Up and down the tunnel he would run. Then, totally exhausted through cold and lack of food, he collapsed next to the big chest near the foot of the ladders. He had given up. Finally, he had realised that she was not going to come. She obviously couldn't come for some reason or she would stand and beckon him to jump up into her arms. Perhaps she too, was dead? With a soft whine of surrender he laid his stubby snout upon his paws and closed his eyes, never intending to open them again. But then after a few moments, he heard the familiar creak of floor boards in the house above. Booted human feet banged noisily upon the wood. Oh, the great bones of a lamb shank! She had come to take him away finally. He dragged himself to his paws and with what energy he had left, he began to run backwards and forwards along the tunnel. He whined as he realised that when she did come down the ladder and into the tunnel, she would have to pick him up for he just didn't have the energy to leap into her arms now. His breathing was wheezy and erratic, and he now grunted for breath in the ice cold air. Finally, he collapsed again at the side of the chest at the foot of the ladders. It was now silent in the house above. Had his mistress gone away now? He whined again. Then for a moment he thought he had fallen asleep, for he had often dreamed about the thin light that grew wider and wider. But it was not a dream, for above him there appeared the thin ray of light. It grew wider and then a dark figure appeared, slowly descending the ladder. He rolled over slowly and then managed to stand for one last chance to see his mistress. He managed to loop his forepaws on the bottom rung of the ladders. His tail wagged slowly as he tried to welcome her but all that came out of his mouth was a distraught, wheezing, half bark, half-grunting noise. His cold was so bad that he couldn't smell her or anybody else's scent. His eyes were bloodshot and resembled the colour of a deep red, fiery furnace.

*

"What do you see, Mr Smith?" asked Peabody as he stood on his tip toes to look over Smith's shoulder and into the great darkness beyond.

"Nothing," came the blunt reply, "and I don't want to see nothing either." He continued muttering under his breath. He was frightened and highly agitated; his breathing heavy and ragged. Beads of sweat trickled down the back of his neck and then down along his spine.

"What was that?" questioned Peabody, still trying to see around Smith.

Smith was at the end of his tether. Peabody frightened him these days. Not in a physical sense, for that would have been a joke, but in a way that Smith couldn't quite understand. He was Mr Winston Peabody only some of the time these days; most of the time, he was like a shadow that was growing wider and longer.

"I said Mr Sillykop, or whatever your name is now that ... ah ... ah ... ah ...!"

Smith's voice changed from a positive tone of descent to a high-pitched tone of terror. "The eyes!" he cried, his voice rising to a shriek, "don't look at the eyes!"

He had now turned back to look up at Peabody with such a look of terror on his face that Peabody himself began to shake with terror.

"Wa... wa ... what eyes?" Peabody responded in barely a whisper. He began to back out of the cupboard, then turned and ran for the door of the dining room. Smith shot up out of the trap door, which slammed shut, and also made for the opening. They both reached it at the same time and were jammed in the doorway briefly. But Smith's strength and power won the day and he burst through, leaving Peabody to collapse on his knees, winded and whining. But not for long, for the sound of the wheezing breathing and grunting had begun again. Smith had not made the slightest attempt of concern on his part, for he could clearly see his coat tails flying behind him as he shot through the dining room, with one of the great cumbersome chairs crashing to the ground as he passed, and then down the main stairs and to the front door. Whatever resolve Peabody had left was now drained away completely and he shot after him. With typical 'scolded cat' speed he made it to the front door at the same time as Smith. Fortunately, it was wide enough for both of them to race through without touching the sides, or even each other.

Both guards looked up in amazement as the two senior officers flew past them with looks of utter terror on both of their faces.

"I told you it was creepy in there," said the guard to his colleague.

*

It was evening and the green glass shade of the desk lamp in Peabody's study gave the room a soothing ambience. It looked cosy, warm and normal. Peabody sighed while he wiped the sweat from his forehead with his handkerchief. "Phew, Smith!" he exhorted, "I am getting to old for this sort of thing." He put the timer down sharply with a bang on one corner of his desk. "It's playing games with us, I tell you!"

"Games?" asked Smith, eyeing the brandy in the decanter on the sideboard.

"I mean, you clown, what is the little swine to put us through next. It never sends us where I ask it to these days. It only sends us where *it* pleases. I've had enough, I tell you! He strode over purposefully to the decanter and poured two brandies, one very large and one 'just' large. He handed the 'just' large one to Smith. "I am ready to give up, Mr Smith," he said, looking into the swirling contents of his glass. "It will just not take me to either her or the tiny crown or even the eggs." He sat down in the leather chesterfield chair and took a large gulp. Smith joined him, but drained the glass in one go and remained standing. The excellent brandy soothed his very soul as it warmed the pit of his stomach and then down to his toes.

"I have an idea, Mr Peabody!" he exclaimed excitedly. Peabody remained silent, deep in thought, still gazing into the light golden liquid of his glass. He moved it again in a circular motion and then watched the film run down the sides of the lead crystal.

"Why don't you let *me* try?" Smith continued, too excited to think what such a suggestion might have on Peabody's already delicate disposition. "I mean," he said, "You, Mr Peabody, are so pure and good that maybe that is why it ain't working for us. Why, it's not sending us where we want it to. I, on the other hand, am not half as decent a bloke as you, Mr Peabody. I mean, you even mentioned that my socks had become evil only the other day. Maybe it'll work if I ask it."

"Not," Peabody answered.

"Not, Mr Peabody?"

"Yes, Mr Smith, it is *not* working for us. How many times do I have to ask you to speak correctly, and what is a block?"

"You see, Mr Peabody," Smith continued, ignoring the question, "you are so good and clever and everything; maybe it's jealous of you, that's why it won't do as you ask."

Peabody put his finger to the side of his nose. "Mmm," he said "you may have a point there," he tapped the side of his nose three times. "So what do you have in mind?"

"Well, I was thinking, we are always on the trail of Fanny because we think that she knows where all the stuff is. Well, isn't one of her sisters just as likely to know where the stuff is, too?"

"Possible, possible," answered Peabody, taking another large gulp and then nodding his head, "which sister are you thinking about?"

Smith put his hands to his temple. The question was very difficult for him. A picture of the four of them picnicking on a blanket on the lawn at the front of their Livadia palace came to his mind. But he had no idea what any of the others were called, never mind which one might know where any jewels or whatever were.

"Never mind, Smith," said Peabody patiently for once. He thought on the matter for a second or two. "I know! Let's try the youngest one. She wasn't so arty farty or airy fairy as the others by all accounts. Perhaps we can even come to a deal with her?"

Smith looked up with shining eyes full of admiration. "Cor, boss! You really are clever, you know!" He looked through the bottom of his empty glass.

"Yes, I know this," answered Peabody, "I know it." He tapped on the arm of his chair thoughtfully. "Now listen! We know now from what Natalia told me that the girls and mother escaped to Perm at the very least, so why don't you ask the little swine to take us to see Anastasia in Perm in 1918?"

Smith looked at the decanter again. "I am not so sure that I am really up to such a task, boss," he said. Peabody filled his glass with a very large one. "Let's see now; what date should you head for?" Again he tapped firmly on the arm of his leather chair with his forefinger. "I should say you should aim for September! Say the twenty-first, at Berezin Rooms on Obvinskaya Street, Perm."

Smith took another large gulp from his brandy. "I hope it didn't hear, boss," he whispered loudly, glancing swiftly to where the little culprit still stood on the corner of Peabody's desk, "or it might think it was *your* idea!"

Peabody looked out of the large picture window at the cultivated farm land. He raised his chin to adjust his tie. "Try it, Mr Smith," he said mischievously. "Just try it."

CHAPTER 11
EVERY PHOTO TELLS A STORY

Anastasia whistled softly to herself as she sat on the creaking, rickety wooden cot. It served as both her bed and a place for her to sit, for there were no chairs in the room. She swung both her legs to the beat of the music that she could hear in her head. She leaned forward and spied the big round chamber pot clearly visible between her feet and half hidden beneath the cot. Her mother and Marie were still asleep, both their pale faces reflecting the trauma of the last eighteen months. The death of her brother had hit her and Marie terribly hard, though not perhaps quite as hard as one might expect. After all, they had lived with their sickly brother for all of his and most of their lives, and the probability that he would die young had always been great. Her lip quivered. A great tear rolled down her cheek as she whistled one of Alexei's favourite marching tunes. Bewildered and frightened, she had no idea if either of her two older sisters were still alive. Olga she hoped had managed to get away with Plant, but where to, and for how long? And where on earth was Tatiana? It was so uncharacteristic of her to run off with a complete stranger! She had always been the sensible one. Unlike Olga, who the sisters had always teased as being the romantic

297

dreamer, Tatiana or 'the governess' as they called her, was quite the practical one. It had been Tatiana and not Olga who had been most suited to the rigorous duties as a nurse at the hospital. She had even taken part in some of the appalling operations during the war. Anastasia remembered the amputation of that poor soldier's leg. She missed the 'completeness' of them all being together. They had *always* been together, but that had now changed forever. Another tear rolled down the side of her face as she looked at her aging mother. Her world had now completely collapsed. She had lost her beloved husband and now her beloved son. Her face was sallow and her eyes hollow with grief. Anastasia's thoughts were disturbed momentarily by a low noise just outside the door, as if somebody was standing on the other side listening. It was never locked for it was not allowed to be. Nobody ever knocked before entering either, therefore all three women slept with their clothes on. Their soldier's overcoats served as their blankets. Anastasia stared passively at her sleeping mother and sister. Marie was laid on her back with just the top of her forehead visible above the collar of the trench coat. Her mother was laid on her side clutching the small mauve pillow which bore the ex-emperors monogram; embedded into this was a tin soldier of the Imperial Guard. It had been Alexie's. They were so soft and vulnerable, she thought; there was no resistance left in either of them. She knew that they believed all was hopeless and that all was now lost. What kind of future lay ahead for them, if any future at all? They had asked no questions. Their mother, it seemed, had given up on any chance of being released or rescued. Their only responsibility now was to die a death with dignity and one honourable to God, for it *was* God's will, she had told them both. Well, if that was the case, Anastasia reasoned, why had Olga and Tatiana managed to escape? Had that also been God's will? Why had she, Anastasia, not been able to get away? She looked at the grey dull sky through the grimy window pane. Even if she could manage to escape, where would she go? She had overheard one of the guards talking at the Ipatiev House that most of her surviving relatives, including her grandmother the Dowager Empress, had managed to get away safely, at least for the time being, to the Crimea. Our dear Livadia, she thought. She longed for the sound of the ocean, the sunlight on the palace courtyard walls, the lengthening shadows in the late afternoon; especially her dear papa's shadow. Perhaps what Plant had told her had been a lie and that he wasn't dead after all, but had gone ahead with the rest of the family to wait for them there! But how on earth would she make such a journey? It was such a long way away! She glanced again at Marie. Oh dear gay, vivacious Marie! How she had been transformed by the terrible recent events! The first real change had begun when she had been caught with that Red Guard on her birthday in the Ipatiev house. He had smuggled the cake in especially for her and she had rewarded him with an innocent little kiss in that little cupboard on the landing by the back stairs. But they had been caught, and that Yurovsky pig didn't think it innocent at all. The guard was relieved of his duties immediately and both mama and papa were informed of their third daughter's indiscretion. Of course, mother and Olga from then on gave her the cold shoulder and wouldn't even talk to her. Poor Marie! She was perhaps the least suited to their confinement as it was, without the added unpleasantness. When the three girls had left for the train station, her papa had hugged all three of them as normal but her mother had refused even then to say goodbye to her properly. Even now, the talk between her mother and Marie was strained and puritanical. Just because of one little sin, Anastasia thought. Marie had also given up, but no wonder, listening to mother's defeatist banter! She stood up and pulled the big coat over her shoulders. She licked the palm of her hands and then pushed back what there was of the short, prickly bristles of hair on the top of her head. If she could only get out of this place and out onto the streets of Perm, she would be able to blend in with the bedraggled groups of redundant, hungry soldiers. If she *could* get away perhaps she would even be able to find Olga and Plant, or even Tatiana and the stranger. She had to try! She just *couldn't* give up – it wasn't in her nature. She picked up the empty chamber pot and tiptoed towards the door. "I really do need a pee!" she exclaimed loudly.

Vladimir Mutnykh was indeed, as his sister had claimed to 'Sokolov,' the secretary to the Ural Soviet. He was also the personal aide to Beloborodov, the Chairman of the Ural Soviet. Beloborodov was in the confidence of Vladimir Lenin and it was he that Lenin trusted with the secret of the Romanov women being kept in Perm. In turn, Beloborodov trusted Mutnykh with the secret information, and appointed him specifically to keep all trace of the women's presence in the Excise Office on the corner of Pokrovskaya and Obvinskaya Streets highly confidential. He personally was to take command of the situation; even the few men that guarded the house were unaware of why they were guarding it. Mutnykh was also fully aware of the proposed swop for the Romanov women of the German-held revolutionary leader, Karl Liebknecht. Now that Olga Nicolaevna as well as her sister Tatiana had gone missing, this exchange was in serious jeopardy. He was also fully aware that Lenin himself at that very moment was on the train from Moscow and hurtling towards Perm, for Lenin was convinced that the Romanov women that had *not* managed to escape knew exactly where the others were and he meant to get the information out of them one way or another. Fortunately or unfortunately as the case maybe for Anastasia, Vladimir Mutnykh informed his sister of all the facts.

*

"Who is Boris?" Olga asked, marvelling at Plant's expertise as he doctored his injured arm. She was rather squeamish when it came to blood and though she really wanted to help, she found herself looking away as he stitched the wound himself with thread from the hem of his trousers and a needle that he mysteriously produced from his wallet. She had, of course, also been a nurse in the hospital with her sister Tatiana, but the tragedy of the maimed and broken lives of the young men that were brought in to the hospital had been too much for her soft and sensitive nature. She soon began to spend less and less time in there, and more time engrossed in her books in her room at the Alexander Palace, as the war raged on and her world slowly crumbled around her.

"One never knows when one may be required to sew something up, or even back on!" Plant declared dryly, ignoring her question. The blood ran down the length of his forearm, onto his wrist and then dripped onto the wet grass. They had been running, walking, running, walking for over an hour, and Plant had decided it was safe for them to take a rest. He was alarmed at how weak Olga had become; he would have to carry her before too long. He was still undecided in which direction to go. As long as they ventured west, things would eventually get better, for that was 'Whites Territory' and if they were being followed, their pursuers would not want to go very far into that. But was he to continue on and try and make it with the help of the Whites to Odessa and whatever awaited them there? Or should he change course and go to Perm, as ordered? If he was to seek help from the Whites, he would have to explain who the young girl was. She would then undoubtedly be handed over to the British Intelligence Service. He remembered his conversation with Tudor about her being 'predestined' to the mysterious American politician without being given any choice in the matter. He glanced at her as she stared up at the canopy of branches under which they had sheltered. The water was dripping from leaf to leaf. There was something about this quiet, extremely introverted girl that had begun to melt the ice in his heart. She deserves a choice, he decided, excusing his own feelings. He groaned silently at the sky. It was alone, no moon or stars. There would be no relief from the intermittent downpours in the near future. To make it to Odessa on their own, without any help, would be one hell of a feat, even for him, Reginald Plant. Either way, they would need food and a horse, at least. He clenched the fist of his injured arm. Satisfied with his work, he stood up abruptly. "Stay here," he said curtly, "I am going for a look around."

Olga sat down on the wet grass. She shivered in the cold predawn hour but was thankful for the rest. She decided to push herself backwards and further into the undergrowth, concealing herself completely from view. She sat with her back against a tree and closed her eyes. She didn't really care if she ever opened them again. A lone star had suddenly appeared. The north-star, she thought. It shed just enough light for her to see her hand in front of her. She shivered against the silence. Even the dripping of the raindrops from the leaves had stopped. There was not a sound. No birds, no crickets, no wind or breeze. All was deathly still. Had nature itself finally succumbed to man's folly?

When she awoke, the sun was already high up in the sky; she found that she had been laid flat amidst a thicket of soft, green ferns. Another trench coat, much larger than the one she was wearing, had been laid upon her. She closed her eyes again. Her dry mouth began to water; someone was roasting a chicken. This time when she opened her eyes, she saw the rugged, heavily lined, yet rather handsome face, she thought, of Reginald Plant, peering anxiously at her. He was talking to her as if she had been awake and attentively listening for hours.

"Do you always sleep so late?" he asked gruffly.

"Only when there is no chance of breakfast in bed," she answered, yawning and stretching.

Plant watched her. At least she seems in better spirits, he thought.

"According to my calculations," he informed her, "we are just east of Kazan." He stopped and shaded his eyes as he stared at the marching outline of grassy hills to his right. "We can either journey a thousand miles southwest to Odessa and a *possible* rescue ship, or a thousand miles northwest to Saint Petersburg where there are some of our chaps on the ground, or ..." He stopped again, looking at her intently.

"Or?" she asked, the hopelessness beginning to overwhelm her again.

"Follow orders and take the relatively *short* road to Perm and certain death," he answered, grinning like a Cheshire cat, "for east is out of the question," he concluded. Olga pushed herself up onto her elbows, her nostrils searching out the delicious aroma. "And just how do you propose to get us to *any* of those places, Mr Plant?" she enquired a little airily. He had, after all, been holding a very large and menacing pistol to the back of her head only a few hours previously.

"When we have eaten breakfast, I will show you," he answered, suddenly a little more cheerful. He helped her to her feet, and showed her to where a little stream flowed, gurgling merrily in the morning sun. She knelt down and cupped her hands so that she could drink the cool fresh water. After she had rinsed her neck and face, she looked at the spiralling smoke and saw that Plant had built a low fire; the embers glowed orange in the ash. Above the fire, a rather puny chicken was skewered between two sticks. Though it did look perfectly roasted, she concluded, and puny or not, it smelt delicious and she was ravenous. She watched as he strode over to the fire.

"Breakfast is almost served, Duchess!" exclaimed Plant, and with a single, swift swipe from the keen blade of his Bowie knife, he removed one of the legs from the chicken and tossed it to her.

"Oh dear!" he exclaimed sarcastically, "I forgot to steal some serviettes."

Olga burned the end of her fingers as she held on to the little limb, but managed a smile as her teeth pierced the lightly browned skin and then the fleshy white meat. When she had stripped the little limb completely of its flesh, she licked her fingers and watched Plant expectantly as he detached the remaining leg with his knife. She threw away the bone with one hand and caught the hot sizzling chicken leg with her other. He laughed at her. Again, she smiled as she bit into it. About twenty minutes later, all the chicken had been demolished. Though neither Olga nor Plant felt contentedly full, they both certainly felt a little better. He sat back and plucked a Gauloise from its packet, lit it and blew out the smoke contentedly, watching as it spiralled up towards the racing clouds.

"Don't you think we should be moving?" Olga asked, also looking at the sky. "Aren't we still being hunted?"

In answer, Plant stretched his legs out in front of him, resting on his elbows. He blew out the most impressive smoke ring she had ever seen. He sighed heavily and turned to face her. "If we are to go to Odessa or Saint Petersburg, yes," he answered simply. Olga looked at him in confused agitation.

"Will you stop talking in riddles, sir!" she cried, "and please tell me where you intend taking me. My family and I are deeply indebted to you and your men, Mr Plant, for at least attempting to rescue us, but whatever plan you or your superiors had has gone completely haywire. My father is dead, my brother also," she swallowed with emotion. "Yes, Mr Plant!" she exclaimed, seeing the surprise on his face. "I didn't sleep as soundly as you supposed." She pulled out a piece of paper from the inside pocket of his great coat. "I have read the note from Mr Preston." Plant cursed himself silently, but Olga continued, "My line is ended with his death, Mr Plant; our dynasty is finished." Her voice broke with the emotion, "But I do think that we should try everything in our power to try and rescue mama and my sisters."

"And how do you propose I do that, your Imperial Highness?" he answered quietly. "This whole place is crawling with one army or another and either one would love to capture us for *one* reason or another." The hope of the new morning was beginning to lie rather thin with him, and once again the enormity of their predicament began to make him despair. He also hadn't slept properly for almost forty – eight hours. He had lost two of his charges to the enemy as well as one of his colleagues. He had also witnessed two of his best men being mercilessly executed. Repeatedly, his thoughts were filled with Peabody whose accursed face seemed to be hiding behind every bush, tree and thicket and he couldn't understand why. Just the fact that Winston Peabody was here in Russia and turning up at the most inconvenient of times was now tremendously puzzling. Something just wasn't right. Nothing was!

Olga studied him. She thought herself rather good at weighing up a person's character just by watching that person, the way they spoke, and their mannerisms. She was usually very accurate, but was having trouble with this strange, brooding and a little arrogant character that she was now *alone* with.

"Do *you* have a wife and family, Mr Plant?" she asked, pretty sure of the answer, "at home in England."

Plant scowled at the trees in front of him. "I have neither a wife nor family," he said abruptly, "I have a house," he continued, "but not a home!" His throat had become dry. He stood up and made his way to the stream. He drank the water and then looked over his shoulder at her. "You might call me 'The Gypsy Assassin.'"

"You mean you kill people for money?" she responded, shocked.

"No," he answered, "I only kill for king and country, but is there a difference? There is money involved somewhere along the line, no doubt; it's just a question of the beneficiary."

Olga was silent as she pondered his response.

"I am tired, Olga" he looked at her mournfully, "there comes a time in every 'gypsy assassin's life when they really would like a change of career. You know: slippers, woolly jumper and Sunday newspaper; in fact at this moment I would *kill* for that."

She laughed at the irony of his unintended humour. She also appreciated his openness.

"The sacrifices I have made to become who I am …" his voice quietened into a sad whisper.

"I know," she said. The pity she felt for him drew tears from her eyes.

But Plant laughed loudly. "Ha ha! What would a poor little daughter of the man who was once probably the wealthiest individual in the world know about sacrifice?" He shook his head in disbelief as he poked the pebbles in the bottom of the stream with his forefinger. But when he stood up to face her again, she was sobbing.

"Sorry, luv!" he exclaimed awkwardly, "I didn't mean to upset you. I am just a little strung out at the moment."

"No, no," she sobbed shaking her head. She began to violently shake. She embraced herself with both her arms and began to rock back and forth, tears pouring down her face.

He knelt beside her and placed a comforting hand upon her shoulder. "You can talk to me luv, if you need to," he said tenderly. Then he became a little angry; not with her, but with what had obviously happened to her and with the people that caused her such anguish. He felt ashamed at his callous outburst. He knew she had been through absolute hell for the last few months. "Spit all the crap out," he snarled, "rid yourself of it! It doesn't belong to you."

His rough and abrupt manner caused her to regain her composure a little.

"Papa gave me a revolver," she began, her chest heaving, "when we were first held under house arrest at Tsarskoe Selo. I hid it in one of my boots when we were moved to Tobolsk." She heaved again as she struggled to release her pent up emotions. "If only I hadn't relented when Kobylynsky begged me to give it up before we were transferred to the Urals." Her face hardened now at the memory. "Mama, Papa and Marie went before us to Ekaterinburg as Alexia was not well and couldn't travel, so we followed a few weeks later." She took a deep breath before continuing. "The first part of the journey was on the steam boat, 'Rus.' They locked my brother and his diadkas, Derevenko, in their cabin." Her voice rose and became shrill as she spoke quickly. "They refused to let us lock our cabin doors ..."

"The bastards!" interrupted Plant, guessing what she was about to tell him.

"He came to me and promised me that he would make sure that my sisters would be left alone if ... if ... "

"Okay, luv," Plant said as tenderly as he could, "There is no need to carry on ..."

But Olga was insistent; she needed to tell *somebody*. "He ... he touched me ;his breath stank, his skin was horrible ... he forced me to ... who would want me now?" She broke down again into almost uncontrollable weeping. As usual when Plant was confronted with an intolerable sadness, he reacted with anger. He cursed and shouted expletives to the sky, shaking his fist. This beautiful, pure young woman had made perhaps the ultimate sacrifice a woman could make – she gave her virginity to a dirty slob in order to keep her sisters from the same fate, and yet she was probably the least capable to cope with such a burden. If he ever came across that son of a bitch, he would make sure he made a couple of very painful sacrifices of his own.

"Listen," he said kneeling down by the side of the utterly distraught young woman. He lifted her jaw between his hands so that her flooded eyes looked into his. "You are no longer who you were five years ago, five weeks ago or now even five minutes ago. The good or bad things that happen to us make us who we are meant to be. I don't believe in any religion or anything like that, but I just know from personal experience that what happens to you makes you either stronger or weaker." His piercing blue eyes penetrated hers and for a split second she saw into his heart. "And that diabolical atrocity," he spat the words out, "will make *you* stronger, not immediately, but it will, and until then I am going to look after you."

Her breathing had become steady again as she lay with her head upon his chest. His shirt was wet with her tears. Again, a hot wet tear rolled down his own cheek. He had finally found something worth living for. A pale, skinny undernourished young girl of twenty-three, who had no home, no money, and quite probably now, no name either. Just like him.

""I just want to get married and be happy," she whispered, "live in the country always, through both winter and summer and never ever have to deal with officials."

"Is that a proposal, my dear?" he asked, grinning broadly, "For if it is, I can certainly go along with the 'never having to deal with officials' bit."

He closed his eyes. He touched her delicate finger tips with his own surprisingly long, artistically defined digits.

"I know I could never be easy to love," he said quietly, "even my mother had great difficulty with that! I have a fearsome temper, an absolute unpredictable disposition and an unquenchable love for these things." He held the cigarette for her as she drew lightly on the stub of his Gauloise, "but one thing I can promise: I would give my life before I let anything happen to you."

Olga sighed deeply. "My heart has been broken twice, Plant. Five years ago, I fell in love with Pavel. He was a junior officer on the Standart, so of course any meaningful relationship between us would have been impossible. But my heart in particular tends to be unpractical and when he married one of the ladies-in-waiting a few months later, I was devastated. I know time heals most of love's injuries, but still to this day I think of him with great fondness and I pray that God will grant him good fortune in these terrible times." Plant was silent, and she could sense that he had grown a little tense, but she had to tell him. "The second

308

time was two years ago when 'Mitya' was brought into our hospital, wounded. I grew so close to him that I confided things that I couldn't even to my own father. I told him I was worried about the influence that Father Grigori wielded over mama, and that the most disgusting rumours were being spread about them. He told me that all I had to do was to say the word and he would kill Father Grigori himself. As I am sure you know, it wasn't necessary for me to say the word."

Plant was surprised. "Do you think it was good that he was murdered?"

"Not 'good'" she answered, "but I understand why and I think it was necessary. Though I abhor the way in which he was killed, and I am ashamed that it was done by one of our own family members."

Plant shifted uneasily. It could so easily have been him assigned to deal with the mad monk Rasputin, if Yusopov had failed.

"I suspect now that he was evil," she continued. "He meddled in affairs that shouldn't have concerned him; he took advantage of mama due to the faith she had in him to be able to heal Alexei, especially when father was away at our military headquarters at Mogiliev. I fear he was one of the causes of our ruination."

"He certainly helped," said Plant.

"The evil that has entered our world has become even more powerful now and unrestrained," she continued, "and it will grow more powerful still. But evil will not conquer evil; only love can do that!" As she recited the words of her father, the tears formed again at the thought of him. "I could see how much people had grown to dislike mama and papa in the end, though neither of them seemed to realise the consequences of such animosity …
" She broke down again and sobbed. Awkwardly, Plant put one of his powerful arms around her and pulled her closer to him. Again, Olga's sobbing subsided. Though she was sure she would never be able to really love such a menacing, military machine

of a man, he made her feel safe. The clouds in the sky seemed to be racing even faster; the diluted sun was as high as the day would allow.

"We need to go in one direction or another," Plant expressed his thoughts aloud.

"You said you had something to show me?" Olga said expectantly. She could sense his trepidation and though she herself had lost all hope, something about this man, even in his own apparent hopelessness, made her want to cling onto him; something that she could not quite identify. Plant looked at her briefly then sighed heavily again as he rose to his feet, stamping out the half smoked cigarette. He strode across to the other side of the fire and disappeared into the long tall grass. In a moment or two he reappeared, pushing the strangest machine on two wheels that Olga had ever seen. Its appearance was very angry looking, from the aggressively tilted handle bars to the bright orange, thick and chunky 'saddle.'

"A bicycle?" she enquired, not convinced.

"Watch," he instructed her, a brief smile returning to his face. He threw one leg over the motorcycle and sat fully astride it. Looking down to the right hand side he pressed the small red button with his thumb. Immediately, the engine burst into life like an angry wasp.

Olga covered her mouth with her hand. "I know that sound!" she cried. "It is the same sound that we heard the night Tanechka and the stranger turned up at the train station in Ekaterinburg! Where on earth did you find this thing?"

"In the barn, along with the chickens," he answered. He revved the engine loudly, and smiled at her, "Let's go to Perm!" he said.

"Not until you tell me who Boris is," she said.

*

The sky was a canvas of grey shades when Natalya Mutnykh walked with urgency along the sidewalk of Petropavlovskaya Street. Already the trees were heavily laden with autumn gold, and even the first chills of winter whispered in the breeze. She pulled her shawl higher up around her shoulders and shivered slightly. The railway station to her left, known in Perm as 'Station Number Two,' was crowded with forlorn, almost destitute soldiers waiting for trains to take them away from the onslaught of the White Army. Weren't they supposed to be protecting us and the city? Her brother had told her that it was only a matter of time before the city would fall and so what was left of the army was being ordered to regroup on its outskirts. When their numbers had been replenished, they would be strong enough for a counterattack. Some of the soldiers turned as she walked by. She was a young, fresh faced, pretty woman and they leered at her, shouting suggestive remarks. Stony faced, she continued, wishing that she could board one of the steam boats that occasionally came up the Kama, the river that lay a little further away to her left, and escape all this madness. But not before she had witnessed what her brother had promised her: a look at the remnants of the imperial family. For her brother had confided in her that the ex-tsarina and some of her daughters had been secretly brought from Ekaterinberg to Perm. They had not been executed along with the tsar, as had been rumoured. She had always been keenly interested in the imperial family, especially the ex – tsar's four daughters. They had always looked so elegant and pretty. She had seen many pictures of them in magazines and newspapers as she was growing up. She remembered a particular photograph that had been her favourite. They had all been dressed alike in the same floral dresses and wide-brimmed hats and were crowded lovingly around their father who had been dressed magnificently in full military uniform. She couldn't remember the occasion but she remembered, like many other young Russian girls who also idolised them, that the scene looked so ideal. The four fairy tale princesses together as always it seemed with their devoted and loving father. But the years that followed were unkind to Natalya and her family and they fell upon hard times. Her father and brother, Vladimir, swayed by other workers at the factory where they worked, joined the Socialist Revolutionaries and it soon became forbidden in the house to even mention the names of any of the imperial family. Their hearts hardened towards the Russian aristocracy with their wealth and lavish balls. Their hardships grew even worse in the war years when their father was killed in the trenches. Like her brother and many others, she began to hold the tsar and especially the German born tsarina personally responsible for their plight. Yet the ideal of that picture of the young girls and their father always managed to pull a little at her heart strings, and deep down inside she knew that another force was taking control of Russia's destiny; a dark and powerful force that would not stop until every young Russian girl's 'ideals' had been destroyed. She remembered learning with an almost sardonic indifference of the family's arrest soon after the tsar's abdication, for the hardships of the war with Germany had taken its toll further. Still, a great sadness entered her heart when it was reported that the tsar had been executed in Ekaterinburg, and then shock and horror at the rumours that the girls, their brother and the tsarina had also been executed. She had therefore heaved a sigh of relief when her brother informed her of his secret. She hadn't believed him at first, so he promised to smuggle her inside the house in which they were being held, and so at last she finally saw what was left of her ideal. A tremendous pity entered her heart, for what she saw was not a picture of arrogant haughtiness but humble togetherness. She only caught sight of two of the sisters and their mother, but they all looked so terribly tired and downcast, obviously struggling to cope with yet another change in their circumstances. The sad, mournful and truly heartbroken shadows that lay upon their faces made her want to reach out to them, help them. But what could *she* do? That had been the previous evening and now that morning, she had moped around in a daze. She wondered what the revolution had in store for them. Did they really deserve to die? She understood the need from the Bolsheviks point of view to execute the tsar, and quite possibly the tsarevich and tsarina, but the girls? They were now no threat, for the laws dictated that as women none of them could ascend to the throne. Their only crime had been to be born into the world's richest family. Were they to be murdered for that? She feared the worse though, for though Vladimir claimed that he didn't know what was to become of them he had informed her that Lenin himself was on his way to personally see them, in particular the ex-tsarina. Her heart was filled with dread, for she disliked Lenin and thought him a traitor to the revolution. He was merely a puppet of their German foes – the very foes that her father had died fighting against. She and most other Russians knew that the Treaty of Brest-Litovsk, which had been signed the previous March, had through Lenin basically given precious Russian soil away to the central powers of Germany, Austria Hungary, Bulgaria and the hated Ottoman Empire, and granted independence to the Crimea. Most Russians were outraged! Some even suspected that he had been planted by the Germans to orchestrate such a treaty. She had told her brother as much, but he had shrugged his shoulders and walked away abruptly. She also knew that Lenin hated the imperial family. After all, Tsar Alexander III had condemned his brother to death by hanging for a thwarted assassination attempt.

Beneath her feet, large leaves of brown, yellow and gold were pasted to the road. The fine rain of the previous evening still hung in the air. She felt so sorry for the girls, even though as she had stood in the doorway to their room with her brother, who had stood slightly in front of her, one of the girls, she thought it was Anastasia, looked at them both with the most utter contempt and scorn. But Natalya understood. The eagle is a proud creature and when on display, especially before its enemies, it must relay no fear or weakness. Natalya knew her father would have been proud of Anastasia. If only she could help them!

Her thoughts were unexpectedly disturbed by the presence of two soldiers walking toward her. What seemed a little odd and peculiar about them was that one of them was not only very tall but also very powerful looking. Most of the soldiers now left in Perm were a rather bedraggled lot. Their near defeat clearly reflected in their stature and minds. This man walked as if he was about to conquer the world, if he hadn't already. He looked proud and almost contemptuous of his surroundings. There was certainly no hint of anything but 'victory' in his gait! Even from that distance she could see that he was watching her with keen, startling blue eyes. His companion looked much more like the normal soldier, though. He was thin, almost purple pale and sickly looking, and he stared down at the ground in front. Natalya was sure that he was being supported by his companion. Even though she felt intimidated by the tall soldier's stare, she continued to look at them when they passed each other; there was something strangely familiar about the sickly looking soldier. Then, at the moment of passing, she realised that the sickly soldier wasn't a 'he' at all; nor was 'she' a soldier. She could not fail to recognise that high forehead and those eyes, so like her father's. Unable to help herself, she gasped with shock.

"How did you escape?" she cried, as she turned around. The 'soldiers' ignored her and began to walk away a little quicker; she could see quite clearly now that Olga was clearly being supported by her tall companion. Or was she his captive? Though she certainly hadn't seen Olga the night before in the excise office, her brother had led her to believe that all the girls and her mother were held captive there. Had this soldier taken her away without anybody knowing? An escape? Or was this part of the

Bolshevik plan to split them up and perhaps murder them one by one. "Stop!" she demanded. "I am Natalya Mutnykh, the sister of the secretary to the Ural Regional Soviet and I demand that you tell me where you are taking her." Her outburst she knew was a little naïve, but it seemed to work. The powerful-looking soldier stopped and looked over his shoulder, still supporting the grand duchess, who simply stared ahead, with his other arm. He stared at her a moment, his eyes coldly intense. He had an aura about him, like a great lion about to attack. Then he seemed to change his mind. He turned again and they began to resume their walk. But Natalya could not help herself; one way or the other, Olga was surely in terrible danger.

"Please, your Imperial Highness," she cried after them, suddenly deciding that the large soldier was definitely not a Bolshevik. "Please, I can help you! Please wait a minute!" She ran after them blindly. In a swift and incredibly threatening movement the tall powerful soldier turned around so that she almost bumped into him.

"You are mistaken," he hissed, "be on your way."

But Natalya could not be put off. "I know who you are, Olga Nicolaevna," she said now in a low voice, gathering her wits and concealing her fear, "I can help you ..." But without further warning, she felt a blow to her temple, her legs gave way immediately and she knew no more.

*

"Mama told us that it poured with rain during the whole time of her visit here," Tatiana remarked as she hurriedly unfolded the umbrella over her own and Arty's head. They linked arms and sped past the 'first world war' monument trying as best they could to dodge the puddles of water. They reached the arched entrance of the church. Her mother, the empress, had been here as well, she informed him. Her hosts had been Mr and Mrs

Allen, who'd recently had twins and they'd asked her to stand in as a godparent at their christening. On 13 June 1894, the twenty-two year old Alexandra attended the said christening at Saint Peter's church.

Unbeknown to them, they had 'arrived' upon a fairly busy Parliament street, seemingly unnoticed as usual. As if being guided by their own inward thoughts, they took their first left turn and strode up the hill. It was a cobbled road. Tatiana exclaimed that perhaps they had gone back to a time where some of her family could still be alive at least. But then of course, Arty pointed out the obvious like the modern 'Fords' and 'Vauxhalls' parked end to end along both sides of the road, and of course the clothes that people were wearing, though most were concealed beneath rain macs and thick woollen coats. All the cars seemed to be rather old models; they certainly hadn't 'landed' in Harrogate in 2014. Once again, they found themselves in the old and very beautiful spa town; they were informed of this by a plaque on the wall of the church at the entrance. Arty shook his head. "Of all the towns in all the world," he said in his best Humphrey Bogart impression, "it has to keep sending us to this one!" Tatiana smiled broadly but shivered slightly. The thought of herself standing in the footsteps of her mother at roughly the same age yet one hundred – and-twenty years later was positively eerie. She remembered that her mama had told her that she had thoroughly enjoyed her stay in the town as she had been quite able to roam around quite inconspicuously at first. In the mornings she would freewheel on a bicycle down the hill from the terraced villa where she stayed in High Harrogate to the Victorian Baths. Carefree and laughing, her teeth chattered as the wheels shook violently, shuddering and trembling over the cobbles. Here she would take baths in sulphur and peat, hoping to ease the chronic sciatica from which even at such an early age she already suffered. She even endured drinking glasses of the foul smelling sulphur water. Later in the afternoon she was able to cycle on to some of the local beauty spots, followed of course at a discrete distance by a policeman. However, these visits soon came to an abrupt end as word spread that a granddaughter of the queen was in town. The crowds were soon congregating outside the villa hoping to catch a glimpse of her. She was forced to cut short her visit abruptly, journeying by train to Walton by the river Thames, to be with Nicolas who was by now her fiancé and visiting his royal relatives in London. In Walton they found relative seclusion, staying with her sister Victoria and husband Louis of Battenberg. After a few days of glorious privacy they then travelled together to visit the Queen and the Prince of Wales at Balmoral. Tatiana looked up at the pale yellow glow of the familiar Victorian-style street lamp. A ghost wanders these streets, she thought. A dear ghost that still lives!

"Yoga classes in a church!" exclaimed Arty looking at the advertisements pinned to the notice board in the entrance, "quite ironic when you think that we are standing in a place of Christian worship and yoga is basically a spiritual, physical and mental representation of Hinduism and Buddhism."

Tatiana shook the rain drops from the umbrella and then stood by his side. "I can't believe it," she cried, shocked, "how can the king allow it?"

Arty looked at her wryly.

"Well my dear Anne Teak, first of all they have a queen on the throne at the moment who I believe would also be a relative of yours and secondly, you are visiting the 'Age of tolerance' which in my opinion is an age where every*thing* is just totally confused and every*body* even more bewildered."

"Oh," she replied a little indifferently, for she was now looking through the glass door of the inner entrance to the church at her own reflection. She observed closely the face that stared back at her. It was generally noted that she of all the girls resembled her mother the most. "A ghost indeed!" she exclaimed aloud.

"Sorry?" Arty said, not understanding what she meant.

She took a few steps closer until she could see through her reflection and on into the church, at the very same pew where her mother had once stood. "I think I prefer Fanny," she answered him mischievously.

They left the church and made their way up the steep pavement, the cold, damp, muggy air in their nostrils. They jostled to get past the bustling crowds of shoppers. Tatiana (and Arty) was glad that she was an unknown in Harrogate in 2014. Although neither knew why they were in Harrogate, nor where they were going, both strangely felt completely at ease. It was as if they were being directed and even though they were holding each other's hand rather tightly, they needn't have done.

All the doorways on either side of the road were tall and arched at the top. Most of the terraced villas were three storeys high; each had its own set of steps bordered on either side by glossy black, wrought iron railings leading up to the brightly painted front doors. Number ten had a red door and it reminded Arty of that British emblem, the post box. The letter box high up was brass and misted by the fine rain. Above this was a large brass knocker in the form of a lion's head. Arty stood up onto his toes. "Wow!" he exclaimed, "I didn't think people were quite so tall in England." He gave three loud knocks. The rain started to pour a little harder.

"If you're from that newspaper, I've gone out!" It was the voice of an old woman, shaky but adamant and magnified by the echoes of the obviously spacious empty hallway inside.

Arty peered at Tatiana through the rain drops, screwing up his eyes in consternation. He opened the letter box.

"Errr... We're really sorry to trouble you, but we'd just like a few words. I'm doing some research for a book, and I believe this house has an interesting tale to tell," he said.

Tatiana rolled her eyes at him. "Well, *that* should do the trick," she said sarcastically.

There was silence from inside. The rain began to pour even heavier.

"Come on Arty, let's go!" cried Tatiana, pulling her scarf tighter around her neck. "I mean, would you let two strangers into your home?"

Arty looked confused. "But we have been lead here for some reason!" he said, then sighed. "Perhaps you're right; especially when one of us is an antique."

As she was in the process of elbowing him in the ribs, they both suddenly stepped down one step, for with a creak the door opened slightly.

"Is it about Reggie?" said the voice.

Arty looked at Tatiana and nodded his head in satisfaction. "Yes," he said, "It's about my friend Reginald Plant."

The door opened a little wider. Two gnarled and very white fingers were clearly visible.

"Your friend!" exclaimed the voice, "I doubt it! He's been gone for well over sixty years!"

She was thin, bent and gnarled with age. Her long, white, rather scraggy hair fell loosely over her shoulders. The skin on her face had yellowed with the years, yet underneath her silvery bushy eyebrows, her blue eyes were clear and bright. Her dark green, knitted woollen cardigan hung up at the back as she showed them down the black-and-white tiled hallway, muttering to herself. As they followed, Arty looked with amusement at one of the old lady's stockings that had fallen and wrinkled at her left ankle. At the end of the hallway on the right they entered a sitting room littered with comfortable, dark green easy chairs. The colour contrasted sharply against the tiles that had flowed in from the hallway. The high-arched, ornate fireplace was the central attraction of the room and was crowned with a large brass-framed picture. It was an image of a room in a house of what looked like old colonial India. There was an abundance of tall, green, stooping ferns in brass pots around the edge of the room, with screens decorated with all kinds of colourful exotic birds. There was also an easel standing just to one side of the honeycomb-cane coffee table.

Arty and Tatiana stared at the canvas and then at each other in amazement, for upon the white canvas the image of a large gold-coloured egg timer had been beautifully and masterfully painted. All the artist's attention had been given to the object and nothing else, for there was no background; the whole canvas had been taken up by its form. It stood alone as if suspended in a pure white cloud. Yet the painting also seemed to give the impression that it was a reflection of the room in which they were standing – a reflection coming from within the image of the egg timer. Both Tatiana and Arty were completely exhilarated by the painting, as though the reason to be brought once again to Harrogate was just to observe it. It looked so lifelike that Arty immediately thrust his hand into his pocket to make sure his timer was still there. All three of their faces seemed to be lit up in gold from the glow of the painting.

"I've been waiting so long for you to come," the old lady said quietly. No sooner had she spoken these words than the glow from the painting ceased as abruptly as if turned off with a light switch.

Though the gold-coloured chintz curtains were open, the mid-afternoon winter light outside hardly penetrated the glass window and the room had now become very dim. The old woman collapsed with relief into one of the chairs and reached over to switch on a lamp. It was a warm yellow glow that seemed thin and shallow compared to the light they had just very briefly experienced.

"He said you would come, you know!" she exclaimed, looking at them both curiously. "He also said that I would forget that he said it, but I haven't." She chuckled to herself now at some long ago memory.

"Sorry errrr… Mrs … errrrr, but who said that?" asked Arty awkwardly.

"My heart said it," she answered, looking at them in amusement, "my dear heart."

"She looks a little familiar," whispered Arty so close to Tatiana's left ear that his unshaven chin scratched it. "Have we met before?"

But Tatiana ignored him; she could not take her eyes off the face of the old lady.

"You would like to know a few things wouldn't you," the old lady answered her gaze, "well I can enlighten you!"

"You know who we are, don't you!" Tatiana whispered softly.

"Well, I guess you, my dear, are Miss Fanny Dodger, and this I believe is your uncle Jamie Dodger," she answered, "two of the most unlikely aliases imaginable." She stared at Tatiana, her eyes twinkling with amusement. Tatiana realised that the old lady knew *exactly* who they were, but how? And who was she? She opened her mouth to say something but the ancient old lady changed the subject quickly.

"You like my painting, I see," she said, her clear heavy-lidded, blue eyes gazing at them steadily. She indicated for them to sit down. "You are the first people to see it. This old age of mine is full of surprises. I have not painted anything since I was a young girl, not because I didn't want to, mind you, but because I seemed to have lost any talent I may have had for it. Then inexplicably, a couple of months ago I had a dreadful need to express myself in some way. I tried to write down what it was but it was so deep that I couldn't find it. I played my piano and tried to release it that way but again it was buried away, as if in a tomb. So, I began to doodle with a pencil and it was as if my hand and arm became on fire. I looked at what I had but I couldn't tell what it was. It just looked like a monstrous entangled wig. I knew I could do better, so I bought some paints and things. When I got home I got to it straight away and couldn't stop until I had finished. When I stood back to study my vision, I saw this picture of an egg timer, of all things." She smiled gravely, though for a fleeting moment it seemed to Tatiana that her face became young again. Tatiana gasped in recognition. Arty looked at her with concern for all the colour had drained from her face.

"I have no idea what it means, or represents," the old lady continued, "But since I finished it, I feel immensely contented and I even seem to sleep at night now!"

Tatiana put her face in her hands as if she could not bear to look at the old lady.

Seeing Tatiana in obvious discomfort, Arty plucked up some courage.

"Look, I don't know what is going on here or who you really are, but we would like to know what happened to our friend, Plant." He had stood up and was hovering over the old lady with one hand in his trouser pocket.

"And I shall tell you," she said calmly, "but first, let's have some tea".

The cup that Arty sipped the strong sweet tea from was so delicate that he was scared to hold it too tightly for fear of crushing it. It felt like a porcelain shell. Tatiana seemed to have recovered from whatever had shocked her and sipped her tea silently as the old lady began to talk.

"Of course, it was Anna that escaped, my heart saw to that …" the old lady began

"Anna?" interrupted Tatiana, "do you mean our …?"

"Heart?" interrupted Arty.

The old lady rested her tea cup back on its saucer. "I have waited many years to tell you both this," she said without any form of emotion, "so the least you can do is listen until I have at least finished."

Both Arty and Tatiana closed their mouths with a snap. The old lady stared steadily at Arty, "My *Lionheart* saw to it, of course." This time, Arty kept quiet and the old lady continued.

"He sent word to her brother Vladimir Mutnykh who was the so-called Secretary to the so – called Ural Soviet, that he must 'assist' him in the rescue of the remainder of the imperial family and release a certain officer called Owen Tudor from *his* confinement somewhere in the city of Perm. Otherwise he threatened to cut his sisters throat from ear to ear. He never minced his words, Reggie! They met secretly the next day and it was arranged that the back door to the house would be left unlocked and that the guard on that side of the house would be, shall we say, 'distracted' by my Lionheart in order for them at least to make a run for it. This Tudor fellow would also be released at the same time. Coincidentally, Plant had also received word from an undercover agent in the city that all that had been planned by the king, for the rescue was now finally in place. The plane was waiting in the field a mile or so out of the city and we were all to climb aboard for Vladivostock. The territory on that route was mainly under the 'Whites' control and we would be able to land and refuel. At Vladivostock, a Japanese destroyer was waiting to take us all to Tsuraga in Japan ..."

Arty couldn't help himself. "But such a rescue plan could only come from the very top!" He exclaimed, "For another power to be involved like that!"

"But it was, young man," confirmed the old lady. "Though Lloyd George had declined to help them, their relative the king could, and did not just stand by to see them *all* murdered." Tatiana shifted uneasily on her chair again, staring intensely at the old wrinkled face. "From Tsuraga, we were to make the short journey by road to Kyoto where the prince was waiting to escort them aboard another Japanese battle cruiser, the 'Kirishima', and on to Canada ..."

This time Tatiana could not help herself. "Prince?" she asked. "Which prince would that be?"

"Prince Arthur, the king's cousin," the old lady answered patiently. "His 'excuse' for being in Japan was to restore confidence to the Japanese that Britain was capable of winning that terrible war and to bestow the rank of Field-Marshall in the British army on the Japanese Emperor Yoshihito with the presentation of a baton. But as you now know, his real mission was for something a little more humanely pressing. Anyway, so much for plans!"

Tatiana put her head in her hands. "Please tell me what happened to my family," she cried. "Don't hide anything away from me! I just need to know!" Arty slid closer to her and put his arm around her shoulders.

"We have all suffered, my darling," the old lady almost whispered. She wiped a tear away before it evidently rolled down her cheek. "Reggie left Olga, your sister, guarding the hostage," her voice was low now, barely audible as if the words she was speaking should never be spoken. "The moon was fat and full that evening; both good and bad for his mission. The two guards were dispatched of their miserable lives silently and quickly with the old piece of cheese wire that he always kept looped around his belt, their bodies hidden in the bushes just to the side of that house. Then he waited. But the agreed time for them to exit by the back door came and went. He looked at his watch anxiously. It would soon be day time and then all the plans would be torn apart. He had just decided to go in and bring them out himself, when shrieking and hollering erupted from the house followed shortly after by gunshots. Reggie's mind was made up in an instant and he darted forward towards the back door, but suddenly that back door opened and out staggered the recipient of the gun shot. His face was deathly pale, but Reggie still had no trouble recognising him; it was our good friend, Vladimir Lenin. But Reggie didn't have much time to wonder at the wonder of it, for immediately behind him Anna appeared in the doorway with the intended murder weapon in her hand. She was screaming of course and in a dreadful panic. She took one look at the back of our old adversary who was by now on his knees in shock and pain and then bolted past him and also through the grasping hands of Reggie. It was then that he made a decision that would haunt him for the rest of his days; instead of chasing after her, he decided to enter the house.

CHAPTER 12
ANASTASIA

Anastasia bolted up Obvinskaya Street, Lenin's Mauser pistol still in her hand. The passersby scattered before her as she raced over Pokrovskaya Street past the Cheka Head Quarters on her right, up over Petropavlovskaya Street. She stopped at the railway line, breathing hard. She dropped the pistol onto the tracks and looked at the swollen expanse of the Kama River. Its murky, dark gray waters gave her no comfort; there was no escape by that route. She looked to her right to see a train rolling towards her, its black smoke spewing upwards and into the cobalt-coloured sky. She waited for the train to pass. She looked back over her shoulder again. Nobody seemed to be following her. They could have come with me, she thought; it must just be God's will. Her thoughts were broken by the sound of angry shouting as three soldiers of the Red Guard suddenly appeared where the road met the railway line. "There she is!" one of them shouted. She ran down one of the smooth, polished rails balancing like a tight rope walker. She wore only her fine cotton blouse and her long black skirt; that made it a little difficult for her to run quickly, but she didn't care – she was free at last. Then amidst the shouting, she heard the blast of a gunshot. She felt something that sounded like a very angry giant mosquito whiz past the right side of her head. She darted to her left and onto the grassy plain that led down towards the river bank and the safety of the sheltering trees.

*

Life as a signalman for Pavel Utkin was pretty mundane these days, and he was feeling pretty bored once again at noon on 21 September 1918, a chilly, windswept autumn day. His yearly update of the safety programmes and manuals were thankfully completed and behind him now. So too was his monthly report for August on any incidents or accidents upon the line. There had only been one accident involving a badly mutilated dog and no incidents to speak of. He pushed back in his chair, and placed the heels of his short leather boots up on the old wooden desk. His tin cup of weak tea sat at his elbow. Likewise, two thick wedges of black bread lay on a plate on the desk next to his boot heels. Yes the signal box at siding 37 was a pretty lonely and very boring place to spend time. He told people that he had been too old to be called up for the war, but that he was too young not to have the jaw of consciousness gnawing at him when he saw the blooded and maimed soldiers returning from the front and disembarking at Perm. They seemed to be appeased with that. He swatted a lazy fly on the table with the palm of his hand and then rubbed his palms together to rid them of the crushed insect. He crushed the remnants violently on the floor boards with the heel of his boot.

"I see you're very busy again today, Pavel."

The voice startled him, though it shouldn't have, for Serge had been a frequent visitor to the signal box for over a year. Pavel almost overbalanced off his chair as he jumped in surprise. He soon settled himself again with a groan as he recognised Serge's toothless grin in the open doorway to the signal box.

"That is probably the most exciting thing that will happen this week," Pavel replied, with his own grin of nicotine stained teeth, "last of the summer flies deserves a good headache!"

"I think you gave that more than a headache," answered Serge, observing the two halves of the fly in printed into the grain of the wooden boards, "But listen to me! I think I have the news of the year for you," Serge continued, looking out through the window on the left.

"Another defeat, I suppose," answered Pavel dully. All the news from the front these days was usually bad.

"Oh sure, sure," confirmed Serge, "nothing surer. But I've something else for you. They've caught a daughter of the tsar."

Pavel put both feet on the ground. "Who has?"

"The Red Guards. They saw her in the woods, yelled at her to stop but she attempted to run away so they fired a shot at her," Serge replied.

"You mean they shot one of the grand duchesses? One of the same grand duchesses that they were already supposed to have shot, back in Ekaterinburg?" Pavel asked incredulously.

"Who knows what to believe these days," answered Serge, "but old Shilova swears it's one of them and they have her in a sentry box just down the road there." He pointed through the window. "Come, let's go see!"

When Serge and Pavel reached the sentry box, there were no sentries; only a small group of Red Army soldiers. Three of them were peering in from the doorway and jeering at a young girl who looked to be about eighteen or nineteen. She was sitting on a three legged stool near the stove, shivering from both fright and cold. Though she was utterly dejected and tear stains like train tracks upon her grubby dirty face, there was still a proud look and air about her. Her long black skirt had been torn up on one side so that her pale white leg was exposed up above her knee. Serge leered at the spectacle, but Pavel grabbed him by the shoulder.

"She has done no wrong, comrade!" he snarled, disgusted with his friend, and the predicament that the young woman, whoever she was, was in. "Even if she is one of them, she is just an innocent young girl born into turmoil."

Pavel ran back to his signal box, determined to help the young girl in any way he could. When he returned, he was clutching one of the thick wedges of black bread that he had taken from his own plate. But as he approached the signal box again, he could see that there were now more soldiers inside.

"Please," he shouted, "let me tend to her! I was once a doctor!" She was now facing the doorway and he could see that she was injured; there were blood stains upon the white blouse across her chest.

The soldiers made way for him to enter. "Tend to her quickly!" ordered the most senior of the soldiers, "and be quick about it; they are on their way to take her back."

Serge was also trying to get into the signal box, but the soldiers wouldn't allow him. As they manhandled him and turned him away, Pavel clearly heard one of the soldiers say:

"If you breathe a word about this to anyone, you will join her in front of the firing squad."

As Pavel entered the box, he could see the young girl clearly. Her hair was cropped very short and the bruises on the side and back of her head were already turning a nasty shade of purple. There was blood on her face and more bruises around her eyebrows. Her lip was cut and there was an angry red lump on her nose. Pavel gritted his teeth. "For heaven's sake, man!" he said, looking up at the soldier, "what on earth have you done to her?"

"Only what the bitch deserved," the officer answered with a snarl, "a harmless little girl you think?" the soldier continued. "If you knew what our little friend here has been up to, perhaps you wouldn't be so compassionate."

Before Pavel could answer or ask for the bowl of soap and

water that he needed, another six Red Army soldiers turned up. They said nothing as they entered the sentry box, but the young girl looked up fearfully at them, finally losing her proud composure.

"What will you do with me?" she cried.

Saying nothing, two of the men lifted her to her feet.

"Be careful with her!" cried Pavel. "She is badly injured! You shouldn't really move her."

"And who are you?" asked the captain, fixing Pavel with a dull blank, grey-eyed stare.

"A ... a ... doctor," Pavel stuttered. "Please, she needs help."

"Come with us, *doctor!*" the captain ordered

They carried the young woman out of the sentry box and into the back of a waiting automobile. The driver sat behind the wheel; a soldier sat in the front and another sat in the back on the girl's left side. Pavel was shoved roughly into the back seat to sit beside her on her right.

"Eat this," he said to her, thrusting what was left of the black bread under her nose, "it will help you to regain your strength a little."

She shook her head, "I cannot eat anything," she mumbled softly through her swollen lips. Then she turned to look at him. Her incredible bright blue, sad eyes pierced his heart. "Are you really a doctor?" she asked simply.

"I was," he answered, "a long time ago before the war." He reached discreetly for her finger tips, "who are you?" he asked.

"I am me," she answered this time managing to speak a little clearer, "the daughter of the ruler."

The Peasant land bank was in Perm on the corner of Petropavlovskaya and Obvinskaya street. It was a large, tall building of three floors and during the first half of September it was occupied by the Cheka, the recently formed, ruthless secret police in the service of the revolution victors, the Bolsheviks.

At first they only occupied the ground floor where the bank was housed, but then as their operations increased, more space was needed and they evicted all the apartment dwellers that occupied the second and third floors. It was to the second floor that Pavel and Anastasia were taken.

"You wait there," the captain ordered. He was led to a small wooden chair opposite a closed door. He watched as the two soldiers who had now been joined by the young woman disappear with the injured young girl up the flight of stairs at the end of the corridor.

As the door opened, Pavel immediately recognised the face of Lobov who beckoned silently with his finger. He had seen Lobov and the other hard men of the Cheka many times at the train station. As Pavel entered the cigar-smoke-filled room, he recognised the other two Bolsheviks. Vorobstov stood impatiently on one side and in front of the large official looking desk, Shlenov sat on the other. Behind the desk sat the stony faced Malkov.

"Mr Utkin," Malkov exclaimed dryly, "we were aware of your many talents, but the fact that you are also doctor escaped us, it seems!" His tone was also rather threatening, and Pavel knew he had some explaining to do. The Red Army had been short of doctors and the fact that there had been one under their very noses in Perm that could have been tending to their injured soldiers was not a fact that pleased them. Pavel held out his trembling hands.

"The hands of an alcoholic are not the hands of a doctor," he answered.

Malkov smiled. "How many time have we met, Pavel?" he asked slowly. "As many times as I have been at the station," he confirmed, answering his own question before Pavel had time to respond, "But that is the first time I have seen your hands shaking like a bride's on her wedding night."

"The hands of an alcoholic are not the hands of a signalman,"

Pavel answered, beginning to wonder if he would ever see his signal box again.

"Precisely," answered Malkov. "If you can stay away from the vodka long enough to perform your duties as a signalman, I am sure from now on you can do the same in order to honour your medical responsibilities."

Pavel grew silent and stared sullenly at the floor.

"You are in a lot of trouble, comrade," Malkov declared, "but perhaps I can lessen the consequences in return for your discretion as to the young girl you have just met, or should I say who you have *not* just met."

"They say she is one of the ex-tsar's daughters," Pavel answered, still looking at the floor, "but we all believe them to have been shot in Ekaterinberg."

"Do *you* recognise her as such?" Malkov asked slyly.

"I have never seen the imperial daughters, comrade," Pavel lied. "I would not know what any of them looked like, but as I said, they were all shot in Ekaterinburg, so obviously she is an imposter."

"I am glad you see it the same way we do, comrade," answered Malkov, "but we need to keep this under wraps anyway. We demand your co – operation in the matter."

"You have it," answered Pavel simply.

Lovov, Vorobstov and Shlenov escorted Pavel up the stairs and into a long corridor at the end of which Pavel could see a low light from the paraffin lamp escaping through the door that was slightly ajar. The young woman he had seen accompanying the girl and soldiers up the stairs was standing rigidly in the corner to the right of the bed. Upon the bed lay the young girl. The woman in the corner was between twenty and twenty-four years of age, Pavel estimated. He did not recognise her. She was of average build and height and her braided, light brown hair was swept back from her face in the Grecian style. What he noticed

331

most about the woman was that her face was hard and stern, her lips were thin and pursed, giving him the impression that she was guarding, rather than caring for the patient. The woman indicated with her cold eyes for him to attend to the girl.

"The doctor needs to perform his examination of the prisoner," she said to the men. "Please leave the room."

The three Bolsheviks sneered at the patient and then filed one by one through the door where they stood. The woman pushed the door shut with her boot.

"Get on with it, doctor!" she ordered.

Pavel knelt down besides the patient. She was not conscious, and was shaking quite violently.

"She is in shock!" he exclaimed, turning to the woman in the corner.

"*Tend* to her!" the woman insisted loudly.

Pavel's hands now genuinely began to shake. Of course he had seen all the imperial family in photographs and in person. He remembered distinctly them visiting the Naval Cathedral at Kronstadt; the girls in their famous white dresses, white hats and parasols were accompanied by their father, resplendent this time in his Cossack uniform. They were all beautiful, he thought, the flowers of Russia! But which one of them was his patient? He heard the woman in the corner sigh loudly and he proceeded to examine the girl quickly. The left eye was swollen by a large bruise that ran from the corner and along the cheek bone. That side of her face was now a mottled purple. The left side of her lip bore a superficial cut; like the injury above, he had no doubt that it had been caused by a beating. A fist, he thought. And the lip, probably a finger nail. As he pulled back the blanket the patient opened her eyes; her voice trembled through chattering teeth.

"Who are you?" she asked.

Pavel raised his hand to his mouth in a signal for her to be quite.

"More to the point," he answered quietly, "who are *you*?"

A tear rolled down from her damaged eye, "I told you," the girl answered, recognizing him, "the emperor's daughter," she said, "Anastasia!"

The woman walked across to the other side of the room and poked her head through the door to speak to the three men outside in a hushed voice.

"What have they done to you," asked Pavel, "Did they …?"

"They tried," the girl whispered back, "That's why they beat me."

He heard the door close again as the woman returned to her corner.

The patient gasped as he pulled back the blanket to reveal her naked torso and chest. There was another long superficial scratch down the right side of her neck but her chest showed no signs of violence. He made to pull the blanket down further but the women immediately stepped forward and took the blanket, covering the patient again.

"Doctor, that is not part of your examination," she said, then facing the door she shouted, "Comrades!"

Immediately, the door opened and the three Bolsheviks stalked back inside the room.

"The examination is over," confirmed Shlenov, "come with us!"

Pavel glanced at his patient. She stared back at him with the eyes of her father. Another tear rolled down her face.

They led him out of the room and into the adjoining one which looked as if it was being used as a makeshift bedroom. Though stark, it was habitual. All four men stood by the solitary single bed.

"What do you prescribe, *doctor*?" asked Vorobstov with a sneer.

"First of all, she needs sweet, strong tea to help her overcome the shock from whatever has been done to her." Pavel struggled to restrain his emotions, then taking a pencil and a small note

pad from Shlenov, he continued, "and she needs this urgently."
As Pavel wrote he noticed that the paper bore the letterhead of
Doctor Ivanov.

"Was Ivanov not available?" he asked, continuing to write
the prescription.

"He died of dysentery yesterday," answered Lovov, "Perhaps
you'll be next."

Pavel finished writing and handed him the note book. "Yes,
perhaps," he acknowledged.

"Iodine, Goulard Water, bromide salts with Valerian and
bandage material." Lovov read the list out loud.

"Give me that," said Shlenov and snatched the paper out
of his hand. He wrote something quickly on the back of the
prescription and then handed it back to Levov.

"You can have the honour of performing what I suspect to
be the last service for that little bitch, my comrade," he said,

Levov smiled sardonically. He gave the girl one last leer then
turned on his heels and left the room.

"You will stay here," said Shlenov to Pavel. "We will need you
again shortly."

Pavel sat upon the bed. He was well aware that the events of
the last few hours were going to change the course of his life. He
had no doubt that Malkov at that very moment was organising
a place for him as a doctor in one of the Red Army regiments.
The Whites had taken Ekaterinburg and now they were coming
for Perm; everybody knew it. It was only a matter of time before
the order was given to evacuate the city. What was to happen to
the girl, the one that called herself Anastasia? Is she indeed to
be executed, as one of the soldiers had implied? The old springs
creaked as he lay back upon the bed. He was tired and for the
first time in many months, he wished he had a bottle of Vodka
at hand.

He was awoken by Shlenov who, much to his surprise, had
brought him tea, which was to his distaste, very much like the

one he had requested for his patient. He sat on the edge of the bed and sipped it gingerly. However, the sugar revitalised his senses immediately and he was soon wide awake.

"That imperialist dog, Kolchak, and his army is on his way, *doctor*," Malkov was saying, "so as I am sure you have guessed, we will be drafting you into our service with immediate effect. We are to evacuate the city shortly, but our army will regroup on the outskirts for we are to make an immediate offensive to take it back. As I am sure you have heard, we have retained Kazan so don't get your hopes up too much that we will suffer the defeat for you to go back to your bottle."

"I am at your disposal for as long as you need me, comrade," answered Pavel, "and as you say my medical duties are now at the top of my priority list and I am very concerned for my present patient."

Malkov cleared his throat and glared at the doctor. "This will be one patient that you will not have to be concerned about after this day has passed," he answered, "I thought you understood that."

"Merely showing concern for my first patient in my new position," answered Pavel indifferently, "though if she is to be shot, can you at least tell me why I am bothering to treat her?"

"I can see you are only going to be trouble, Utkin," Malkov answered angrily, "but *we* have the remedy for troublemakers. Now, follow me!"

Pavel knew he had to get out of there and fast. If he could get out of their clutches perhaps he could make it back to Saint Petersburg and the possibility of finding his uncle if, of course, his uncle was still there. For he was well aware of the fact that most of the bourgeoisie had been relieved of their wealth and had been left as destitute as the ones they had previously apparently exploited. Many had to flee the country. He was sure he would have to flee the country himself sooner or later, possibly to Finland or Denmark where some of his distant relatives lived. He could never serve the Bolsheviks and a cause he did not believe in. He recognised that the injustices of the imperial reigns had been unacceptable for a modern society, but from what Pavel could already see, injustices already taking place and those to come under the Bolsheviks were going to be far worse. 'Rather serve the devil you know,' was his motto; but what of the grand duchess in the next room? Was he even sure that she was Anastasia? Her face, her manner and lastly her eyes certainly made him think so. It was said among the Russian people that Anastasia had the most unusual blue eyes, seemingly filled with a light from the stars. But her previously privileged position was now the noose around her neck. She and whoever was left of her family were now caught up just like him and all the rest, in the madness of a civil war. They would surely execute them all for fear of the Whites using them as a rallying point. But her problems certainly weren't his. He had enough of his own.

"You need to administer the medicine," the woman 'guard' said curtly from the corner of the room where she still stood, as taught and rigid as a sentry.

Pavel washed the girls face carefully. She seemed to be slipping in and out of consciousness. She would open her eyes and look at him as if from afar and then close them again. He was worried. "How long has she been like this?" he asked, looking at the woman. Malkov had now left the room.

"It is your duty to administer the medicine only," the woman answered coldly, "not to ask questions."

"Is it my duty to keep her alive as well?" Pavel asked sternly. "For if it is, to enable me to attempt that, there are certain things I need to know."

The woman did not answer him, but merely scowled at him with uncaring eyes. Pavel returned to his task. He applied the iodine to her injured lip; it trembled as he did so. He suspected then that she was faking her state of consciousness. He thought her face quite beautiful despite her injuries and her almost shaved head. Her nose was long and perfectly straight apart from the small lump. Her forehead was high and slightly oval above the dark eyebrows that framed those mesmerising eyes. Like corn flowers, he thought. He cleared his throat a little nervously and was relieved to find that she was now fully clothed beneath the blanket. She wore the same fine silk blouse that had obviously been cleaned but was still soiled by a light rust-coloured mark across the chest. It was cut low so that parts of her breasts were visible. Her long dark, thick woollen skirt reached down to her ankles; her feet were bare. He applied the Goulard Water and then poured the Valerian mixture onto a teaspoon and waited for her eyes to open again.

"Wake her up!" the woman demanded.

The girl immediately opened her eyes and attempted to smile at him with her swollen mouth. The moment captured his heart. He helped her sit up until she was propped against the pillows. He gave her two spoons of the mixture. "Now you really will be unconscious," he whispered winking conspiratorially. He wondered briefly if anybody had been kind to Anastasia Nicolaevna recently for she looked at him with overwhelming gratitude.

The woman now came forward to stand directly behind Pavel where he knelt at the bedside.

"Your services are no longer needed here," she said as coldly as ever, "You must now leave!"

But Pavel could not leave just like that. He had made up his mind that the girl was indeed the daughter of the late tsar as she had told him. All the Romanov women were also noted for their beautiful hands and the girl before him did indeed have the most exquisite hands. Also why would she claim to the Bolsheviks to be a daughter of the tsar if she wasn't? Surely such a claim would put her life in extreme danger?

"I cannot leave until I know that my patient is out of danger," he answered, without bothering to turn to face the woman. He remained kneeling at the side of the bed while Anastasia looked up and past him at the woman's face.

"You are a Jew, are you not?" the woman said, bending down mouthing the words accusingly into his right ear. Pavel continued to stare at Anastasia, who continued to stare above him at the woman, and remained silent.

"I think," the woman continued, "If you knew the identity of the one you are treating you would not perhaps feel so compassionate."

Pavel rose slowly to his feet. "This doctor does not discriminate," he said staring at her with unblinking eyes.

"Even against the one who shot Vladimir Lenin?" she said accusingly.

Pavel was caught completely by surprise by the sensational statement. What was she talking about? Everybody knew that Lenin had been shot three weeks previously outside a Moscow factory by the Social Revolutionary Fanya Kaplan, who had in turn been executed by firing squad for her crime three days later. He turned now in bewilderment to look again at the girl on the bed. Could she be Fanya Kaplan?

"Who are …?"

Pavel's question to the girl was interrupted by an onslaught of shouts, shrieks and even hysterical screams from downstairs.

"What the …" the woman made her way to the door and just as she placed her hand on the handle, four loud bangs reverberated off the walls of the downstairs entrance. Putting her hand on the handle of the pistol on her hip, she disappeared through the door.

Quickly, Pavel ran to the sash window. He had no idea what was going on but he could certainly use the confusion to make his escape. He groaned as he tried to lift the window, but it wouldn't budge. He groaned again with frustration as he looked down; it had been fixed shut with screws and brackets.

"Don't leave me!" the voice from the bed was soft and pitiful. "They will kill me if you leave me here. Please, wherever you are going, take me with you!"

Pavel turned to see that the girl was attempting to stand. But she was groggy and could not stay on her feet. She swayed momentarily and then collapsed back onto the bed. Her eyes were still open and they stared at him impassively.

The shooting began again downstairs. Pavel forced himself not to panic. "Look," he said forcefully, "you had better tell me the truth. Which one is it Fanya Kaplan or Anastasia Nicolaevna? Are you Lenin's assassin or the daughter of the tsar?"

"Both!" she answered weakly. She closed her eyes. The Valerian was taking its full effect. Pavel was totally bewildered. He ran from the door to the side of the bed. He propped her up against the pillows as before, shaking her by the shoulders.

"Are you crazy?" he shouted at her.

She opened her eyes again as her head lolled back against the pillows. "No," she answered drunkenly, "they are definitely going to kill me for I am Anastasia and I shot that pig."

Pavel stared at the badly bruised face, wondering if he had made a serious error in his diagnosis. She managed to open her eyes again. "I speak the truth, doctor," she mumbled, "He came to tell us that the Germans are on the verge of losing the war and that we were no longer needed, and that it would certainly be better for Mother Russia if we were out of the way." She closed her eyes again. He splashed her face with water from the bowl that still lay at the side of the bed.

"I need you to speak quickly, whoever you are!" Pavel demanded, shaking her again.

"He wanted to know where the governess and Olushka are," she mumbled again. "Who knows?" she continued dreamily, "and even if I did know, I wouldn't tell him or anybody else. He ordered us to pack our few things, but I knew what that meant. He had come to take us to the woods where he and his men were going shoot us like dogs. Mama pleaded with him to at least let Marie and I go but he was adamant. As mama fell on her knees he was distracted and I managed to lift the gun from his holster. He wasn't expecting that and neither was mama or Marie. All three of them told me to put the gun down."

The girl's eyes grew wide and frightened now with the memory. Her speech became more clear and urgent. "I really would have been crazy, Mr Doctor, if I had put the gun down. The pig had just told us all he was going to take us to the woods and blow our brains out."

"So you shot him!" cried Pavel, barely concealing his grin even under the circumstances.

But the girl was now becoming distressed.

"He tried to grab it back," she continued her voice now rising, "then three shots went off and he fell forwards to his knees. There was blood on the lower part of his face and his shoulder, I…"

"Okay, okay!" Pavel shouted, making up his mind. "I believe you, you crazy girl!" Sweat was dripping off his brow. The shooting was still continuing downstairs, interspersed with intermittent shouts and hysterical screams. He lent forward and lifted her; she flopped both arms around his neck, and the side of her face lolled against his shoulder.

"You shot Lenin!" He exclaimed again, the enormity of the fact preventing him from bursting out in joyous laughter, at least for the time being. He made his way to the door, which was still slightly ajar, and opened it with the toe of his boot.

"I'm so tired," she whispered in his ear.

"Then sleep," he told her, wondering if he was the only one able to hear the raucous downstairs. There is no way around this, he thought; the only way is through. He carefully stepped down the stairs with the sleeping girl in his arms.

*

"What was the name of that guy and his room, Mr Peabody?"

Peabody and Smith were staring expectantly at the little egg timer still perched upon the corner of Peabody's desk inside his study at Stony Hurst College. Peabody was smirking broadly at his 'vacant' employee. "I've just told you, Mr Bumbling Bread roll!" Peabody exclaimed rather smugly. "Do you really expect it to work for one as thick as you?"

"Benzene Room, Mr Peabody?" Smith asked, ignoring the criticism.

Peabody picked up his smart gold pen from his desk and began to write the instruction, "Just in case it hears, eh Smith!" he said sarcastically. He handed Smith the piece of paper.

"Okay boss! Are you ready?" Smith asked theatrically.

"Ready, you fool," answered Peabody, looking out the window again and wondering if more rain would fall before morning.

"September 21st 1918 at Berezin Rooms on Obvinskaya Street, Perm," Smith chanted the words slowly.

"Precisely," said Peabody, still staring out the window, "and just remember you clown, that if it is as you say and that little swine is no longer my friend, then I won't have a hand in it! You, mister clever arse, will be the leader of *this* little trip."

Of course, Peabody knew that the timer would only work for him. For in all the years he had been using it, that had been the case, apart from when it just hadn't worked at all, of course. He smiled inwardly as he looked up at the darkening sky, but his thoughts were interrupted by a loud outburst from Smith.

"Look, Mr Peabody! It's working!"

Peabody turned to see the familiar glowing from the timer where it still stood upon his desk, but miraculously, Smith, who was standing at the other side of the room, was beginning to 'fade.' Indeed, Peabody could clearly see *through* the considerable form of Smith's body.

"You blithering clown!" he exclaimed urgently, "you need

to take the timer with you or how on earth do you propose to come back!" Peabody darted across his office. With one hand, he grabbed hold of the joyously glowing timer and with the other he took a firm grip of Smith's wrist to prevent him 'leaving.' But inconceivably, Smith was leaving anyway, but not in the usual 'quick' fashion they were used to. He had certainly faded but he had not disappeared entirely. Also, the hand that he had gripped Smith's wrist with was, like Smith, *fading*. Peabody thought for a moment that all was okay and that the rest of him would follow but he soon realised with horror that the rest of him was not following at all but was staying firmly put in his office. He looked down at his shiny patent leather shoes and trouser legs to see them firmly and quite solidly planted upon the plush Persian carpet. He couldn't even move; he was literally frozen to the spot. Only his eyes it seemed could perform any sort of movement and they soon irresistibly located the face of the grandfather clock in the corner, proudly displaying 6pm. But he couldn't hear any chime above the familiar roar and crash of the sea that was in his ears. Still though, he failed to be transported. Then he noticed with further horror that the hands of the clock began to move *backwards*, slowly at first but then they gathered speed faster and faster. They rotated to such an extent that the fingers became blurred and barely visible. Then suddenly and very violently, his handless arm began to shake up and down. The shaking soon gathered momentum and before too long Peabody himself was being flung up off his feet and then down again repeatedly. He began to scream hysterically.

Mr Smith, on the other hand, seemed to be transported quite as usual. He was standing in what looked like a large entrance to a large building. The tiles on the floor were black and white and laid in a diamond formation. It was only when he looked at the palm of his hand, as he had seen Peabody do on countless times, that he realised that there was something wrong. For unlike Peabody who usually clenched his fist with the timer in it and then slipped it into his jacket pocket, there *was* no timer in the palm of his hand *for* him to pocket. It was also at this point that Smith realised that things certainly *weren't* as they should be, for gripping very tightly onto the wrist of the hand that should have been holding the timer was a *decapitated* hand. It was very white, which made him think that its owner was probably dead already, and its fingers were almost as thin as a big bodied spiders legs, though not quite as hairy. The fingers gripped his wrist with the strength of a vice. Indeed his wrist was already beginning to turn purple from the pressure. Even though there did not seem to be any raggedy bits of skin or blood dripping from the wrist, even for Mr Smith the sight was quite unnerving, so he immediately turned to tell his boss about the bothersome member. Of course, this now brought him another shock and surprise for his boss had not come along for the trip. He swung around in a circle in a mild panic and scratched his head in consternation with his free hand.

It was at this moment that Lovov emerged from one of the offices to Smith's right. He was carrying a report that he had just completed for Malkov when he saw the apparition. The bundle of papers immediately left his hand and floated slowly across the large entrance way to the Cheka head-quarters. Each leaf of paper was marked in bold red letters: 'TOP SECRET.' Lovov turned back to the open door of his office. He walked back inside as if in a trance, then poked his head back out of the doorway just to confirm what was before him. It was a very large completely bald-headed person, dressed as a clown as if from a travelling circus. His head was completely white, as if painted. Around his eyes were large black circles. In the centre of his face was the customary round red nose, except in this case it looked to be the size of a billiard ball. Beneath this was a large red mouth, the lips of which looked to have been coated with great dollops of strawberry jam. He was dressed in an enormous suit of yellow and green check; the trousers were at least six inches too short and revealed one bright green sock and one bright yellow one. On his feet was a pair of furry bunny slippers. His jacket and trousers were at least four or five sizes too big for him so that when he turned or moved without actually moving his feet, the jacket and trousers did not move at all but stayed in their same position. This sight for Lovov was alarming enough but what totally unnerved the hardened Bolshevik was the fact that he could see directly *through* the 'clown.' The picture of Lenin on the wall momentarily clashed with the apparition's own head making it look as if the recently and critically injured Lenin had indeed passed away and had come back to pay them a visit. The apparition was carrying a very large hand gun strapped to his waist. Levov was a very rational and level-headed person. He therefore at first could just not accept what he *thought* he was seeing. He removed his round-framed glasses from his nose, turned to face the inside of his office and cleaned them swiftly with a handkerchief, hoping against hope that the gallon or so of vodka that he had drunk the previous evening was playing tricks on him. Alas, it wasn't. His distress was even increased tenfold by the realisation that at the end of one of the apparition's hands was another totally separate hand, so white that its owner must be dead. It was standing in mid air, holding onto the apparition's wrist with a ferocious grip. That was now just too much for Levov. With what sounded like a cross between a scream of terror and a shriek of disgust, he pulled out the Mauser from its holster and fired four rapid shots at the clown. Two hit him squarely in the forehead while the other two disappeared into the cavern of his great belly. Nothing happened. The clown hadn't even seemed to have noticed him. It seemed rather to be highly irritated with the hand that was holding on to its wrist and was obviously now losing its temper and had begun to shake his arm with the offending hand attached vigorously up and down, trying to dislodge the unsightly and thoroughly annoying appendage. The commotion had now obviously come to the attention of the other Cheka men and one by one they had reacted in much the same way as Levov, so that pretty soon the entrance to the Cheka headquarters was filled with a cacophony of shrieks, shouts, screams, cries for help and general hysteria, permeated of course by the odd gunshot for good measure.

Meanwhile, Winston Peabody, who was still stuck in his study, was no longer rooted to the spot. He was being yanked up and down by his arm with the force of an unseen assailant, like a manic string puppet. His screaming became even louder.

Smith, amidst all this confusion could now hear another sound above the roaring of the sea and the wind that, unusually, was still in his ears. It sounded like his boss was in trouble. Big trouble!

"Is that you, Mr Peabody?" he shouted at the top of his voice, for he could quite clearly hear the terror-stricken screams of his boss. "Hold on, boss! I'm coming to save you. I've first just got to get rid of this blasted hand!" He grit his teeth in unabated anger as he doubled his efforts to get rid of the tiresome thing. Smith suddenly became aware of what was happening behind him. He certainly didn't take kindly to the 'nasty little Bolshies' taking pot shots at him either. He couldn't believe what hopeless shots they were. With his free hand he reached across his waist and drew out his incomparable 'Colt 45 super deluxe, modified to cannon status' model. He had absolutely no qualms about returning their fire. With each explosion from his immense firearm he expected to see parts of nasty Bolsheviks coating the stark white walls, but amazingly it was not to be, even though he could see without a doubt not one of his shots went astray and that each one definitely hit their mark. The older more senior Bolshevik for instance, who was firing at him from behind an overturned chair, was hit in what Smith termed the 'Cyclops' – in the centre of the bridge of the nose. Smith was not sure who was the more shocked or surprised as the bullet clearly hit its mark. The room was a litter with men falling to the floor and then standing up again in utter shock and wonder; they had not been injured at all. Now that Smith's full attention was on the gunfight, he also began to realise that the bullets aimed at him were indeed also hitting their mark. He also began dropping to his knees when one looked to have buried itself in his enormous body, only to jump up again with surprising agility when he saw that he was totally unharmed and shouted with an exaggerated "Ha Ha! You nincompoops!"

It was amidst all this mayhem that the doctor with the sleeping girl in his arms made a dart for the front door. Not surprisingly, nobody even noticed.

CHAPTER 13
I LOVE YOU

As the old lady told her story, Arty had been unable to take his eyes from the painting of the timer. The fact that she had painted it so incredibly accurately and lifelike amazed and bemused him. Though he listened attentively to what the old woman was saying, at the same time he couldn't take his eyes from the painting. The harder he stared at it, the more lifelike it became; he blinked continuously, quite unable to believe what he was seeing. For now the picture looked to be slowly changing. The gold shades of the timer were slowly melting into reds and greens and then with a sudden eruption of colour, burst into life as if throwing sparks, just as the real one in his pocket had a mind to do. He closed his eyes and then shook his head from side to side. It was 'normal' again, if that was the word to describe it. He remembered the dream-like incident that he and Tatiana experienced when they somehow entered a song and discovered that what the song described had really happened. He suddenly realised that the timer was not only a way of travelling through time, but was in fact much more. He thrust his hand into his trouser pocket. It was cold and yet, as sometimes happened, seemed to have increased in weight. He looked at the old woman; who the hell was she? Why had the timer guided them to her and this house? He looked again at the painting and saw two letters painted with a thin sweeping brush stroke in the bottom right hand corner. He was sure the letters had not been there before. 'M. B.' He played with the letters in his mind. Could one of them stand for 'Marie,' he thought. Could this old lady actually be Tatiana's younger sister, Marie? But then, what would the 'B' stand for? His mind also pondered that the old lady had said it had been Anastasia shooting Vladimir Lenin and not Fanya Kaplan as the history books had recorded, and that the shooting had actually taken place three weeks later than it was supposed to have. Now that really would be just too sensational for his book. His racing thoughts were all at once invaded by the anguished voice of Tatiana.

"Please finish the story," she pleaded. "What happened to dear Anna?"

The old lady herself was now becoming distraught as if the memory was too painful to put into words.

Tatiana leaned forward.

"Who *are* you?" she whispered. It looked to Arty that she had already guessed who the old lady was but could not accept it.

"She was so sick, you know," the old lady continued with difficulty, her voice breaking with emotion, "they had beaten her so hard and Pavel and Reg and …"

"You mean Plant found them?" Arty interrupted, wondering what the hell was coming next.

"As soon as Pavel ran out of the doorway to the Cheka headquarters with Anna in his arms, he was 'accosted' by two 'Red Guard' soldiers, who of course were Reggie and Tudor. Owen had by this time been released. He was soon tracked down by MI 1 who in turn took him to Plant, for of course they were constantly monitoring the situation. For Owen was …" the old lady stopped abruptly, looked at Tatiana and then at the painting. "The rest of the story," she sighed heavily, "is not mine to tell."

"But please, please, did Anna escape? Did mama and Marie get to safety?" Tatiana was becoming almost hysterical. Arty again leaned over and tried to hold her tightly around the shoulder, but she wriggled free and stood up.

"Olga!" she cried, "you must tell me that, at least!"

Arty closed his mouth with a snap. He was dumbfounded. The old woman was *Olga*!

Olga stared at the painting again almost as if she was asking its permission to say more.

"I can only tell you this, darling," she said, tears rolling down her face, "the rest will be revealed to you in due course."

"But why?" cried Tatiana, her eyes desperately looking for the answers in Olga's face. She turned, staring accusingly at the painting of the timer. "What happened to them?" she cried, "I will go mad if I don't find out!" she continued, turning back to look at Olga.

"The plane was waiting for us," Olga continued, her breathing had become ragged and strained and talking had obviously become more difficult. She took a deep breath, and for a moment Tatiana saw the familiar light that used to shine in her beloved older sisters eyes. "But Pavel was afraid for dear Anna. We all were, for she had become very drowsy and wanted to sleep all the time. Pavel told us that it could not be the medicine for too much time had passed. We knew that somehow we had to get her to a hospital. It was agreed that Pavel would take her and that we would wait three hours for him to meet us. The plane and the pilot were waiting for us about a mile away on the outskirts of the city in a field on the far side of the woods. Pavel told us not to worry and that he would get dear Anna there. Reg insisted he go with him to the hospital, but Pavel quite sensibly pointed out that they would be much less conspicuous if he took her alone, pretending to be her husband. He promised us all he would protect her with his life. Somehow, Reg and the boys organised *two* planes so that Pavel would have been able to come with us, for Anna would need a doctor on that long journey to safety. When we arrived, we were greeted very cautiously by two of the 'Intelligence' men. The pilots were already seated in their cockpits and impatient to take off. I remember Reg swearing outrageously at both of the agents, shouting at them that Pavel would come and that we just had to wait a little longer. But Pavel didn't come and it was now over an hour past our schedule. Everything had been planned meticulously for the escape of whoever was in those two planes," Olga finally broke down, "we had to leave," she cried, "we had to leave poor Anna."

Arty stood up, impatient, and not understanding why.

"What about her mother and her other sister?" he blurted out a little callously without really meaning to.

Olga had covered her face with her hands as she sobbed silently. Tatiana knelt at her feet, weeping. Arty looked away. He could only imagine what each of them must be feeling. Olga dabbed her eyes with a handkerchief. "If only the prime minister, Lloyd George, had had a heart, they may have had a chance," she sobbed, "the king could only do so much in secret! The last we heard of them was that they were taken to Kazan." Tatiana looked up at him, her eyes drowning in grief. "Will you please leave us alone for a while, Arty?" she asked softly. Without any hesitation, Arty said that of course he would and he strode from the room, feeling the dead weight of the timer in his trouser pocket. As he closed the door quietly, he sighed with both sadness and relief. He was certainly glad to be out of there for a while, but he felt so terribly sad for Tatiana and for Olga. As he strolled down the hallway towards the front door, he stared at the photos on the wall; he now noticed that many of them were of Plant and a fine-looking young woman whom he knew to be Olga. In most of the pictures, they were always dressed in some sort of military combat gear. In one they were both seated in an old style fighter plane from the 1920s. Arty thought it looked like a Czech Army Air force plane, possibly the Aero A.11. They were both grinning broadly; she had been crammed in front of him and was obviously sitting on his knee. "Well, at least one grand duchess found some happiness," he said to himself, surprised but rather glad. The next picture startled him a little more. Both Plant and Olga were standing in what obviously looked like the African bushveld. Plant rested his boot heel upon the matted mane and head of an exceedingly large but very dead lion. They were both dressed in typical safari attire and neither of them faced the camera. Again they were laughing as they gazed lovingly at each other. Both of them were holding large calibre rifles in their hands, or Elephant guns, as they were called in those days. "It certainly looked like my crazy friend also found what he was looking for," Arty said. He then turned away from the pictures, for he could look at them no more. They were lucky, he thought. At least they had *time* to live in and the *time* to love *in* it. Unlike us, he thought, we are only engulfed in sadness and sorrow in no time at all. He was just about to turn back along the hallway when he saw the shadow of someone's feet at the bottom of the front door. Probably one of those damn newspaper men, he thought as he strode towards the door. He had a good mind to vent some of his own anger on the poor chap on Olga's behalf. As he strode quickly back down the hallway, the timer that he still clutched in his hand inside his pocket became noticeably heavy, but it was too late to take his attention from what he was doing. A sudden onslaught of heavy rainfall hit him as he thrust open the door to reveal the very unwelcome figure of Winston Peabody sheltering beneath a large black umbrella. Behind him stood the equally unwelcome statue-like form of the drenched but still grinning very broadly, Charles Henry Smith, with bars of rain behind him. "Hello, Blew Eyes!" he growled. "We thought you might be here, didn't we, Mr Peabody?"

"I certainly did," said Peabody, staring at the horrified Arty. "Now, aren't you going to invite two old friends in out of the rain?"

Arty tried to slam the door shut, but Smith wedged his monstrous boot in the way and the door sprang fully open again with such force that Arty was unable to hold it. He was thrown backwards and almost lost his balance. As tended to happen when Arty became under extreme pressure in one form or another (emotional stress usually started it) he burst out in hysterical laughter. What on earth would happen next? They had been whisked off to the old gray town of Harrogate again and for the first hour or two they had absolutely no idea why. Then they are inexplicably led through the bustling crowds to an old Victorian villa only to find Tatiana's older sister waiting for them. But *older* is not the word for she looks to be at least sixty or even seventy years older than when they had last seen her! Olga proceeded to enlighten Tatiana with as much as she was allowed by the timer, it seemed, about the fate of the rest of her family. The damn thing was in his hand. It was constantly on his mind and now he saw it inexplicably painted on a canvas. The thing was everywhere! He felt it again now in his clenched fist still in his pocket. It now felt so heavy that he was afraid it would burst through the lining of his pocket. Now, Peabody and Smith turn up, and right on time as usual. Time! That was another thing! Everybody else seemed to have it, except himself and Tatiana. He laughed uncontrollably, not really caring what happened next. He was knocked even more out of his senses by a ferociously powerful blow to the side of his head and then all became darkness.

Fortunately, it seemed he had only been out for a few seconds, for when he came to, he found that he had been unceremoniously dragged back inside the house and laid face up on the tiled floor in the middle of the hallway. He could hear the voices of Peabody and Smith whispering above him.

"Oh, she's here alright, bumble brain," Peabody was saying. "Remember what he requested in his will? Remember he asked her to wait for her sister here, in his house. He *also* knew, somehow, that she would come and seek her out. Really, Smith do you ever take notice of anything? It was just a case of figuring out when she and her loser friend here would come, but as usual I got it right. Now, come on!" Peabody stared down the hallway at the only door. "I think that would be a good place to start," he said, nodding towards it. He clipped the ties around the umbrella and then pulled on the pearl-inlaid handle. He drew out the long, thin, cruel steel blade. Smith looked at his boss in admiration. "Wow, boss! Where did you get that from?" As usual, even in the most pressing of moments, Peabody could not help but brag about his wonderful self. "I converted another of my walking sticks, Smith," he said, with obvious glee, "by the time we had made the fifth trip here looking for these two fairies, I thought it a good idea to bring something to defend against the rain and to attack the fairies with."

"The fairies won't have a chance, boss!" exclaimed Smith, staring at the fine, tempered, quivering blade. Arty had to think of something very quickly. A fight was out of the question. He was unarmed and the thought of tackling Peabody with his quivering blade and Smith who no doubt had that monstrous canon strapped to his hip, in the confines of the hallway was not very appealing. He was going to need help. It came. The timer had, as mentioned, been growing intolerably heavy as he gripped it in his right hand which was still inside his trouser pocket. It was beginning its colourful display of exotica, for it glowed through the material. At first he was alarmed, for he knew that it would attract the attention of Peabody and Smith and they would undoubtedly and very quickly, finish him off. But as he took his hand out of his pocket and looked at his clenched fist, he became aware that he was unable to unclench his hand. As he stared at it, he saw that not only were the radiant colours of red and green bursting through the skin of his hand, he also became aware of thin wisps of white smoke, almost like steam, escaping through the gaps of his clenched fingers. The smoke or steam was white – so white that he could barely look at it. He soon became aware that Peabody and Smith had stopped in their tracks halfway to the door at the end of the hallway and were irresistibly drawn to stare back at him and the phenomenon that materialised before their eyes. As Arty watched the wisps of steam; they floated upwards as if they had a mind of their own, then hung from the wall downwards in straight lines. There were seven of them. All three men were glued to their respective spots. None of them could take their eyes from the strange manifestation taking place. Then each line began to twist within itself so that it became the shape of a plait of hair, or a rope. Then miraculously, all the 'ropes' of pure white 'steam' left the wall and formed the shape of an umbrella joined in the centre at the top by another plait. On each of the fourteen ends there appeared a shiny little brass object. Arty looked closer and realised with shock that they were little egg timers, exactly like the one he had in his clenched fist. He again tried to open his hand but still could not. He continued to watch in utter amazement as the 'umbrella rope' then rose up higher until the binding 'plait' touched the ceiling. It then slowly floated over to where Peabody and Smith still stood rooted to the spot, gawking at the incredible sight. It hovered innocently above them.

"Look, boss!" Smith announced solemnly," it's just like an umbrella!" Then with a whoosh, and much faster than any of them could see, it dropped like a thunderbolt through the air from the ceiling. It covered both Peabody and Smith just as a gladiator's net might. They both sank to the floor, either in fright or because the thing was so heavy, Arty could never decide which. The end of the rope where the little egg timers dangled then proceeded to wrap around the arms and legs of both Smith and Peabody so tightly and so quickly that within a second or two, neither of them could move an inch. Arty could feel their eyes of silent terror staring up at him as he slowly edged past them.

"Good day, gentlemen!" he said, and kicked Smith violently on the shin as he passed, "never kick a *good* man when he is down!" He grinned quickly and then ran to the door of the sitting room.

Tatiana was still kneeling on the floor by Olga, her head in her lap. He almost thought she was asleep. "I think we had all better get out of here!" he cried. "Our friends are in the hallway, a bit tied up at the moment, but not for long, I think." He again tried to open his hand so that he could look at the timer and ask it to take them away, perhaps even Olga.

"She's gone, Arty," Tatiana answered softly. Arty looked at the ancient old lady that had once been Tatiana's pretty elder sister. Her head had slumped forward onto her chest; her eyes stared lifelessly at her sister. He held her wrist and felt for a pulse. There was none. "Oh, Tanechka!" he said, "I'm so sorry!" He felt his eyes water for her. Surprisingly, Tatiana stood up. "It's alright," she said "I understand now." She leaned forward and kissed the cold brow of the old woman. "She is waiting!" she said simply. "She told me. They all are! In no time at all."

Arty stared at her. Something had happened apart from the obvious while he had been gone. Tatiana was clearly very distraught at the passing of her sister, but that distress was counterbalanced with a strange sort of peacefulness, brought about by whatever Olga had told her. She had even become a little dreamy. But there really was no time to ask any more questions. "We have to leave," he said firmly. She took his hand, "The window?" she asked. He nodded.

"Where on earth did you get that from?" Arty exclaimed in surprise as he glanced sideways at Tatiana. They were dodging the shoppers along Cambridge Street, their feet splashing in the puddles from the never-ending rain. He had noticed that she carried a small black umbrella. Unfortunately for him, it was only large enough for one person. "It was lying by the window as we left the house," she cried, "I feel a little like Mary Pippins."

"Poppins!" he corrected her, relieved that she seemed to be coping with the trauma, but again he was also puzzled. Most people on the cold wet street were either heading for the large coffee shop on the left that they had just passed or for the cover of the Victoria Shopping Centre on the right a little further down. Arty pulled at her hand, forcing her to stop. He thrust his clenched fist under her nose. "Look at this thing!" He declared. He was becoming frantic, for still he was unable to open it. Together, they both pried at his fingers but still the hand that held the timer would not open.

"Arty," Tatiana said steadily, she looked deep into his eyes, "be patient. There must be a reason. Just trust it."

"Let's just find somewhere quiet," he responded, sighing heavily.

"Yes," she answered, "we need to talk."

Talking wasn't really what Arty had in mind at that moment. His fingers were really becoming quite sore and were now beginning to ache. She stared longingly as he led her past the church again. The yellow lights that glowed through the stained glass windows seemed to beckon to her, offering her safety. "Oh, do let's go back inside!" Tatiana cried.

But Arty refused, and pulled her forward.

"There's probably a yoga class going on, anyway."

Reluctantly, Tatiana let him lead her to where Cambridge Street became Cambridge Road and then down to a large busy intersection. She looked at him expectantly. "If you don't know the way," she said, "just let *me* show you."

"Look," he cried angrily, "I'm the one in the rain." He stared at her sarcastically from the tip of the umbrella down to her toes. She was hardly wet at all. "Let *me* show *you* the way!" He pulled on her hand and they turned into Montpellier Parade. As they trotted down the wide pavement, Arty continuously looked over his shoulder for any sign of Peabody and Smith.

"Okay," he said, the rain now dripping off the end of his nose, "It should be quiet down here." He took a right turn and they found themselves in a narrow, cobbled street. Tatiana looked up at the sign on the wall.

CRAVEN COURT

It was an old part of the city that had been turned into a quaint little shopping arcade but due to it not being under cover it was at that moment quite deserted. On either side were cheerily lit little shops with white cottage pane windows. There was an exclusive clothing and camping equipment shop, and even an exclusive home décor shop. Arty peered inside one of the windows, admiring a pair of walking boots, but for once Tatiana showed no interest in window shopping. "It would have been just as quiet in the church, Arty," she said softy.

"Ah, at last!" he cried, ignoring her. He had turned to look up ahead. He beamed at the warm cosy light of a small coffee shop. "I wonder if they have any Jammy Dodgers?" he cried enthusiastically.

It wasn't as quiet inside as Arty had expected, but thankfully they were shown to a relatively private, small table for two in the corner by the window. It was practically dark outside. He looked at his watch. It showed 6:00 p.m. Well, I guess it should be dark, he cried. Then he realised that his watch always read 6:00 p.m. these days no matter where or what time they were in.

As they took their seats, Tatiana uncharacteristically reached across the small table and took his hand in hers. Arty blushed a little, but was pleased. So she wasn't angry with him after all.

"Arty," she said her eyes looked almost as dark as ebony

in the dimness. The flickering light of the candle on the table before them danced upon her high pale cheek bones. "I have figured out why time has stopped for you, just as it has for me."

He smiled at her warmly. "Please enlighten me, Einstein," he said. He was enjoying the sudden intimacy that she had orchestrated between them.

"It's because you have got yourself wound up with me," she said. She squeezed his hand lightly.

"I thought you were going to tell me something other than the obvious." He smiled again. "And I wouldn't have it any other way."

Her eyes grew even more troubled. She looked down at the surface of the table. "What I am trying to say to you, dear Arty, is that if I wasn't around I am sure things would soon get back to normal for you."

"As I said," he answered again, his throat becoming a little dry, "I wouldn't have it any other way."

Tatiana still stared at the table. She slowly withdrew her hand from his. "What I am really trying to say Arty, is that I love you!" Her hand trembled as she rested it on her lap. He had longed to say those very words to her! He couldn't believe that she had said them to him first, but something was wrong.

"But?" he asked. His heart should have been bursting, but her words only sounded like words.

"I think you getting involved in all this was a mistake and that ..."

"You know that isn't true," Arty interrupted, his voice rising a little so that the couple at the table next to them both stared for a moment. "Harry said that it doesn't *make* mistakes, remember?"

"I don't think dear Harry knows everything," she answered, "if you remember he was the first to admit that very fact. He was very confused by the whole thing. Me being able to come back with you, for instance ..."

Now they were interrupted by the fresh-faced waitress.

"Just two cappuccinos!" Arty ordered bluntly.

"Arty, you have to listen to me," Tatiana said urgently, "we may not even have *time* for a cup of tea now."

"Not a cup of tea now," he exploded, "I said CAPP U CCIN OS," he continued angrily spelling out the letters." This time the couple at the next table raised their eyebrows at each other and smirked into their own coffee cups.

"You are not making sense, my dear duchess," Arty carried on, lowering his voice and leaning across the table searching for her hand.

"You have been wonderful, my darling," she said softly. She so desperately wanted to hold his hand again but if she did that she would not be able to say what she knew she had to. Instead, she reach across the table again and gently stroked the side of Arty's bruised and swelling face.

"You have protected me and looked aft ..."

"What has happened?" he interrupted her again furiously. "Did something happen when I left you alone?" Even now, he did not want to mention Olga's name, thinking that it may upset her even more.

A large solitary tear rolled down her cheek and splashed onto the wooden table top. "She told me something, dear, dear Arty," she answered him, "she spoke about someone. Someone who I thought I had forgotten; someone with whom I was very, very close. But just the very sound of his name suddenly made my heart ache."

Couldn't she at least lie to him a little, he thought. Did she have to be so truthful?

"Look," he cried raising his voice again, "We are stuck to each other whether you like it or not, remember." He thrust his still clenched fist under her nose. He could feel the shocked and penetrating gaze of the couple again to his right. Then much to his surprise and relief he found at last that his fingers sprang open. There stood the little brass egg timer, lifeless and dull, balancing in the middle of his palm. "Unless of course you want to go traipsing off with him here in nineteen hundred and who knows when …" He struggled to lower and soften his voice. "It's me and you, Tanechka," he said, "the timer has brought us together and we need to stay with it. Belong to it, until it finally makes up its mind what it's going to do with us."

Another tear rolled down her face. The cappuccinos arrived; the young waitress looked embarrassed. She set the two cups down carelessly in front of them and walked away quickly.

"That's just it, "she continued, "Olga told me something." She stopped and looked at him again, now her eyes were gray and sparkling. "A certain thing was stolen from my family, long ago when I was only a little girl. It was something very dear to us. Olga told me that in order for our family to put right what is wrong it must be returned to us. This she said is *my* task. *He* knows who took it. She had waited for me Arty, to tell me when I turned up at her house. She told me that it was revealed to her as she painted … painted the timer." She had become a little breathless now and she stopped and looked at the little egg timer on the table in front of them. Her eyes reflected the tiny red and green sparkles from the top phial of the egg timer. "He is going to come for me, Arty, and together we must seek it so that it can be returned." She could not help herself now as she reached across and touched the back of his hand. "So you see my Arty, no matter what our feelings are for each other, I fear the timer has got different plans for us."

"This thing is just about pain," he hissed, pointing at the little object, "It brought you to me. Let me fall in love with you and now determines that you must be wrenched away from me." He stared at the timer coldly. "So anyway," he continued, "when is Sir Lancelot arriving? Do we have time for our last cup of coffee together? Tell you what: I will order some Jammy Dodgers so that we can end our love affair in *real* style."

She took hold of his hand forcefully, becoming angry herself.

"You are in my soul," she flared at him, her eyes awash with sorrow, "you are my everything. What you love, I love. Love *is* us! But we can't go against it. Oh my love, I just wish you could see that."

"Who *is* it that is coming for you?" he asked jealously, refusing to understand anything except the way his heart felt.

"His name is Vassilli," she answered quietly, this time looking at the heart of her own cappuccino. "I knew him when I was a little girl. He lived in the palace with us. Papa loved him so much." She talked quickly, her voice trembling with emotion. "He was just a little older than I …"

"Well, then!" he cried emphatically, "I'm sure you're going to make the *perfect* couple!"

"Oh, please don't Arty! This is bigger than us! Can't you see that? Just for once, can't you open your eyes and really see? Can't you also see that I can never now be *really* happy without you?"

"Then tell him to bugger off when he turns up," he declared stubbornly and rather bluntly, "and just stay with me." The couple at the next table looked across at him again. The young lady shook her head and whispered something to her partner. "It's because I'm so much older than you, isn't it?" he continued childishly. Tatiana remained silent, refusing to be goaded into an all-out argument. "That's it! Isn't it?" He yelled at the top of his voice. The couple sniggered.

"I was only six or seven when we met," Tatiana answered him.

"Then it was *obviously* true love," Arty declared again at the top of his voice.

The couple giggled.

"You even remind me a little of him, in a funny sort of way." Tatiana looked at him sadly.

The couple burst out laughing. They stood up quickly as Arty glared ferociously at them both. They edged past Arty's and Tatiana's table slowly. When they reached the front counter where they were to pay their bill, Arty clearly heard the young woman say to what looked like her husband. "Well, he looks older than six, that's for sure, but he certainly doesn't act any older." Her husband hooted with laughter as they grabbed their umbrella from the stand and left.

"You know what," Arty said determined now to act like a six-year old, "you remind *me* of XP8!"

Tatiana looked up at him, her eyes very dark and troubled. "XP8? What's that?"

"A cold hearted, manipulating computer program," he answered cynically, "and what's more, it's bloody atrocious, just like *you*."

"Arty, please!" she said quietly. He watched her lips as she spoke. The lovely lips he loved and longed to kiss. "What's more," he continued, "you've got lips like a bloody frog. You've got great big, froggy lips!"

The group of people behind Tatiana suddenly grew silent. She stared at Arty, her eyes streaming with tears. The people pushed their chairs back from their table and one by one began to make their way to the pay counter. One of the men stared at Arty with a cold hard look and mumbled under his breath.

Arty's anger slowly simmered down into the sorrow that had caused it. He just wanted to hold her in his arms, wipe all her tears away. He looked at the timer. He wondered briefly if they should just get up and leave it there; set out on their own and leave the damn thing behind. Let it find some other unsuspecting idiot, he thought. But then he knew Tatiana. Of course he did, and he knew that she would not refuse what she thought she had been called to do.

"Just how do you propose we break up?" he said. "I mean, even in our confused state of existence neither of us belongs here, and we aren't exactly independent, are we?" He looked at the front of a newspaper that had been left on the table next to them. He took it and read the date. "February 4th 1986. Not a good year," he said, "but I guess none of them were when I was a kid."

They had been so engrossed in their terrible predicament that even though Arty had positioned himself facing the front door, neither of them had noticed the arrival of Peabody and Smith.

"May we invade your intimacy?" Peabody asked. He immediately pulled up a chair. The small table suddenly felt very crowded. Tatiana lifted her chin and challenged his very unwanted presence, proudly.

"Always the plucky miss, aren't you?" Peabody declared. He grabbed hold of her wrist in his spider fingered, vice-like grip. Arty attempted to stand, but Smith, who had made his way to stand behind him laid both his enormous hands upon his shoulders and began to push down with all his might.

"See how *you* like it, Blew Eyes!" he growled in Arty's ear.

"Now, now, Mr Smith! Don't go breaking his neck just yet!" cried Peabody. His yellowed teeth were even more repulsive than Tatiana remembered. He lit a large cigar and then blew the smoke directly into Arty's face. "You are just as beautiful as ever, my dear!" he said, turning back to face Tatiana. "I, on the other hand, have matured a little since we last met." He flicked his greying temples with his fingers dramatically. Tatiana could certainly see that he had aged since she had last 'bumped,' into them. His face was heavily lined and rather craggy, his hair still thick and shaggy but now flecked with white and grey streaks. There was something different about his eyes that hadn't been caused by any amount of aging; something in their depths that made her gasp. It was a haunted almost frightened look, akin to that of a child who was being exceedingly naughty, doing something incredibly daring and he just couldn't help himself.

"Have we met?" she said aloofly. Arty wondered what she was up too. Much to his relief, Smith had released the pressure from his shoulders a little, but still he could not move.

"Yes, I am afraid we have, Tatiana Nicolaevna," he answered in his best suave tone. "And I have been so dearly wanting to meet you again, for it is time for you to tell me a few secrets."

"But my name is Mary!" she declared, straight faced.

"Not Fanny?" asked Smith, rather surprised.

From the corner of his eye, Arty could see that the timer had begun to glow. It was concealed from the view of Peabody and Smith by his elbow but he knew that Tatiana was also aware of it.

"Oh, I get it!" Arty cried, realising that she was playing a game to give them the few seconds or so that they needed before the timer whisked them away to safety. "You think that she's that Tatiana chick, the one I used to hang about with."

"What happened to her?" asked the hapless Smith.

"Oh, you know what young girls are like," Arty answered, "she ran off with the first young guy she fancied. Let me introduce you to Mary Pippins!" The timer was taking a little longer than usual. Where was the sound of the sea and the wind?

"Smith! Shut up!" demanded Peabody. "And you," he continued, facing Arty squarely, "Button your lips or I will slice them off!" He laid his umbrella on the table with his hand clutching the pearl handle, ready to draw out the razor sharp blade. He stared at Arty, threateningly. Smith giggled. He then returned his glare to Tatiana. "You have got precisely ten seconds to tell me where the little crown is and all the missing eggs or I will instruct *my* friend here to jerk *your* friend's neck with force that will snap it like a chicken bone!"

Smith growled.

"Super coloured-froggy's lipstick-XP eights-atrocious," Tatiana cried, trying to remember her favourite line from the 'Mary Poppins' movie she had watched with Arty, and getting it mixed up a little. While all three of them looked at her as if she had gone totally mad, her eyes suddenly lit up with the glow from the timer. "Go, my darling!" she cried, "Go, let it take you. Go! I love you. I always will." Peabody now grabbed her other wrist. "You aren't going anywhere, my dear!" he shouted at her menacingly.

Arty tried to stand but the weight from Smith pushing down on his shoulders prevented him. The familiar ear-splitting roar of sea and wind began to crash inside his head. "No, no, no!" he heard a voice scream. He realised it was his own voice. The room, the lights, the faces of Smith, Peabody and that of Tatiana began to swirl as if in a whirlpool. The roaring became louder and louder. Never had it been so loud. He reached out blindly with his hands to try to grab hold of something to prevent him leaving – the table, even Smith's thick forearms. But it was no good. The thunderous roaring continued. The swirling of room and faces began to blur. Then suddenly, silence!

He lay still, keeping his eyes shut. He could distinctly hear a sort of heavy breathing sound in his ears. He smiled. She had told him that she loved him. He opened his eyes and was disappointed to find that Tatiana was not there. Her head laying on his shoulder, one arm and sometimes a leg as well strung across him. He looked up at the ceiling and then he closed his eyes as he listened to the heavy breathing of the not too distant sea. Suddenly, he opened his eyes again. Abruptly, he leaned over to peer down at the floor at the side of the bed. She wasn't there. The timer lay as usual on his bedside table next to his watch. The hands were pointing vertically opposite from each other. He grabbed the timer and sprang off the bed and drew back the curtains. He could see a faint amber light on the horizon of dark, moody water. He knew it would be light in just a few minutes. His old jeans and t-shirt clung to him in the humid pre-dawn air as he opened the door to his bedroom, walked quickly across the hallway to the door of the spare room.

"Tatiana!" he called gently, at the same time knocking softly with his knuckles, "are you awake, Tanechka?" He opened the door to find the room in perfect order as usual, her favourite long, mauve skirt folded carefully over the back of the chair. A book that she had been reading was placed neatly on the bedside table. The bed had been made with her usual precision, pillows and duvet perfectly tended to. Of course she wasn't there, but the bedside table lamp had been left on. He nodded to himself. He knew where she would be –the same place as when the timer separated them the last time. He leaned over to turn off the lamp and then noticed a single piece of paper that lay upon the book. Immediately, he recognised Tatiana's handwriting.

Look for me in that sunset evening
Look for me as the rain drops fall
I'll be there with the autumn leaves
Waiting for you, 'in no time at all'
Dance with me 'neath the light of a street lamp
Dance with me, at the emperor's ball,
Seek me in the valleys of the roses
I'll be waiting for you in no time at all
In the years of shadow from the moonlight
You will surely hear a lonesome owl call
Climb on the rungs of the ladder to the starlight
I'll be waiting there, in no time at all.
One day we will come to rest
Under the timeless blanket we will crawl
We'll stare at the heavens and our God in wonder
Together forever, in no time at all.

He read it again, this time out loud. He wondered if she had a tune for it.

He raced down the stairs, then out through the back door. He leaped over the short wooden fence of the small garden and on to the path that took him down to the beach. He couldn't wait to tell her that he loved her, too; to hold her in his arms, finally. To tell her that they would brave whatever the timer had in store for them together, no matter how dark it looked up ahead. They would be together. Their love would conquer all! He smiled again as he saw the familiar set of long slim footprints in the shadowy sand, heading out to where the rocks met the dancing water. The sea breeze was strong as he traced her footprints with his own and made his way to the blanket of rocks. He could see her now, a huddled figure with her back to him, staring at the great burning sun that was peering over the water's edge. She was wearing his large waterproof wind jammer and she had wrapped herself nicely inside it, even tucking her knees up inside.

"I thought for a second or so that I had lost you," he shouted against the breeze, "I wish it wouldn't do that." He paused. "I love you so much, you know." The huddled figure didn't move, though the plastic material of the jammer flapped angrily against the rock. "You see," he continued, "we are *meant* to be together! I think maybe Olga misunderstood her painting." He stepped forward a little closer and gently touched her shoulder and then stepped back in horror and disbelief; the wind jammer crumpled and fell to the rocks in a misshaped heap. Even as he watched in complete shock, the wind took hold and caught the garment, lifting it high up. It hovered for a moment, then another gust of wind catapulted it towards the horizon and it was gone.

"Tatiana," he cried up at the bruised sky raising both of his arms in anguish, "Tanechka!" He fell to his knees and wept.

*

Harry's shop was closed. Arty looked at the dusty front door. The sign that usually read 'gone fishing' had been removed. On closer inspection, Arty realised that the frame of the door was thick with cobwebs. He could barely see through the dust-covered window, but as he framed his face with his hands and peered in he could quite clearly make out that the shelves once jam packed with antique wot nots were now bare and also very dusty. It looked as if the shop had been deserted for months, even years.

As Arty drove towards the coffee plantation, his throat was dry. He could barely swallow the sorrow. His eyes for some reason had become tired, red and sore as if from lack of sleep. He had of course asked the timer to take him back to the little coffee shop in Harrogate. He had given it the exact date and time but of course its brass-coloured case merely glinted at him while the powder inside the phials remained dull, damp and lifeless. Then he remembered with an aching in his heart that one of the rules of the timer was that you could not return to a place until a year had passed in the present. Tears welled up in his eyes. But he wasn't even in the present, was he! He was in time suspended. So even if he could have borne to wait a year to get back to her, it would be impossible. He looked at his watch. Like the clock in his lounge and the small digital clock in his kitchen it still read 6pm. If only he could find Harry! He would know what to do.

Arty didn't wait for an answer to his knock on the door of Harry's wooden cabin. It creaked loudly as it swung inwards. At first Arty thought that the place was also deserted, for again there was dust and grime everywhere. Then he heard the sound of an old weak voice from the chair that faced the opposite window.

"Thank the Lord!" it said simply.

Arty walked quickly across the room, shocked at the state of the place. As he reached the back of the chair, the hairs on the back of his neck began to rise. The hand that clutched the arm of the chair was so old and thin that it looked like that of a skeleton. The yellowed skin had tightened on Harry's skull. Only a few thin, white strands of hair hung from his head, the top of which was covered with large brown marks of age. His eyes had sunk deep into his head; though his spectacles still balanced on the end of his nose they did so precariously. His ears seemed large and now out of proportion with his head. Harry's frame was also decimated from its former portly glory to skin and bone. The belt holding up his trousers was wrapped almost double around his waist.

"You're here, my boy!" he gasped, his voice was ragged and hoarse with age.

"Harry!" Arty cried, engulfed in a mixture of horror, pity and sadness, "what does all this mean? What has happened to you? I thought time had ceased for you, too! How long have I been away?" He knelt down beside his friend on one knee.

Harry waived the questions away with his shockingly bony hand. His face crinkled into humour, his eyes for a moment lit up to how Arty remembered them. "You daft sod," he chuckled asthmatically and then broke into a fit of dry coughing. He wiped his mouth with a loose handkerchief. "No need to be upset. I haven't been waiting long. All this started the moment I realised."

"Harry! You look bloody ancient!" Arty blurted out, unable to contain himself. Much to his consternation, Harry chuckled again. "Well, I guess it's *time* for me to go then, isn't it?"

"Well, you certainly haven't lost your gift for talking in riddles, my friend," answered Arty affectionately, "and please, you don't need to be going anywhere just yet. I don't think I could bear it, even if you do look like an unwrapped mummy."

"Ah, but I do," said Harry. Again, Arty noticed the gleam in Harry's eyes. "My clock began to tick again when I realised, quite rapidly I guess, from the look on your face."

"Realised?" Arty asked puzzled, "realised what?"

Again, Harry lifted his bony hand from the arm of the chair. "There is a jewellery box over there," he said pointing to the sideboard against the wall, "Bring it to me."

Arty picked up a small wooden ornament shaped liked a piano. "This?" he asked. Harry beckoned with a bony finger. "This was once Magda's," he said holding the piano-shaped jewellery box in his hand affectionately. "But first," he continued, "I need to make sure. Arty hold out your hands, palms upwards." Still very puzzled, Arty did as Harry asked. "What *is* this all about?" he asked. With a long and rather sharp finger nail, Harry traced a red line that ran from the bottom of Arty's index finger through the centre of his palm and ended at the wrist of his right hand. As he did so, he sighed with relief. "Any idea how you got this?" he asked.

Arty shook his head. "I've no idea," he said, still very puzzled, "and what's more, neither my mother nor anybody else, for that matter, could tell me either!"

"She couldn't tell you, Arty," Harry said quietly, "because she really didn't know. For you already had the scar when she first saw you …"

"What are you blabbing on about, Harry? Are you trying to say I was born with this mark?"

"It's not a birth mark, Arthur," Harry answered a little more firmly, "It is a scar, and it was made by this!" He opened the lid of the little jewellery box to reveal what looked to be a broken bit of pottery. Arty lifted it out and found that it was in fact the head of a soldier, wearing a military hat of the time of the Napoleonic wars. The head had been broken off at the top of its shoulders. Arty winced as he ran his middle finger against the broken edge and saw that it cut him just as easily as a very sharp knife.

"You were adopted, Arthur," Harry said as sympathetically as he could, "*you* are the boy! The boy we brought back or rescued if you like, from the 1905 Saint Petersburg massacre!"

Arty fell from his knees onto the seat of his pants. "But that's crazy!" he cried. "I mean, I remember living with my mother and a few of her husbands in England before we came over here. I'm really sorry, Harry, I know how much you need to find this boy but …"

"Tell me, Arthur," Harry interrupted quietly, "can you

honestly remember anything about your life before the age of nine or ten?"

Arty hummed loudly and shook his head in frustration. As a matter of fact, he couldn't. He had always put it down to some sort of safety mechanism kicking in. Unpleasant times are best forgotten. His childhood and indeed young adulthood had in general been rather traumatic for one reason or another. "But … but … this is crazy. You are trying to tell me that I am not even of this time. That I was born back in eighteen hundred and who knows when." He suddenly felt sick.

"Take a grip on yourself, my boy," said Harry firmly, "don't you see this explains everything? Though we can never know everything about the timer and the reason it allows certain things to happen and how and why it orchestrates them, at least we know now why time has ceased to tick for you also."

"But why all of a sudden? Why am I allowed to live in this time until the age of forty two and then all of a sudden time ceases to exist? Why couldn't it just let me go back straight away? Why put me through forty-two years of living in the wrong time?"

Harry pushed his spectacle back onto his face. "It is part of your story, Arthur. I am sure it will be revealed to you sooner or later, though it makes sense to me that it is certainly something to do with Tatiana coming back with you. Just think the way it has panned out now. She has been saved from that dreadful mess that happened in that dreadful house and *you* have even been saved from yourself. From what I could see the last time we were all together, there certainly seemed to be a nice 'rapport' developing between you two. Where is she, by the way?"

"That's just it," Arty answered glumly. "I've lost her, Harry! Or should I say, the timer split us apart."

The old man looked up at Arty; tears welled up in his eyes. "It is hard my friend, when the timer gets hold of your life. But you must trust it. There is a reason for everything."

Arty delved into his pocket and brought out the culprit. "I guess this is yours now?" he said sadly, holding it out on the palm of his hand. Harry took it slowly. Immediately, the egg timer began to glow. It began to glow in a way that Arty had never seen before. Sparks the shape of stars began to burst forth from the phials; stars of every colour imaginable. The little stars would rise up at the same time as growing in size and radiance. One by one, they would hover above Harry's head and then extinguish themselves in another extravaganza of light and colour. As Arty watched in unbelievable fascination, he noticed with each star that burst over Harry's head a change began in Harry's appearance. Firstly, the hair on his head grew in a sudden rush. It became thick and dark and rich. At the same time, the skin on his forehead changed from mild yellow to a brown tan of the utmost health. The belt around his waist unravelled so that he was neither bone thin nor portly. The spectacles on the end of his nose fell off completely. His eyes sparkled with happiness and laughter. To Arty's amazement and utter happiness also, a young and very handsome Harry sprang out of his chair. "I must take your leave, my friend," he said, "she is waiting!"

Arty looked down at the floor, downcast. "But what am I to do?" he asked.

"Believe, Arthur!" Harry cried in a voice almost unrecognisable, "If you cannot believe in something, how on earth will it ever become real? Truly believe and it shall be given to you." Harry gripped the timer in his hand tightly. He looked one last time at Arty with eyes of indescribable love and then in a colossal burst of colour and light, he was gone.

As Arty drove down the winding pock-marked road, bordered on each side with the lush foliage of KwaZulu-Natal in early summer, he saw the incredible blanket of a sea the colour of gun metal laid out before him. It was already mid-morning and the sun was intermittently hiding behind the racing clouds above. He pulled into the side of the road and turned off the

372

engine. He looked at his watch. 6pm. He raised his wrist to his ear and listened to hear the faint workings of a tiny precise Swiss made mechanism. He was still in limbo. He had lost his love. He had lost his friend. He had also lost the only thing that was capable of orchestrating a meeting with them all again, and he was still stuck in a vacuum of time. Who am I? He thought. Where was I born? Who were my real parents? There were so many unanswered questions. He knew that Harry was not mistaken, for how else could he have been released from his captivity in no time at all? He had no idea what to do next. He gripped the steering wheel in both of his hands, leant forward and wept again.

Even with an utterly broken heart one can only weep for so long, especially to the silence. When he looked up again, the air had become filled with mist. This was unusual, as the mist normally rolled in from the sea in the evening. But these days, Arty did not think anything that happened as being 'unusual,' anymore; his normal was very 'unusual.' 'He decided to return back to his cottage immediately. He would write all of it down. He had enough material for two or maybe even three books. That would keep him busy at least. Who knows, the clocks may start ticking again and Russian immigrant or not, he just may be able to go back to his previous normal life of being the lonely, almost broke unpublished writer. He pushed the start button on the dash and felt the V-8 roar into life reassuringly. "Today," he said aloud, "is going to be a good day!"

Even the powerful fog lights were rendered useless as the thick mist swirled around on all sides. The Jaguar growled softly as it tentatively searched for safety with its headlights. He looked at the speedometer and realised that the car was only moving at 10 km per hour. He had never seen such thick fog before. As he could no longer see his surroundings he began to feel completely lost, yet commonsense told him that sooner or later if he stuck to the road he would eventually reach home. Commonsense also told him that the *further* down the hill he drove the more likely the mist would clear. But it didn't. It also began to feel cold. Not just a little chilly as can happen in that part of the world even in summertime, but positively *cold*. The breath from his mouth became a vapour of steam as he continually gasped in frustrated confusion. He reached over to the passenger seat for his jacket. It had had a tear in the lining and Tatiana had mended it for him only a couple of days previously. For some reason, she must have put it in his car. As he put the jacket over his shoulders, he felt something heavy and hard knock against his leg. Something was lodged in the bottom lining of the jacket. It had been neatly enclosed so he was unable to see what it was, but as he traced the outline with the tips of his fingers he could feel that it was a small and rather dense little box shape. His investigation was interrupted however by the distant glow of two red lights spaced closely together, up ahead. As the Jaguar came closer, he realised they were the tail lights of a car that had pulled over to the side of the road, probably in distress. He braked to a very lazy stop, close behind the car and could just make out the 'wings' emblem of Aston Martin at the base of the boot lid. A yellow light suddenly appeared to the right of the car. The driver had got out and was coming towards him, lighting his way with a torch. The dark shape of a man tapped firmly on the passenger window. Arty recognised him immediately. It was Alex.

"Hello, mate!" his voice was muffled. Arty opened his door and climbed out. "We were worried about you, son!" Alex exclaimed, thrusting out his hand. Arty took it and shook it tentatively. Tatiana's words were in his ears. "He is one of them," she had said, "Alex is not who you think he is."

Alex attempted to peer inside Arty's car at the passenger seat. "Where is Aphrodite?" he asked, but there was an usual tone to his attempt at humour.

"Who is 'we'?" Arty asked, "You said *we* have been worried; have you brought somebody with you?" He looked over Alex's shoulder to the sleek lines of the Aston. He could clearly see the dark shape of somebody sitting in the passenger seat.

"Who is with you, Alex?" Arty asked suspiciously. An indescribable fear had unexpectedly sent shivers down his spine. Every muscle in his body tensed.

"Just tell us where she is, son," Alex said soothingly, "and you'll have nothing to worry about."

"Who?" answered Arty pathetically.

"Arty," said Alex with sudden menace, he leaned forward conspiratorially. He pointed over his shoulder with his thumb. "The guy in the car is not one to be messed with, my son," he whispered. Arty could see there was fear also in Alex's eyes. "He is my boss," he continued in a shaky whisper, "In fact, he is *the* boss. Just tell us where you left her, the place, the date, the time and you can be on your way. Forget about it all. In fact, we also came to tell you there is a nice allowance provided for you until you finish your book, so you have no money worries mate. Just give us what we want."

Arty again peered over at the figure in the passenger seat. It sat perfectly still. Its silhouette seemed to be an impenetrable black. His fear was almost overwhelming. Arty wanted to turn and run; run as far away as he could from whoever or whatever was sitting in the passenger seat of Alex's car.

"What do you want her for?" he managed to ask.

Alex looked at his watch. "It is nearly time Arthur, and then there will be nothing I can do!"

Again, Arty wanted to run, but his jelly legs were rooted to the spot. Suddenly, the image of the timer came into his mind. Oh, please help me, he prayed. I have been trying to hide from you, I know. I am so sorry! Please help me.

The passenger door of the Aston Martin slowly swung open. A dreadful odour of rotting flesh engulfed the air. 'Believe Arthur, truly believe.' Harry's final words entered his mind. He looked up at the sky. "Please!" he cried. The blackness was at the side of the car. He could not tell front from back, but he knew it was looking at him. *Searching* him. Immediately he felt a great weight in his jacket side pocket and red, green and silver sparks began to burst from his jacket. Alex sprang backwards in alarm. A noise like a wild animal in a rage emanated from the blackness. But the roaring of the wind and the sea came upon him wild, untamed, beautiful. It drowned out all other sounds. Even though he could feel a terrible rage from the direction of the black silhouette, his fear subsided. Louder and louder. Then he felt as if he had been plunged into the sea itself, for he was engulfed in water. Down and down he went until he thought his lungs would burst. Then as his toes touched the very bottom, he sprang back upwards. As he burst out of the water, he could see a lone dazzlingly bright star above him, and from its five points it spread its light and opened up the darkness of the black sky.

*

His suit was of the early nineteen-twenties style. It was immaculately tailored from Saville Row. The jacket fitted perfectly and naturally across his broad shoulders. It was hip length. He slipped the timer into one of two large pockets on either side. All four buttons at the front were fastened, and as he looked at the other men in the room, he realised that this was the correct way to wear it. As he sat down at a small round table, he could feel the very high waist trousers hug him uncomfortably around his middle. He squirmed in his seat and crossed his legs, admiring the jet black shiny brogues. He patted the timer affectionately through the material of his jacket pocket. The club or bar in which he had arrived was humming with low conversation. Most of the tables scattered carelessly around the room were occupied by either a couple or by a single man. In the very centre was positioned a white Baby Grand piano. The walls were white also. There were large Picasso prints hung at various intervals and the paddle-like ceiling fans propelled themselves lazily, dispersing both the warm air and the considerable cigar smoke. The bar took up the whole width of one side of the room. Its front was wood panelled. An impressive assortment of liquor lay behind it. Every style of glass imaginable was stacked upon the mirror-backed shelves. Arty had no idea where he was or why he was here. He decided to head for the bar and perhaps get some information out of the barman.

"You're looking dapper, young man," the white jacketed, middle-aged barman observed as he approached. He looked Greek or Turkish, Arty thought. His big black moustache complimented his dark olive skin. Likewise, his large black and very thick bushy eyebrows protruded from beneath the rim of his Fez.

"Thank you, young man," Arty returned the pleasantry. "I would like a Glenmorangie, if you have one, please."

The barman suddenly scowled at him. "I presume you *are* of age?" he asked. He stepped to one side and turned his back to Arty, polishing a glass and looked suspiciously at Arty through the reflection of the mirror.

Arty laughed hollowly. "Thanks," he said, not understanding the question, "I can see you don't have any, so I'll just try one of those." He pointed at a bottle labelled simply as 'French Cognac.' "You might as well make it a double."

"Papers," The bar man demanded airily, "show me your papers."

"Papers?" Arty raised his eyebrows in surprise, "you mean identification papers?"

"What else *would* I mean?" the barman answered impatiently.

Arty searched inside the inside pocket of his jacket and to his relief he produced a document folded in half along its length. He glanced at it just long enough to see that the name on it was Vassili Kharitonov, before it was snatched out of his hand by the barman, who studied it intently. He glanced up at Arty and then back at the paper.

"Russian?" he asked.

"I guess so," Arty answered, remembering just in time that he was in fact a Russian from eighteen nineteen who knows when!

"You still look too young to be in here!" the barman declared, handing back the paper to Arty, who immediately returned it to his inside pocket. The man poured a small measure into a large brandy glass. "You can have a single, young sir," he said smirking, "we don't want you getting up to too much mischief in here, do we?"

Arty returned the smirk and took a sip from the glass. Obviously, the man had a complex about aging. Arty watched him as he stood again in front of the mirror and tried to tease the few strands of hair that lay upon his seriously balding head. It was Arty's turn to genuinely smirk. He took another sip of the brandy. It relaxed him a little. As he turned to observe the room again, he noticed a slight figure of a man dressed as Fred Astaire in one of his dance movies, complete with coat tails and hat, glide across from an internal side door and seat himself at the piano. His top hat looked a little too tall for the rest of him. His black and white spats immediately pumped the pedals of the Baby Grand. The lights dimmed and the room suddenly hushed.

"Thank you, fans," the pianist said in a very familiar voice. "Tonight, I would like to perform a song that I wrote only last night, and it is dedicated to my darling Fanny."

Arty paled and froze. It was Peabody! It was then that he noticed the large burley figure of Charles Henry Smith. He was standing as if on guard at what looked like the entrance to the establishment. He looked across in unadulterated admiration for his boss. Arty was suddenly appreciative of the trilby hat he was wearing. He pulled it lower over his face, shielding his eyes.

Peabody meanwhile began to play a very familiar tune. It was one of Arty's favourites: "*They can't take that away from me.*" Arty wondered for a moment how on earth Peabody could get away with claiming the tune to be his own. Then he realised that he had obviously gone to the future, heard the song and now claimed it for his own before the rightful owner wrote it. George Gershwin will not be pleased, Arty decided. As Peabody tinkled on the piano, Arty concluded that the song was written in or around nineteen thirty seven which meant in all probability that he had indeed arrived some place in the early 1920s. He wondered longingly where Fanny Dodger was, and why Peabody had called her *his* darling. As the tune finished and a diluted applause emanated from the tables, Arty looked around wildly for either somewhere less conspicuous to place himself, or even a way out, at least for the time being. But he decided the only way out was through the door, keenly guarded by his old friend, Smith. Peabody began to play again and this time, unfortunately, Arty thought, sing. His voice though tuneful was thin and quivering. Arty shook his head in disbelief as he clearly recognized "*My Heart Will Go On.*"

"The boss is so talented," observed the barman from behind him. "He wrote this one this morning. I watched him do it in *ten minutes.*"

"You mean, he's the manager of this place?" Arty asked, ignoring the barman's admiration concerning Peabody's song writing talents.

"He *owns* the place," the barman said, "so you better not let him see you and that fake set of papers that you carry, 'ses.'"

Arty was now really becoming irritated with the barman's obsession with his age.

"Look, if this is an 'over fifties only' establishment!" he exclaimed, "there is a serious number of perpetrators sitting out there!" He pointed at the scattered tables where most of the men and women didn't look a day over thirty.

"Don't say I didn't warn you, ses," the barman answered, "his bodyguard over there is a particularly mean character."

He pointed to where Smith stood, silent and brooding. Arty pulled his hat even lower over his face. He certainly didn't need reminding of that fact. One thing was sure: as he was the only one sitting at the bar, he needed to sit somewhere else. As Peabody continued to destroy *My Heart Will Go On*, Arty slowly edged along the bar moving from stool to stool. As he did so, he happened to catch his reflection in the mirror. He was so shocked that he missed sitting on the next stool completely and only succeeded in pushing it over. He then became so disorientated and off balance that he fell backwards onto the seat of his pants. The barman peered over the bar at him.

"Just be thankful I only gave you a single!" he said. Then as he looked up, his face clouded over and he quickly turned his back and began polishing the whisky tumblers.

"Ere, what you doing?" growled a familiar voice. He was lifted easily and very roughly to his feet to stare directly into the large purple face of Smith. For a split second, Arty saw a vague look of recognition in his piggy eyes, then just as suddenly, it passed. "The next time you fall, it will be on your arse," the vulgar Smith declared loudly, "For I'll throw you out the door and down the front steps!" he snarled, covering Arty's own face with garlic breath and saliva. He then turned around smartly, not wanting to interrupt his bosses 'superb' performance with another unpleasant incident, and returned to his position at the front door.

Arty seated himself on a stool again at the far end of the bar. He peered slowly at the mirror opposite. He understood completely how Smith had failed to recognise him for he had barely recognised himself. He looked at least twenty years younger. He could clearly see the dark hair of long ago just visible under his hat. His eyes where larger and brighter and shone with the vitality of youth. The lines of 'care' on his face as Tatiana had so subtlety described to him once, had vanished. He was young again! He quickly fished out the paper from inside his inside pocket.

Vassili Kharitonov
Birth: Nov 4th 1895
PLACE OF BIRTH: SAINT PETERSBURG – RUSSIA
STATUS: RUSSIAN CITIZEN

If he was now in the early 1920s, that would make him in his mid-twenties, though he conceded that his reflection looked even younger.

His thoughts were interrupted by the arrival of a young woman. She wore a cream tubular dress dropped low at the waist. A thin circlet of silk was wrapped around her forehead, dividing the short, mousey brown hair. Her large round, brown reindeer eyes looked to be in a constant state of surprise. Her small mouth was painted pink. Her perfume was strong and overpowering.

"Are you looking for me?" she asked with her mouth and her eyes. She spoke in English with a strong Russian accent. Arty looked over his shoulder at the barman who winked at him conspiratorially.

"Nnn... No," Arty stammered, "I am looking for somebody else." The barman shook his head chuckling to himself.

"Well, if you don't find her, or she is busy," the girl answered, "I am Lushka, and I will be waiting over there." She pointed to one of the larger tables at the far end of the room around which sat another young woman and a man, one of the few in his fifties. Arty turned pink and mumbled into his brandy glass.

Peabody stood up again, bowing theatrically to the slightly more enthusiastic applause encouraged no doubt again by Smith.

"Now my fans," he cried loudly, "Now is the time that you have all been waiting for! So let me introduce you once again to the lady of the house herself. The incomparable! The inconceivable! The ravishingly beautiful and of course, my very own darling: Fanny Dodger!"

381

Her tallness had always amazed him. She also looked a tiny bit older, though it complimented the bone structure of her face even more. She also wore a tubular dress. The low waist was decorated with a band of cotton and metallic gold thread in a brocade design, as were the bell-shaped sleeves. The dress was three-quarter length and her slim white calves showed seductively beneath the gold-tasselled hem. She wore a thick headband of gold around her head. Her auburn-tinged wavy hair had been cut just below the ears in the fashionable 'Bob.' It framed her high cheekbones perfectly. But now Arty saw that instead of displaying the natural beauty of her face, she had drawn a thick black line of mascara around her eyes and her lips were painted ruby red. Her face was deathly white, though her cheeks were red with rouge. As graceful as ever, she took her seat at the piano. The murmur of voices quickly dispersed to silence with no encouragement needed by Smith.

As she began to play, the notes created a vision for Arty of the time they had spent together at his cottage. Their time together listening to music, watching movies, Carlo's restaurant, the beach and of her coming to lay with him in his room at night, when he would trace her eyebrows with his fingers and hold her tightly until he himself dropped off to sleep, only to wake the next morning to find that she had returned to her own room. It had been something they had never talked about or mentioned; each heart's own secret. His heart yearned now for those moments again. As he watched and listened to her play, he sensed that something had happened to his Tanechka; that something perhaps was not quite the same. Then she started to sing in her low sweet and beautifully in tune voice. In shock he lifted his hand to his mouth, for she was singing the words that she had written on the paper he had found by her bedside table. Not a person moved. Everybody was mesmerised by the beautiful woman and her song. Her long fingers caressed the keys as her voice caressed the words. When she had finished, she put her hands on her lap and waited for a few moments. The complete and amazed silence that followed was broken by a solitary hand clap, for Arty could not help himself. Tatiana looked up slowly and directly at him. He stopped clapping. Then a thunderous applause followed, complete with hoots and hollers, as she made her way gracefully towards him. He lifted his hat a little, wondering if she would recognise him. As she sat down next to him, Arty was immediately aware of her scent and her soft white arms. He also immediately felt the eyes of Peabody on them both. Then with a blow that hurt, shocked and surprised him, she slapped him smartly across the face. His hat flew into the air.

"Well, Sir Lancelot! I've been waiting over two years for you!" she cried angrily.

NOT THE END...